THE SHANGHAI INTRIGUE

THE SHANGHAI INTRIGUE

MICHAEL S. KOYAMA

LONDON NEW YORK CALCUTTA

Seagull Books, 2016

© Michael S. Koyama, 2016

ISBN 978 0 8574 2 383 2

British Library Cataloguing-in-Publication Data
A catalogue record for this book is available from the British Library

Typeset by Seagull Books, Calcutta, India
Printed and bound by Maple Press, York, Pennsylvania, USA

Authors' Note

The international financial conspiracy that takes place in this novel can befall any country. It is one you should hope will never occur, but which has actually happened in the past with horrendous and multifaceted consequences. How the conspiracy in our book was organized and how it imperilled both the financial world and the economy of a nation are portrayed as authentically as possible to give readers a vivid ringside view of both the conspiracy and its consequences, with all of the attendant human drama.

This is an international novel about events taking place in a dozen cities in Asia, Europe, the United States and Africa. We hope the story will be captivating enough to help readers learn painlessly how the complex and internationalized financial markets of the world work. However, with regard to the trading of stocks and bonds, and various kinds of crime, ranging from murder and kidnapping to corruption and money laundering, which are used to heighten the suspense, we chose to prioritize readability over technical correctness. We have also taken some liberty with various facts relating to China. However, we are confident that neither of these decisions has compromised the essential authenticity of the plot which was first conceived in Shanghai.

Although both the Japanese and Chinese put the family name before the personal name, we have followed what seems to be standard convention and have used Western order for the Japanese names and retained the order of using the last name first for Chinese names.

1

Beijing, Early May

'Just wait, I'll crack you yet!' Belinda Lin muttered at the 10 strings of numbers on her computer monitor currently defying her best efforts to decipher them. Belinda had managed to crack several codes that had stymied even the elite, veteran cryptographers working at the Pentagon for G2, the Army's intelligence branch. But these were proving to be an unaccustomed humbling experience. Frustrated, she stood up, yawned and stretched her arms to relieve the stiffness in her shoulders. After nearly three hours of work, she was tired and hungry. She shut down her computer, turned off the lights and walked out of her small office—no more than a cubicle with a desk and two filing cabinets—located on the second floor of the US Embassy in Beijing. As she locked the door, she smiled as she often did when she read the title on her door: 'Cultural Affairs Officer'.

There were only four officials who knew Belinda was a G2 captain specializing in cryptography: the ambassador, the deputy chief of mission, the head of cultural affairs, Mrs Wade, and the military attaché, Lieutenant Colonel Unger, her immediate superior. Others only suspected she was 'undeclared embassy staff'—someone doing intelligence work under an assumed title. Thanks to her near-native fluency in Chinese, she often helped the ambassador and other senior officers with various 'cultural affairs', but still it was impossible keep her real job totally secret.

At a little past seven, the embassy was quiet. Even Mrs Wade, whose office was next to Belinda's, had left. As Belinda started down the deserted hall towards the elevator, she met Colonel Unger emerging from the men's room.

'Belinda, you know the Army doesn't pay overtime. You're doing a remarkable job, but please don't overdo it. I can't afford one of our best cryptographers getting sick on me. Why are you working so late?'

'Those coded messages we talked about a few days ago, sir. The ones I started getting about 10 days back? I got another one today. I've tried everything—the Lehmann program, the programs I came up with to crack most of the coded messages of the Chinese military . . . So far, none of them work.'

'Our NSA satellite lifted them over Shanghai—right?'

'At first, yes, but some of the most recent ones were picked up over the east coast of the US.'

'Don't worry too much about them, Captain. They don't look like they have anything to do with the Chinese military. Maybe they're just messages a multinational corporation is sending, using a "one time pad".'

Belinda had already thought of a 'one time pad'—a code that could be used many times despite its name. Because it was based on a specific book or table, it was impossible to break without 'the pad'. But her experience and instinct told her that this particular code was different.

'You may be right, sir. But—'

'But they bug the hell out of you when you can't crack 'em. Right? Well, keep at it if you want to. But don't overdo it. That's an order.'

Colonel Unger gave her a mock salute before continuing up the stairs. Belinda saluted back and then hurried on out of the embassy complex. As her stomach emitted a low growl, she was forced to turn her thoughts to dinner.

The next day Belinda went back to her usual tasks but she couldn't get those messages out of her mind. At about 11, she took a break and poured herself a cup of coffee, and decided that it was time to stop going in circles. It was time to get some perspective—it was time to call her father. A Harvard professor, he was one of the world's leading scholars of what mathematicians call 'differential equations' and his hobby was cryptography. It was her father who had got her interested in breaking codes.

Belinda had sparred with her father many times over the years, everything from how someone with her cultural heritage should behave to arcane aspects of cryptography, but he remained both her inspiration and her guide. This wouldn't be the first time she was seeking his advice about deciphering a code.

Belinda called him on the pre-programmed scrambled phone number they'd set up at the behest of a G2 general. 'We know your famous father,' the general had said, 'Talk with him as often as you want. We've just got to make sure your conversations remain private.'

As she'd expected, her night-owl father was awake and working. He picked up the phone after the very first ring. Belinda told him about the messages. After a few questions, Professor Lin said, 'I remember my grandmother telling me about trying to send a telegram to a friend in Yunnan when she was young. The post-office clerk gave her a table with about 2,500 characters on it and told her to write her message using only those characters. He then converted each character into a number. I don't remember how many digits. I'm sure the post office in Yunnan converted the numbers back to characters before it sent my grandmother's telegram to her friend. She was amazed at being able to send a written message through a wire, but what amazed me was how time-consuming and cumbersome the process was.'

'You're sure she said her message was coded into numbers, not letters? The current telegraphic code uses the letters of the alphabet. It's more efficient since there are 26 letters and only 10 digits if numbers are used.'

'Yes, I'm sure. Since you haven't gotten anywhere, why don't you look into earlier numerical codes? There must be books describing how telegrams used to be sent. You know, a clue in breaking a code often comes from an unexpected place.'

After they hung up, Belinda knew she had to see if this was the clue she needed. The most likely place for information on outdated codes was the National Library of China, one of the largest libraries in the world. She checked its opening hours on her computer, then gobbled down a tuna sandwich, sent off a message to Unger telling him where she was going and set off.

This was Belinda's first visit to this library and she was overwhelmed by its size. The registration process was swift enough but soon after she was totally lost. Eventually, she found her way to the rare-books section and was introduced to a bespectacled and wizened curator. When she explained that she was looking for information on the early telegraphic codes for a study she was doing, he said, 'Ah, we have several books you might be interested in. We also have a copy of the Viguier code. You ought to take a look at it.'

'The Viguier code?'

'Viguier—Septime Auguste Viguier—a Frenchman and a customs officer in Shanghai. He devised the oldest known code and published it in 1872. It used four numbers to represent each Chinese character. Zheng Guanying later revised it but it continued to be known as the Viguier code. Then, in the 1920s, after it became technologically possible to code each Chinese character in Roman letters and other symbols, it fell into disuse for it was thought to be too clumsy and time-consuming.'

'How amazing that you know all this!'

'Well, I've always been interested in codes, but not many people know about the old ones any more. Although, come to think of it, you're the second person this year to inquire about the history of telegrams. A few months ago, a man came and asked for the same thing. I told him about the Viguier code too. He got very excited and took out one of our two copies but never returned it.'

'I thought no one could take anything out of the collection,' Belinda asked, puzzled.

'I told him that was the rule, that he could only read it here. Though he didn't say much, I got the feeling he was some kind of a high-level official. Sure enough, he came back with the head librarian who told me to let him have a copy. And as I said, he never returned it. So we now have only one copy, which you must look at here.'

'Thank you so much. I'd love to have a look at it. Why do you think the official wants a code which has been replaced long ago?'

'I don't know. Since the Viguier code uses a four-digit number for each Chinese character, it's more cumbersome than the Standard Telegraphic Code adopted later. The STC code uses just three Roman letters for each character. But the original Viguier code would be more difficult to break because almost no one knows about it.'

Belinda almost said 'Hallelujah!' Her father's suggestion was turning out to be a great lead. Under the watchful eyes of the curator, she used her phone to photograph the 72-page code and then returned to work.

Back at her desk, Belinda noticed that all the strings of numbers were divisible by four. Dividing all the numbers into groups of four to see if a pattern emerged, she spotted quite a few duplicate sets. She grouped those together. Then, with the help of the supercomputers and several experts at G2, she tried to see if combinations of the four-digit numbers could produce coherent Chinese. But nothing worked, even though there were only 24 sets of numbers.

I must be missing something obvious, she thought. *Why would anyone write messages using just 24 Chinese characters when there are thousands of them? And you need to know at least 900 to be able to read most of a newspaper?*

Then it suddenly hit her! 'It can't be—no way! But that's hiding things in plain sight!'

Smiling broadly, she emailed all the messages to Dr Greg Harrison at the NSA, and explained her 'hunch'. Could he please check them out using the NSA's six 'linked' computers?

Two days later, Dr Harrison replied by email:

'Captain Lin, that was easy. As you suggested, one of our programs assigned a random letter to each of the four-digit numbers. And then went through the routine process of switching the letters systematically. As you also suggested, we assumed the messages were in English—and you were right. In only a few minutes we figured out which four-digit number combinations stood for which letter, since the programs know the relative frequency of each letter used in writing English. We quickly discovered that there was no Q or Z. I'd say the guy who came up with this code was an intelligence officer but no genius. Even though the messages are in English, they make little sense to me. I hope you can make something of them. GH'

At last, she'd been able to crack the code! All the messages were in more or less coherent English but cryptic. And, to her great disappointment, none of them sounded even remotely like they involved national security or military intelligence.

Belinda went over the messages yet again in the order in which they were received, adding spaces to divide them into words. But all she got was:

can you use this code
takes time but will work send to jf
is code necessary too time consuming
yes billlons at stake
st very interested joining
meeting dresden possibility
st expects mof and boj to meddle

ask st to explain how also report on mtc

arriving day before meetings

bring estimates

Five messages had been picked up over eastern China, the other five from the eastern US. She got the impression that the plot involved something financial, but there was no real evidence in the messages to support her surmise. Deciding ST and JF were people's initials, she looked up MOF, BOJ and MTC on the Internet. But nothing came up that could help her.

In her opinion the messages were unrelated to America's national security but, since she had talked to Colonel Unger about them more than once, she decided she'd play it safe. She printed them out and took them over to his office.

'You look like the cat that swallowed the canary,' he said as he took the list from her. 'What's up?' He glanced down at the sheet of paper and then looked up at Belinda, astonished.

'You broke that darn code! Congratulations!'

Then he read the messages. And read them again while Belinda stared silently at the top of his balding head.

'Belinda, you're a great cryptographer, but the hours you've spent breaking that code look like a waste of time. These messages I'm damn sure have nothing to do with the Chinese military or with American security. How did you break the code anyway?'

Midway through her explanation, he interrupted her. 'These are just private communications. Maybe some guys are scheming something, but they're clearly not related to national security in any way. I suggest you ignore them. Although I do appreciate your showing them to me. I'm glad to know that nothing gets past you.'

Belinda returned to her office. She had expected nothing more from Colonel Unger.

But ignore the messages she could not.

OK, so they're of no interest to G2, but 'billions at stake' *means it's something big and it's just getting organized. China, the US and Germany are most certainly involved. That's why the plotters are creating a new code based on one nearly a century and a half old. The main conspirator could be Chinese, someone very important if the curator was right in guessing the identity of the person who borrowed the Viguier code.*

She went back to work but thought about the messages off and on all day. There was a lot for her to do, now that her code-breaking efforts were over, and by the time she wrapped up work and got home it was after eight. A packet of instant noodles and an apple later, she wrote a long email to her father and told him about how his clue helped her decipher the messages. Then she turned on the TV and scanned the news on CNN while she packed a small suitcase for her trip to the Shanghai Economic Forum the next morning and finally went to bed.

2

Shanghai, 12 May

On the second day of the Shanghai Economic Forum, Nick Koyama met his old friend, Ken Murai, at the Nadaman Restaurant in the Shangri La Hotel, located in the Pudong District on the bustling 'East Bank' of the Huangpu River. Since Nick lived in New York and Ken in Tokyo, they rarely had a chance to meet. They had been delighted when they discovered both would be attending the meetings in Shanghai.

'Thanks for inviting me,' said Ken. 'The Nadaman in Tokyo is too expensive for a bureaucrat like me, so it's a special treat to eat at the branch here in Shanghai.'

'You're not just a bureaucrat, Ken,' protested Nick. 'You're the deputy director of the International Bureau in Japan's Ministry of Finance. You're so important that the ministry sends you here every year to stay *au courant* with what's happening with Japan's biggest trading partner.'

'Yes, but we have a tight budget. And even though I'm the deputy director, I don't get paid like people in the private financial sector . . . like you.'

The two men had first met nearly two decades ago at the doctoral programme in economics at Harvard, where their classmates had dubbed them 'the doppelgangers'. Though Nick was only half Japanese, with their dark hair and lean faces, they were almost twins. But the two no longer looked so much alike. Ken had joined Japan's Ministry of Finance, and the responsibilities of his position and the precarious state of the Japanese economy had put lines on his forehead and strands of white in his hair. Nick was the head of the Asian division at Rubin-Hatch International, one of the leading international financial consulting firms in New York. Despite working long hours, he had somehow managed to remain fit and now looked younger than Ken.

The session they had just attended had been on the Chinese policy on oil. Neither man was directly concerned with China or oil but with the financial implications of world energy conditions: Ken, because of his position in the Japanese government, and Nick, with regard to his advising many 'high net worth' customers with international investments. Today both men were frustrated with what they felt had been a wasted morning. After ordering sushi sets with beer, they continued the conversation they had begun on the walk over from the Shanghai World Financial Centre.

'I agree that the president of the Sino-African Energy Corporation seemed to be obfuscating rather than clarifying China's intentions,' said Nick.

'I thought we might get a scoop on China's assessment of the new oil reserves found in West Africa, off the shores of Benin. But all we got was the warmed-over official line on China's energy policy.'

'I was disappointed too, though I'm not sure what we can expect from the president of a state-owned enterprise. But I got the impression he was trying hard not to let the audience know how important these finds are to the Chinese.' Ken sighed. 'I'd really like to know what the head of SAEC plans to do. What China does relating to oil affects the world price of oil and therefore Japan's trade balance, which is one of my biggest concerns.'

'I know why you're frowning. Japan has had to spend so much money importing energy sources since the Fukushima nuclear disaster. The only solution your government seems to have is to sell more government bonds. You know, your debt to GDP ratio is the highest in the world. And, worse, it's been steadily creeping up towards 300 per cent, isn't it?'

'Yes, I'm afraid it is. That's precisely why I'm so concerned about energy. I'm really puzzled why the president of SAEC seemed almost secretive about those new African oil fields.'

'Say, speaking of puzzles, did you see those two guys the president was talking to when I went back to my seat to get my umbrella?'

'I couldn't get a good look at them from where I was standing. I did see the president stop talking and stare at you as you walked up to them.'

'He seemed unnerved. I wonder if he thought I was going to try to join them. But when I stopped at the second row of seats and picked up my umbrella, he relaxed. I was curious, so I tried to get a good look at the men he was talking to. One guy was Asian. But the other was a New York hedge fund owner. Why would he want to talk to the CEO of SAEC?'

'A New York hedge fund guy? So you know him?' asked Ken.

'I don't know him personally, but I recognized him. He's Joshua Fried, the owner of a middling hedge fund. To put it mildly, he has an unsavoury reputation in the financial community in New York.'

'The Asian you saw . . . could you tell his nationality?'

'Could be Japanese, could be Korean, even Chinese. Hell, I don't know, Ken. You Asians all look alike!'

Ken smiled briefly. 'My guess is that he is *not* Japanese. President Fan could very likely be getting advice from the hedge fund guy. I can't imagine why he'd want to talk with a Japanese, someone from a country competing with China to get more of the world's oil resources.'

At the same time that Nick Koyama was having lunch with his friend, his wife, Bess, was at another Shanghai restaurant with Belinda Lin, a friend from her college days. Two Chinese waitresses dressed in Japanese kimono set down before each woman a large lacquered lunchbox and added bowls of *miso* soup and rice, then bowed slightly and smiled as the two Americans thanked them with a 'Xièxie.'

'Delicious! My favourite Japanese foods,' exclaimed Bess Koyama, whose short brown hair curled around her smiling face. 'Nick said I was going to find the Japanese food here at the Okura Hotel in Shanghai authentic.'

Her companion laughed, her jet-black hair swinging forward as she leaned over her box lunch. 'The only difference is that the waitresses here speak Chinese. I swear, Bess, you have a Japanese stomach. Is that your husband's influence?'

With her mouth full, Bess shook her head and swallowed, 'No, Nick's always begging for spaghetti instead of rice. He says I'm just like his mother. She doesn't have any Japanese blood either, but she loves Japanese food even more than I do.'

'Right,' said Belinda. 'Acquired taste trumps blood. My father prefers coq au vin to Shaoxing drunken chicken.'

As they savoured the various delicacies in their lunch boxes, they caught up with what had been happening in their lives since they had last met two years ago, when Belinda was on home leave from Beijing.

'Strange things do happen in our lives, don't they?' commented Bess. 'Here we are, two of the six members of the nutty club you organized when we were undergraduates to see who could write a firewall program that the others couldn't breach when they tried to hack into one another's computers. Who'd have thought we would be meeting in Shanghai!'

'That's true. But I'll bet no one'll be surprised to learn what our jobs are now. Especially you, working in the financial world as an electronic communications expert.'

'And anyone with Alan Turing as a role model was bound for a career involving computers. I've always wondered, though, how with a father who's a professor of mathematics you ended up in the military?'

'Blame it on Turing,' mused Belinda. 'Since high school I've been fascinated by how an English mathematician became the World War Two hero who deciphered the German naval code. My father did hope I would go into academia, but I guess I was bound to end up in military intelligence.'

Bess paused, her chopsticks held in the air. 'But tell me—if you're permitted to—why is it the job of a captain in military intelligence stationed in Beijing to check out web security for American politicians and business leaders attending the Shanghai Economic Forum?' Bess paused. 'I probably shouldn't ask, but what exactly is your job anyway?'

Belinda laughed. 'Bess, you never change. Still as snoopy as ever.'

'I call it being interested, not snoopy. But you're avoiding the question.'

'All I can tell you is that I'm the aide to a lieutenant colonel who is the military attaché at the embassy in Beijing, and I was sent here to Shanghai because the US doesn't want anything to happen that might compromise the cyber security of the participants in the forum. For example, we don't want any of the laptops of the participants taking home malware. Someone might well try to install software that's infested with viruses that make computers leak all kinds of information.'

'Like politically sensitive communications and trade secrets?'

'Right. And you know China's reputation.'

Bess let out a brief laugh. 'Why do you think I've spent the better part of a week here in Shanghai upgrading the firewalls of the computers in the Shanghai office of Rubin-Hatch? Financial consulting firms like ours have to be equally concerned with cyber security.' She paused. 'You're going to call me snoopy again, but I sure am curious about what you do in Beijing.'

Belinda laughed. 'You're right. I can't tell you. Since you know my main interests and so can guess my job, there is one thing I can tell you, though, without breaching national security.'

Bess stopped eating and stared at her friend. 'Yes?'

'I've found messages that I've been told to ignore because they don't concern national security. They use an outdated Chinese code to communicate in English. It was quite a challenge for me to figure them out.'

'An outdated Chinese code to send messages in English?' queried Bess, frowning. 'How could anyone come up with a code based on Chinese that uses thousands of characters to communicate in English, which uses only 26 roman letters?'

'Actually, it was so simple that it completely fooled me. The thousands of Chinese characters can't be transmitted by telegraph without first encoding them. So back in the late nineteenth century, a code was developed that gave a four-digit number to each character. But it was obviously very time-consuming to look up the numbers for each character when encoding or decoding a message. So a revised code was established in 1925 that substituted roman letters for numbers, enabling coders to use three letters instead of four numbers. This was more efficient because there are only 10 digits but 26 letters. This change enabled the Chinese to code 17,576 characters—26 by 26 by 26.'

'Wow! I'm impressed. Tell me more.'

'Well, it turns out that someone is using an old Chinese code from the nineteenth century to code the alphabet, identifying each letter by four numbers. It took my dad plus an elderly curator at the Chinese National Library to put me on to this. But it's interesting that someone in China's found it and decided to use it.'

'What were the messages that you were told to ignore?'

'I've only got 10 so far. The first ones simply verified that the code could be used. They didn't say what the purpose was. These were within China—I probably shouldn't be telling you this, so keep what I say under your hat.' When Bess nodded, Belinda went on. 'The other messages also involve someone on the East Coast of the US, who confirmed he could use the code and said that he—could be a she—would be arriving "the day before the meetings". I'm only making a wild guess but it's possible that meant arriving in Shanghai the day before the Shanghai Economic Forum began. If I'm right, the plotters could be meeting here today!'

'Hmm. But why? And why were you told the messages aren't important?'

'Well, there's nothing related to any military concerns. And the first messages were almost childish, like kids playing with a code. The rest included two- or three-letter acronyms or initials. I tried my best to figure out what the three-letter ones could mean. But no dice. Colonel Unger, my superior officer said they were unrelated to security, so I should just ignore them.'

'But you don't agree?' said Bess, smiling.

'No. Why would someone go to all the trouble to invent a new code if it weren't for something very important? Since they're using English, and since one or more of the people sending them is in the US and one includes the word "Dresden", it means these guys are plotting something international. The word "billions" was in one message, but billions of what?'

'I can see why you're intrigued.'

'Intrigued?' Belinda gave a short laugh. 'It's more like I'm obsessed! Oh, well, I'll just have to wait and see if more come in and what they say.'

'Keep me posted, Belinda. If you think either Nick or I could help you with them, let me know.' Bess looked at her watch. 'I've got to go get Mikey a present after lunch. Do you want to come with me?'

'I'd love to, but I've still got stuff to check out here. What're you getting Mikey?'

'I thought a panda. He's into stuffed animals.'

'I'd love to see him,' Belinda said wistfully. 'It's been two years. He was just a toddler when I last saw him.'

Bess laughed. 'He's quite a handful now.'

A server came to refresh their tea, but the two women declined and prepared to leave.

Belinda said, 'This is my territory, so lunch is on me.'

'*Xièxie*. Or should I say *arigato* since this is a Japanese restaurant?' smiled Bess.

As Bess walked through the old French Concession afterwards, she wasn't thinking about a stuffed panda for her son but Belinda's codes. *An international plot involving billions of . . . what? China? US? Dresden? What's it all about? Damn, she's got me obsessing about them as well.*

3

Dresden, 15 May

The retired professor sitting in the corner of Paulaner's looked over the top of his newspaper at the two middle-aged men settling in at the next table. One of them was a little over six feet tall with a full head of grey hair and dressed in an obviously expensive suit. He was speaking colloquial German but with a strong American accent. His companion, a head shorter and pudgy, wore a cheap ill-fitting suit. His thinning hair was carefully combed over his pate, and his German had a Dresden accent.

The two men asked for beer on tap and said they'd order their meals when their friend joined them. As the only other people at this end of the restaurant were two young women chatting softly in Russian, the professor could easily hear every word the men spoke.

The Dresdener looked across the table at his companion. 'Josh, you're staying at the posh Taschenbergpalais, so why come to this little bistro? And why are you travelling from Shanghai to New York via Dresden? Not that I don't enjoy seeing you again.'

'Well, Markus, when in the land of my forefathers, I like to enjoy their food. The restaurant at my posh hotel, as you call it, doesn't have good, honest German food. And I stopped here just to see you. Too bad you couldn't attend the forum.'

'I don't see any reason why I should have. Besides, the head office in Frankfurt wouldn't think it necessary to pay its local manager to go to a meeting in China.'

'Hmm. You know, I was really surprised when you were made manager of the branch here. Quite a different career path for you, to go into management after being a "quant" for so many years.'

The professor in the corner wondered what a 'quant' was. It certainly wasn't a German word. But the meaning was made clear soon enough.

'Josh, I think I can truthfully say that I was the best analyst they ever had. I could come up with the canniest algorithms based on higher mathematics for trading tricky derivatives. I made tons of money for the bank, so I expected to become the head the derivative trading division at Frankfurt. But I was passed over—because I'm an Ossie, from former East Germany. I was exiled to head the Dresden branch . . . sent back to the East. I was told it was a promotion. But, *scheiss*, that isn't the way I see it.'

'But surely, Markus, having been the top quant, you still must have some clout at headquarters . . . and being the manager of a major branch, doesn't that allow you to make decisions as you see fit?'

'Well, the answers are "no" and "maybe". The ungrateful executives at headquarters don't listen to me. As to what I can do as manager of the branch here—not a hell of a lot. All I've done since I got here is build up the private accounts. Their total assets have increased substantially since I began managing them because I'm still a good quant.'

Before Markus could say more, a tall, slender and rather handsome Asian man appeared at the table. Josh looked up at him and with a broad smile of welcome switched to English. 'Shig, you're just in time. Markus, let me introduce my good friend, Shig Tanaka. He's the senior vice president of Sumida Bank in Tokyo, Japan's fifth largest. I've known him for years, ever since he was manager of Sumida's New York branch. Like me, he's en route—he's off to London. I asked him to stop by and meet you.'

Josh turned to Shig. 'Shig, my friend here is Markus Adler, one of the best quants there is and now manager of the Deutsche Wiederaufbaubank in Dresden. We met at the World Economic Forum in Davos years ago. I've told you about him.'

Deutsche Wiederaufbaubank! Suddenly the professor remembered a stray bit of talk from a party—a friend who worked at the Deutsche Wiederaufbaubank had told him, 'Our new manager was one of our bank's traders at Frankfurt headquarters. He traded a risky derivative using his fancy program and our bank lost over a billion euros because of it.'

Meanwhile, Shig acknowledged the introduction in excellent English, and then Josh took over.

'Gentlemen, I'm delighted we could meet here tonight. I have . . . '

But before he could continue, the waitress approached again and the three men spent the next few minutes ordering their food. Josh went for *wurst* and sauerkraut, Markus for *Kartoffel Gemuseauflauf*, a huge vegetable casserole topped with a mound of melted cheese. Shig asked for *Wiener Schnitzel* without looking at the menu.

The man in the corner glanced at his watch—he still had time before his appointment with the small group of salesmen to whom he was teaching English. So ordering another beer, he retreated behind his newspaper once more and continued to listen to the three men talking, in the hope that something important would finally come up.

The waitress finally left and Markus asked, 'Why did you two go to the Shanghai Economic Forum?'

The American laughed. 'Not for the speeches, that's for sure. We went to make contacts which will, we hope, lead to big deals. Shig and I had a good meeting with President Fan of SAEC.'

'*Sa-yek*? What's that?'

'There's no reason why you should know it. It's the Sino-African Energy Corporation, the state-owned enterprise that handles all energy-related business with African nations. And given the Chinese need for energy, SAEC is one of the largest of the state-owned enterprises.'

'So why is the owner of a hedge fund in New York meeting with the president of a Chinese state-owned corporation?' Markus asked, still perplexed.

Josh answered so softly that the professor could barely hear him.

'We've done some very profitable business since we met three years ago. But this time Shig and I met him about something else. That something else is also why I wanted to see you tonight.'

Shig, who'd been silent so far, murmured something that the professor in his corner couldn't hear. Josh looked to his left where the two blonde women were still carrying on their talk in Russian, and the professor lowered his head further, as if he was totally engrossed in his newspaper.

'You worry too much, Shig,' said Josh, 'Those women aren't paying any attention to us—they're jabbering in what sounds like Russian. And look, the man in the corner is reading the *Sächsische Zeitung*, and Ossies of his age don't know English. Let's finish eating, then I'll take you to my suite at the Tauschenbergpalais where we can all enjoy some of the duty-free cognac I picked up. And then Shig and I can tell you what we want to talk to you about.'

I wonder what they're plotting, thought the man in the corner. He smiled at their assumption that he didn't understand English. *Well, I'm not going to learn any more now. It's time to go.* He raised his hand and called for the bill.

Some hours later, Markus lay in bed, unable to sleep. Somewhere in the distance, a church bell tolled once. He got up and took another antacid pill. But it wasn't just indigestion that was keeping him awake—it was the amazing proposition that Josh Fried and Shig Tanaka had put to him.

The plan was brilliant. And foolproof. But Markus needed to raise at least a few hundred million euros if he wanted to participate. *Scheiss, this isn't going to be easy.* He'd lost his own considerable fortune at the same time as he'd lost all those euros for the bank. Now he was within a decade of retirement, with no family, no future, no money. *I really have to get those euros back into my retirement nest egg, and then get the hell out of Dresden!*

Josh had seemed to assume that he could persuade his bank to join in the plan. But the strait-laced head office wouldn't be interested in a project that was not *völlig rechtlich* . . . totally legal. Josh had said the plan was 'not illegal'—only 'some elements of it weren't strictly above board'. But *wird es lukrativ sein wie die Hölle!* . . . they'd hit the jackpot if they could pull it off!

And what a team they already had! The head of one of the largest state enterprises in China, a hedge fund owner in New York, and the vice president of one of the largest banks in Japan. There were others, equally big, Josh had hinted. Markus certainly wanted in on this plan, but how was he to raise the funds? *Mein Gott! At least two hundred million euros?*

The problem was, according to Josh, that to make the plan sure-fire they needed at least eight, if not 10 billion dollars. Fundraising was going well—they already had more than half—but they were looking for more 'members'. The more money they could raise, Josh said, the greater the chance of the project succeeding. Josh had hoped that Markus, along with his bank, could provide at least several hundred million dollars. Hence his Dresden detour.

Well, the Deutsche Wiederaufbaubank would never consider a scheme like this, so it's up to me to come up with the money. Given the projected profits, I could easily pay back the bank whatever I 'borrow' for this short period and still have some left over for my retirement fund. How about 'borrowing' from the private accounts I've been managing? No, those accounts check their balances regularly. But, wait, there are some who don't. I'll have to check the accounts one by one to see how much money I could 'borrow' for them.

But what can I do about Trudi?

Trudi Vögel handled the bookkeeping for these accounts. She looked over them with an eagle eye and not the tiniest irregularity ever escaped her.

He would have to do something to take her away from them.

Well, there's nothing more I can do tonight. In the morning I'll look into how much money I might be able to come up with after I check all the 'borrowable' accounts. And then I'll consider the problem of Trudi. Josh has given me a few weeks to tell him if I can participate in the project and, if so, how much I'm able to contribute. And by God, contribute I will!

Markus fell asleep with a faint smile on his face and didn't hear the church bells chime twice.

4

Shanghai, 25 May

Mimi thought she was the luckiest young woman in Shanghai. At 26, she was the personal assistant to Fan Zhipeng, president of SAEC. She was very grateful to the president not only for her position, but also for sending her to the US for a year to 'polish' her English and become 'international', and this only a year after she was hired. She was aware that it may have been partly due to *guanxi*, the personal relationships that are so important in China—she had been introduced to the president by SAEC's CFO, Lei Tao, an acquaintance of her father, one of Shanghai's senior vice mayors. However, she preferred to think it was due to her degree in international studies from Fudan University and her excellent command of English.

But even if she dismissed the importance of her father's influence, she was grateful to him for the lessons in English he had provided when she was a child. The vice mayor had foreseen the importance of English for China, and when his only child was just 10 years old, he had hired an American woman to give her private lessons. As a result, and because of the year abroad, she spoke English nearly fluently and with only a slight accent. It was her tutor who finding her name, Xia Mingxi, hard to pronounce, had dubbed her Mimi.

Although many found him intimidating, Mimi respected Fan Zhipeng's dedication towards bringing more energy resources to China. An imposing figure of a man, Fan Zhipeng had been a colonel in the People's Liberation Army and his pedigree was impeccable— son of a retired commanding general in the Beijing Military Region and grandson of a participant in the historic Long March of 1934– 35 led by Chairman Mao.

Mimi was very pleased by the president's confidence in her. In addition to having her go over the speeches and letters he wrote in English, he had her sit in on his meetings to take notes as well as prepare coffee or tea for his visitors. A few weeks ago he had even entrusted her with the intricate coding of his confidential messages. Although she had to be very careful, she found the coding of these short and cryptic messages not terribly difficult once she'd done the first few. There was only one thing she was unhappy about—she was no longer asked to sit in on meetings between the president and Professor Du. She couldn't forget about it because her dismissal had been rather humiliating.

Back in March, Mimi had gone in as usual to the small conference room to prepare for the president's meeting with the professor. She pulled open the drapes, and then went into the adjoining kitchenette to make coffee. By the time she took the coffee into the conference room, both men had arrived. After serving them, she quietly seated herself at the far end of the table and opened her laptop, ready to take notes.

Though Mimi enjoyed most of the president's meetings she sat in on, she didn't like Professor Du. Unusually short, unattractive with beady eyes and thinning hair, he dressed in expensive dark suits and looked more like a gangster than a professor. He constantly boasted of his 'very good English and nearly fluent French', his job at Fudan University and his PhD in economics from Beijing University, ranked number one in China. Every time she heard him brag about his degree, Mimi thought, *You know full well that most of the people around here have a degree from Fudan or some other Chinese university. What a stupid snob you are!*

Mimi didn't know how her boss felt about Du, but she knew that the professor of international trade was useful to him. She was also not blind to the fact that Du had cunningly ingratiated himself to President Fan and become a well-paid advisor while continuing to earn a full salary at Fudan University.

On that humiliating morning, the president had begun to question the professor about his recent trip to Benin. Was the report by the head of SAEC's office in Cotonou accurate?

'The head of your Benin office did a credible job. It's essentially accurate.'

'*Essentially?*' Fan sounded surprised.

'Well, the technical information about the discovery of oil reserves off the coast of Benin is correct. Yes, oil and natural gas reserves have been found in an 80,000-square-kilometre area in the Gulf of Guinea. In the ocean, about 3 kilometres from the shoreline out to about 10 kilometres into the gulf. They—'

Mimi was typing as fast as she could when the president interrupted.

'Yes, yes, I've read the report. What can you tell me that's not in it? We're concerned because Benin has a population of only 8 million or so. Can it prevent the reserves from being claimed by its dangerous big neighbour, Nigeria? How stable is Benin's government? Will it honour any contracts it makes? That's what we need to know from you.'

The professor held up his hand. 'Please let me give you my report. Then you can ask me questions. So—the reserves extend from the westernmost coastal city of Quidah to Porto-Novo in the east. Which means that Benin can stake a legal claim that will stand up to international pressure and scrutiny. Incidentally, I talked to a French geologist who was part of the team hired by Benin to assess the oil reserves. They estimate that the area could produce 3 million barrels a day for the next 40 years. If they're correct, the total amount of oil is only slightly less than Nigeria's. And, as you know, Nigeria is the eleventh-largest oil producer in the world. No one seems to be sure how much natural gas the area has, but the geologists working for Lone Star, the American oil company, think it could be as much as 10 per cent of all the natural gas now produced in the US.'

Fan nodded. 'That's impressive. But if we obtain the rights to extract the oil and gas, do you think the government of Benin will honour the contract? Will the current government stay in power? It's obviously going to cost a lot to win the bid, and to extract the oil from the bottom of the gulf. We need to make certain we won't lose our investment.'

'I believe the Benin government is stable—certainly for the near future—and it will honour any contracts it signs with SAEC. But that's not what I see as the problem.' Du paused, took a sip of coffee and looked hard at the president.

'Yes, go on,' commanded Fan.

'What we don't know is exactly how the area is to be developed. What I mean is that the government of Benin hasn't yet made an official announcement, though the rumour is rampant that it plans to solicit bids for four large tracts, each about 20,000 square kilometres. I'm fairly certain that both PetroFrance and Lone Star, one of the biggest American oil companies, will make bids, but only for one tract each. Mr Chen and I agree that we have to worry most about Mitsumoto Trading of Japan—it will be leading a consortium consisting of Heisei Petroleum, Kanto Gas and and other large Japanese firms. My sources say that this consortium plans to bid for all four tracts.'

'Professor Du, it doesn't surprise me to hear that Mitsumoto Trading will go all out to win all the tracts. Because Japan no longer relies on nuclear power the way it used to, it is essential for it to diversify its sources of energy. And obtain as much oil as possible. So the question is: How do we outbid Mitsumoto and get all four tracts for Sino-Africa Energy?'

'That's just part of the problem,' Du said. 'The seas in the Bight of Benin are quite rough, so extracting the oil and gas is not going to be easy. At least three people have tossed that old saying at me: "Beware, beware the Bight of Benin, for few come out, though many go in." That part of the gulf's very dangerous.'

'So it's going to be very expensive to get the oil from these reserves, both because of the competition from the Japanese and the high cost of extraction.'

'Precisely. But, President, I've put a lot of time into a plan to help us outbid Mitsumoto.'

The professor leaned over the table towards Fan, then he hesitated and glanced down the table at Mimi. 'It would be better to keep this conversation absolutely confidential.'

Mimi saw the president nod in agreement but he said nothing.

'I think,' continued Du, 'that your secretary should be excused.'

Mimi couldn't believe her ears. *I can't be depended on to keep SAEC's business confidential?*

There was a moment of silence, then her boss looked at Mimi and said, almost apologetically, 'Miss Xia, please excuse us.'

Chagrined, Mimi closed her laptop, stood and bowed slightly, then left. She had no idea of the rest of the discussion that took place between the two men.

Since that morning, the president had met more frequently with Du. Every time Mimi was asked to prepare the room and serve the coffee but not to stay and take notes. A 'Dr D' had been mentioned in one of the messages she had encoded. So it was very likely that the secret meetings and the coded messages were related.

As the days went by, Mimi grew more and more curious.

Today, about two months later, President Fan informed Mimi that Professor Du would be arriving at 10 for a meeting and asked her to make the usual preparations. So as usual she served coffee and returned with the tray through the door into the kitchenette. As she tidied up the coffee and the tray, she realized she could hear scraps of conversation—she obviously hadn't shut the door tightly enough.

Should I close the door before I leave? I should. But . . . what if they hear me and then think I'd left it open on purpose?

She turned off the light as softly as she could and went over to the door. Putting her ear to the crack, she could hear the voices just loud enough to understand what was being said.

'Your estimates,' Fan was saying, 'appear to tally with those I've got from New York. I'll study them carefully today. Do you really think this plan will work?'

'It should. Look, sir, if Soros could do it, there's no way we can fail, not with enough participants.'

'How long have we got to raise the funds?'

'We've got to have everything in place by mid-August. Preferably a Monday in mid-August. I don't know when Benin's going to accept bids, but the latest information I have is maybe early September. We don't want to be caught short.'

Mimi pushed her ear closer to the crack and inadvertently moved the door a tiny bit, making a slight sound. She held her breath but the men appeared not to have heard. Du was going on about 'a thin trade on Mondays, especially in summer'. Mimi relaxed and listened on.

'Sir,' Du was saying, 'this is the only way for SAEC to outbid Mitsumoto. A few high-ranking officers in the Benin government told me that the consortium led by Mitsumoto has enormous backing, even from the Japanese government. They are determined to win the bids. So we have to make sure they can't.'

'Well, everything seems to be going as you predicted,' conceded Fan. 'And if we succeed, it'll certainly play havoc with the Japanese economy.'

Even though Mimi had taken courses in economics and finance, the conversation baffled her. She couldn't understand how trading whatever it was they were discussing had anything to do with SAEC winning the bid over Mitsumoto. There was the sound of paper crackling, as if it was being inserted into an envelope. The meeting was nearing its end. Mimi dared not get caught, so she slipped out into the hallway and, to avoid meeting the two men, went down the hall and into the women's restroom. She needed a few moments to collect her thoughts.

What is going on? What is this secret plan that requires the SAEC to raise a huge amount of money? And how is it connected to out-bidding the Mitsumoto bid? Did Du want me out of the room because this plan is illegal? Why else should their conversation be 'absolutely confidential'? . . . And I wonder who So-rose is?

5

Beijing, 28 May, and New York, 29 May

Since Belinda told Bess about the messages in Shanghai, four more had come in—there were now a total of 14. One of the new messages included the word 'firepower'. Belinda was still certain it had nothing to do with anything military but that did nothing to dampen her curiosity about them. *I know it's none of G2's business, but I'm sure something big, international and fraudulent is afoot!*

She went over the new messages again.

> dresden would like to join
>
> provide details of firepower of mtc
>
> will look into mtc st
>
> estimates of dr d same

The newest messages looked as if the plot was progressing. Someone from Germany wanted to join. NSA had told her that the thirteenth message had originated from 'the Kanto region' of Japan, which included Tokyo. That meant that people in four countries—China, the US, Germany and Japan—were somehow involved.

Belinda googled the acronyms MTC, MOF and BOJ, which had appeared in the earlier messages. She started with MTC, which was in two of the new messages. There were more than 10 million hits for MTC. That was no help. Then she tried MOF. This was more promising—it most probably stood for the ministry of finance of some country or other and, if so, it would bolster her suspicion that the plot was financial in nature. But so many countries had a ministry of finance—where could she begin? There were as many hits for BOJ—everything from video games to a dozen local and national banks. If her suspicions were right, the reference could be to one of these banks, but which? Could it possibly be the Bank of Japan?

She knew she was clutching at straws. The Internet wasn't helping her much, but she didn't want to give up. So she decided to do what she'd been thinking about for a while—take Bess up on her offer to look at the messages. Since Colonel Unger had deemed them useless, she couldn't think of any reason to not show them to someone else.

She typed out the 14 messages using the encrypted program she sometimes used when emailing Bess, added a short message, also encoded, and sent them off.

While Nick was dressing Mikey for nursery school, Bess sat down in the kitchen with her first cup of coffee and checked her messages. *Ah, one from Belinda. I haven't heard from her since Shanghai. And it's encrypted. Interesting.* She opened it and was immediately intrigued. But then Mikey ran into the kitchen with his Chinese panda, and Bess didn't get to tell Nick about Belinda's message until noon, when she went to his office for lunch.

'Look what Belinda sent me. I didn't have a chance to show it to you this morning. She's decoded more messages but she can't figure out what they're about. Her superior officer says they have nothing to do with US national security. But the code was so unusual and so hard to break that she thinks it must involve something important. She thinks they could concern an international plot involving finance—right up your alley. But she can't figure out what, so she sent the messages to us to puzzle over. Take a look while I get us some coffee.'

Nick momentarily abandoned his lunch and read over the messages. When Bess returned with two mugs, he looked up at her and asked, 'Did she say she had permission to send you these deciphered messages?'

'Well, not exactly, but since she was told to ignore them, she didn't see why she shouldn't. But she used the encoded email program just to be sure no one else could read her email or the attachment.'

'What does she know about who's sending them? I mean, where did they originate?'

'Some were picked up over eastern China, others over the eastern US and one over Japan. Belinda told me in Shanghai that the code was based on an outdated Chinese code. So at least one Chinese must be involved, most likely the person who made up the code.'

'Hmm,' murmured Nick as he read the messages again. 'Dresden's mentioned, so the messages are certainly about something international. MOF is mentioned—that's likely a ministry of finance. And with a message picked up over Japan, BOJ could possibly refer to the Bank of Japan. There's an MTC that comes up twice. It might be a major corporation or financial institution because one message talks about its firepower. In fact, that's probably the biggest clue we have— that whatever these messages are all about, they have something to do with finance.'

'Isn't "firepower" a strange term to use if MTC is a company or a bank? Sounds more military to me.'

'It's not all that strange to say a company has firepower . . . it just means it has a lot of resources, maybe cash or powerful political connections.'

Nick turned to his computer, his fingers moving swiftly over the keyboard. Knowing he was looking up MTC, Bess asked, 'Find anything?'

'Only that MTC could be anything. A missionary training centre, a metropolitan transportation commission, Microsoft Technology Centre . . . dozens . . . hundreds of MTCs. Damn it. The same with MOF and BOJ—'

'So what should I tell Belinda?'

'Tell her if these messages keep coming, she could send them to us. That is, if her superiors let her spend time decoding them. I might ask James Gao in our Singapore office if he's heard anything. He's usually pretty up to date with rumours about financial scams in Asia. I'll also ask Ken Murai if he can figure out what the messages are about. Do you think Belinda would object to my sending them to James and Ken?'

'I don't see why. I know James is always extremely discreet. But tell Ken to be very careful. He's not to let anyone know where he got the messages from.'

Nick laughed. 'Don't worry. I'll tell Ken just enough. He's a savvy guy. Like James, he won't ask too many questions. And he just may see something in the messages that we can't.'

6

Tokyo, 29 May

Nick's email arrived in Ken Murai's inbox in the wee hours of the night, so he could only read the long letter and the attachment over breakfast the next morning. He pondered both during his hour-long commute to his office and for the rest of the morning, every time he took a break. Then, during his lunch hour, he called his close friend, Saburo Baba.

By 6.30 that evening, Ken was seated in a corner of The Bistro, a small restaurant in the Hotel Chinzanso, a luxury hotel not far from where both Baba and he lived. He nursed a beer while he waited for Baba, a member of Japan's Foreign Ministry, currently seconded as a counsellor on international affairs to the Prime Minister's Office. The friends had met in a music club at Tokyo University, where Baba had been nicknamed Bach because of his love of the composer.

Ken had asked Baba to meet him tonight because he thought the decoded messages should be read by someone other than Nick and himself. Because the two of them worked in the financial sector, they had both had a fairly similar reaction. But Baba would look at the messages from a different perspective. *If he doesn't, we'll still have a great meal together.*

He looked up as a tall figure in a subdued dark suit made his way to Ken's table.

'Sorry to be a bit late,' Baba said as he sat down. 'The PM kept me until after 5.30. I thought Emiko would be joining us?'

'No, Bach, it's just you and me. Emiko's working late again. Anyway, I wanted to pick your brains and I do appreciate your coming at zero notice. Although,' Ken grinned, 'I'll admit that you've spared me a dinner of instant noodles.'

'You're lucky,' said Baba wryly, 'You've caught me on the one night this week I don't have to eat with the prime minister or someone else having an international crisis.'

Ken noticed how tired his friend looked. Baba was still as slim and erect as he had been when they were at university together but his short hair was almost grey even though he was barely into his forties.

A waitress hurried over with menus. Baba ordered a glass of Rhone wine and chose the three-course set menu of the day. 'It's always good,' he said. Ken, looking up at the waitress, said, 'I'll have the same. And a glass of the same wine too, please.'

'I take it that the PM is keeping you busy,' said Ken, as the waitress left.

'That's an understatement,' sighed Baba. 'I never thought when I was seconded to the Prime Minister's Office that I'd end up working far longer hours than I did at the Foreign Ministry. The PM thinks nothing of working 14-hour days. He doesn't look well, but he won't slow down. I'm quite concerned about his health.'

Their wine arrived. Baba took a sip. 'It's a real treat to have a relaxing meal with an old friend.'

'Well, you may not find it so relaxing when I tell you why I wanted to see you.' Ken pulled out a sheet of paper from the slim briefcase that sat beside him. 'Take a look at this.'

Baba took the sheet of paper and read the messages very carefully. Then he looked at Ken over his gold-rimmed glasses. 'What's this? Where'd you get it?'

'They're decoded messages sent to the wife of an American friend. The person who decoded them—an American working in Beijing—was told they weren't important. But the few people who've seen them, me included, think they are.'

'This friend of yours—it's Nick Koyama, your classmate at Harvard. Right?'

'I'm neither admitting it nor denying it. Just humour me. I've already said all I can about how I got them.'

Baba smiled. 'OK, so this is confidential. Well, I've read the messages, but I can't at the moment think what they are about. Why did you want to discuss them with me?'

'I was told that the first messages were picked up over the eastern part of China. The messages were in English, but the code was based on an outdated Chinese telegraphic code. Other messages came either from the same part of China or from the eastern part of the US, but one of the last messages was picked up over Japan, over the Kanto region in fact.' Ken pointed to the message 'will look into mtc st'. 'I could be dead wrong, but they seem to be about some kind of international financial plot. I just want to be sure that whatever the plot is, the target doesn't involve anything Japanese. I can speculate about what a lot of things are, especially the acronyms. But I can't figure out what the plot is about, so I wanted to see what you'd make of it.'

Before Baba had a chance to respond, their prawn appetizers arrived. Ken began to eat, but Baba didn't touch his food. His eyes narrowed as he reread the 14 messages very slowly. Ken chewed on a prawn and waited.

Finally Baba put the sheet of paper down on the table.

'OK, I think there's more to them than I initially thought. I think MTC might possibly be the Mitsumoto Trading Company, which does business around the world. Remember, when we met a few weeks ago, I told you that the PM was working to help the consortium that Mitsumoto has cobbled together? To ensure that it won the bid for the oil reserves off Benin? That's one reason I think MTC could be Mitsumoto Trading.'

Ken nodded and put his fork down, distracted from his meal. 'What other reasons?'

'There could be lots of corporations in the world with the acronym MTC, but the messages also have MOF and BOJ in them. I thought these might refer to the Ministry of Finance and the Bank of Japan.'

Ken leaned back and sighed. 'So we're on the same wavelength. I wondered whether my conjectures were far-fetched, given the scanty evidence in these obscure messages.'

Baba nodded. 'It all fits, doesn't it? There's an international plot originating in China that is focusing on the MTC and that is concerned about how our Ministry of Finance and the Bank of Japan will react. One very reasonable guess we can make is that someone based in China is plotting, with the help of people in the US, Germany and Japan, to grab all four tracts of the Benin oil reserves. And this someone knows that its biggest competitor for those bids is the Mitsumoto consortium.'

A server appeared to remove their appetizer plates but hesitated when he saw that the plates were still full.

'Sorry, we've been talking,' apologized Baba. 'Give us a few more minutes, please.'

The two men ate silently. When they'd finished the prawns, Baba asked, 'So who do you think the plotters are? And how do you think they plan to prevent MTC from winning the bids?'

'If MTC were an American firm,' Ken said, slowly, 'I'd suspect that the plot is about buying up as many shares of MTC stock as possible to control the company. But only 10 to 15 per cent of MTC shares are traded, because here, in Japan, we have *keiretsu*. And those firms in the same enterprise group that own most of each other's shares would never sell their shares. So if the aim of the plot is to prevent MTC from winning the bids, the strategy has to be something more subtle. But I can't think what.'

Before Baba could answer, they were interrupted again by two servers who removed their empty plates and replaced them with their main courses.

'Listen,' suggested Baba, 'Let's enjoy our meal and then talk—OK?'

'You know,' Ken said, when they finally got to dessert and coffee, 'a couple of weeks ago, I attended the Shanghai Economic Forum. And Nick Koyama and I went to a session held by President Fan of SAEC, the Sino-African Energy Corporation, a big state-owned enterprise, headquartered in Shanghai. It's MTC's main rival in the bid for the Benin oil. Nick and I had hoped to hear something new and useful on China's oil policy, but all we got was platitudes. Fan was remarkably close-mouthed about the Benin discoveries. He almost brushed off questions about it. The whole thing turned out to be such a waste of our time.'

'Do you think a state-owned enterprise like that could be behind these messages?'

'It does seem unlikely, given the amateurish nature of the exchanges. And I can't imagine a major state enterprise in China hooking up with a group in the US, in Germany, in Japan in order to do something financial . . . and very likely illegal.'

'So what do you think is going on?' Baba asked. 'You sound like you've something in mind.'

'It's pure speculation, but I do think it's quite possible it's a plot against MTC. I thought, Bach, that you might shed some light on who or what could be involved.'

'I think you have more faith in me that I deserve. I'm not in the world of finance. But I do know how serious the PM is, both about getting more badly needed energy sources for Japan and about keeping his major supporters happy. He pushed for the formation of the consortium because it'll help Japan get more oil from dependable and regionally diversified sources. And MTC and the rest of the Mitsumoto group have long been his major financial supporters, right from his days as the governor of Tottori Prefecture. But given the organization of both the Mitsumoto group and the MTC consortium, I can't think of a way either could be undermined except by China or some other country organizing a similar consortium. You're the financial expert, Ken—what do you think the plan could be.'

'Hell, Bach, I don't know! And that's why I'm so frustrated.'

'Unless we have more information, I don't think we can figure it out. Do you think we can get more of these messages? Assuming there will be more.'

'I suspect so. I'll ask Nick.'

'I knew it was Nick,' Baba grinned. 'Now I've got to figure out how to alert the PM about a possible plot against MTC. It's not going to be easy, because we don't have any firm basis for it. And I can't give away how I heard about it. I think I'll tell the PM's chief secretary that I've heard rumours from my colleagues in the Foreign Ministry about an international plot against Mitsumoto but don't know more than that. I've no doubt Chief Secretary Fukunaga will warn the PM and keep his ears open for any information.'

Ken pushed his coffee cup away. 'I remember,' he sighed, 'the world when we started working. Japan was still No. 2 in terms of its GDP, we had 50 nuclear energy plants and the Chinese economy was just beginning to grow. Now we're No. 3 and steadily sliding, and after the Fukushima meltdown, we've got massive energy problems. China's an economic superpower and Japan's standard of living continues to decline.'

'Let's not despair. We don't know what's going on but, rest assured, whenever someone's trying to pull off something this big, there's bound to be a weak link. That's what we have to count on, and that's what we have to wait for. The more devious and elaborate the plot, the more chances there are of someone slipping up or something going wrong. Those will be our clues.'

'You're right. But what really bugs me is who this "st" is who's going to check out MTC. He must be Japanese. Which means we have a traitor in our midst!'

7

Shanghai, 1 June

Ma Jianrong bit his lips in irritation as he listened to the wailing of his wife and her sister. Why were they mourning the death of their father? When they had so bitterly complained about him all their lives? *Women*, he thought with disgust, *and these outmoded Chinese funeral customs*!

His left pocket vibrated.

Ma surreptitiously pulled his phone out and held it low beside him. His wife nudged him, but he ignored her and checked the latest message. It was from Ye Lixi. *Why does he want to meet now? We're supposed to meet at his hotel this evening.*

Even though his wife was glaring at him, he pointed to the door and indicated he was about to leave. Then he slid to the side of the room and backed out of the door of the crematorium.

Outside, Ma read Ye's message again. He frowned. *He wants to meet as soon as possible.* There were directions to the building where Ye was waiting. *Never been to that part of Shanghai.* Ma walked over to the parking lot, got into his Honda and headed west. As he drove, Ma thought, *Ye is clever. It's good to change the meeting place. Much better than our original plan of meeting at his hotel. Now we'll have no worries about being seen together.*

But as he followed the directions to the meeting place on the outskirts of the city, Ma became increasingly disconcerted. He was driving by shabby buildings and small run-down factories. The streets were mostly empty. *Why did Ye choose to meet at a place like this?*

His destination proved to be a deserted factory. There were no lights, no sound of machinery, not a soul to be seen.

This is very odd.

He carefully checked the address again, then parked. He locked his car and walked through the open fence towards the building.

What a strange place for our meeting! He must be more nervous about the evidence he's uncovered than I thought . . . some big corruption in Nigeria involving SAEC. I knew the books weren't balancing as they should, but is the evidence so hot that it can only be handed to me in this godforsaken spot?

Ma stood in front of the building, staring at the entrance. *Ye must be waiting inside.* Feeling terribly exposed, he went up to the door. It appeared at first glance to be locked but, when Ma gave it a tentative push, it creaked open.

Ma walked in and immediately smelt machine oil and urine. The only light came through the crack in the door. As his eyes adjusted to the darkness, he thought he saw discarded machines and equipment at the far end of the hall. Piles of rubbish lay here and there.

But where was Ye?

Should I wait for him? I need whatever he's got on the embezzlement going on in the SAEC offices in Nigeria. Good thing I asked him to look into it for me. I could have been accused of malfeasance and fired . . . or worse. But if I can uncover who the culprits are, I could finally be promoted to CFO! But where the hell is Ye?

Tired of waiting, and bit unnerved by the strange, dark building, Ma decided to return to his car when he heard a sound.

'Ye Lixi?'

A shadow detached itself from the discarded machines and strode over to him. As it drew closer, Ma realized it was not Ye—it was a stranger.

'Who the hell are you?'

The man said nothing but drew even closer and then, twisting his body in a rapid flowing move, he kicked Ma's side with his left leg. Ma groaned, lost his balance and slumped onto the cement floor.

The man pulled out a pistol, jammed its nozzle into Ma's mouth and fired.

Blood and tissue splattered around what remained of Ma's head.

The dead man was no longer recognizable.

The gunman carefully squatted beside the body and felt for a pulse, though it was obvious the man was no longer alive. Then, nodding to himself, he took out a handkerchief, carefully wiped his fingerprints off the weapon, then carefully put the pistol in the dead man's right hand and pressed his fingers around it.

As he got back to his feet, he felt a pang of regret. Not for the dead man—but for the gun. *I've had that 77 shi shou qiang semi-automatic since my days in the army.*

8

Shanghai, 8 June

'That's blackmail,' shouted a voice behind the door. Mimi took her hand off the doorknob of President Fan's office as if it was red-hot. *What's going on? Who's in there with him?*

'You're being paid enough already!' Fan shouted.

A chair scraped back. Mimi beat a hasty retreat back down the hall, nearly dropping the files she'd been taking to the president.

Blackmail?

Back at her desk Mimi stared at her dark computer monitor. Over the past few months she'd increasingly felt that something was amiss. The first thing out of the ordinary had been her dismissal from the meeting between President Fan and Professor Du. Then there'd been the disappearance of the head accountant, Ma Jianrong. He'd had a message at his father-in-law's funeral and gone off in his car. A patrol car found Ma's auto—and a curious officer had searched the desolate area and discovered his body. From the evidence at the scene it seemed a clear case of suicide. Rumours were rife about why he was at the site, and why he'd rushed out to commit suicide.

None of it made sense to Mimi. What distressed her most was that things at work had changed in the last month. Professor Du was now coming for meetings with her boss more than once a week, and she was still not allowed to sit in on those meetings. She couldn't help wondering, *If everything is above board, why are their meetings so secret?*

Even more puzzling was the president asking her to encode and decode short messages in English. Shortly after she'd been dismissed from the meetings with Du, the president had asked her to come to his office to encode a message in English that was 'top secret.' She was to work at a small table in his office, using his personal laptop and she was not to talk to anyone about them. The coding was tedious though simple enough—all she had to do was to convert letters into four-digit numbers, using a table the president gave her. She didn't know what the president did with the messages she encoded, but she assumed he was sending them over the Internet.

The day after she encoded the first message, she was called into President Fan's office to decode a message he had received. She had to use the same table and, like the message she'd coded, this one was cryptic and made little sense to her. Since then, every few days she was called in to encode or decode a message, all still cryptic but using more acronyms and initials. She often wondered, *What are all these messages about? Why should they be in code? And what do they have to do with SAEC?*

Then there was the surprising way the president had treated her. He'd never spoken to her sternly before, but when she encoded the first message, he'd said, very severely, 'Mimi, I must make one thing very clear—this message is absolutely confidential. That's why it's in code. This means you are not to discuss the content with anyone— not even with your family or colleagues.' When Mimi said, 'Of course, President, I never talk to anyone about this work,' he'd replied, 'Be sure you keep your word.'

His expression had been so cold that Mimi had felt a chill run down her spine.

And then there was that strange meeting at Fudan University the day after the Shanghai Economic Forum had ended. She got a phone call from President Fan, asking for the file marked 'Estimates'. She was to bring it to the faculty lounge at the Department of Economics. The file was in the top drawer of his desk in a sealed, buff envelope. So she had no idea what was in it. As instructed, she had taken a taxi out to the university and gone up to the top floor of the building, to the department. She had never been in the faculty lounge before and was surprised at the rather luxurious furniture and the students serving drinks.

She found President Fan talking to Professor Du and two middle-aged men, one a grey-haired Caucasian, the other a handsome Asian who Mimi guessed was not Chinese. They were speaking in English but stopped talking when she walked up to give the president the envelope.

In a taxi on her way back to SAEC, she wondered why her boss was having a meeting at the university instead of in the SAEC conference room? Were the two men professors? *But they were wearing such expensive suits! Who were they?*

She hadn't been able to answer any of these questions, nor the one that kept nagging at her: *Why is the president using me for the secret coding?* He was bypassing his senior staff. And he was telling the administrator that she was 'helping write confidential letters in English'. *Does he think I'm so young and naive that I can't tell there's something strange going on?*

The only good thing in the past month had been a meeting with Lei Tao, the chief financial officer of SAEC. Lei Tao was her father's acquaintance, who had got her the interview with President Fan. The president had immediately hired her without going through the usual personnel search. Her father's guess was that Fan had taken into consideration that Lei Tao was a nephew of Lei Shuo, the minister of ethnic affairs and a member of the Politburo.

Mimi had talked to Lei Tao only once before, when she had come for her interview. Then, a couple of weeks ago, Lei had sent word that he wanted to see her and she had gone to his office with some trepidation. But it turned out to be just a social visit. She had been served tea and Lei had chatted with her about her work and how she liked working at SAEC.

'Since I'm the person who introduced you to the president, I feel responsible for your welfare here.'

Mimi had been a bit surprised—because she had joined SAEC three years before and this was the first time they had had a conversation. But Lei totally disarmed her. He asked her in detail about her work and she replied as best as she could. She did not, however, mention the coded messages. She wanted to keep her promise to the president, though she suspected that the CFO probably knew about the messages she was coding.

She found Lei utterly charming and very different from the authority figure that Fan presented. Lei was in his early forties, slim and with a full head of wavy black hair. Later she was surprised to learn from Han Bingbing, her closest friend in SAEC and who worked under Lei in the Financial Office, that he was unmarried. And that there was a despicable rumour about why he was single, but she just couldn't believe it.

But that hadn't been her only chat with Lei. A week ago he'd been to see Fan, and Mimi had run into him in the corridor. He'd stopped her and again chatted about her work. *Maybe I'll get somewhere in this organization, after all, if the CFO's interested in me.*

And so Mimi, hoping for a great future, had gone back to her coding work in a more equable frame of mind.

Until this morning.

She'd come in a few minutes early today so she could return to President Fan the file of letters she'd worked on yesterday. He'd said he wanted them first thing in the morning, but when she reached the door of his office, she heard him shout 'Blackmail'. So Mimi went back to her office and was now sitting at her desk, wondering what to do.

Her thoughts were interrupted by someone wishing her good morning. Her colleagues were arriving, one by one. She checked the time—she'd better get those files back to her boss or risk a reprimand.

But instead of going directly to Fan's office, Mimi went to his chief assistant, the one who maintained his schedule.

'I went to return these files to the president but someone's with him. When do you think his meeting will be over?'

'Shortly, I should think. It wasn't a scheduled meeting but Professor Du asked to see him about something first thing. Why don't you give me those files and I'll hand them over as soon as the president is free.'

Mimi returned to her desk, looking troubled. *So it was Professor Du as I guessed. But why did he ask for an unscheduled meeting with President Fan? And why did the president shout 'Blackmail!' and 'You are paid enough already.'*

These thoughts niggled at her all morning, and, by the time she went to lunch, she was aware that her feelings about her job had undergone a rather abrupt change. A job she had thought was so good one had somehow become fraught with worries. For the first time since she began to work at SAEC, she sat silently at lunch, not tasting a morsel of her food.

Things did not improve by the time she got home that evening. She was in a quandary. She badly wanted to consult someone. *Should I talk to Father or not? If I do, I'll have to tell him about the coding I'm doing. The president has forbidden it, but if he's up to something he shouldn't be, why am I honour bound to keep silent about the coding? Maybe I should talk to Father. After all, he's vice mayor.*

She finally made up her mind, and after dinner, she went to her father's study and asked to talk to him. 'I'd like some advice.'

Her father looked at Mimi's distraught expression and beckoned her to sit down.

'What's happened to make my daughter look so worried?'

'I've become very disturbed by things going on at SAEC that don't seem normal. Something's not right. I think something secret, and possibly illegal, may be going on. I don't know what, but whatever it is, I'm very sure that the president's advisor, Professor Du is involved. I used take notes of their meetings, but now I'm "excused" from them.' She hesitated. She didn't want to tell her father that she had eavesdropped.

'OK, I can see why that bothers you. But that can't be the only reason you wanted to talk to me.'

Mimi sighed deeply. 'You're right, Father. What really worries me is something I am not supposed to tell anyone. President Fan made me promise. He was very stern about it.'

'But I gather you are worried enough that you think you have to break your promise. Is that right?' Mimi's father spoke in a kindly tone but with firmness, a characteristic that made him popular with all his subordinates. 'Mingxi, if I think there is nothing in what you have to say, I won't mention it to anyone. I promise. And you know I keep my promises.'

'Yes, I do. Well then, for several weeks now I have been asked to encode and decode messages that the president writes and receives in English. I think the code is almost impossible to break without the table President Fan gave me. But the messages are very short and cryptic and with so many two- and three-letter abbreviations that I don't understand them. I can't understand why the business of SAEC needs to be in code.'

Clearly surprised by what his daughter had told him, he didn't respond immediately. Then he said slowly:

'Are you sure the reason for the coded messages isn't that President Fan is concerned about commercial spying? I'm told there is a lot of what's called industrial espionage. There's so much hacking of computers and email accounts that he might feel he has to keep some sensitive things relating to his business secret.'

'Yes, I've thought of that,' Mimi replied. 'But there are too many things that make me suspect this isn't just normal business practice.'

'Why do you think that?' Her father asked sharply.

'Well, first, his telling me all these messages I encode and decode for him have to be so totally secret that I'm the only one who works with these messages. And I'm the most junior member of his staff. Isn't that odd? If these messages are related to SAEC's business, why did he tell his chief assistant that I was helping him write very confidential letters in English when I was working on these messages? And then, I've always attended and taken notes in the president's meetings. But now when he meets with Professor Du, his advisor, I'm excused because they have something "very confidential" to talk about that I shouldn't hear. Father, there are some other reasons as well that make me think that something is wrong . . . '

Seeing how surprised her father was, she suddenly stopped. She wanted to tell him more . . . about how she had overheard Fan yell 'Blackmail' to Du and about Fan meeting mysterious foreigners at Fudan University. And then there was the inexplicable 'suicide' of the chief accountant. But before she could decide how much more to reveal to her father, he commented:

'Hmm, now I can understand why you're concerned. So, let me make some inquiries through my friends in the Party. I have to be very careful because President Fan has many friends among the leaders of the Party in Shanghai.'

The vice mayor leaned over and patted his daughter on the knee. 'Mimi, you are an intelligent and well-educated young woman. But remember that you are still a novice when it comes to business. It's a tough, dog-eat-dog world out there. What you told me surprised me, but we have to remember that the president . . . and SAEC . . . must have especially difficult and delicate problems to deal with in the very competitive international energy business. I suggest you keep your eyes open and your mouth shut and stop worrying so much until you or I find something more about what's going on at SAEC.'

Mimi nodded. Her father still seemed to be thinking. He slowly added:

'As I said, I'll make inquiries. And you keep me informed if you learn anything new.' Then he paused and went on. 'Offhand, I really can't think, though, that there could be any malfeasance involved. From everything I hear about President Fan, he is a very able president of SAEC and above reproach. And I've been involved in various matters for several years now with the CFO of SAEC, and I can't believe that Lei Tao would be doing anything not above board. So, I understand why you are very worried but let's not make any hasty presumptions. OK? Do stop worrying and put that smile back on your face.'

Mimi smiled wanly at her father. Although she still felt anxious, it felt good to have her worries off her chest and to have her father now as a confidant.

9

Dresden and New York, 9 June

Markus Adler finally had his plan in place on 9 June, his 54th birthday.

It had taken him three weeks to figure out how he would come up with the funds for Josh's project—he would abscond with the money from the accounts in his bank. *I can't just 'borrow' the money and stay in Dresden—eventually the auditors would catch me. And why stick with the job when the project is going to make me fabulously rich?*

He would have to disappear. The more he thought about living somewhere in the US, or even Paris, the city he had long wanted to visit, the easier became the decision to leave Dresden for good. He was sure he could 'disappear' out of reach of the German authorities, even Interpol. *I'll be a multimillionaire—I can live wherever I want. I could get a new face with plastic surgery—I'll do some research on that. I think Josh can get me an American passport . . .*

His only problem was how to circumvent the numerous 'prudential' rules and regulations of the bank. Finally, he was sure he'd found a way to get 250 million euros. *Even though Josh was hoping I'd come up with 300 million, 250 should do it.*

Markus grinned as he checked the list of 52 accounts belonging to individuals and organizations, each a 'private, high net worth equity investment' account. He knew the name of every one of the individuals and organizations and the amount in each account. To make sure each account was earning the highest possible income, he had used all his skills as one of Germany's best quants with his complex algorithms consisting of advanced mathematical equations.

Looking at the names, he knew he had chosen the 'best' accounts to plunder—they were large accounts whose owners were unlikely to realize that funds were missing before he was gone. One group, the Frau Braun group, as he'd named it, consisted of 22 accounts belonging to wealthy individuals, mostly elderly females, who had entrusted Markus with the management of their money. They rarely asked questions as long as they were getting good returns.

The second group, the Pension Funds, consisted of 17 institutional accounts, such as the Transportarbeiter Rente Aktienfond or the Transport Workers' Pension Equity Fund. The officers of these accounts were not familiar with the stock and bond markets, and Markus' trading decisions had rarely been questioned, particularly since the returns had been good.

Markus decided that he wouldn't touch the 13 remaining accounts because he knew their owners frequently checked their performance records on the Internet or by calling Trudi Vögel. And every so often they withdrew money. In any case, he didn't really need those accounts—he could get nearly 90 million euros from the Frau Braun category and another 160 million from the Pension Funds. The money would be transferred to Josh's New York firm via accounts he'd create in Singapore where few questions were asked. Josh's ideas, some of which he said he had got from his 'genius friend in Singapore,' were extremely useful.

The only obstacle to the plan was Frau Trudi Vögel. Markus had to get rid of her. *Aber wie?* But how? He had puzzled over the problem for hours until yesterday when he'd finally cracked it. His bank's head office in Frankfurt had just sent a memo demanding that all branch managers reduce their payroll costs. Thanks to this new policy, he now knew what to do. He smiled, knowing that the way was clear for him to invest in his future, in the life of a multi-millionaire.

He called Trudi Vögel into his office.

'Frau Vögel, congratulations! You've earned a well-deserved promotion.'

As Markus had expected, she looked bewildered—she was aware that no one in the branch was retiring. And since the bank was trying to reduce the number of employees, a new position was highly unlikely.

'You may have heard that the manager of our Quedlinburg branch is resigning due to ill health. You have such an excellent record that you clearly deserve a promotion. As the head of the Dresden branch, I am empowered to name the head of our Quedlinburg office. So, I've decided to have you head the branch.'

Markus hadn't expected Trudi to be particularly grateful for this 'promotion', but he was surprised by her dismay at the news.

'Herr Adler, I am perfectly happy with my position here. Have I given you any reason to be dissatisfied with my performance?'

'No, no, Frau Vögel, your performance has been exemplary. But we need a loyal and experienced person to replace him. There will be an increase in your salary too, along with your increased responsibilities. All well deserved, I may say.'

'But, sir, I've had no experience in handling personnel. I've always worked with accounts, mostly on my own. I'm not sure I could handle the job as you would expect me to. Is there no possibility of my staying on here?'

'No, your promotion is also a part of the cost-saving organizational changes that I've been ordered to make by the head office in Frankfurt. Your position here is being eliminated.'

Trudi was desperate not to go. 'Sir, I'm responsible for my ageing parents who live here in Dresden. I'm their only child—I'm needed here.'

'But you don't live with them, do you? Quedlinburg isn't far away. You can come spend weekends here.'

Adler stood up, indicating the meeting was at an end. Trudi thanked him and trudged desolately out of the room.

As she closed the door, Adler thought, *That's done. Now all I have to do is wire the money to Singapore.*

Josh Fried grinned when he received Markus Adler's message that he would be soon sending him 250 million euros via several banks in Singapore, just as Nelson Ing, a banker in Singapore and his close friend had suggested.

Josh knew he could count on Shig Tanaka to raise money in both Japan and the US. And he would get Fan's promised 2 billion dollars by early August. He had advised Fan to use Ing's bank in Singapore as 'the relay station' for the money he was gradually sending, well ahead of the deadline, from his accounts in the Union Bank of Benin to Josh's hedge fund in New York. Even though Josh was paying a modest amount of interest on Fan's deposits, he was making good money already, using them in his hedge fund activities.

He closed his eyes and recalled with pleasure his conversation with Peter Scheinbaum at lunch. Peter was the CEO of a hedge fund almost twice as big as Josh's and the largest shareholder of one of the largest brokerage firms in New York.

'So . . . you want our brokerage firm to let your group do a 10-to-1 margin trade?' Scheinbaum asked.

'Yes, Peter. I now think the project I've told you about—the one Fan and I are planning—will have the necessary cash. But I need your brokerage to let us do the margin trades and all the other trading as well, here in New York and Tokyo . . . maybe even London, Shanghai and Singapore. You can charge our group a hefty interest rate and commissions for all it. But remember, you need to give Shig Tanaka a little extra something for bringing in a bundle for the project. And you agreed to give me a third of the money you make through your fees from the group.'

'Sounds good to me, Josh. I'll still come out ahead. I've discussed your project with a few of my most trusted traders and quants. They tell me the trades you're planning to do in August sound virtually foolproof. My hedge fund will do some trading too. . . exactly the same ones you guys do . . . it should help you make even more.'

'Great. How much you think you'll trade?'

'At least 2 billion. Could be more.'

'That'll help immensely. Thanks, Peter.'

'Don't thank me. I'm going to make a pile thanks to you.'

Josh could still hear Peter's exuberant laugh.

After that conversation, Josh was even more confident that the war chest would exceed the 6 billion dollar minimum he'd considered absolutely necessary for the project to succeed.

He couldn't stop smiling.

Shigeru Tanaka couldn't stop smiling either. In New York on Sumida Bank business, he was also soliciting funds for 'the project.' This afternoon he was visiting Charles Patrick Dugan—a well-known developer of large-scale projects from Dubai to Hawaii—and his wife, Devra Berger—owner of a small but fast-growing fashion house, DevraStyles. He had been introduced to them by Tim Ogilvy, a multi-billionaire and an international investor with whom Shig had done many lucrative deals during his time as the manager of the Sumida's New York branch. Shig had been invited to the Dugans' home. As soon as he looked at their Manhattan address, he realized how rich they must be, even before he stepped into their luxurious penthouse with its breathtaking view of Central Park.

Shig found the couple charming though a rather odd pair. Dugan was tall with light hair and seemed rather laid back. Devra was an alluring beauty, slim and dark and very intense. She wanted to expand DevraStyles internationally but lacked the funding. She had started out making a sun hat for a friend, and from hats had successfully branched out into clothing. Next to Devra, Ogilvy was the largest shareholder in her company.

Tim had told Shig that he had concluded several real estate deals with Dugan over the years, each of which had rewarded the men with tens of millions of dollars. Tim said Dugan was always on the look-out for new ventures and both he and Devra would be ideal investors for the project.

Dugan came straight to the point as soon as they'd finished their small talk and coffee. 'I understand you've known Tim Ogilvy since you were the head of Sumida's New York branch. He says you have a big project you want to tell us about.'

'Yes, Tim and I go back a long way,' said Shig, smiling, 'He mentioned that the two of you have worked together. When I told him I had a major project in the works and was lining up investors, he said you and Ms Berger might be interested.'

'Devra, please. Yes, I'd like to expand into the international market but I need more capital. So, what is this project?'

Aware that he was speaking to a financially astute couple, Tanaka carefully explained his plan. Charles interrupted now and then with questions about the size of 'the war chest' and the 'margin trades', and Devra wanted to know about who would be doing the trades and on what terms.

Finally, Charles turned to his wife. 'Well, what do you think?'

'It sounds like a winner. I know the Japanese are going to hate us when we make a huge amount of money on this project. But that's capitalism for you. And everything's legal—right?'

'Well,' said Charles before Shig could speak, 'some people, especially the Japanese, might not like the ethics of it, but you're right—it's legal all right.'

'And Tim's investing in your project?' Devra asked, smiling at Shig.

'Yes, and that's why he suggested I should talk to you two. I've no doubt about the high return on your investment. How big a killing you'll make depends only on how much cash you put up and how you structure the contracts on all your trades.'

'I think it's a great idea,' said Devra, 'I'm in, although I'm going to have to think about how to raise that kind of money.'

'And what about you, Mr Dugan?' asked Tanaka.

'It's very tempting but, unfortunately, my working capital is completely tied up with a project I've got in Seattle. Tim isn't involved with it, so I guess he didn't know my situation. Sorry.'

Tanaka was disappointed because he knew that Charles Dugan had many times more working capital than his wife. After promising to get together with Devra when she had the funds ready, he said his goodbyes and left.

As he made his way down the teak-lined elevator and out past the doorman, Shig was not a happy man. Here he was, the senior vice president of the fifth-largest bank in Japan, and instead of a luxury apartment like the Dugans', he lived in a modest house inherited from his wife. Granted it was in central Tokyo, off a small lane lined with cherry trees and near the Edo River, but it was only half the size of the Dugans' apartment. And, by rights, he should have been the bank's president, and not that fat idiot Honma who'd won over the board by convincing the members that the bank should continue to buy more government bonds. Shig had argued against it—it was a risky move because Japan already had the world's highest ratio of government debt to GDP. But no one had listened to him.

But, hey, by the end of August, when the project is over, I'm the one who's going to be a very, very rich man!

10

Shanghai, 11 June

It was nearly midnight when the Fengs were jolted awake by the insistent ringing of the doorbell. Feng struggled into his robe and went to the door. As he drew closer, a man yelled out from the other side, 'Mr Feng, I'm from the security company employed by SAEC. Mr Cao sent us.'

Mr Cao? He's in the communications room and must be doing overnight duty. Feng quickly unhooked the safety chain and opened the door. 'What's the problem?' he asked the gigantic young man who stood on the doorstep. The new chief accountant of SAEC was still too drowsy to wonder why Cao had sent someone to deliver a message in person instead of just calling him on the phone.

'One of SAEC's oil tankers was grounded in the Gulf of Guinea near the mouth of the Niger River a few hours ago. The captain has asked for 20,000 dollars to be wired to him immediately so that he can bribe the Nigerian officials for immediate help. And for repairs. Mr Cao said you'd know what to do. We need you to come with us. We've got a car to drive you to SAEC.'

Cao must have panicked, thought Feng, at the news of the disaster. He was a new recruit and hadn't experienced a crisis like this before. But neither had Feng. Promoted to chief accountant only a week ago, just after Ma's death, he was feeling his way in his new job, still surprised that he had been promoted over two seniors in the department. *This is my chance to prove myself and show the CFO that I'm up to the job. I'll go to the office and wire the money. With a car and no traffic in the middle of the night, it shouldn't take me more than an hour.*

'All right,' Feng said to the messenger, 'just give me a couple of minutes to get dressed.'

Still bleary-eyed, he threw on some clothes, told his wife about the emergency at work and said that he'd be back in about an hour.

He went outside and joined the huge young man who pointed to a car parked across the street where the driver was smoking a cigarette.

Feng knew neither the big young man nor the driver. But then, he thought to himself, it really wasn't possible to know everyone who worked for SAEC's security company.

The men sat silently as the car sped west on Huaihai Road. Feng dozed off until the car took a sharp right to the south, into Zhongshan Road along the Huangpu River, and jolted him awake. He looked outside and realized they were way off course.

'Hey, where are we going?'

'I'll explain in a minute,' said the driver.

The car sped along a dark road between the river and the Yuyuan Garden. Suddenly it swerved off onto the grassy bank of the river and came to a stop.

'What is this?' asked Feng, confused and alarmed, 'Why are we stopping here? What's going on?'

'Get out,' said the driver, stepping out of the car, carrying a paper bag. The big man got out too and opened Feng's door.

Feng slowly clambered out of the car. They seemed to be in the middle of nowhere. There were no other cars on the road. The river flowed silently past them, and the place was eerily quiet.

The driver pulled out a bottle of *shaojiu*, the very strong cheap liquor Feng liked to occasionally drink. Then he took three small cups from the paper bag, placed them on the hood of the car, opened the bottle and poured a drink for each of them.

'Relax. You're among friends. Friends who need to talk to you. To show we mean no harm, first we'll have a drink together.' The big man and the much shorter driver smiled and raised their cups in a toast to Feng.

Feng was suddenly terrified. *Something's very badly wrong. I've got to get out of here*!

At that moment Feng heard a car approach. He threw his cup to the ground and ran to the edge of the road, 'Help! Stop! Help me! Stop!'

But the car sped on without slowing down. Feng didn't think the driver had even seen him. Before he could take another step, the big man had clamped an arm around his neck, twisted his arm behind his back and dragged him back to the car.

'We offered you a drink,' snarled the driver, 'and drink you will.'

'Why are we here?' Feng shouted, frightened and enraged, 'Who *are* you?'

Neither man said a word. The giant of a man forced Feng to the ground, flat on his back, then sat on his legs and pinned his hands on the ground. The driver brought over the liquor bottle and poured a stream of liquid into Feng's mouth. Feng gasped and choked but had no option but to swallow. The driver kept pouring until the bottle was empty. Fighting to breathe, Feng could already feel his head beginning to reel from the alcohol he'd been forced to drink.

While the big man held Feng down, the driver went to the car and pulled a huge metal bucket out of the trunk. Then he brought out a very large metal canister and poured its contents into the bucket.

The big man grabbed Feng's feet and hoisted him upside down. Feng shrieked at the top of his lungs, but his shriek was stifled when the big man lowered Feng's head into the bucket. In a panic, Feng arched his back to try to prevent his head from going into the water. It was to no avail. As Feng's head got submerged, bubbles rose to the surface of the water.

The big man continued to grip Feng's jerking legs until at last they stopped moving.

'He struggled more than I thought he would,' said the short man. 'Good thing we came earlier and collected river water. Much less risky than trying to do the job in the river.'

The big man grinned and momentarily lost his grip. Feng's head hit the bottom of the bucket and a lot of water splashed out. When it was clear that there were no more bubbles and Feng's legs were absolutely inert, the driver said, 'OK, Corporal, you can pull him out now.'

Feng's body lay still on the ground. 'No cars in sight,' said the driver, looking up and down the road, 'no sound of any vehicle or boats. Let's get it over with.'

Together the men carried Feng's body to the edge of the bank and hurled it into the river. With a loud splash it was gone, into the depths of the Huangpu.

The two men got back into the car and headed back north.

'That wasn't so hard,' the big young man said with a smile.

The driver exhaled a lungful of smoke and smiled back.

'The police'll find the body somewhere downstream tomorrow morning. If they do an autopsy, they'll find his lungs full of river water and plenty of alcohol in the rest of him. SAEC's chief accountant got drunk, fell into the river and drowned. *This* time nobody will think it was anything but an accident!'

11

Shanghai, Mid-June

Mimi's mother was astonished when Mimi came back home just after two in the afternoon, rushed into her room and shut the door behind her without saying a word about why she was home in the middle of a workday. *Something must've happened at work. I guess she'll tell me when she's ready.*

When Mimi's father came home shortly after six, Mimi emerged from her room and told her parents she wanted to talk to them. Once they were all seated in her father's study, she announced, 'I'm going to quit my job!'

'Why? What's happened?' Mimi's mother couldn't believe her ears.

Mimi didn't respond and looked at her father.

'That's a big decision, Mingxi,' he said, slowly, 'What happened?'

Mimi explained. An hour after she got to work this morning, the police had arrived. The new chief accountant, Feng Tongbin, had drowned in the Huangpu River.

'The police interviewed President Fan Zhipeng, CFO Lei Tao, then everyone in the accounting department. And then everyone in all the other departments. Did anyone know why Mr Feng might have committed suicide? Was he depressed? Was he a heavy drinker? What problems did he have?

'I barely knew what Mr Feng looked like and I've never spoken to him, so I couldn't answer any of the questions. No one else in the office had any explanations either about why he'd commit suicide. We told the officers we were all shocked at the death of a second chief accountant so soon after the first.

'After the officers left, I was called into the president's office. He gave me another secret coding assignment and—'

'Another secret coding assignment?' Mimi's mother was having a hard time grappling with all this alarming information.

Mimi explained what she'd been doing for the last few months. 'I talked to Father about it, but he convinced me that President Fan had legitimate business secrets connected to SAEC. The messages are in English, so I'm sure the recipients are foreigners.'

'Well, if your father thinks it's all right, why are you so upset? Upset enough to want to quit your job?'

'Something's very wrong at SAEC.' Mimi was emphatic. She turned to her father. 'Father, you told me earlier that President Fan might be trying to prevent industrial espionage. Maybe he is. But why is he using me, the most junior person, to do the coding? And why have two chief accountants died in less than two weeks? And both under very strange circumstances?'

'After we were questioned by the police, I went to lunch with Han Bingbing, my friend in the finance office. She told me that Mrs Feng came to SAEC, demanding to know why her husband had left home in the middle of the night on SAEC business and didn't return. She said someone came to get him around midnight to take him to SAEC. He told her he'd be back in an hour. But he never came home. Bingbing said no one in the office knows of any emergency that could've needed Mr Feng coming to the office so late at night. And if someone went to take him to SAEC, how did he get to the river? Everyone in her department is wondering if the deaths of the two chief accountants are connected.'

'But,' her mother said, 'I thought Mr Ma commited suicide with a gun?'

'True. But both were chief accountants at SAEC. Mrs Ma insists that her husband left in the middle of a funeral service after getting a message on his phone. And Mrs Feng said her husband left home in the middle of night because someone came in a car to get him. I think it's very possible that the person who called Mr Ma away and the person who came to take Mr Feng are one and the same.'

Mimi's parents stared at her, speechless.

'One more thing. Bingbing told me that Mr Feng had been very concerned about something. He'd been checking and re-checking the financial records, and he'd scheduled a meeting with senior management, including CFO Lei Tao, for yesterday morning at 10. So why would he go out in the middle of the night and drown himself? All this, and my worries about the coding I'm having to do—it's all too much! I just can't take it any more. I used to love my job but I just can't work at SAEC any longer.' Mimi looked as if she was trying to hold back tears.

'You walked out?' Her mother was dismayed.

'No, no. I said I had a migraine and needed some rest. No one was surprised because everyone's been so upset after hearing about Mr Feng and undergoing the police questioning.'

'And so you're throwing away the position that both your father and Mr Lei worked so hard to get you?' Clearly, her mother didn't approve of her impulsive decision.

'Mother,' Mimi snapped, 'do you really think I should keep on working there? The police were so persistent with their questions— I don't think they're convinced at all that Mr Feng committed suicide. One person being killed might have nothing to do with SAEC. But for two of its chief accountants to die under suspicious circumstances within such a short time?'

Mimi looked at her father, hoping for some sympathy. He didn't disappoint her.

'It's understandable for you to be upset—the secret coding, the president's attitude towards you, the two suspicious deaths . . . If you're asking for my permission to quit, you have it. It sounds like it's time for you to leave SAEC.'

Relieved, Mimi wanted to know what she should give as her reason for leaving. Her parents believed it had to be something harmless enough so as not to arouse President Fan's suspicions, particularly if he was up to something illegal or unethical. Nor should he begin to worry about Mimi spilling the beans about his coding assignment. Mimi's father also admitted to being concerned about what he'd say to Lei Tao, who had got Mimi her position.

What they finally decided was that Mimi would say she was leaving because she wanted to do something else, not because she was unhappy with her position.

But what was that something else?

Mimi wandered over to the window as she listened to her parents discuss her future. She looked past their green hedge and across the narrow lane to the row of identical brick houses. Usually she loved the view, loved looking out at the quiet, little settlement built in the French Concession a century ago, but this evening she wished she were far away.

'Father,' she said, her mind suddenly made up, 'what if I were to leave Shanghai for a while . . . go away . . . to America to study again?'

Her parents were stunned into a few moments of silence. But then her father slowly smiled and said, 'That may not be a bad idea. Then I'll have no problem explaining to Mr Lei why you decided to quit. President Fan too will understand, I'm sure.'

Mimi's mother suggested they continue the discussion over dinner. In the end it took them less than half an hour to come up with a plan for Mimi's second stay in the US. She would say she wanted to study in America again, to take courses in English, economics and international relations. They would pretend this had been in the works for some months. She would resign as soon as she could and then go back to Minnesota where she'd spent a year at Macalester College in St Paul, the alma mater of her American tutor.

'Your stay at Macalester was paid for by SAEC. Even though I'm a senior civil servant, I don't know how long I can finance your studies there. But I can certainly afford a year if you're careful with money.'

During the weekend, Mimi did some online research and found that there were summer courses at the University of Minnesota for non-matriculated 'visiting students', so she could go back to Minnesota to study. She phoned the Petersons in Minneapolis who had hosted her during her holidays at Macalester. Much to her delight, Mrs Peterson invited her to spend the summer with them.

Mimi returned to work on Monday, and on Wednesday presented President Fan with her letter of resignation. She had no trouble at all in convincing him that she had changed her future plans, though he was a bit taken aback by the suddenness of her decision. She had after all been so eager to come to work at SAEC. She gave two weeks' notice, but the president said that she would need time to prepare and suggested she leave by the end of the week. Much relieved by his reaction, she gratefully thanked him for everything he had done for her and left his room.

President Fan seemed rather distant in the days immediately following, but she thought that only natural. After all, she was leaving after working at SAEC for such a short time. He didn't have her do any more coding or decoding, but perhaps there was no more to do. All in all, she was quite relieved when her last day of work came and she made her formal thanks and farewells to her colleagues. The only person who seemed at all sorry to see her leave was Han Bingbing, who hugged her with tears in her eyes and made her promise to stay in touch.

12

Tokyo and New York, 18–23 June

'I can't get the prime minister to seriously consider the possibility of an international plot against the Mitsumoto Trading Company,' Baba grumbled to Ken Murai on the phone. 'I need something more specific. Have you any more news about the coded messages?'

'Nick sent several more to me yesterday. I meant to call you today.'

'Anything I can use to convince the PM?'

'Could be. The messages continue to mention MTC.'

'If there's anything more specific, the PM would be interested. What do they say?'

'That's the whole problem, Bach,' said Ken, sounding frustrated, 'there's nothing specific in them! If you think they can make a difference to the PM, you'll have to read them yourself.'

'Are you free for lunch?' Baba asked.

'I have a meeting at two, but if you come over at noon, I'll order in some lunch and we can talk in my office.'

An hour later the two old friends were at Ken's desk. Handing a box lunch to Baba, Ken said, 'Bach, before getting to the messages, do you think the PM has contacted Mitsumoto that some group may be trying to block them from getting the Benin oil?'

'No, I don't think so, and that's been worrying me. The MTC group is his biggest financial supporter and he helped MTC put together a strong consortium to get the finances needed to acquire the Benin oil. The PM would certainly want to warn them if there was an international plot against the bid. I only wish we had more evidence . . . '

'Who's in the consortium? For some reason, the media's been totally silent about the group.'

'Anything related to the consortium is *sub rosa*. They don't want any potential competitor to know how strong it is. The members are all companies with deep pockets,' replied Baba, putting down his chopsticks for a moment. 'There are five key members: Heisei Petroleum, Kanto Gas, Kotobuki Life Insurance, the Omori Construction group and Sumida Bank.'

'That's quite a line-up!' commented Ken. 'Japan's largest oil and gas companies, its largest insurance company since the merger of three large firms, and one of our country's two biggest construction companies. Only Sumida Bank isn't at the very top in its field.'

'Yes, but it's our fifth-largest bank. And I've heard its president, Daisuke Honma, is one of the PM's strongest supporters in the banking community. There's no way the PM wants to lose the confidence of this group. But neither does he want to needlessly worry them. So let's see those new messages.'

Ken nodded and pulled out a sheet of paper out of his top desk drawer. As he handed it to Baba, he commented, 'One thing that's new is that more of them have been picked up over Japan. It could, of course, be a foreign plotter who happens to be in Japan. But if a Japanese is involved, which I think is more likely, he can get a lot more information about MTC and possibly about the consortium than a foreigner could.'

'I agree. What's even more worrying is that the Japanese plotter could be a mole in a company that's a member of the consortium.'

'Hey, let's not get carried away. Although you could very well be right. Take a look at the messages that have come in since we last talked.'

Baba read the messages carefully while Ken finished his lunch. After a few minutes, Baba looked up: 'I see why you couldn't tell me what they mean. "Brokerage", "margin trades" and "short selling"— but they're all so cryptic that I can't figure out what's going on.'

'Well, we can assume the group now has a brokerage firm lined up, and I'll bet the firm isn't in China. They could be planning some margin trading. Maybe they're planning to buy a large amount of MTC stock or sell MTC stock short on the margin? I don't see, though, how they could do either since almost all MTC shares are held by other companies in the MTC group. And none of them would sell their MTC shares. This means they're planning something so devious that you and I can't even begin to guess what!'

Baba let out a huge sigh. 'Yeah, even I know that doing margin trades means you can trade in many multiples of the money you have. So what now? What could we possibly do to find out more about these people and what they're plotting?'

'I've been thinking,' said Ken. 'It's a long shot, but when I was at the Shanghai Forum, my friend Nick Koyama and I happened to see a couple of men go up to the CEO of SAEC after his session. Nick recognized one of them, the president of an American hedge fund, a guy called Joshua Fried. Nick wondered why Fried, who apparently has a shady reputation in New York's financial world, would want to talk to the CEO. And some of these messages are signed JF. I've been thinking of asking Nick to look into Fried. Nick and his wife Bess have done this kind of thing before and had some unbelievable success. What do you think? Should I ask them?'

'Please do. We've got to do whatever we can.'

Seeing Baba's disconsolate expression, Ken smiled. 'You really seem down in the dumps today! What's the matter? Apart from all this, that is.'

Baba stopped eating and sighed again. 'I had no idea what I was getting into when I was seconded to the PM's office. He spends so much time worrying about party politics—how to please his sup-porters, how to raise more money . . . He's so busy with all that, he's paying no attention to all the important things, especially to the many difficult issues we have now with other countries. I can't tell you how frustrating it is. And now this plot looming out of nowhere, like a spectre. We have no idea who or what we are dealing with.'

'Spectre is the right word. And the spectre is so illusive because the plotters' messages are so cryptic and confusing,' Ken commented, sighing.

Baba said wryly, 'But don't forget that Nick's friend in Beijing wouldn't have sent the messages to Nick if the code wasn't convo-luted. Well, I'll tell the PM what we've gathered from the new mes-sages. He should be interested in the possibility of at least one Japanese being involved, if not more.'

Baba covered his half-eaten lunch with the lid, drained his teacup and stood up. Ken got up as well, came around the small table and clapped his old friend on the shoulder.

'Cheer up, Bach. I'll contact Nick as soon as you leave.'

'Bess, Ken's got an assignment you're going to like,' Nick said to his wife as she came out of the bathroom, wrapped in a huge blue towel. She stifled a yawn and sat down on the bed next to her husband who was checking his phone for messages.

'What is it?'

'He wants us to check out Joshua Fried, the New York hedge fund guy I saw at the Shanghai Forum. He says he wants to know if there's any connection between him and the plot that we all think is the subject of the coded messages.'

'Check out a New York hedge fund guy? Really?' Bess grinned as she stood up to get dressed.

'Bess,' Nick warned, 'you're not to do this yourself! You'd have to use the computers in the office. That's strictly illegal!'

'I know, I know—calm down,' laughed Bess, 'I was just thinking what fun it would be to get through the tough firewall the hedge fund guy's computer must have.' She ruffled her husband's hair by way of reassurance.

'What about putting Charlie DeMello onto it?' she suggested. 'Can Ken find the money to pay him? Thanks to his FBI background and his computer skills, Charlie can find out almost anything!'

'That's a good idea. I'm sure Ken and his friend Baba can find the money to pay him. You contact Charlie, and I'll ask around about Fried. I haven't heard any gossip about him lately, but who knows what's out there.'

The next Tuesday, Bess' phone rang just as she was thinking it was time she stopped for lunch. Before she could say hello, a familiar voice asked, 'Bess? It's not much, but I've got something I think you'll want to see. Can I bring it over?'

'Charlie? Already? Fantastic! Can you come now?'

'I'll see you in 20 minutes. Maybe less.'

And the line went dead.

Bess called Nick, then ordered in three turkey sandwiches and coffee. She and Nick were waiting in the small conference room in the Rubin-Hatch suite of offices when a rather scruffy figure with windblown grey hair, clad in jeans, sneakers and a windbreaker sauntered in.

'Hi, Charlie.' Nick shook DeMello's hand. 'Bess says you have something for us?'

Charlie put a manila envelope on the table and sank into a chair.

'Thanks for lunch!' Charlie said, reaching for a sandwich, 'I have another meeting after you guys, so I didn't think I'd get any.' DeMello began to unwrap a sandwich as Bess pulled out a sheaf of papers from the envelope.

'I think it would be quicker if you tell us what you found,' said Nick. 'We'll go over the report later.'

'Well, the bad news first,' began Charlie, reluctantly putting the sandwich down. 'Fried's firm has a really good firewall—I couldn't breach it with my ordinary programs. Didn't know if you wanted me to pull out the big guns, so I've left it for now. But he does have a free Yahoo account. And, for a hedge fund guy, a really crap password. It was a cinch to crack it. I got a lot of his emails in my report, but there are two kinds I should tell you about.'

Bess stopped going through the report and stared at Charlie. 'What?'

'One: he's arranged some kind of deal with a guy called Peter Scheinbaum. I assume you've heard of him?'

'Yes,' nodded Nick, 'we have. He heads one of the bigger hedge funds in New York. What kind of deal?'

'Not a very straight deal, I'm sure, because Fried used his private email account to set it up. They're going to short sell something and Fried's asked Scheinbaum to use the brokerage firm he owns or controls to handle it. I didn't have time to check who owns the brokerage, but I got the impression that Scheinbaum's hedge fund has a majority share. Several emails made it clear that the brokerage handles a lot of Fried's trade and that the two men meet often.'

DeMello took a bite of his sandwich, then swallowed and continued.

'Two: lots of Fried's emails are just strings of numbers. All from anonymized accounts. I've tried several sophisticated decryption programs but none of them worked. I did note that the numbers in every message are divisible by four.'

'Bingo!' exclaimed Bess, smiling from ear to ear. 'That proves Fried's in the plot! Fantastic, Charlie!'

Charlie was puzzled.

'You know what the numbers mean?'

'The plotters we're trying to trace communicate in code using anonymized email accounts. The code's in four-digit numbers. A friend of mine's managed to break it, so she can convert those numbers into English. We were only guessing that Fried was one of the people sending and receiving the coded emails. You've just proven he is!'

'This is a big help, Charlie,' Nick said and asked, 'Anything else?'

'I tapped into Fried's personal phone records. Nothing. The guy hasn't made any international calls recently. Just to Scheinbaum's office. Lots of email and texts to his mother, his daughter in Israel and to friends for social arrangements. Also several calls to the St Regis Hotel during the week of June 7. That's about it. Do you want me try and breach his firewall?'

'Not right now,' said Bess, as Charlie paused for another bite of his sandwich. 'We've got enough for now. Give us a day to read the reports—we'll let you know if we need more.'

'OK.' Charlie looked up at the clock on the wall. 'Mind if I take the rest of the sandwich with me? Great, and thanks for the quick payment. Someone called Saburo Baba wired it into my account. I've sent a copy of the report to him by DHL. Thanks, guys—see you sometime.' And with that, DeMello was up and out of the door.

Nick and Bess looked at each other and smiled broadly.

'Ken is going to be so hyped! At last we know that Fried and maybe Scheinbaum are in the plot. Too bad that Charlie couldn't tell us the source of the coded messages.'

'What I want to know,' Ken said, slowly, almost to himself, 'is who the third man is. The Asian talking to Fan and Fried after Fan's session, the man neither Ken nor I could identify.' Nick paused and looked at his watch. 'Just after one. That means it's 2 a.m. in Tokyo and Ken must be fast asleep. I'll text him to call us at home when it's mid-morning his time. By then we'll have had gone over Charlie's report.'

'This is all so mysterious—I wish we were working on it,' said Bess rather wistfully as she picked up her uneaten sandwich and took a bite.

'Who knows? Before it's over, we may well be,' said Nick as he began to read Charlie's report and bit into his own sandwich.

13

Minneapolis, 10–11 July

It was 11 days since Geoff Mitchell first met Xia Mingxi. It had been the third Monday of the eight-week summer session at the University of Minnesota. Twenty minutes after his class started, he heard the door of the classroom open. A department secretary poked her head into the room.

'My apologies for interrupting, Mr Mitchell, but I have a new student for you.' She opened the door wider to reveal a petite Asian woman.

The usually placid Geoff Mitchell was more than a bit annoyed at the interruption and at the late entrant to his course. *This class has already run for two weeks. I hope at least she is a native speaker of English.* But he hid his irritation and spoke as pleasantly as he could to the new student. 'Please come in and sit down. I'll talk to you after class.'

When the young woman was seated, he returned to his lecture on the art of describing characters in a short story. The woman took copious notes. After finishing his lecture, he gave a 20-minute assignment to write about 'a despicable character'. He saw her write busily again. As he collected the papers, he was surprised to see that she had written almost twice as much as the others had.

After class she came up to him and introduced herself. Surprised to learn she was Chinese, Geoff asked her how she wanted to be addressed. She said to call her Mimi. Geoff discovered in her an interesting mix of innocence and determination. In very good English she apologized for joining the class late and earnestly promised to catch up with the assignments. Later, when he read what she'd written, he was surprised to find that not only could she write in English, she had also described with real flair a senior government official who had the air of a gentleman but was possibly a conspirator in some dastardly international plot.

Today was a perfect summer day, the kind of day that made Geoff forget Minnesota's mosquito-ridden summers and Siberian winters. As he sat in his office, he found that he couldn't stop thinking about Mimi. She wasn't beautiful—her nose was a bit too wide and her chin rather pointed—but she had lovely dark eyes and gorgeous long, black hair.

Shaking himself out of his daydreaming, he decided to eat his lunch outdoors. He walked out, across the campus lawns dotted with students, to the Northrop Auditorium. As he approached its steps, he spotted a familiar elfin figure. Her arms wrapped around her legs, Mimi was sitting alone, lost in thought.

'Mimi,' he called. Her head jerked up, she looked at him blankly for a moment and then smiled. 'May I join you?' he asked.

She said nothing but nodded.

Geoff sat down beside her and pulled out his lunch. 'Not eating lunch today?' he asked.

'I'm not really hungry,' Mimi said softly, her thoughts clearly elsewhere.

'But you have a long class this afternoon. Here, have one of my *ikh* sandwiches.'

'*Ihk?*'

'Sorry. *Egg*—it's an egg sandwich,' Geoff replied, smiling. 'I try to talk American, but sometimes my New Zealand accent slips out.'

Mimi laughed and accepted a sandwich. He saw her relax at last.

To Geoff's surprise, once she began to talk, Mimi had a lot to say. She told him she was from Shanghai, that she'd spent a year at Macalester College in St Paul. Geoff told her he was from Christchurch in New Zealand but working for his doctorate at the

University of Minnesota. The more they talked, the more beguiled Geoff was by Mimi. As they finished their sandwiches, Geoff decided to take the plunge.

'I was wondering if you'd like to go swimming,' he asked rather diffidently.

'Swimming?' Mimi was a bit taken aback by the suggestion.

'The weather's supposed to stay like this over the weekend. I know a nice spot at Cedar Lake. Maybe we could take a picnic. How about tomorrow?'

Mimi thought for a bit and then, surprisingly, agreed. 'OK, I'll bring the sandwiches. Tomato and *ihk*?'

Geoff chuckled. 'Great, and I'll bring some cold drinks.'

Promptly at 10 on Saturday, Geoff picked Mimi up in his old VW Rabbit and they drove off to Cedar Lake. Mimi was delighted with the secluded point he'd found, and immediately took off her clothes to reveal a bikini. Small and slim, Mimi had the perfect figure and Geoff had to fight not to stare. The two had a long swim and then relaxed on the shore with their picnic lunch. Mimi seemed much more at ease, so Geoff thought it safe to ask her a few questions about herself.

'Are you just here for the summer?'

'I'm applying for the MA programme in economics, and I'd also like to take some courses in international relations. I thought it'd be easier to apply from here so I could be available for interviews. And I wanted to take your course to improve my English-writing ability.'

'Reading the essay you wrote on a despicable character, I got the feeling you had a specific person in mind. Or do you just have a lively imagination?'

'The man I wrote about? There's some imagination there, but what I said about him is true.' Then abruptly she stood up. 'Let's go for another swim!'

An hour later, as they lolled on beach towels in the shade of the wooded point, Mimi was very quiet. Geoff thought she seemed pre-occupied but he decided to not ask any more questions for now.

Mimi was grateful to Geoff for his silence. She was still very nervous about the situation at SAEC. Han Bingbing had sent her several emails reporting on events since Mimi's departure. Despite his wife's protests, Ma's death had been declared a suicide because the police could find only his fingerprints on the pistol used to kill him. Feng's death too had been officially declared a suicide or an accident because he had been 'clearly intoxicated'. Plus no marks of any kind were found on his body to indicate foul play.

Mimi, though, remained convinced that both men had been killed.

Bingbing had also written that Lei Tao, the CFO, was doubling up as chief accountant for now—her guess was that he thought it unlikely anyone would want the position after two predecessors had died under suspicious circumstances. She also wrote that 'Morale is low in my office because when Lei Tao took over, his colleagues felt that what he was really doing was going over the books to look for their errors.' Mimi had not been replaced, as far as Bingbing knew. In her last message, she'd signed off saying she wished she could go abroad to study too.

After getting Bingbing's last email, Mimi phoned her father to ask him what he'd found out about the two deaths. But his answer hadn't been helpful at all: 'I'm writing you a long letter that I'll send by email. I'm checking into the investigations of Ma's and Feng's deaths. Both cases have been closed by the authorities because they had found no evidence of "foul play". So I have to proceed very carefully. Fan Zhipeng is the respected president of a big state-owned enterprise and has a lot of connections with high Party officials in Beijing. I can't risk alienating the police by even hinting that they aren't doing their job. Please give me some more time.'

He ended by saying that Mimi was well out of SAEC. And since she hadn't told anyone where she was, he couldn't imagine that she was in any danger. She should stop thinking about the past and concentrate on her studies.

Mimi understood her father's position, but the lack of knowledge frustrated her. Two people had been killed, and there was some kind of an international plot that could harm the company, maybe even the country. Today was already 11 July and President Fan's plot was to take place soon—she remembered Du saying 'by the end of August but preferably before the middle of the month'. She felt utterly helpless. *Should I go to Washington and try to meet the Chinese ambassador? But what if he's a friend of President Fan? What on earth can I do?*

Mimi badly wanted to talk to someone. Her host parents were sweet but ageing, and they wouldn't be able to do anything other than lend a sympathetic ear. Her friends from Macalester had all moved away. But Geoff—Geoff seemed sensible. She looked at him sitting on the towel beside her, staring out at the lake.

'There's something I'd like to tell you,' Mimi said, hesitatingly. 'I'd like your advice. Would you mind if I told you about something that's bothering me?'

'No, go ahead.'

Her voice gaining confidence as she talked, Mimi told him everything—from the coded messages to the shouting about blackmail in the president's office to his meetings with Du to the two suspicious deaths. Geoff listened, by turns fascinated and alarmed. But by the time she finished, he was seriously worried. 'Good grief, Mimi, you ought to do something!'

'I know, but what? My father's a high official in Shanghai but even he doesn't seem to be able to do anything, not even to find out what's really going on.'

'How about writing up everything you've told me and sending it to a big newspaper in China? Something like the *New York Times?*'

'That won't work. They won't print it—I have no hard evidence to give them. They're not going to accuse the president of one of the largest state-owned companies based only on my suspicions. President Fan is also a member of the Communist Party and a former colonel of the People's Army. And even if I tried to hide my identity, I'm sure they'll find out. And then my father will be in big trouble.'

'Surely there's *something* we can do.'

'I just can't think of anything.'

Geoff looked pensive. Finally he suggested, 'How about writing up as much as you can remember . . . and . . . Hang on—which country do you think is the target of this plot?'

'Well, Fan and Du talked about Benin and how to obtain the rights to the oil. That's when they sent me out of the room.'

'Benin? I've never heard of it. Any other place mentioned in the conversations or the messages?'

'Benin's a small country in Africa. But yes, they mentioned Japan, so I think Japan could be a target.'

'Why?'

'Before Professor Du had me sent out of the room, he emphasized that the major competitor for winning the Benin oil bids was going to be Mitsumoto of Japan. I went on the Internet and found out that there are a few dozen companies named Mitsumoto-something. One is the Mitsumoto Trading Company, one of Japan's largest international trading companies. MTC. It makes a lot of investments abroad and exports and imports a lot of things, especially petroleum. It's such a huge corporation that it's not surprising that President Fan and Professor Du were worried about MTC outbidding SAEC for the Benin oil tracts.'

'Is that the only reason you think Japan is the target?'

'No, but once I found out what Mitsumoto was, then many other things began to make sense. One of the messages I coded mentioned BOJ. I checked that out on the Internet too, and it can mean the Bank of Jamaica or the Bank of Japan. It's not likely that President Fan is planning a big scheme involving Jamaica, so I'm guessing it's Japan. Another message mentioned the MOF, probably the Ministry of Finance. Then, again, most countries have a ministry of finance.'

'Mimi, Japan makes sense. It's a very large importer of oil. If you think the plot affects a company like Mitsumoto, and you know it involves something financial, why not write everything and send it to the Ministry of Finance or the Bank of Japan? Yes, that's it!'

'I suppose I could,' said Mimi, turning the idea over in her mind. 'One of the messages also mentioned "countermeasures by the BOJ and MOF".'

Geoff, nodded. 'It means that your former boss and his group are worried about or expecting possible countermeasures against their plan by the Bank of Japan and Japan's finance ministry.'

'Right. So if we alert the bank or the ministry, they may be able to take the countermeasures Fan is worried about to stop the plot! But where should I send my message? The bank or the ministry?'

'The central banks are usually too stuffy—they might not even do anything about it. How about the minister of finance? Someone there should be concerned. Write up everything you've told me and send it to the minister. They must have a website that gives you the ministry's address. Be sure you explain who you are and why you're writing what you're writing. Or the minister's secretary who'll open your letter will think you're a crackpot.'

'Crackpot?'

'Sorry. A nut . . . a crazy person.'

'I see what you mean. I'll write it up tomorrow. Could you go over my English, please?'

'No, just write it as well as you can. It will be more authentic if it's in your words and not edited to sound like someone else. But leave out your suspicions of the chief accountants getting murdered. Focus on the financial angle.'

Mimi was relieved—at last there was something she could do.

14

Tokyo and Benin, 16–20 July

Shigeo Tanaka sighed with pleasure as he accepted a flute of champagne from the Air France flight attendant. It had been a hectic day and he could have done without that unpleasant meeting with the president of Sumida Bank. His own position as vice president was becoming increasingly untenable. *The day of reckoning is coming soon for that fat Honma. I can't wait to tell him I'm quitting! But right now I'm going to enjoy this trip that's First Class all the way, from Narita to Paris and on to Benin. This is going to be the easiest 50,000 dollars I've ever made!*

Tanaka had a snack and then slept for a full seven hours, cocooned in his First Class pod. He was one of the lucky few who could sleep on planes. When he awoke, he was treated to French roast coffee and croissants. At Charles de Gaulle Airport, an agent escorted him to the First Class lounge and left his side only after making sure he was comfortably ensconced. But he was in for a shock when he realized he'd landed before four in the morning European time, and that he had a 10-hour layover in Paris before boarding his flight to Cotonou. Wondering why the travel agent had given him this terrible schedule, he checked air routes on the Internet and discovered, to his amazement, that it really did take 30 hours to get from Tokyo to Benin. *I guess this is the best the travel agent could do.*

So despite the First Class service, Tanaka was absolutely exhausted when he finally arrived in Cotonou that evening. An airport cab, an old Peugeot, took him to the Novotel, a three-storey hotel, not far from the airport. The travel agent had assured him that it was 'the best in Cotonou', but it was a far cry from the five-star hotels he usually stayed in.

An attractive young woman with dazzling white teeth escorted him to his third-floor room. As soon as she left, he slid open the windows in the hope of a breeze—the room was terribly stuffy. The night air was fresh and cool against his face, a welcome change from Tokyo's heat and humidity, but he could see nothing. Leaving the window open, he turned back and got ready for bed. But once he turned the lights out and lay down, he couldn't sleep a wink. The travel, the exhaustion, the jet lag—and the mosquitoes no one had warned him about! By dawn, he was cursing the moment he'd imagined this turning out to be a wonderful weekend. He hoped fervently that everything would go according to plan. He wanted nothing more than to catch the next flight back home.

Watching the sun rise, Tanaka mulled over his last conversation with Fan in Shanghai. 'Mr Tanaka, it's crucial we get all possible information about Mitsumoto's plans for Benin. Otherwise we have no hope of outbidding them. Which is why I need you go to Cotonou and talk to someone at MTC. I'm sure your chances of getting information in Benin are better than at the head office in Tokyo. I want to know as much as possible so that I can then make sure SEAC will get the Benin oil.'

Tanaka had been nonplussed. Japan needed the oil so badly that in asking him to make sure SEAC got all the four bids, Fan was in fact asking Tanaka to betray his own country. *Is this something I really want to do?*

'I'll make it worth your while, Mr Tanaka,' Fan had added, correctly sensing his hesitation, 'Just a day or two, and we'll pay you 50,000 US dollars and all expenses, including First Class travel.'

Fifty grand for chatting with someone from MTC? Of course he'd go!

'Just leave me your account number,' Fan was saying, 'and the Swift code of your bank in Tokyo—or anywhere else for that matter. The money will be waiting for you when you get back.'

Fan planned to be in Benin at the same time, and Tanaka had agreed to meet him before he took the flight back home. As Tanaka stood up to leave, Fan said, 'Since you've agreed to go to Benin, Mr Tanaka, I have a special request. You need to see the head man in the Benin office of MTC and give him the following message.'

The message Fan then spelled out was so devious that Tanaka, accustomed though he was to various unscrupulous dealings in the banking business, was shocked. But he agreed to pass the message on. *As the Japanese saying goes, 'Doku wo kurawaba sara made.' If you're going to swallow poison, why not swallow the container too*!

Tanaka's first appointment in Cotonou was at the Japanese Embassy. He hadn't told Fan he'd be going there, but from his experience he knew an ambassador in a small country like Benin would be a mine of information. He arrived at the embassy just before the 10 o'clock appointment he'd scheduled from Tokyo and was greeted with the deference due to a senior banker from Japan.

Ambassador Kazuo Hattori was in his late 50s, and Tanaka surmised he was an undistinguished career diplomat serving his final post. Hattori seemed delighted to have such an important visitor. After a few minutes of polite conversation, Tanaka said he hoped that the MTC-led consortium would get the rights to the offshore Benin oil field 'for the sake of energy-starved Japan'.

The ambassador, nodding enthusiastically, launched into a lecture. 'Indeed. Mr Tanaka. I too hope so. About 10 days ago, I dined with Mr Nagano, the manager of MTC's local office. He told me he had "reliable enough intelligence" that none of his potential competitors —an American, a French and a Chinese company—would be able to outbid MTC which, as we all know, has deep pockets and plenty of government support. But he did say he was worried about the high cost of getting the oil from so far deep in the ocean. Not only is the Gulf of Guinea notoriously rough all year round, but they'll also have to hire very expensive specialist OFS companies.'

'OFS companies?' asked Tanaka, who knew nothing about the oil business.

'Oil field service companies. I didn't know about them either until Nagano told me. Until very recently, it seems, oil companies drilled for oil by forcing a well shaft into a gentle arc into the ocean bed. But now shafts can be drilled vertically to a depth of several kilometres. Then they are made to turn sharply and continue horizontally for up to 12 kilometres. Because of the new technology the OFS firms have, you can extract almost all the oil from under the sea. What is troubling MTC is that these companies are extremely expensive. Apparently there are only four or five OFS companies in the world, and they charge at least a few million dollars per day!'

'The MTC consortium doesn't have this technology?'

'No. So they are between a rock and hard place. They desperately want the oil here, but they aren't sure they can afford to get at it profitably. So they may have to let the Chinese win the bid for some of the oil fields.'

'The Chinese?'

'Yes, the Sino-Africa Energy Company, SAEC. It's already getting a lot of oil from Nigeria and elsewhere in Africa. It's a state-owned company that can get the government to pitch in with a lot of money.'

Tanaka was surprised that the ambassador made no mention of the Mitsumoto consortium. Or was it so secret that the ambassador didn't know about it? Even Tanaka hadn't been in on the talks when his bank had joined the consortium, but he had thought that had been because he was out of favour with Honma, Sumida's president.

Tanaka thanked the ambassador for his time, and left. He was sure Fan would be delighted to hear that the MTC, despite the consortium, would be faced with financial problems should it obtain the bids. *This will increase the chances of MTC accepting Fan's devious proposal.*

Tanaka went back to the Novotel and had lunch. Then he arranged for a taxi to take him to MTC for his two o'clock appointment with Nagano. The office was located some distance away, across the Lagune de Cotonou, the waterway that connected Lac Nokoué, the large lake to the north of the city, and the Gulf of Guinea.

Nagano, MTC's manager in Benin, was most cordial but very curious about why Tanaka wanted to meet him.

'Mr Tanaka—welcome! To what do I owe the honour of meeting the vice president of one of Japan's largest banks? And, if I may ask, sir, what are you doing in Cotonou?'

Tanaka gave his prepared answer—his bank was exploring 'investment opportunities' in West Africa.

'I realize my bank isn't your main bank, but our branch offices in Kobe and Yokohama have substantial dealings with your branch offices in these cities. So I decided to tell you something that might be extremely useful to MTC. I'm sure your company is devoting a lot of time and money to prepare for the oil bid in September.'

The manager sat up straighter. 'Yes, we certainly are. What do you know that might be helpful?'

'Before I tell you, I need your promise that no one in your office here or in the Tokyo head office will reveal where you got this information.'

'Of course not, Mr Tanaka!' The manager could barely contain his excitement. 'I'm sure the head office will oblige me if I tell them my source is confidential. You have my word.'

'You know who Fan Zhipeng is?'

'Indeed. Fan Zhipeng is the president of the Sino-Africa Energy Company, our toughest competitor for the bid.'

'Well, the president and I go a long way back. When he found out I was coming to Cotonou, he asked me to get in touch with you and give you a message.'

Nagano raised his eyebrows in surprise.

'President Fan said his company would like to make a bid as low as possible in September but still win the bid for half of the fields—for two tracts.'

Nagano looked even more surprised. 'Two tracts only?'

'Two tracts only. SAEC plans to bid low, but high enough to out-bid the Americans and the French. President Fan thinks that the French and Americans don't have the funds that the Japanese and Chinese have. So SAEC and MTC will submit high bids in order to outbid them. But if SAEC and MTC come to an agreement, then each company can make lower bids than they would have to if they were competing for all four tracts. This way, each will not only win two tracts but also save an enormous sum of money. Which means that SAEC and MTC must first negotiate how much each will bid and for which tracts.'

The manager was dumbstruck.

'Negotiate the prices each of us is to bid,' he said a few moments later, still clearly struggling with the whole idea, 'I gather you're to be the go-between . . . between SAEC and us?'

'Let's say I'm just a *kuromaku*—a behind-the-scenes intermediary between MTC and SAEC. I'm doing this only because I've known President Fan for a long time, and because, as a Japanese, I want to help MTC. You communicate to your head office in Tokyo what I've told you, and if they agree, get in touch with Mr Chen, the manager of SAEC's Cotonou office. And tell him you want to settle on the MAB. He'll know what you're talking about.'

'M . . . A . . . B?'

'The Mutually Agreed Bids.'

'How much time do we have?'

'Enough time to discuss this arrangement with Tokyo.'

Nagano fell silent again. Then he gave a hard look at Tanaka and asked, 'Why haven't you contacted Tokyo with this proposal?'

'This was a personal request from the president of SAEC. It's obviously a very delicate matter. So he must've thought it unwise to go through all the layers of bureaucracy in Tokyo. He knows how seriously Tokyo takes recommendations from you, the head of such an important branch office.' Tanaka said, desperately hoping that flattery would tip the scales in his favour.

It did. Nagano smiled with pleasure at his words, and said, 'I understand everything. I'll contact my superior in Tokyo immediately.'

Looking at him, Tanaka felt a twinge of pity. *I wonder how he would've reacted if I told him that it doesn't matter what he decides. Because Fan is planning to bid only a sliver more on each of the two tracts MTC is supposed to get and grab all four tracts.*

When Tanaka got back to his hotel, he went into Orisha, the restaurant, and then out onto its terrace. In the late afternoon light, Fan was alone, sitting at a table and drinking what looked like iced tea.

Tanaka joined him, with a satisfied smile on his face.

'I trust everything went well,' said Fan.

'Exactly as planned,' replied Tanaka, still smiling.

Tanaka recounted his conversation with the ambassador and Nagano, and Nagano's surprised but pleased reaction to Fan's proposal. 'Because of the high cost of getting the oil from the bottom of the Gulf, and because they want the oil very badly, I'm pretty sure Tokyo will jump at your proposal.'

'Excellent. You've more than earned your fee. I'll contact my office right away to have the money wired to your account today. Many thanks. Have a good trip home.'

Fan stood up, smiled, and left.

Tanaka was relieved that Fan hadn't suggested they dine together. Though he knew he had succeeded in his mission, he wasn't exactly proud of his accomplishment. As if to subdue the odd pang of guilt, he hoped the MTC executives in Tokyo would be smart enough to see through Fan's outrageous bid-fixing proposal.

Tanaka went back to his room to pack and rest before his ordeal of flying back to Tokyo. As he tried to eat an overdone room-service steak, he smiled at the thought of the 50,000 now in his bank. *Not bad pay for what I've done for that devious bastard Fan . . . even with these damn long flights.*

But when he finally landed in Tokyo, at eight on Monday morning after 25 hours of travel, he was no longer sure if the money Fan paid him had been enough.

Fan left the restaurant and phoned Chen, the manager of SAEC's Cotonou office, and warned him to expect a call from the MTC office to discuss the bids. Even as Fan was talking to Chen, the Japanese ambassador was busy sending a message to Saburo Baba, the prime minister's counsellor on international affairs. The email was automatically encrypted as the ambassador typed:

Counsellor Baba:

Thanks for alerting me to be on the lookout for any plots against the bid for the four tracts of oil. Mr Shigeo Tanaka, senior vice president at Sumida Bank, came to see me today and later met with Mr Nagano, the head of the MTC office in Benin. Tomorrow I'm sending you by diplomatic pouch the recording of the conversation between Mr Tanaka and Mr Nagano. You will note that Mr Nagano proved himself to be an exceptional actor. Especially grateful for the warning that such a visit may occur, he was, nevertheless, shocked that a senior officer of a bank in the Mitsumoto consortium is trying to subvert the interests of his own bank and the consortium. Mr Nagano and I await your instructions or advice after you discuss the contents of the recording with others.

Hattori.

15

New York, 23 July

The new Mark Arnold sucked in his belly, stuck out his chest and smiled in approval at his reflection in the full-length mirror in his luxurious apartment overlooking the Hudson. The expensive sessions in the gym were paying off. He was 15 pounds lighter and had shed most of his beer belly. *Life's been real good since I left Dresden. No one can tell I'm the Markus Adler who absconded with nearly 300 million dollars from the Deutsche Wiederaufbaubank.*

He also sported an expensive toupee now, and contact lenses instead of his thick glasses. And an air of confidence that he hadn't possessed since he lost those billion euros of his bank's money several years ago because a trade in derivatives using his algorithm had gone terribly wrong.

The journey from Markus Adler to Mark Arnold, from Dresden to New York, had been a long one. First, he'd had to send his share of the funds for Fried's project. Fried had connected him to Nelson Ing, who had created 18 accounts in Singapore to which Adler could wire the money, nine accounts at Ing's own bank and then three each at three banks in Singapore with which Ing had 'a working arrangement'. Ing had warned him not to send too many euros at a time because the US Treasury Department, working with the NSA, was constantly on the watch for money being laundered or sent to terrorists or both. Adler had had to move the money into a new account at his bank, and then, the day he left, wire the 250 million euros in nearly two dozen batches to the banks in Singapore.

At the same time that he was moving the money around, he was planning his own disappearance. He wanted to make certain that

Markus Adler disappeared from the face of the earth. In preparation for his trip, he had withdrawn 15,000 euros from his own account. He regretted leaving behind almost 10,000 euros, but he didn't want to ring any alarm bells by emptying his account at one go. After his American passport and credit cards arrived from Fried, he waited until Wednesday, 17 June. That afternoon he'd wired all the money to Singapore. Then, late in the day, he asked his secretary to book a seat for him on an ICE express train to Frankfurt around 10 the next morning. He told her the head office had asked him over for a meeting and that he'd be back at work on Monday morning.

After his secretary printed out his ticket, Adler hurried home to pack a change of clothes and a few objects he couldn't bear to part with—his grandfather's watch and a photo of his dead mother. At Dresden's main station, Adler followed the 'disappearance strategy' he had carefully worked out. He got on the train to Frankfurt but got off at Leipzig. He spent the rest of the night taking three more trains that ultimately got him into Paris just before 10 the next morning. Every new ticket he bought, he paid for in cash. In Paris, he checked into a small hotel near the Gare de l'Est, ate lunch at a brasserie round the corner, slept until six in the evening, then had a huge platter of *choucroute* for dinner. He saw no irony in the fact that though he was finally in Paris, the city of his dreams, he still chose to eat sauerkraut.

On Friday he changed into Mark Arnold. He cut into small pieces any and every document that could identify him as Markus Adler and deposited the pieces in trashcans around the Gare de l'Est. Using his new credit card and American passport, he purchased a one-way ticket on Air France to New York. At JFK, he had answered all the questions as simply and carefully as possible, lest the immigration officer pick up on his German accent—because his passport claimed he was born in New Jersey. To his great relief, the officer only cursorily examined his passport and then waved him through.

Now in New York he had a studio apartment with a spectacular view, was working out daily and, best of all, writing algorithms for

Fried's hedge fund. He was back to being a quant, to doing what he loved. And by the end of August he expected to be a billionaire! Mark Arnold turned away from the mirror, patted his pocket for his keys and left the apartment.

Shigeo Tanaka was the second member of the group who was satisfied with how things were going. Though not fully recovered from his trip to Benin, he had had to travel yet again, this time to New York on Sumida Bank business. Today, however, he was meeting Devra Berger in her office in Manhattan.

This time, Devra didn't waste time on small talk.

'Thanks for coming again, Shig. I've talked to my husband and Tim Ogilvy. Although Chuck can't invest in your project, I've decided to put in 50 million. Tim's going to put up 450. He said he'll talk with you tomorrow before you leave New York.'

That Ogilvy would put up so much money was very welcome news. But all Tanaka said was: 'Excellent! I hope it isn't going to be too difficult to get your hands on the 50?'

'Well, I'm counting on my luck,' smiled Devra. 'My bank's going to help. Credit Helvetica's main American office in Stamford, Connecticut.'

'A Swiss bank?'

'They put up some money for Chuck's first project in Dubai years ago. I met Bruno Eisner then—he's such a nice guy. And he was the chief loan officer in the Stamford office just about the time DevraStyles went public. He handled our initial public offering and he's now head of the Stamford office.'

'Eisner's letting you have 50 million?' Tanaka asked, rather surprised.

'Yes. Against all my shares in DevraStyles, all the investments my mother and I have . . . and with my mother's house in Clifton Park and our own apartment as collateral. And I'm using up the 10-million credit line I have with them. I have to pay interest on the 50 million but I can handle it because I'll be using the bank's money for only a month at most.'

'Right. As I've told you, the deadline for sending the cash to New York is August 3. You can short sell the Japanese stocks of your choice, and your contract can be for as many days as you wish . . . a few days, a week or even longer.'

'Let me make sure I have this straight. I send 50 million to Mr Scheinbaum by August 3. He uses the money for the project. At the same time I can also short sell 500 million dollars' worth of the Japanese stock of my choice? He's letting me do a 10-to-1 margin trade without putting up margin call money, which means my money can be used for two separate investments at the same time. Correct?'

Even though she's running a successful company, Tanaka thought to himself, *she clearly hasn't engaged in any short selling. I'd better be careful with how I explain margin trades without embarrassing her!*

'Yes. I realize it sounds odd to be able to do both at the same time using the same capital, but Mr Scheinbaum has arranged it. Usually you're required to put up the margin call deposit with the brokerage that's letting you do margin trades. This is because if the price of the stock you are short selling goes up instead of down, as you are betting it will, your brokerage will lose money. Say you're doing a 10-to-1 margin trade, and the price of the stock you asked the broker to trade goes up by 3 per cent. When this happens, the brokerage will lose 3 per cent times 10—that's 30 per cent of the value of the trade it's doing for you. So, it makes a margin call on your margin deposit, that is, it takes money out of your deposit to cover its loss.'

'I understand. If the price of the stock goes up 10 per cent when I'm asking the brokerage to do a 10-to-1 margin trade, the firm can take all my deposit. But that's not likely to happen . . . I mean, the price of the stock I'm short selling going up as much as by 10 per cent when I'm betting it'll drop? I can see the possibility of the price falling a little. So . . . if that happens, Mr Scheinbaum could lose money. Then why is he letting me short sell the stock of my choice without depositing the margin call money with his brokerage?'

Just as I thought—the lady really doesn't know how things work, so I better take it slow. Patiently, Tanaka explained: 'Mr Scheinbaum is trading the stock for you on a 10-to-1 margin trade for two reasons. First, he's very sure, as am I, that the price of Japanese stocks will go down when our project starts. Second, Mr Scheinbaum's brokerage will make money even if you don't deposit anything for margin calls. That's because he's going to charge you commission and interest for using his money during the period of your short selling contract. Both the amount of the commission and the interest rate could be slightly higher than the going rates. But that's to be expected. Scheinbaum has to keep other shareholders in the brokerage happy when it is permitting "double use", as it were, for the contribution each member is making to the project.'

What he didn't tell her was that many unscrupulous traders in the US and Japan didn't bother owning or borrowing from some brokerage, bank or even an individual, the stocks they short sold for their clients, as they were legally required to do. The chance of getting caught and fined was extremely small, so they were free to play around.

Devra was now all smiles. 'OK, I got it. I'm just thinking . . . my doing a 10-to-1 margin trade using my 50 million . . . that's a 500-million-dollar trade. If the stock goes down even by only 3 per cent, I'll make almost 15 million dollars after paying the commission and interest! That's a return of over 30 per cent on my 50 million for the short period of the contract!'

Tanaka, nodded. 'And when the project is over, you'll get back your contribution—all 50 million, by the end of August. *Plus* your prorated share of the profits. And whatever you make by short selling stocks of your choice. I could be wrong, but my guess is you'll make at least 30 million from this venture.'

Devra was quiet for a few moments. 'Shig, come to think of it, it's almost ludicrous . . . making 30 million in such a short time. My mother would never believe it! Even I'm having a hard time believing it. I know my husband will tell me this is how capitalism works . . . but 30 million in a month?'

'Well, you better believe it, because our project is foolproof and I'm as sure as I can be that when it starts, the price of Japanese stocks is going to take a nose dive. Have you decided which stocks you're going to short sell?'

'Yes. Only one.'

'Only one? Which one?'

'KLOZ. Tim thought it would be a good idea. I'm sure he'll tell you when you talk to him that he's planning to do the same.'

Tanaka was taken aback but said nothing. Devra explained. 'KLOZ is one of the largest clothing companies in the world, with a foothold in at least 40 countries. My major line is sun wear, known mostly in the US. My annual sales volume is puny compared to KLOZ's. I'd love to own a bit of KLOZ. I know I can't buy enough shares to get on its board, but I might be able to own enough to be able to ask it to let me learn how their merchandise stays ahead of the market trends and how it's able to manage its suppliers in China. I need to learn all that if I want DevraStyles to become as big as KLOZ.'

Tanaka thought it unlikely that KLOZ would give away any of its trade secrets but he held his tongue.

'If Tim's also buying KLOZ shares, the two of you might end up having enough to make KLOZ put you on their board. And, once you're on the board, anything can happen.'

Beaming, Devra said, 'That's right. I'm keeping my fingers crossed that all goes well.'

'Devra, remember: it's not *if* all goes well but *when* all goes well. With all the work being done by our team, and all the money coming in, our project's going to be a megahit!'

'My mother told me we have to be extra careful when something sounds too good to be true. But in this case I'm sure I have nothing to worry about.'

'Nothing at all,' said Tanaka, and smiled.

Only a mile or two away, Fried sat in his Manhattan office reading an email from Nelson Ing, the head of the International Section, United Trust Bank of Singapore, the city's fourth-largest bank. Nelson's message was terse as usual:

Joshua, another batch of SAEC's dough got here via our Hong Kong branch. Will arrive in Scheinbaum's account in a few days through the usual relay banks. It's like magic. No one can follow the money. Nelson.

Fried had met Nelson almost a decade ago when he'd been in Singapore and visited the United Trust Bank to open an account. Nelson had immediately understood what kind of an account Fried wanted and why. His work done, Fried had then invited him for dinner and that had been the start of a mutually lucrative friendship between two men who had no qualms about cutting legal corners to make money. Three years ago Nelson had been promoted to the head of the bank's international section. Now he had more authority and could even more easily move money around. Over the years, Fried had met Nelson more than a dozen times and every time they met, he was even more impressed by Nelson's extensive and arcane knowledge of 'the blind spots' in wiring money internationally and 'the pliable banking laws' in some countries.

Fried smiled as he read Nelson's message. *Good, now Fan's got his wish . . . the SEAC money will keep going to Scheinbaum. Fan hinted he might leave China after the project ends in August. Well, we'll let him dream on for a little while longer.*

He leaned back in his comfortable chair. At 6.30, both his secretary and his assistant went home. Only a few traders were left in the office; those handling the Asian markets had yet to come to work. Because he wasn't meeting his wife for dinner until 7.30, he decided to stay on a bit longer and work on a lucrative insider trading deal involving a Taiwanese auto-parts maker.

Fried's profits had rolled in once he got rid of his puritanical partner, Tom Redgrave, almost 15 years ago. Redgrave had joined Fried's hedge fund with 2 billion dollars of his clients' money. He was an extremely talented but also extremely foolish—and unusual—hedge fund manager who wanted everything to always be 100 per cent legal.

Fried remembered the day a professor from a top-notch medical school and an advisor to a large pharmaceutical company in Connecticut had walked into the office and told them he wanted to sell some insider information for 500,000 dollars. Redgrave flatly refused to hear what the professor was selling.

'Josh, I went along with some of the things you've done before, including the Ponzi-scheme-like thing last year. We got out of that one OK only because the price of the euro suddenly tanked. But, Christ, if you trade on the information the professor says he has, it is a blatant case of insider trading. Illegal as hell.'

'*If* we get caught, Tom. But we won't. Besides, all the hedge funds do insider trading . . . in one form or the other. It's how our system works.'

'You don't know that. We have to make money by being smart . . . finding things others don't . . . and taking risks. Insider trading is a cowardly . . . criminal . . . way of making money.'

'Tom, all we'll be doing is to cash in on the opportunity the professor is offering us. I'm tired of you calling me a criminal—I'm only doing what most guys on Wall Street do. We should do everything we can to make money for our clients.'

'What you really mean is that this insider trade will line your own pockets . . . satisfy your greed. In addition to charging 2 per cent for managing our clients' money, we are also taking a hefty cut . . . 20 per cent . . . out of what they make.'

Fried had insisted he was doing only what everyone was doing. 'That's what makes capitalism work as it has for centuries.'

The next morning Redgrave left the hedge fund. Fried had immediately called the professor and paid for the information—a promising cancer drug the company was developing, but which had just been found to have 'too many side effects, including death'. Fried short sold the company's stock and made nearly 24 million dollars. He found he was far better off without the morally righteous Redgrave.

Fried nearly laughed out loud when he thought how well he'd done since then. Just then he heard a tentative tap on his door.

'It's open.'

One of his senior traders, Ben Larson, poked a worried face in. 'I need to report on a trade we did following your instructions . . . '

'Sure, Ben. Come on in. What is it?'

'If you remember, we bought long the stock of that German machine-tool company. You said the price would go up. But our seven-day contract just closed. And we lost 3.2 million dollars because the price suddenly dropped by some 4 per cent during the last two days. I'm sorry.'

'Of course, Steinhaus AG in Duisburg. I was sure the price would go up. It's my fault. Well, we win some and lose some. That's how things go in this business. Thanks for letting me know.'

Fried had a hard time keeping the smile off his face until Ben left. He couldn't be happier to hear the 'bad' news—because he had 'bought' for 100,000 euros a tip from one of his 'contacts' in a bank in Frankfurt that Steinhaus AG was 'going to lose a big contract it has with a state-owned Chinese company' and had done 'the trick' he often did: he had short sold 20 million euros worth of stock of the German company using 'the dark market'—off-hour trading done by large brokers and banks—pretending to be six different foreign buyers. His contracts would be closed tomorrow and, since he was doing a 10-to-1 margin trade with the help of the brokers and banks, he knew would make almost 10 million dollars.

The SEC and Treasury can look for the six foreigners who used phoney W-8 tax forms and ask as many questions as they want about some hedge funds short selling stocks using insider information. But my hedge fund lost 3.2 million dollars buying the stock long and is squeaky clean as usual!

Fried found himself thinking again about Fan and about getting his hands on more than 2 billion dollars of SAEC money and the profit it would make in August. The money would be sent to Scheinbaum's brokerage via Nelson's 'magic' string of banks—the relay stations that would wipe the footprints off the money. He stood up, grabbed his briefcase, locked the door to his office and left. *Fan told me he plans to disappear with his money in August . . . But I've arranged with Scheinbaum's brokerage to have all of Fan's money, including the profit, turned over to me when the project is over. What a sucker! He'll be a poor man soon!*

More than satisfied with Fried's arrangements, President Fan found himself grinning at the oddest moments—reading a boring report from an underling, in the toilet, in the middle of the night—as he went over the golden future awaiting him.

I've sent to Singapore nearly 8 million dollars of kickbacks from the Nigerian officials who are so grateful to SAEC for buying their oil and for making major investments in their country. It's much safer to keep it in Singapore than in Benin. And if all goes well—and I'm sure it will—and if my calculations are correct, our project should make upwards of 20 per cent or more of the 2 billion dollars SAEC is putting into the project! My God, that's a lot of money! Clearly enough to win all four bids for the Benin oil fields. And make me very rich as well!

Fan was positive that the project would succeed. The plan was foolproof and the money for it was already in New York or would be very soon. Josh and his friends Adler and Scheinbaum, Tanaka and his friends, and, of course, SAEC—the total everyone had managed to come up with was more than the minimum needed to assure success.

But once in a while, in the wee hours of the morning, when his stomach bothered him, he would fleetingly think of Lei Tao and his powerful uncle. And Mimi. *Why did she leave so suddenly? Did she really want to study in the US? Or was it something else?* But then he'd take an antacid and his mind, and his stomach, would calm down. And he would soon fall asleep again, dreaming of the money he was going to make.

16

Minneapolis and Tokyo, 23–25 July

Mimi stowed her small suitcase in the overhead compartment and took her seat for the long flight to Tokyo. *I'm not looking forward to being stuck in the plane for more than 12 hours. Well, at least I got a window seat. I hope I don't get one of those talkers next to me!*

The only person who knew about her trip was Geoff. She told the Petersons that she was going back to Shanghai for a few days as her mother was to have surgery. She told her parents nothing.

As the cabin filled up, the aisle seat next to her remained empty. She wondered if she'd be lucky enough to have two seats to herself. Then the last few passengers trickled in and, to Mimi's disappointment, a short, coarse-looking Asian man, probably in his 30s, took the seat beside her. He neither looked at her nor greeted her, but put on his seatbelt, sat back and closed his eyes, waiting for take-off.

The hours passed slowly. When the drinks and then the dinner cart came along, the man pointed out his choices, still not saying a word. Mimi wondered if the man spoke any English at all. He wore an ill-fitting brown suit and certainly didn't look like either a businessman or a tourist.

Mimi tried to watch a movie but the comedy she'd chosen did nothing to distract her—all she could think of was her meeting at the Ministry of Finance.

A week after she mailed her letter to Japan's minister of finance, she had received an email from a Mr Murai, deputy director of the International Bureau. He said they'd taken her letter very seriously and would like to discuss its contents with her in person. Could she come to Tokyo if they sent her a ticket and paid her expenses?

Delighted by the response, Mimi had let them know that she was more than willing to make the trip. And in less than a day, a round-trip ticket to Tokyo had arrived in her inbox along with her hotel reservation. Now, two days later, she was on the afternoon nonstop flight for Narita.

As the hours passed, Mimi dozed off. She was sound asleep when she felt a tug on her arm. She jerked awake to find herself looking into the beady eyes of the man beside her. He spoke to her in a low voice in Mandarin with what she thought was a Beijing accent. 'Xia Mingxi, I'm a man of few words. Please do as I say. If not, your parents will face the consequences. Do you understand?'

Mimi was stunned. Her eyes opened wide in fright, and she gripped the armrests of her seat for support. 'I know where you are going,' the man continued, still speaking softly but threateningly. 'I know who you are going to meet. There is something you need to do. Are you listening to me?'

Mimi felt sick. She could feel the bile rising in her throat. She didn't trust herself to speak, so she merely nodded. He handed her two small objects, one with two holes in it.

'Good. Then fasten these pins to your jacket.'

With unsteady fingers Mimi pinned two small grey discs to her light summer jacket. As she struggled to do so, a flight attendant came around with glasses of water and snacks. The man immediately closed his eyes and pretended to be asleep. Mimi froze in her seat, and could barely shake her head at the woman's questions about food and water. The attendant looked at her quizzically but passed on to the next row of passengers.

Questions rushed through Mimi's mind.

Who is this man? Who sent him? How did he know I'm going to Tokyo? Has there been a leak in the ministry? Can I talk to a flight attendant and get this man arrested when we arrive in Tokyo? But who's going to believe my story? He'll probably accuse me of being a mad woman. And I can't put my parents in danger. Oh God, how did I get into this?

Mimi gave a soft moan and the man opened his eyes and continued his instructions. 'Keep the pins with you at all times. Take them with you even when you're in the bathroom. I'll be monitoring your every move until you leave Tokyo. If you try to get rid of them, I'll know. And that won't be very nice for your folks back home in Shanghai.'

A wave of nausea swept over Mimi. She quickly got up and dashed to the lavatory. She barely closed the door before she violently threw up. As she came out, the flight attendant looked at her, concerned. 'Are you all right? Can I get you something?'

'Thank you,' Mimi said, her voice trembling a bit. 'I'm OK now.'

'I'll bring you a cup of ginger tea to settle your stomach. Let me know if you need anything, all right?'

Mimi tried to smile as she said, 'Thank you,' and returned to her seat.

The plane landed in Narita at 5.30 in the evening, Japan time. Mimi was still in shock, so she obediently followed every command the man gave her. She bought two tickets to the Tokyo City Air Terminal. There, she hailed a taxi to the Ginza Nikko Hotel. The man refused to speak, so she had to do all the talking. She was even more convinced that his English was rudimentary at best and that he spoke no Japanese.

Mimi checked in and was told that a room had been reserved for her. To her surprise, the man finally spoke, asking in barely passable English for a room directly across from hers.

'Don't forget,' he whispered, as they parted ways in the corridor, 'that your parents' lives depend on you!'

Mimi nodded, and entered her room. She immediately locked the door, put on the safety lock and checked it twice. Then she sat down on the bed and struggled to hold back the scream that was rising up in her. *I have to keep my head. I've got to think of some way out.*

Emotionally exhausted and dead tired, Mimi crawled into bed and was asleep in minutes. But by four in the morning, she was wide awake and starving. She took a shower, made herself a cup of green tea and went back to bed to think. Finally able to get her thoughts into some order, she concluded that the man or his cohorts must have hacked into her email and obtained her itinerary, down to her plane seat. If that was so, then they had also read the email containing instructions from Mr Murai's office. *What else does the thug know?*

She booted up her small laptop and checked her email. The man had said she must act naturally, so she had to email Mr Murai with news of her arrival. She had a message from him saying that a ministry car would pick her up at nine for her 9.30 appointment with him. *At least I won't be in a taxi with the creep*!

She made herself another cup of tea. She packed her small suitcase, then ordered a room service breakfast. She had almost two hours before her appointment. Ordinarily, she would have gone out exploring but she didn't dare leave her small room even though she found it claustrophobic.

At 8.30 there was a knock on her door. She opened it; it was the man; he wanted to tell her that he'd be waiting outside the Ministry of Finance for her. *Now I know he's hacked into my computer*!

At last she thought of a plan. Mimi took the small pad by the phone in her room and began to write furiously. Before she could finish, it was time to go down to the lobby to wait for the car sent by Mr Murai. The man was standing just outside the hotel, smoking a cigarette. Finally the car from the ministry arrived. As Mimi drove away in it, she saw the man walk over to the doorman. She was sure he was going to ask for a taxi to follow her. All the way to the ministry, Mimi continued to write, finally stopping as the car pulled up in front of an imposing six-storey, grey stone building.

Mimi gave her name to a young woman at the Reception desk who told her to go up to the International Bureau on the fourth floor.

Ken Murai was waiting for her. He was tall and slim and quite handsome. Somehow she'd been expecting to a pudgy bureaucrat with thinning, grey hair.

Murai bowed slightly and said, 'Hello.'

Mimi said 'Hello' back as she shoved a sheet of paper at him and put a finger to her lips.

Taken aback, Murai looked down at the message written in big print: 'I'm wired. Please read my notes.' He was so disconcerted that for a moment he was speechless. But he caught on immediately and realized he needed to say something.

'Thank you for coming all this way, Ms—' he said and halted as Mimi handed him a sheaf of small notes.

Mimi smiled, 'My family name is pronounced *She-ha*, but don't worry, like everyone else you can call me Mimi.' At the same time she pointed to the two pins on her coat and her laptop. Murai nodded that he understood.

He then invited Mimi into a small conference room next to his office. As he escorted her in, he looked over to the corner where a taller man was standing. The man started forward but Murai put a finger to his lips and shook his head. The man, slightly perplexed, stepped back into the corner. Murai offered Mimi a seat as he hurriedly scanned her notes while asking her pleasantries about her trip. Then he sat down across from Mimi and began the interview.

'I've brought you a report that is much more detailed than the letter I sent to your ministry,' Mimi said. 'That's why I have my laptop with me.'

Murai hesitated for a moment. 'Let me get my assistant. If you boot up your computer and open the file, I'll have her print it out. The ministry is old-fashioned—we still like things on paper.'

As he left the room, he detoured to the man in the corner and handed him the notes. Within a few minutes he returned with a young woman who had clearly been briefed about the situation. Murai introduced her as Saya. Mimi said she had the file ready and Saya took the laptop away.

Murai said that he would read the report shortly but could he ask her some questions first. Aware that everything he was going to say was being overheard, he phrased his questions carefully. The last thing he wanted to do was to let the Chinese man know that he knew as much as he did. Nor did he want to get Mimi into more danger. He asked Mimi about her job at SAEC. He wanted to ask about the coded messages that Bess Koyama had sent him, but couldn't because that would let on to the Chinese that the code had been broken.

'You contacted us because you thought something SAEC was doing would cause serious problems to our economy?' Murai asked, looking at her closely to see how she would respond.

Very much aware of their eavesdropper, Mimi replied, carefully summarizing her report. She told Murai her guesses about what seemed to be 'some kind of a big plan' involving the Japanese economy. She couldn't figure it out, and she had been excluded from meetings in which it was discussed. But she had decided, based on the little that she knew, that it would be best to tell the Japanese minister of finance all about it. Mimi left out any mention of having talked to her father about her concerns. And she told Murai that she'd gone to the US because she wanted to get an advanced degree rather than work in an office as a secretary for the rest of her career.

As he asked his questions and listened attentively to Mimi's answers, Murai was writing on a notepad. Saya entered the office with Mimi's laptop and a hard copy of her report. Murai asked her to bring some coffee for Mimi. When Saya had gone, Murai gestured to Mimi to stand up, take off her jacket and place it on the table next to her. At the same time he handed his notepad to the man in the corner. Aloud, he said, 'I am going to leave you for a few minutes so that I can read through your report. Please enjoy your coffee, and I'll give you an English newspaper to read.' Mimi said that would be fine. She wasn't in any hurry.

Saya returned almost immediately with a cup of coffee on a tray along with sugar, cream, a few cookies, and the *Japan Times*. As she left, Murai motioned to the man in the corner to come to where Mimi was sitting at the table. Then he gestured to Mimi to leave the office with him. She wondered what was going on but understood immediately when she saw the tall man move to the chair she had vacated and rather noisily start to add sugar and cream to the cup of coffee.

Murai said, 'Mimi, I'll be back in a few minutes,' and led her into the hall, closing the door, carefully but audibly. When they were well away from the conference room, he spoke hurriedly. 'I'm sorry to have put you and your family at such risk. I hadn't realized until I read your notes that you suspect that employees in SAEC have been killed. I'm going to do everything I can to ensure your safety. First, do you know if the man plans to fly back to Minneapolis with you?

Mimi bit her lip. 'He hasn't said so. I have no idea what he plans to do next.'

Murai nodded. 'You wrote that he was sitting next to you so I'll find out his name from the airline. If he's planning to go back with you, I'll have him detained long enough to miss the flight. I don't want you to ever be alone with him, so I'll arrange for a ministry car to take you to back to your hotel and to T-CAT—the air terminal where you'll catch the shuttle to Narita. OK?'

Mimi said, 'Thank you,' with a catch in her voice.

'And I am going to have an American woman, someone who works in computer security, contact you in Minnesota. Her name is Bess Koyama. She's the wife of a very close friend. Both of them can help you while you are in America. Can you give me some way Bess can contact you that you're sure can't be hacked into?'

Mimi pulled out her small pad and jotted down the Peterson's address in Minneapolis and handed it to Murai. 'This is where I'm staying. No one but my parents know this address.'

Murai pocketed it and continued with his instructions.

'Do exactly as the man tells you to, but go nowhere alone with him, not into an elevator, not into a taxi. Be sure there are other people near you, but don't get into a crowd with him either. And be aware that neither your computer nor your email nor your phone—nothing you have used to contact us or your family—is secure. Bess will help you to obtain a safe means of communications.

'I am sure you'd like to get rid of those two pins as soon as you can. But keep them on until you're in the boarding area for your flight. Then throw away the one with the holes in it before you board the plane. That's the microphone. It's very important that no one hear your conversations after you board. Someone is going to contact you on the plane and we don't want the people spying on you to hear. Do you understand?'

Again Mimi nodded.

'It's also important that you leave the tracking device on until you are on the plane. You can toss it in a waste bin then, but the man watching you must be sure that you get on the plane back to Minneapolis. If you throw it away at the airport, the people tracking you won't know where you are—whether you got on the plane, flew to China or are still in Japan. We'll be in touch again when it's safe.'

Mimi said 'Thank you' in a small voice.

'Now, let's go back in. The Chinese listening to you should hear your voice. You've been very helpful to us and I can't thank you enough. But I have just one question before we go. I scanned your report and the date you've given us for this plot to unfold is "by the end of August". Do you have any more precise information than that?'

'The professor emphasized that it should be by mid-August, no later than that. Oh, and he also said it should be a Monday.'

'Thank you, that's important. Is there anything else at all that you might have overheard, but that you didn't understand or thought was not important?'

Mimi thought for a moment. 'I did hear a name that sounded like "so-rose". It sounded like he did the same thing or something very similar to what President Fan was planning.'

Murai mumbled to himself, 'So-rose . . . Sorose . . . Could it be George Soros?'

'I don't remember hearing his other name. Just so-rose.'

'Thank you. Nothing else you can think of?'

Mimi paused as if thinking over everything she had heard or overheard at SAEC. Finally she said, 'No, I think that's everything.'

Back in the conference room, Mimi put her jacket back on while Murai thanked her for her report but in a very different tone from the profuse gratitude he had expressed out in the hall. Mimi was taken aback, but then she realized that Murai was talking for the benefit of their eavesdroppers, deliberately trying to create the impression that he didn't believe her conspiracy theory.

Finally, Murai said, 'I know you must be anxious to go back to your studies in Minneapolis, but we do appreciate your coming all the way to Japan. We'll have a car take you back to the hotel and then to the city air terminal. I'm sorry we can't drive you to Narita, but the shuttle bus is probably more comfortable for the long ride.'

Mimi was escorted to a waiting car by Saya. Back in the hotel, she scurried up to her room before the man could return. She took her things down to the lobby and was checking out when he walked into the hotel.

As she left the counter, he came up to her. 'Where do you think you're going?'

'I thought you were listening. The ministry has a car waiting to take me to the Tokyo City Air Terminal, so that I can catch the shuttle to the airport.'

'Wait for me there. You're not free yet. Buy two tickets for the airport and wait for me at the ticket counter.'

Now she was sure his comprehension of English was limited. At T-CAT, she waited for him for nearly half an hour and then they set off on the long ride to Narita. At the check-in counter, the man stood right behind her and she wondered if he would manage to get on her flight again. When he didn't check in for her flight, she stifled a sigh of relief. He walked with her to the security checkpoint where he issued his final warning: 'This is as far as I go. But I'll be here until your flight leaves. Be sure you keep the pins on—I'll know if you take them off, talk to someone you shouldn't or go somewhere you shouldn't. May your parents have long lives.'

Mimi looked at him and nodded. Then, without a word, she disappeared into the security area. Waiting to board her flight, she nervously stared at everyone who came to her gate. Then, when her flight was announced, she threw the microphone pin into a dustbin and hurriedly joined the queue. When she got to her seat and was about to stow her suitcase in the overhead bin, a flight attendant came up to her. 'Miss Xia? You've been upgraded to Business Class for this flight. Please come with me.'

Mimi was led to a window seat in the third row. Before the flight attendant left, she handed Mimi a small packet, about the size of a paperback book. 'A small gift from a Mr Murai,' the woman said with a smile.

Inside was a paperback on Japan and a thick envelope. Mimi tore open the envelope and pulled out a letter wrapped around American money. She put it all in her lap and slowly counted out 10 100-dollar bills. *A thousand dollars*! She stuffed it into her handbag and unfolded the letter.

Dear Mimi,

I'm sorry that our request for you to come to Tokyo turned out to be such a horrendous experience. Since you could not enjoy even a few days in our country, I am enclosing a token of our appreciation and a small book on Japan in the hope that you can visit us for pleasure in the future.

I trust you have already disposed of the microphone and will leave the tracking device on the plane. I suggest you communicate with no one until Bess Koyama has contacted you and can give you advice. You can trust her implicitly.

By the way, the tall man in the corner was Mr Saburo Baba, a high official in our government.

My best wishes for a safe trip back to Minneapolis.

And our many, many thanks,

Ken Murai.

17

Shanghai, 27 July

Shortly after nine in the morning, a young woman pushing a stroller greeted her neighbour, as he was striding to a black Audi parked on the street next to Fuxing Park in Shanghai's former French Concession.

'*Nin zao*, Professor.'

He looked at her coldly and brusquely returned her 'good morning', then walked on towards his car. Annoyed, the woman quickened her pace towards the park entrance. *I know he's a professor at Fudan University, but we've been neighbours now for three years and he always looks at me as if he's never seen me before.*

Just as she reached the entrance to the park, a thunderous explosion deafened her and a scorching wind swooshed by. She screamed and instinctively bent over the stroller to protect her baby. Then she began to run as fast as she could, pushing the stroller before her.

Soon out of breath and with her baby screaming, she stopped and picked up the child to comfort him. An elderly man with a cane approached her and asked, 'Are you all right?'

Still panting, she wheezed 'Yes,' and looking back at the flames and thick black smoke rising near the entrance to the apartment complex, she gasped out, 'What was that?'

'A pretty powerful bomb! You sure had a close call. I saw a man start to get into his car just after you passed him. Then there was an ear-splitting explosion and the car was instantly a huge ball of fire.'

The woman shuddered and hugged her crying baby tighter. *How lucky the professor hadn't been friendly. If he had stopped to exchange a friendly greeting and I had walked towards the car with him instead of rushing away, my baby and I could be dead too!*

As her baby finally stopped crying, she thought, *I didn't like him, but no one deserves to be killed like that!*

18

Minneapolis, 27–28 July

Mimi awoke to someone calling her name, softly but insistently. It took her a few seconds to recognize the worried voice of Mrs Peterson. Her own voice still slurred with sleep, she said, 'Just a minute, please' before getting out of bed, grabbing her robe and opening the door. Mrs Peterson, looking troubled, spoke in a rush. 'Sorry, dear, to wake you up when I know you're still jetlagged. But your father wants to talk you . . . he called half an hour ago. I told him you were asleep. He said to call him at his office as soon as you got up. I hope your mother hasn't taken a turn for the worse? I thought I'd better wake you.'

'Um, what else did he say?' Mimi had no idea how she was going to get out of this. Neither the Petersons nor her family knew she had gone to Japan.

'Nothing, except that he'll stay in his office until you call. I'll go fix you some breakfast while you dress.'

As soon as Mrs Peterson left, Mimi sat down on the bed and tried to think about what to do. She couldn't use her computer to skype or email, and she was afraid to use the Petersons' landline in case it had been tapped. She'd spent an anxious day yesterday, Sunday, dead tired and afraid to contact anyone. But now her father had called her. She had to call him back. She couldn't wait until Mr Murai's friend got in touch with her.

Suddenly she had an idea. She hastily dressed and went into the kitchen. 'Mrs Peterson, my phone is dead—I forgot to charge the battery last night. You said your husband insisted you keep a phone in your car for emergencies because you often forget to take your iPhone with you. Do you still have it?'

'Yes, dear. Why . . . ?'

Mimi hurriedly went on. 'Can you make calls to foreign countries with it? Could I borrow it to call my father?'

'Yes, I'm sure you can. But you're welcome to use our landline.'

Although she had no idea if it was true or not, she said, 'I'm pretty sure it would be cheaper if you let me use the phone in the car.'

'Well, whatever you wish, dear. Would you like scrambled eggs or boiled?'

Mimi said 'Scrambled, please,' and ran to the garage. She found the phone and, going out to the small terrace, she put through the call.

Her father answered on the first ring.

As soon as Mimi said, 'Father,' he cut her short. 'I'm sorry to call you so early, but I really wanted to talk to you as soon as possible.'

'Why? What's happened?' Mimi asked anxiously. *Had they harmed her parents? Or threatened them?*

Mimi's father sighed. 'This morning Professor Du Yifu was killed by a car bomb. When he got into his car, it blew up. He was incinerated . . . murdered.'

'What!'

'It's being investigated. This now makes three deaths.'

Mimi was dumbstruck.

'Mingxi, are you there?'

'Yes, Father. I'm just so shocked.'

'I thought you should know. This third death is going to spur our authorities to action. I was told on the QT that SAEC and the president are going to be the subjects of a thorough investigation. Three people connected to SAEC dying under strange circumstances . . . something is very wrong. So, I called to warn you not to come back to Shanghai until I let you know it's safe. You should be OK in Minneapolis. I know you didn't tell the president where you were staying. Does anyone in SAEC know where you are?'

Mimi could hear the concern in her father's voice but there was no way she could tell him now that Fan's man knew exactly where she was.

'Thank you for warning me, Father. No, I haven't told anyone where I'm staying. Han Bingbing knows I'm in Minneapolis but not my address. By the way, I'm going to get a new phone so I'll call you when I have it working and let you know my new number. And do you still have that phone I gave you when I bought one for Mama?'

'I don't think I've ever used it. Good idea. I'll find it and turn it on.'

After the call ended, Mimi sat in the car for a few minutes, slumped in the seat, the phone in her hands. *What am I to do? Should I tell the Petersons what's going on? No. I have to talk to Geoff as soon as I can.*

Mimi went back to the kitchen and Mrs Peterson. She quickly finished her breakfast and reassured her hostess that her mother was doing very well. Then she set off to the university to try and find Geoff.

Geoff was in his office and delighted to see her but perturbed to find her so upset. When Mimi told him about her encounter with the man on the plane and her experience in Tokyo, Geoff was aghast.

'OK, we both have to buy new phones. I'll get them in my name so they can't be traced back to you. But don't call your parents on their home phone using it.'

'Thank you, but I'll pay for it. My parents are going to use new phones as well. But what about my computer? And my email? I'm so worried—what's the word? Paranoid? I'm even afraid the Peterson's house may be bugged. How can I keep my parents safe from Fan? It's not just me the man threatened.' She burst into tears.

'Mimi, you have to tell your parents they may be in danger. Not the story of your trip to Tokyo, but that you've found your email has been hacked into. If your father was worried enough to stay late in his office and call you, he does need to be warned.'

'I'll warn him as soon as you get me a new phone.'

'And though you're reluctant to use your computer, I suggest that you continue to use it as you would for your assignments. So if the thug is still monitoring your computer, you won't seem to be doing anything to worry about.'

'But I'm sure they still know where I am, and someone they hire could be spying on me.' Because the idea so petrified her, Mimi began to cry uncontrollably.

Geoff gave her a hug for the first time. Mimi, overwrought, hugged him back. 'Stop worrying! I'll think of something, but now I have to prepare for class this afternoon.' Mimi nodded as Geoff reluctantly left her.

Mimi was oblivious to everything in class, busy trying to concoct a story that would warn her parents but not frighten them unduly. And wondering what she could do about her own safety. After class, Geoff took her to buy new phones for both of them. Even with a new phone in hand, she arrived back at the Petersons' feeling frazzled.

Mrs Peterson met her at the door with a FedEx packet. 'This was delivered an hour ago. From New York.' She was brimming over with curiosity, but Mimi just thanked her warmly and went to her room.

Once she'd shut the door behind her, she tore open the envelope —Mr Murai had come through with the promise he'd made to her about his American friend getting in touch with her. Bess Koyama had written her a short note, asking Mimi to call her as soon as possible, at home or at work. She gave Mimi a warning Mimi didn't need—to make certain she had a secure line.

After dinner, Mimi announced to the Petersons that she was going for a walk because it was such a nice summer evening. She walked down West Elmwood to Gladstone Triangle, a small park where she could sit for a while, to call Bess. She was thankful that Geoff had already got her a new phone.

Bess' voice on the line sounded warm and lifted Mimi's spirits. She said her husband's good friend, Ken Murai, had asked her to do everything possible to make sure Mimi was safe. She had Mimi recount her trip to Tokyo. Then she asked her if anyone had gotten in touch with her since her return. Mimi told her of her conversation with her father that morning.

Bess was silent for a long moment. Then she asked if she could call Mimi back in 15 minutes—she wanted to check some things before she gave her any advice. Mimi agreed, stood up and stretched her legs and took a stroll down the tree-lined West Elmwood Place. When Bess called back, what she had to say both surprised and relieved Mimi.

'Mimi, I think it might be safest if you were to disappear for a time. For you to go somewhere no one can find you. Of course, you can tell your parents. I'd like to offer you the guestroom in my mother's apartment in New York—it's in the same building I live in. Would you like to come here until things settle down? You mentioned that your former boss is being investigated, and from the information Mr Murai has been getting, it seems likely that the president's plot is scheduled to take place within weeks. I don't know how it's going to play out, but if you stay in Minneapolis, it could be dangerous. Can you trust me?

'Oh, please, yes! But if I just disappear, Fan's men could harm my parents.'

'You're right. So, before you come you should warn them.' Bess went on to give Mimi the details of what she was to do. When she had booked her flight, she was to call Bess and someone would meet her at the airport in New York.

It was now growing dark, but Mimi had two more phone calls to make. First she called Shanghai and spoke to her father at his office.

She didn't tell him of her terrifying trip to Tokyo, only that Fan had had someone hack into her email. Hearing how worried her father was when he heard this, she wasn't able to tell him how insecure she now felt in Minneapolis. Neither could she tell her father about her talk with Bess without telling him about her trip to Tokyo, so she said she was thinking of visiting Mrs Peterson's sister in Chicago. Fortunately he didn't press her too closely about her plans. 'It sounds like a good idea,' he said, 'I think your mother had better disappear for a time also. I'm going to have her visit her cousin in Jilin.'

Her last call was to Geoff. When she told him about her conversations with Beth and her father and her plan to 'disappear', he offered to get a ticket for her because she couldn't use her computer. As Mimi walked back to the Petersons' and climbed up the long flight of stairs to the house, she decided it would be best to tell her host parents she was going back again to Shanghai because of her mother.

At five the next afternoon, Geoff took Mimi to the Minneapolis–St Paul International Airport for her flight to New York. She left her computer and the phone she had brought from Shanghai with Geoff, who was delighted to store them in his apartment.

'That means I'll see you again!' he'd said, smiling.

Geoff parked and escorted Mimi through the check-in procedure. She couldn't help looking around for the man who'd been on the plane to Tokyo but he wasn't in sight. When Geoff handed over her carry-on at the entrance to security, he said, 'You're no longer my student, so I hope you'll let me do what I've wanted to do since the first day I met you.' Then he put his arms around her and kissed her. By the time he let her go, she was blushing deeply. *I kissed a man for the first time in my life . . . a foreigner and in public*! As if to spare her and possibly his own embarrassment, Geoff said, 'Take care! Come back when you can.' And he turned and walked away quickly before Mimi could say a word.

19

Tokyo, 1 August

Nick Koyama paid the cab driver, grabbed his bags, dashed through the rain to the Murais' front door and pushed the doorbell. Within seconds, it opened to reveal Emiko Murai smiling warmly. 'Oh, Nick, do come in! I hope you didn't get drenched.'

Nick followed Emiko into the small entryway and handed over his bags. Removing his shoes for the slippers Emiko handed him and stepping up into the hall, he said, 'This weather is certainly better than the heat of Singapore. It's good to see you!'

Ken appeared in the hallway. 'Welcome, Nick. Sorry about the deluge. I can't thank you enough for stopping in Tokyo on your way back to New York. I'm sure Bess and little Mikey wish you'd gone straight home.'

Laughing, Nick said, 'I'll admit that after a seven-hour flight, it's nice to know I'll be sleeping in your guest room tonight instead of on another airplane.'

Ken ushered Nick into the sitting room. A slim, tall man with short grey hair stood up to greet the newcomer. 'My good friend, Saburo Baba, is joining us. Since you met him a couple of years ago, he's been seconded from the Foreign Ministry to the Prime Minister's Office as the PM's senior advisor on international issues.'

'Congratulations,' said Nick as he shook hands, 'Good to see you again, Baba-san.'

'Likewise,' smiled Baba. 'But don't be so formal. Just because I'm in the PM's office doesn't make me important. Please call me Bach.'

Nick laughed and said, 'OK, Bach it is. Now I remember it's your nickname.'

Emiko entered to tell them that the sushi had arrived and asked their choice of drinks. 'Some *sake* with the sushi,' said Ken, 'and then tea. We need to keep clear heads.'

The three men ate quickly while Baba talked about his work: 14-hour days trying to stay on top of one crisis after another in the world and advising the old prime minister 'who always sees everything from his scheming and cunning perspective'. But as soon as they finished eating, Ken said, 'Let's move over to the comfortable chairs and talk about that damn plot that's been worrying the hell out of me. The target date's only a couple of weeks away. I don't really know who all the plotters are, except that they seem to be all over the world!'

'And two of the main players are American,' said Nick.

'Yes, we know about those hedge fund guys thanks to you,' said Baba.

'Why don't you fill me in on what you know now and if you've done anything,' suggested Nick. Ken nodded and began telling him about Mimi's letter to his ministry and then her visit to Tokyo. 'Under ordinary circumstances I wouldn't have brought her to Tokyo. But after I read that she had worked at SAEC, I had to see her, even though some of what she mentioned sounded pretty far-fetched. A very good thing that the minister's office is scrupulous about handling every piece of mail that comes in. So her letter was sent to the director of my bureau, and since the letter was in English, he turned it over to me.'

'And what did she tell you?' prompted Nick.

'Well, thanks to Mimi, we can confirm that Fan Zhipeng of China's SAEC is a key conspirator. It's possible others in the company are in on it too. Most important, Mimi said that the target date for the plot has to be a Monday in mid-August. That would be August 17th. And that's just two weeks from now!'

Baba had been listening quietly, sipping his tea. 'Ken,' he finally said, 'tell Nick about overhearing something that sounded like "so-rose" when Fan and his advisor were talking.'

'That's right,' Ken answered, slightly chagrined. 'How could I forget? Mimi thought she heard what to her sounded like "so-rose". But I realized she must have overheard the name George Soros—'

'The hedge fund guy who attacked the British pound,' interrupted Nick, looking worried, 'and made one billion dollars back in 1992. So we can conclude that these plotters are thinking of something similar. The question is what do they plan to attack?'

'It's a damn shame,' commented Baba, 'that we know several people in the plot, we know the date, but we still don't know what they're planning to do.'

'So you think this Chinese woman, this Mimi, is reliable?' asked Nick. 'I was in Singapore when she arrived in New York, but Bess said she seems trustworthy. Can we assume that her information is accurate?'

'Well, we shouldn't rely totally on the date she gave us and her overhearing the name Soros. But we've a confirmation of sorts from another source,' said Ken.

'Another source?'

'We didn't trust electronic communications to tell you. We think we've uncovered a Japanese who's in on the plot. Shigeo Tanaka, the vice president of Sumida Bank. He made a short visit to Benin to make a proposition to the Mitsumoto people in Cotonou on behalf of Fan who, he claimed, was a long-time friend.'

'He's the ST,' exclaimed Nick, 'the initials in the coded messages we got from Belinda. I bet he's the guy I saw talking with Fan at the Shanghai Economic Forum.'

'Well, let's confirm it, if you really got a good look at the guy.' Excusing himself, Ken went to his study and came back with a photo.

As he handed it to Nick, he said, 'This is a printout of Tanaka's photo I found on the web.'

Nick stared at the photo. 'That's him. I've no doubt. I was only a couple of metres away from him when he was talking to Fan.'

Ken said, 'Good. Now there's absolutely no doubt Tanaka is part of it. The VP of Sumida Bank . . . a bank in the consortium led by Mitsumoto to get the Benin oil! Bach, tell Nick what Tanaka did in Benin.'

Baba smiled. 'I couldn't convince the PM there was a plot against MTC, given our lack of evidence. So I decided that, as a member of Japan's Foreign Ministry, it was my duty to contact our embassy in Benin and warn them to stay alert for anything that might go against our national interests, especially involving our obtaining oil from the new fields. I told the ambassador to keep his eyes and ears open.'

Baba went on to tell Nick about Tanaka's visit to the head of the Mitsumoto office and his proposal about the bids. 'Fan's a devious bastard,' concluded Nick, after Baba finished.

Ken nodded. 'The proposal that SAEC and Mitsumoto collude to get two tracts each is fishy as hell. It's got to be a sham gambit, a double-crossing gambit, so SAEC can get all four. And Tanaka is the VP of a bank that's a major partner in the MTC consortium.'

'So let's consider what we know,' said Nick. 'We know the identity of four of the plotters: Fan of SAEC, Joshua Fried and Peter Scheinbaum who have hedge funds in New York, and Shigeo Tanaka of Sumida Bank.'

'I'm wondering about the involvement of Sumida Bank,' said Ken. 'The bank is in the MTC group and the president, Honma, is an ardent supporter of the PM, but what the hell is Tanaka up to? Is he trying to get revenge on the bank for keeping Honma on as president? Is he just trying to make his millions? I'm guessing—both.'

'OK, back to our main concern.' Nick was tired and wanted to stick to the point. 'What do you think the group's targeting, Ken?'

Ken thought for a minute. 'Well, first, I think Fan's proposal for the price-fixing of the bid is just a side plot. And they can't be aiming to buy up MTC stock since most MTC shares are held by the companies in the same enterprise group, and they'd never sell the MTC shares they hold.'

'OK, Ken,' said Nick with a smile, 'you've told us what they won't do. Now what *will* they do?'

'I don't know. But I'm thinking about Soros, which makes me think along the lines of an attack on a currency—'

'Like the Japanese yen?' interrupted Nick, 'You think that with a much depreciated yen, the Mitsumoto group would be hard pressed to outbid SAEC? That's something I hadn't considered.'

'What worries me is that the people we know about—Fan, Fried, Tanaka, Scheinbaum and someone from Dresden—could be just the core members in the plot. There may be many more people in on it. But even this handful of men that we do know about could do very large-scale short selling. If they did, say, a 20-to-1, or even a 10-to-1, margin trade with billions in capital, they could really affect the international market. And—'

'Wait a minute!' This time it was Baba who interrupted, 'Ken, I know short selling is *kara-uri* in Japanese. But I have only a vague idea of exactly how it works. And I think I know what margin trades mean. But I'd be hard pressed to explain exactly how that works either.'

'Sorry. I keep forgetting your degrees are in law,' apologized Ken. 'Short selling is betting that the price of a currency, stock or bond will go down. Here let me use the example of trading a stock. You agree to sell 100 shares of a stock at 100 yen on a specific day in the near future, say, in three days. If on that day the price does go down, as the short seller was betting it would, to 95 yen, then he buys the stock at 95 yen and sells it at 100 yen as agreed. In the process, he makes 500 yen. Usually short sellers don't actually own the stock they short sell. Legally, they are required to own or rent the shares but it's very difficult to enforce the law. Bach, this is the gist of what short selling is . . . without getting into some technical details. '

Ken paused. 'Nick, now it's your turn. You explain margin trades.'

Nick laughed and said, 'OK, Bach, margin trades can be a very convoluted affair. For now, all you need to know is this—a 10-to-1 margin trade means you have 1 million dollars but the broker lets you trade 10 million dollars' worth of stocks or bonds. He charges you interest for the money he lets you use for the duration of your contract . . . say, for a few days, even a month. Your 1 million dollars is what we call margin capital or a margin deposit. If the trade goes against you—if the price of the stock or bond goes up when you're short selling or goes down when you're buying long—then the broker makes a 'margin call'—he takes money from your margin capital.'

Seeing Baba's slightly bewildered expression, Ken tried to explain further. 'Let me give you an example. The broker may let you do a margin trade of as much 20 to1. That's because it's extremely rare for the price of a stock to go up as much as 5 per cent. Even if it does so, the broker won't lose—he'll just keep all of your million dollars which he lost when the price went up. That's 5 per cent times 20, since you've done a margin trade of 20 to 1. But he'll also charge you a commission and interest on the money you've borrowed from him. So if you're doing a 10-to-1 margin trade, the price of the stock you're short selling has to go up by 10 per cent before you lose your million dollars.'

Baba nodded. 'Got it. So . . . the price of whatever these guys short sell has to fall in order for them to succeed. What could they short sell that would give them enough money to make certain that Mitsumoto can't win any of the bids for the Benin oil? And what makes them think they'll have enough capital . . . even doing 10-to-1 or 20-to-1 margin trades?'

'I think' said Ken, 'they might first try to make the price fall of whatever they plan to short sell—a stock, a bond or a currency. They'll want to do as big as possible margin trades, so first they'll try to spook the market and start a tsunami so that the market for what they're short selling will be seriously affected and there will be a drastic drop in the price. Since we know they can't buy up Mitsumoto stock, they must be planning to do something that will gravely undermine the Japanese economy and thus make it impossible for Mitsumoto to win any of the bids. As a result, they'll get all the bids *and* get rich in the process.'

Baba nodded thoughtfully and then frowned.

Nick asked, 'What's the matter, Bach?'

'Well, don't laugh at me for saying this. But almost two years ago . . . before I was seconded to the PM's office . . . I attended a meeting with some OECD officials visiting the Foreign Ministry. One of the Americans told us that Japan has the highest national debt to GDP ratio among the 34 OECD countries. Our debt was approaching 300 per cent of our GDP. And unless we did something soon, the Japanese government bonds could collapse. So couldn't the plotters make the JGB collapse . . . I mean . . . by suddenly short selling those bonds?'

'It's possible,' Nick said, 'but not likely. The JGB market is huge because the amount of JGB outstanding is well over 15 *trillion* dollars. And at least a few hundred billion dollars worth of bonds are traded daily in the Tokyo market and elsewhere. Even if the plotters did big margin trades, they wouldn't have enough money to succeed in bringing down the price of the JGB. Right, Ken?'

Ken agreed. 'It's possible but improbable. Although because we've continued to sell more and more JGB, I've often wondered whether our government bonds could be successfully attacked. I have talked about this in the ministry, but almost all my seniors tell me I'm crazy and give me a hundred and one reasons and numbers to back up why they think so. So, if I had to bet, I'd have to say the target is not our government bonds.'

'So—what could it be?' Baba was still frowning. 'If they can't buy up any Mitsumoto group stock and the JGB is too big a target, what could they be planning to attack? The yen?'

'No, I'm pretty certain it's not,' said Nick. 'The foreign exchange market trades at least 5 *trillion* dollars' worth of currencies daily. And, depending on the day, as much as 10 per cent of the trade involves the yen. So we're talking about a 500 billion yen market . . . give or take, depending on the exchange rate. They can't possibly be targeting the yen.'

'I'd thought of the yen too,' said Ken, 'but Nick's right. George Soros did attack the British pound but it was under very unusual conditions. I just don't think anyone can pull that off against the dollar, the yen or the euro. Not any more.'

Baba looked sceptical. 'Then why were those men talking about Soros?'

Ken shook his head and Nick raised both hands up and shrugged. Neither had an answer.

'I think,' said Nick, 'that we need to keep a very close eye on Tanaka.'

'He's been under surveillance ever since we heard the tape of the conversation between him and the head of the Mitsumoto office in Cotonou,' said Baba, 'When I told the PM about it, he was livid. So he's asked the National Security Agency to keep an eye on him. The NSA said they'll do what do what they can . . . even though the PM's request is, strictly speaking, illegal.'

'One question, Bach,' said Nick. 'What do you know about Fan? He seems to be at the centre of this plot. Ken and I have talked about him but we haven't really checked up on him.'

'I did some checking up through my contacts at the Foreign Ministry. Fan is a former army colonel in intelligence. Rumoured to be shrewd and ruthless. Speaks good English and is well travelled, especially in Africa. Very well connected with the people at the top of the Party . . . Too bad we don't have Miss Xia Mingxi in SAEC, still coding Fan's messages and eavesdropping on his conversations!'

Nick stifled a yawn. Baba noted it and said, 'Well, it's getting late. I'm going to give the PM the gist of what we've discussed tonight. I want him to know that we have to take this thing very seriously.'

'I think that's wise,' agreed Ken. 'After Mimi's visit, I talked to my director and we went to our minister about forming an ad hoc committee to try and stay on top of the situation. But things move slowly as do most things in our bureaucracy. I don't if that committee will ever be formed!'

Ken turned to Nick. 'I'm wondering if someone in the financial community in New York has heard anything about this?'

'I'll put some feelers out when I get back,' said Nick, no longer able to suppress a yawn, 'but don't get your hopes up.'

'Nick, you must be exhausted. Let's call it a night,' said Ken. 'Would either of you like a nightcap?'

Both men declined. As the three stood up, Baba said dejectedly, 'The title of Senior Counsellor on International Affairs to the Prime Minister sounds impressive, but tonight I feel like I'm a bumbling greenhorn—of little use to anyone.'

Ken patted Baba on his shoulder. 'Bach, don't be so hard on yourself. We're going to do our best to find out what as much as we can. Who knows—we may soon get lucky and find out what's going on and stop it.'

Nick knew Ken well enough to know that he was just whistling in the dark.

20

Minneapolis, 3–4 August

As Geoff Mitchell walked into his office, his officemate looked up. 'Some woman called you about half an hour ago. Sounded real agitated. Wants you to call her back immediately.'

Geoff put his briefcase down on his desk. 'Did she say what she wanted?'

'Nope. Just for you to call as soon as possible. A girlfriend's mother? What have you been up to, Geoff?' Brandon asked with a grin as he handed Geoff a slip of paper.

Geoff looked at Brandon's scrawl. 'Viola Peterson.' *What could she be calling about? It must be about Mimi. Where did she get my number? I didn't even know she knew my full name.* All of this went through his mind in a flash.

Worried and wanting to talk to Mrs Peterson out of Brandon's earshot, he dashed out of the office leaving behind a rather taken-aback Brandon. He made for the shade of a tree, pulled out his phone and called the Peterson's number. Mrs Peterson answered immediately.

'Geoff? Where's Mimi? I don't know what's going on, but something's wrong!'

'What do you mean, "Where's Mimi?"' he asked. 'I took her to the airport on Tuesday. What's happened?'

'I've been told she didn't get back to Shanghai. I'm so worried and I don't understand what's going on,' wailed Viola Peterson.

Geoff tried to be calm. *Are the thugs still after her? We got her out of Minneapolis just in time*, he thought. Aloud, he said, 'Tell me what's happened.'

'Yesterday a florist delivered a bouquet of artificial flowers for Mimi—so lifelike you'd think they were real. I told the deliveryman she'd gone back to China, but he said his orders were to leave them for her. They'd been paid for—he couldn't take the flowers back to the shop.'

'Who sent them?' Geoff asked, trying to stay calm.

'I don't know. There was no card.'

'So, why are you calling me?' Geoff asked.

'Well, an hour ago, a Chinese man came to see me. He was young and spoke good English. He wanted to speak to me about Mimi. I thought he must be a friend of hers. He said he'd called Mimi's home in Shanghai and was told she wasn't there. For some reason he has to get in touch with her, so he came to see me. Do you know where she is?'

Geoff was thinking fast. *Who is sending Mimi flowers? And who is the Chinese guy checking up on her?* He had to be very careful about what he said. He didn't trust Mrs Peterson's discretion.

'I just dropped her off at the airport. I'm as surprised as you are that she hasn't got home.'

'I'm so worried, what with her mother so ill and all, but the only person I could think of calling was you.'

'I'll see what I can do. Don't worry, Mrs Peterson. I'll talk to you as soon as I find out something. I'm sure there's a really simple explanation for all this,' said Geoff, sorry that he had to lie to this nice old lady. When he got back to his office, he found a young Asian man sitting in his chair.

Brandon gave him a queer look and Geoff wondered what had transpired in his absence. But all Brandon said was: 'You have a visitor.'

The Asian man stood up. He was tall and rather stocky. He introduced himself as John Yan, a student from Shanghai. 'I'm here because I've been told that Xia Mingxi didn't get back home and her family is trying to find out where she is. They are frantic and asked me to try to trace her.'

Geoff didn't believe a word of it. Brandon was looking at them curiously so Geoff said, 'We're disturbing my colleague. Let's step outside.'

As soon as they were outside the building, John Yan said, 'I understand you took Miss Xia to the airport. Where did she say she was going?'

'She wasn't my girlfriend, if that's what you're intimating,' Geoff snapped, 'She was my student. She said she was going home to China.'

'So why did you take her to the airport if she's only your student?'

'When she came to tell me she had to drop out of my class, she mentioned she had no one to take her to the airport. Minneapolis taxis are expensive and not always reliable. So I offered to drop her off. Look, I have a class in five minutes. I've got to go.'

Geoff went back into the building, leaving the young man on the steps. He hoped he'd seen the last of him.

Shortly after nine that evening, Geoff went back to his office from a night class he taught. The administrative offices were closed, most of the faculty had left and the hall was deserted. To his surprise, he found his office unlocked. *Shit, the janitor must have forgotten to lock it.* Geoff turned on the light and looked around. *No, the wastebasket hasn't been emptied.* But someone had undoubtedly been there, for things were not quite in their place. Brandon was a neat freak and always had everything precisely lined up on his desk. Geoff checked his own desk drawers. Someone had been through them, he was sure, because the files in the drawers were slightly askew.

It must have been that damn man! Thank heavens I took my laptop and phone with me.

Geoff was angry and just a little rattled. How could he report what he was sure was a break-in by that Chinese guy to the campus police? Nothing had been taken, at least not that he could tell. There was nothing to do but lock up and go home. Which he did, picking up a pizza on the way.

He walked up to his second-floor apartment, juggling the warm box of pizza and his briefcase while trying to get his key out of his pocket. But the key wasn't required because, as he drew closer, Geoff realized that the door was ajar. *I'm sure I locked it this morning. Someone's picked the lock*!

Geoff went in and softly shut the door behind him. The apartment felt empty, but now he wasn't sure of anything any more. He called out, 'Who's there?' but there was no answer. He couldn't hear a sound. Whoever had broken in was long gone.

Geoff looked around the living room. Everything seemed to be in order. Then he remembered the phone he had purchased to keep in touch with Mimi. It was in the drawer of his bedside table.

His heart pounding, he went down the hall and into his bedroom. Halfway across the room he sensed someone behind him. But before he could turn, something hit him hard on the back of his head. Through the blinding pain, he heard someone run through the hall and then the slam of the apartment door.

Geoff lay on the floor for a few minutes, dizzy from the blow. *Someone must've been hiding in the bathroom.* When he finally wobbled to his feet, he nearly stumbled over the bathroom wastebasket, which had been the weapon that hit him. He made his way to the bedside table and opened the drawer—the phone was gone. *Shit!* He sat down on the edge of bed for some minutes—he didn't know how long. Finally he summoned up the energy to go to the kitchen for some ice, which he wrapped in a towel and then held to his head.

I have to contact Mimi and warn her the Chinese are still after her. They have my phone with her number in it. They could call her.

Thank God her number has a 612 area code, so they'll think she's still in Minnesota. But I've got to warn her not to answer her phone!

He pulled out the phone he usually used. *Wait a minute. What's the number of the new phone I got her?* He'd forgotten to memorize it. *How on earth am I going to contact her?*

His head still hurt. He went back to the kitchen and drank a glass of ice water with a couple of Tylenol.

Then he sat down at his kitchen table and tried to think. *Who's Mimi staying with? The name sounded Japanese . . . Kondo? Konya? Something with a K. Aah, her first name's Bess. And she works for an international financial consulting firm.*

He needed help. He called Brandon.

Brandon answered after four rings. 'Hey, what's up?' were his first sleepy words. 'It's nearly one in the morning.'

Geoff explained, and his slurred voice as well as the reason for the call was enough for Brandon to say he'd be over in 15 minutes. He showed up in 12 with his laptop.

Brandon was concerned about Geoff's injury and his bad headache, but Geoff insisted he was OK. Just hungry, as he hadn't eaten since noon. So over cold pizza, they searched for Mimi's contact in New York. Brandon went through the websites of various firms until he finally came across a Bess Koyama at Rubin-Hatch. But he couldn't find a home phone number for her and it was, by then, nearly three in the morning.

Brandon didn't want to leave Geoff, who looked terrible, so he made Geoff go to bed and then he slept on the sofa. At about seven Brandon woke up, made a pot of coffee and then woke up Geoff. They had toast and coffee, waiting until eight to call New York. 'They're only an hour ahead of us,' Brandon said, 'and no one will be an office before nine.' At five past eight Minneapolis time, Geoff called Rubin-Hatch, asking to speak to Ms Koyama.

Bess was on the line within a minute. She was already aware that something had happened because Mimi had called shortly before in a panic, saying that a man speaking Chinese had called her, pretending to be a friend of her father. No one except Geoff and her parents knew her new phone number. When she tried calling Geoff on his new phone, the same man had answered. Mimi had been hysterical, and it had taken Bess some time to calm her down, saying that there was no way the man could know where she was. But what had really worried Mimi was how the man had got Geoff's phone.

Geoff told Bess everything that had happened to him. 'I think you could still be in some danger, Geoff,' Bess said, after he'd finished. 'Since the man could reach her on the phone he stole from you, he knows you know where she is. He's already resorted to violence—who knows what he'll try next. I know you teach, but is there some way you could get away for a few days? You can come here . . . to New York . . . I'll find a place for you to stay. It'll help Mimi too, to know you're out of immediate danger.'

By the time they'd finished talking, Bess had convinced him to leave Minneapolis. Bess gave him her personal number and told him to call and let her know when he'd be arriving in New York. Geoff asked her to tell Mimi he was safe but to not mention anything about the attack in his apartment.

Geoff didn't know what he'd have done without Brandon, though he wouldn't take Brandon's suggestions about seeing a doctor or calling the police. 'What will the police do? The only thing the man took was a cheap phone.' Brandon didn't argue. Instead, he booked Geoff a flight for that afternoon while Geoff went to see his department chair. Geoff said he had to fly back to New Zealand for a family emergency, but that he'd make arrangements to grade his classes. Then he called Bess and gave her his flight number.

Brandon made sure Geoff was never alone. He drove Geoff to his apartment so he could pack a bag and then took him to the airport and didn't leave his side until he was ready to go through security.

Finally, Geoff was seated and buckled up for his flight.

As the plane taxied away from the gate, he leaned back in his seat, shut his eyes and exhaled a small sigh of relief.

Bess was thinking about going to bed when her phone rang. She hoped it was Geoff—his flight should have arrived at La Guardia several hours ago.

It turned out to be a nurse at Mt Sinai Hospital in Queens. She said the phone number had been in the wallet of a Geoff Mitchell who been taken to the ER in an ambulance from the airport.

Startled, Bess anxiously asked, 'What happened to him?'

'He lost consciousness on a flight from Minneapolis and no one could wake him when the plane landed. But he's come around and is quite agitated. Keeps talking about someone named Mimi. Is that you?'

'No, but I'm the person he was to call when he arrived. Can you tell me what his condition is?'

'We performed a number of preliminary tests. The patient told us that he was hit on the head yesterday. This confirms our initial diagnosis of a concussion. But Mr Mitchell is young and in good health. So we don't expect him to be here long. He just needs to rest for a few days. He says he took Tylenol and put ice on the injury, which was the right thing to do, but he shouldn't have got on the flight without having seen a doctor.'

Bess said she'd go to the hospital when Geoff was released the following day and confirmed that the hospital could list her as Geoff's contact.

She didn't say she had never met the man.

21

Tokyo, 5 August

As the black Toyota sped through the night, Baba felt an increasing sense of unease. *Why was I ordered by the PM to accompany him on this secret trip to the western edge of Tokyo? With only a driver and a security officer? Why does he want me at this meeting with the Mitsumoto executives? Why we couldn't have discussed the plot in his office?*

The prime minister had said almost nothing since they left his official residence just after eight, after all the journalists had gone home for the day. Now he sat silently in the corner, across the seat from Baba. Baba glanced at him from time to time. He could see little in the dim light but he thought the PM had rather a pained expression on his face.

Just after they passed through Tachikawa, more than two-thirds of the way to their destination of Akishima, the PM suddenly started and thrust a hand into his jacket. Gasping, he pulled out a small vial, quickly opened it and popped something into his mouth.

'Sir, are you all right?'

After a moment, the PM replied, 'Yes, just a touch of indigestion. I'll be OK in a minute.'

Baba didn't believe him. It was probably an attack of angina and the pills were nitroglycerine. *So the rumours about his health are true.*

Minutes later the car pulled up at the Showakan, or the Forest Inn as it was referred to by international guests, a luxury hotel located at the western edge of Tokyo. Baba could see the PM pull himself together with some effort as the security official sitting beside the driver opened the door and helped him out. A courteous young woman came out to greet them, then whisked them up an elevator to a suite on the sixth floor where she opened a door, let the two men in, bowed deeply and left.

Two men were seated in the living spacious room, nursing drinks, but both stood up as soon as the prime minister entered. The PM introduced Baba, and then said, 'These are my good friends from Mitsumoto, President Noda and CFO Akita.'

Both the Mitsumoto executives were in their early 60s, with thinning coal-black hair, clearly dyed, and wearing dark grey suits. The only difference between them was that the CFO was a few inches taller. The CFO offered drinks to the two newcomers but the PM asked for tonic water. Baba followed suit.

For the next half hour, the two executives politely but closely quizzed Baba about 'the plot the prime minister has briefly informed us of—the possibility of a group led by Fan of SAEC somehow blocking the Mitsumoto consortium from winning the bids for the Benin oil tracts.' They wanted more information about the 'plot' but, unfortunately, Baba was unable to provide any details. Baba emphasized that the plot was international in scope, clearly financial, and most likely involved trades in stocks, bonds or currencies in the Tokyo market and possibly in other major markets as well. The executives already knew of the proposal made by Tanaka for MTC to collude with SAEC but Baba told them, 'I am certain it's not the main focus of what is planned.'

The PM, who looked very tired, had said nothing all the while. Finally MTC's president sat back and said to him, 'Prime Minister, I'm sure we don't need to worry about Fan's group successfully buying up shares in our company. None of the companies in our group will sell their MTC shares. And we have promised all foreign banks and others holding our shares that we'll buy their MTC shares at two per cent above the market price if they want to sell. Since we don't have to worry about the group's getting their hands on our shares, we can pretend to go along with Fan's suggestion of colluding on the bid prices. We'll simply outbid SAEC. We should have no trouble getting all four tracts.'

From what Murai had told him about the long-standing cross shareholding among the firms in the Mitsumoto group, Baba knew the president was right: Fan's group would not succeed in obtaining a lot of MTC shares. But thinking about how devious Fan was, he was sceptical about MTC being able to easily double-cross SAEC in the bidding. However, Baba kept his thoughts to himself.

The CFO spoke up. 'I am concerned, though, about the vice president of a key member of our consortium being in on this plot. Maybe we should speak to Mr Honma, the president of Sumida Bank.'

The PM finally broke his silence, 'Mr Akita,' he began in a tired voice, 'there's no need to do that. I'm having a close eye kept on Tanaka. We'll find out more easily what's going on if we don't run the danger of alerting him.' Then to Baba's surprise, the PM added: 'I'll do all I can to make sure the MTC consortium gets the rights to all of the oil in Benin. You can tell the oil minister of Benin that he can consider MTC a de facto national corporation with 100 per cent backing from the Japanese government. Tell him that the MTC group can be considered financially even more reliable than SAEC. You should also remind the minister that the Chinese government has been trying to privatize the state-owned companies. This means even though SAEC is one of the largest, the company could be privatized any day and lose the backing of the government.'

The CFO, clearly delighted by the PM's categorical assurance, made a small bow to him in gratitude. Smiling, Akita said, 'Just between us, I was in Porto Novo last week and had a long talk with Mr Marcel Edu, the oil minister, who told me a lot of interesting things in exchange for this . . . I handed it to him literally under the table.'

As the CFO said 'this', he spread his right palm indicating 'five'. Baba wondered if he meant 5,000 or 50,000 or 5 million. But the PM just nodded as if he knew all about it.

Baba knew that bribes were not unusual when such big deals were involved but he was both offended and surprised that the men in front of him were discussing it as though it was perfectly above board to do so.

The CFO went on: 'The minister told me he heard from the Union Bank of Benin that for the past several years Fan has been receiving deposits in his account from the Nigerians. The bank says they assume these are kickbacks for Fan from Nigerian government officials for the investments the SAEC has been making in Nigeria. The deposits range from 50,000 dollars to a few hundred thousand. The bank also told the minister that the UBB is being used as a conduit for sending huge amounts of money deposited regularly in SAEC's account to banks in Singapore.'

Before the CFO could say more, President Noda began to thank the PM for all his help in Mitsumoto's efforts at acquiring the oil tracts in Benin. Baba thought Noda was aware of how tired the PM was and was ready to end the meeting. But the PM responded in a bantering tone, 'I will collect your appreciation when the next election comes around.'

Baba was again amazed by how crude the exchange was between the PM and the CEO of the one of the largest companies in Japan. He resented even more having been asked to attend this meeting, thus making him a participant in a sordid trade of political influence and 'appreciation' for influence that would undoubtedly be expressed in cash.

The PM by now was really exhausted, his face grown pale. Baba suspected he was in pain again. Without standing up, the PM thanked the Mitsumoto executives for coming all the way out to Akishima and ordered Baba to escort them to their car. As the three men left the suite, the PM said, 'I'm going out to the beautiful garden of this hotel to breathe some fresh air. Such a treat to be out of the middle of the city.'

When Baba returned to the suite 15 minutes later, he found the PM in the same chair but the colour had returned to his face and he seemed almost back to his usual self. *The PM didn't go to the garden. He stayed in here and took another pill. Those pills seem to work, at least temporarily.*

'Counsellor, I've decided to spend the night here. The security man will stay in the adjoining room but the driver will take you home. Find that woman who escorted us up here and have her bring my overnight bag from the car. Also tell the driver to arrange to have me picked up here at nine tomorrow. Thanks for coming.' And with those words Baba was dismissed. Baba had no doubt that the PM had planned to stay at the hotel for the night and had had his overnight bag packed and stored in the trunk.

When Baba relayed this message to the driver, the driver nodded as if he was expecting the message. He got on his phone and ordered two additional security officers to come to the hotel for the night and a car to collect the PM in the morning. Then the car set off back to the centre of Tokyo. Baba, exhausted after a very long day, hunkered down in a corner of the back seat for the long drive back to town. But he was too agitated to doze. As the car sped on through the dark night, one thought after another raced through his mind:

How honoured I was when I was seconded from the Foreign Ministry to the PMO last year! But now I'm counting the days until I can leave this power-hungry and unscrupulous PM!

The MTC president thinks he can double-cross Fan. Neither he nor the CFO is sufficiently concerned about what else he might be planning. Wasn't I explicit enough in explaining why Murai and I are sure the plotters will do almost anything to derail MTC's hope of getting the Benin oil and making millions for themselves at the same time?

I really should call Murai if only to unburden myself. But looking at his watch, Baba realized it was already past 11 and he wouldn't be home until nearly midnight. His mind full of worries, he was surprised when the car stopped and the driver announced he was at home.

Baba entered his apartment and turned on a light. Always busy and spending little time at home, he had furnished it minimally. Tonight it seemed particularly bleak and empty. He was tired but still not sleepy. He poured himself two fingers of whisky, pulled his tie off, put on a recording of his favourite Bach cantatas and sat down in a black leather chair.

How ironic! As an idealistic teenager, I was determined to join the Foreign Ministry, thinking how I might do my part to improve international relations and Japan's standing in the world. And here I am working for a self-serving, corrupt man. Behaving like a sycophant and turning a blind eye to whatever he chooses to do.

Baba took a sip of whisky and leaned back. *I wish I had some other options. But I need my government salary to help pay for my mother's nursing home. She deserves the best, even if it's bloody expensive. And I have no one else to help . . . the price of being an only child.*

He knew the late hour, the tiredness and the distaste for how he'd spent his evening was making him melancholy. He usually didn't mind his solitary lifestyle, but sometimes a feeling of loneliness came over him.

If only Julia had survived!

After so many years, the memory was still vivid. How they had first met at a diplomatic reception in London. And fallen in love. Within a month they had moved in together. But Julia was a dedicated English foreign-service officer who wasn't at all sure she could give up the job she loved and live as the wife of a Japanese diplomat. So they had parted when Baba was posted back to Tokyo. But neither could give the other up and for several years they had arranged to spend their annual leaves together. Baba had hoped Julia would eventually agree to marry him.

And then Julia had been posted to Egypt. She had been delighted at the thought of being second in command in the embassy in the country that was so important for the UK, struggling to maintain its influence in the Middle East and North Africa. Baba had warned her to be cautious. Egypt could be a dangerous place with religious fanatics attacking foreign tourists and pipelines, attempting assassinations, blowing up car bombs at checkpoints. She had assured Baba that she would be very careful when they parted after their last holiday in Paris. They kissed goodbye at the airport and agreed to meet again as soon as possible.

He never saw Julia again. She had been at the movies in Cairo with a friend when a terrorist group attacked. She was severely injured and taken unconscious to a hospital where she died a few days later. Her name never reached the media because the ambassador wanted it that way; he didn't want to stir up more problems with Egypt. One of Julia's colleagues at the embassy who knew of the relationship between Julia and 'her Bach' called Baba to give him the news that devastated him.

He realized he was getting downright maudlin. He looked at his watch. It was nearly one in the morning. *Snap out of it*, he told himself. *It's time to move on. Julia wouldn't want you to spend your life alone. And it's been six years, no, six and a half. But, damn it! I couldn't even keep a dinner date with a colleague this evening because I am at the beck and call of the PM.*

Baba downed the last of his whisky and stood up. *OK, I am at the beck and call of the PM, but I work for the Foreign Ministry and for the good of Japan. And I am going to do all I can to make sure SAEC and the rest of the plotters don't damage Japan's economy or prevent us from getting at that oil. First thing in the morning, I'm calling Murai to see what else I can do to help foil the goddamned plot!*

22

Tokyo, 8 August

Ken Murai emerged from the Kokkai-gijidomae subway station regretting that there was no easy way to get from his home in Mejiro to the Ministry of Finance in Kasumigaseki. Although today, a Saturday morning at just after eight, the trip hadn't been all that bad because the subway had been only about one-third full. He didn't usually work on Saturdays, and especially not in August when his ministry had a bit of a lull, but today he had come in to go through the box delivered to his office yesterday, and now locked up in a cabinet, waiting for his attention.

He arrived at the International Bureau to find himself alone. As he placed the large box on his desk, Ken recalled the phone conversation with Baba on Thursday. Baba had given him the gist of his visit to Forest Inn with the PM, and reported that the NSA hadn't gained any new information about Tanaka or anything else that could be connected with the plot. Though Ken had tried to keep his voice even, he knew his frustration had got through to Baba, who tried to mollify him.

'Ken, I agree with you. We haven't got anything that can tell us what Tanaka is doing. I'm sure the NSA assigned competent people to poke around to find out what Tanaka is up to.'

'I know, Bach. But the NSA's mandate is to keep watch for terrorists, subversives and other threats to our national security. Their job isn't to spy on a bank's vice president even when the PM asks them to, blatantly misusing . . . exceeding . . . his authority. I'd really hoped they'd find more than what you've told me.' Ken sighed.

'Ken, the NSA guys said the only possibly significant thing they've learned is that Tanaka met the president of an Osaka bank and the chairman of a large insurance company, both men with shady reputations. I read their report of the meetings, but I didn't find anything of interest to us. They found nothing by hacking into Tanaka's computer or listening to his phone conversations. He's either not communicating now with his fellow conspirators or he's doing it in a way that's eluding even the experienced NSA guys.'

'Bach, don't get me wrong. I'm not implying that you missed anything important. But I would like to see for myself what the NSA has gathered. I just might find something.'

'OK. I'll have someone deliver everything the NSA has sent me. As you can guess, the PM asked me to act as a liaison between him and the NSA.'

Although the box of materials had arrived yesterday, Ken had been too busy to even open it and decided to come in today to go through as much of the material as he could. First he spent two hours fruitlessly wading through the written reports on Tanaka. All he discovered was that Tanaka's wife had died four years earlier from a heart attack; there was no evidence that he had formed any liaison since then; he had no children and no close relatives; he had been born in Osaka where he lived until he went to university in Tokyo; and he had joined the bank upon graduation. For 10 years he had headed Sumida Bank's branch in New York and then returned to Tokyo and was promoted steadily to become the vice president.

Tanaka was said to have been in line to succeed the president of his bank, a man called Daisuke Honma, but he had been on the losing side of a dispute over whether Sumida Bank should gradually reduce their holdings of Japanese government bonds. As a result, the board had retained Honma as president. Tanaka had stayed on as the vice president but had been sidelined. Ken already knew that from weekly magazines and the gossip among bankers he met frequently.

The report summarizing what one of the NSA specialists had found by hacking into Tanaka's computer was similarly useless. The only things that slowed Ken's reading were several email exchanges Tanaka had with Joshua Fried, referring to the transfers of money during the first few days of August, the amounts ranging from 50 million dollars to over few hundred million from unnamed Japanese and Americans. Ken speculated that all this money would be used for whatever the group was planning. Still, the amount involved was too small to affect the market in anything from stocks and bonds to currencies. He assumed Fan, a German and possibly some others too would be providing the funds for the plot and the plotters could be planning to do margin trades. *But would they have enough money to do what they are planning? Could be. But I'm just widely speculating here.*

Next, Ken went through the daily reports of the agents doing surveillance on Tanaka. For a senior bank executive, he led a boring social life. The only people he had met in the evening were Fujio Nakai, president of a middle-sized bank in Osaka, and Ryota Seki, chairman of one of the largest insurance companies in Tokyo. Ken wondered if Tanaka had met them in order to recruit them for the plot. Ken knew Nakai was rumoured to have ties with the yakuza underworld and Seki had an unsavoury reputation. Tanaka met both these men individually at a *ryotei*, an exclusive Japanese-style restaurant favoured by politicians and executives. One had to have an introduction to get in, and since every party was served in a private room, the agent tailing Tanaka couldn't get into the building. Using a highly sophisticated directional mike that had a range of up to 100 metres, he had tried from outside to catch some of the conversation between Tanaka and Seki but had been unable to.

But the agent had caught some of the conversation between Tanaka and Nakai. 'See audio,' the report noted. Apparently the two had been seated in a room at the front, so the agent's mike had been able to pick up much of the conversation—most of which, according to the report, had been about Tanaka getting a job for Nakai's son.

Ken stopped to make himself a cup of coffee, and then decided to listen to the audios, especially the conversation between Tanaka and Nakai.

As soon as Ken began listening to the recording, he realized the NSA agent must have had trouble understanding Nakai's thick Osaka accent, rendered even more unintelligible by the sound of traffic outside.

The conversation was intriguing, to say the least. Tanaka and Nakai discussed a job for Nakai's youngest son who was soon to graduate from Osaka University. It was clear that Nakai was hinting to Tanaka for a job for his son at Sumida Bank. But then the conversation turned to a subject not immediately evident to Ken. He knew now why the NSA report had said so little about it. He rewound the tape and listened very carefully.

In his strong Osaka dialect, Nakai asked Tanaka, 'Tanaka-han, mae atta toki jyunen butsu dake yaru to iwahatta kedo sore mada honto dekka?'

Ken paused the audio and translated into the standard Japanese in his head: 'Tanaka-san, mae ni atta toki jyunen butsu dake o suru to iwaremashitaga sore wa mada honto desuka?'

But the question was unclear. Then he remembered that merchants and traders in Osaka and western Japan referred to items they traded in as *butsu*—things. So Nakai was asking, 'Mr Tanaka, when we met before, you said we would only do the 10-year thing. Is that still true?'

Tanaka answered in the same dialect, 'Honto desu wa, jyunen butsu wa mottomo urikai sarete iru butsu dessakai, sorewo naraimasunya.'

Ken had no trouble understanding Tanaka's answer: 'Yes, it is. Because the 10-year thing is the most traded thing, we are going to focus on it.'

The only 10-year 'thing' that was 'the most traded' had to be the 10-year Japanese government bond! Ken knew some corporate bonds had a 10-year maturity but they could hardly be called 'most traded'. And they certainly weren't talking about any stocks or currencies!

Nakai's reply followed: 'Kekkou dosu. Butsu no nedan wa itsu oukuzure ni nattemo okashii koto arahen desakkai.' Or: 'Fine. It wouldn't be strange at all if the price of the thing were to plummet any day.'

They just had to be talking about Japanese government bonds! His heart pounding, Ken listened closely for more clues. Although he was now attuned to the Osaka dialect, Ken almost missed the sum of money that Nakai mentioned—300 million dollars. The tape became inaudible for several seconds and Ken caught only Tanaka's words, 'one of the largest'.

Ken stopped the audio. *This doesn't make sense! If they have that amount of money, and if Nakai is one of the largest investors in the project, then even if the group does margin trades, there is no way they can bring down the JGB. The JGB market is far too huge. Or does 'one of the largest' refer to something else—something other than the amount of money?*

He listened for another 10 minutes. But the subject of the project didn't come up again. Exhausted, he decided to break for lunch. But he was too shaken to concentrate on the food.

What am I going to do now? It's a bit far-fetched that such a small group is planning to attack the JGB. So should I ignore what I've heard? No one at the ministry will believe me if I tell them about this. But . . . could it be possible the group and the plot are far larger?

After two cups of tea and an antacid pill, Ken moved on to check the recordings of Tanaka's home phone. It was more likely he would discuss anything involving the plot on his private line than at work.

To save time, Ken quickly scanned the reports summarizing the findings of the two NSA investigators 'monitoring' Tanaka's phone conversations and daily activities. The phone conversations revealed nothing. All were very ordinary, short conversations. Tanaka seemed to dislike talking on the phone too much.

It was tedious to go through all the audio recordings. Ken was getting tired, and most of what he had heard was both boring and useless. But he plowed on, hoping to hear something, anything, to back up whether 'the 10-year thing' really meant the 10-year Japanese government bond. But there was nothing, not even on Tanaka's personal phones. Could Tanaka have found another way to send messages pertaining to the plot? It seemed unlikely that he was maintaining total silence for the three weeks after his visit to Benin.

Could the agents have missed something crucial? He had been startled to learn that only one agent had been tailing him on each shift. And they hadn't bothered to keep him covered after he got home for the evening. Also there were clear blanks in time, such as when Tanaka took a subway instead of the bank car assigned to him. The agent on duty had no idea where Tanaka had gone. Knowing that the NSA was doing something illegal in responding to the PM's unethical request, Ken was not surprised by the lackadaisical monitoring of Tanaka.

The day was wearing on and Ken hadn't even got as far as checking Tanaka's text messages or emails at the bank. Since banks often monitored their employees, should he even bother?

His phone rang. It was Baba.

'Ken? I've just had a call from the NSA. Tanaka's disappeared.'

'What? When?'

'Yesterday. But I was only told 10 minutes ago.'

'Do the NSA know anything more about it?'

'He was last seen by his NSA tail when he got home on Thursday evening about six. The agent stayed until eight when all the lights went out except in Tanaka's bedroom, and the agent decided it was safe to go home. The next morning, the first-shift agent arrived at seven, just in case Tanaka went for an early breakfast meeting. But Tanaka didn't come out of the house. The housekeeper arrived at 10, but Tanaka still hadn't left the house. The agent thought Tanaka might be sick. To check, he phoned Sumida and asked to speak to the vice president. He was told that Tanaka had taken sick leave. When the housekeeper came out at around a quarter past 11, the agent went up to her and said he had a message from the bank for Mr Tanaka. She looked rather puzzled and then said he wasn't home. He had left her a note that he was going to be away.'

Ken was horrified. 'Have they tried to trace him?'

'Yes. The NSA did all it could yesterday, even getting some help from the Americans . . . the NSA guy I talked to didn't want to tell me who the Americans were. Could be airline people or even CIA agents. Anyway, Tanaka flew on a nonstop flight to Washington, DC. And there the trail ends. They don't know if he took a flight elsewhere. He hasn't checked into any of the major hotels, and he hasn't used his credit cards. Why would he leave and where would he go?'

'I think he may have either known or guessed he was under surveillance,' Ken said slowly.

'Maybe. Did you find anything else in all that stuff I sent over?'

'I haven't gone through everything but I did listen to the conversation between Tanaka and the Osaka banker, Nakai, that took place in a *ryotei* where Tanaka must have thought he was safe from anyone eavesdropping. And they said something I think could be very important.'

Ken summarized the conversation and added that he wouldn't blame anyone for not catching what was likely a discussion on the JGB and the amount of money Nakai was contributing for whatever the two were involved in.

'I think you would have to be familiar with the Osaka dialect and with bankers' lingo to have understood what I heard, given the background noise, the thick dialect and the elliptical references to what I am sure is their "project".'

'The NSA people are professionals, but I was told that the guys who were assigned to Tanaka used to be detectives in the Tokyo Metropolitan Police.'

'I don't blame them for not catching the import of the conversation between Tanaka and Nakai. But why weren't they keeping a 24-hour watch on Tanaka? They had the same two guys on the two shifts, and Tanaka may have caught sight on one or both. And they asked questions about him. Couldn't the people who were mentioned in a report—the neighbour with the dog or the receptionist—couldn't they have mentioned to Tanaka that someone was asking questions about him? Maybe it was time for him to disappear to be personally involved in firming up and carrying out their plot that as far as we know is scheduled for next week. I'd bet money Tanaka's in New York!'

Murai very much wanted to tell Baba his suspicion that the group could be planning to attack the JGB but decided now wasn't time. He looked at his watch. 'Bach, I have a lot more to talk to you about Tanaka and the plot he's involved in. If you're free this evening, could you stop by my place for an impromptu dinner—I'll call in sushi.'

'I'd like that. This bachelor has no plans for Saturday evening. How about seven?'

'Fine, I'll see you then.' And before Baba could ask any questions, Ken rang off and started to pack up the box of the NSA material thinking, *At least my old friend Bach takes me seriously.*

23

New York, 9 August

Bess Koyama was exhausted. She set a mug of coffee down on the coffee table and collapsed on the sofa with a sigh. *I can take a lot of stress, but this is a little too much even for me. Has it been only 12 days since Mimi arrived in New York? Something has to be done . . . and as soon as possible. Thank God today's Sunday and with Nick and Mikey at the park, I can think in peace.* She put her feet up on the table and thought back over the past two weeks.

Ever since Mimi arrived in New York on 28 July, Bess had been trying to juggle her home life, her demanding job, Mimi and, since Geoff's arrival, two visitors. Her mother had been wonderful. Sylvia Browne had met Mimi at La Guardia and taken the anxious young woman home to her apartment in the Murray Hill district of New York City. She had settled Mimi in her extra bedroom, just one floor above the Koyamas' unit. The next morning, at Bess' suggestion, Sylvia had taken Mimi to have her hairstyle changed—the long locks were chopped off—and then bought her a pair of large, funky sunglasses for Mimi to wear outside.

Mimi quickly became friends with Bess' son Mikey and spent hours playing with the boy. After Nick arrived home on last Sunday, he had loaned Mimi an old computer and asked her to write down everything she could think of about SAEC, the plot and her terrifying trip to Tokyo. Bess soon realized that Mimi's dwelling on her ordeal seemed to make her lose her nerve just when it seemed she'd been on the verge of becoming her usual confident self.

Despite her changed appearance, Mimi was rarely willing to venture outside the apartment building. Since she was nearly always indoors, Bess thought she was safe enough. But knowing about the murders in Shanghai and the 'kidnapping' of Mimi on her way to Tokyo, Bess was still worried that when the person masterminding all these acts found out that she'd left Minneapolis, he would find some way to come after her. *Mimi is still in danger. I know it . . . as does Mimi, I'm sure.*

Her thoughts then turned to Geoff who's been attacked in Minneapolis and then flown to New York only to land up in hospital with concussion. When Bess had gone to the hospital and signed for his release, she had taken one look at him and known that he wasn't in any shape to stay alone in her colleague's apartment. Her mother had suggested that a friend who lived in the same building might be willing to put him up in her spare room. Mrs Printz, a former nurse, had taken excellent care of her patient. He spent the first couple of days resting but then joined Mimi in playing with Mikey, who was immediately taken with his new friend who 'talked funny'. But Bess knew she had to relieve her mother and Mrs Printz, both visibly tiring under the responsibilities of looking after their guests.

Bess had talked to Mimi and Geoff about where they would like to go next. Mimi had insisted that it wasn't safe for her to return to Shanghai or Minneapolis. Geoff was clearly enjoying his stay in New York and Mimi's company, but realized that, now that he had recovered, he had better think about getting back to his studies.

'But do you think it's safe for me to return to Minnesota?' he asked Bess and Nick. 'The Chinese thugs know they can find where Mimi is if I'm back in Minneapolis. They will find me easily and they can make me talk. But what I don't understand is why they are so determined to get her.'

The Koyamas had no answer, even after they had read everything she had written up. So Bess decided that they had to come up with a plan to relieve the two older women of their charges but keep Mimi and Geoff away from the distinct possibility of being harmed, or even killed, by Fan's thugs. Bess determined that today was the day they would come up with a plan.

So with her feet up and her mug now empty, Bess turned her thoughts to the rest of the day. First she had to think about Sunday dinner. *I think I'll kill a lot of birds with one stone. I'll organize a Chinese take-out. That way I won't have to cook, and I'll invite Mimi, Geoff, my mother and Mrs Printz. That will relieve them of feeding their guests and we can all put our heads together and come up with a plan.*

The impromptu party was a huge success. And once when everyone was replete and sipping jasmine tea, Bess 'convened' her meeting, rapping her water glass with a knife until the room went quiet.

'OK, everyone. This has been a great get-together, but now I'd like us to think what Mimi and Geoff should do now to guarantee their safety and to get them back to something like a normal life. Mimi can't safely go back home to Shanghai and Geoff can't return to Minneapolis. Not for a while. Any ideas?'

'How about Mimi and Geoff taking an incognito vacation at the lodge Rubin-Hatch owns in La Jolla, California?' asked Nick.

But both Mrs Printz and Bess' mother immediately shot it down, deeming it 'an unsuitable idea'. Nick knew what the women were thinking, *An unmarried young couple vacationing together*? So Nick dropped the idea.

Suddenly Mimi burst into tears. 'I know I can't stay here—I'm a bother to everyone. And I can't go home to Shanghai. Even if I do stay here, the thugs are sure to find me even with my new hairdo and glasses. They found me in Minneapolis when I hadn't told anyone where I was. And look at how Geoff was hit on the head, just so they could find out where I was. I'm never going to feel safe again!'

Geoff got off the sofa and sat down next to Mimi, huddled on a cushion on the floor. Putting his arms around her, he held her close. 'I'm taking you to New Zealand,' he said loudly, surprising everyone.

'But—' was all Mimi could say, looking up at him in astonishment.

'No one will ever find you there. I have a cousin who has a sheep station way out in the country on South Island—that's a ranch to you guys. No one will find us. I'll come with you. But you won't feel alone because he has a big family. In any case, I'll have to take leave or someone will come after me again to try to find out where you are. Right? We'll go to New Zealand. OK, Mimi?'

Mimi seemed overwhelmed. After a few moments of thought, she asked, 'Are you sure no one will find us? Fan's thugs are very clever . . . so they must know already or can find out you're from Christchurch.'

'Yes, but they'll be looking for a Mitchell in Christchurch and we won't be anywhere near there. Let's not even tell our parents where we'll be. Just that we're both safe. We'll fly into Auckland and take the train to South Island, and I'll have my cousin pick us up from the nearest station.'

'That sounds like a good plan for the time being,' said Bess, looking at her mother and then at Geoff. 'But will your cousin really want the two of you to land on him for weeks . . . or longer . . . until the plot is over and we can be reasonably sure no one will be coming after Mimi?'

Geoff responded with a laugh, 'He and his family are really laid back. Kiwis are a friendly lot, and and I get along well with my cousin and his family. It's now winter Down Under but it will be spring there shortly. My cousin can always use help when they shear the lambs for summer. We'll be fine.'

Geoff hugged Mimi gently.

Mimi looked up, a smile on her face, to find all others in the room, even Mrs Printz and Bess' mother, beaming at her. At last a solution had been found.

The mood was broken as Mikey charged into the living room in his pyjamas. 'I can't sleep. I'm *so* hungry. Did you save me a spring roll?'

24

Tokyo, 10 August

On Sunday night Ken Murai hadn't been able to fall asleep. He'd spent much of the day attending the wedding of a junior colleague and all through the reception he debated with himself about what to do with what he had discovered in the NSA material. He had told Baba he now strongly suspected the Japanese government bonds were the target of the plot and why. The two had talked until late on Saturday. They had decided that Ken's strong suspicion was just that. And however strong, a suspicion without unassailable proof was just that. They still had no idea exactly how the group could attack the JGB, let alone what they could or should do. However, when Ken woke on Monday morning after a restless night, he knew he couldn't keep the impending plot to himself. In his mind he was sure the target of the Fan group was the Japanese government 10-year bond.

Ken felt the first thing to do was to notify his immediate superior, the director of his bureau. He hadn't yet said a word about the plot to anyone in his ministry because what he knew about it was so vague, he would end up sounding ridiculous. But it was now only a week to 17 August, which was the only day that fit the information Mini had provided. *And the word 'so-rose' she overheard has to be Soros. The Fan group with the American hedge funds is going to attack the JGB, an international financial attack not on the yen as Soros attacked the pound, but on the JGB!*

So on Monday morning, as soon as his director arrived at the Ministry of Finance, Ken went to his office.

The director was coldly sceptical at first, but that soon changed when Ken told him what he had learned this past weekend from listening to the NSA recordings. The director asked him why the PM's office and the NSA were involved. Ken told him, and then went on, without reacting to the surprised expression on the director's face.

Ken explained why he was now sure the target was the government bonds. He even added what he had deduced from the NSA material he had gotten from his American friend and what Mimi had told him, but it was the conversation between Tanaka and Nakai that had convinced him. 'Director, I know what I've told you doesn't prove the plotters are going to attack the JGB. But, sir, knowing what we now know and considering the fact that we already have the extremely high JGB to GDP ratio, we must conclude there is a distinct possibility that a major, international attack on the JGB is imminent. This means we need to act.'

As Ken finished, his boss closed his eyes, as he often did when he pondered difficult questions. Ken held his breath and waited. Finally the director opened his eyes. 'Murai-kun, I understand why you're so concerned. But as you yourself said, the evidence is far from conclusive. To be frank, a lot of what you've told me is conjectural at best. I don't mean to be critical. I can't blame you if you believe an attack on the JGB is imminent. But we should be prudent. We don't want to alarm anyone when we don't have conclusive evidence. So, this is what I've decided to do. When I meet with the minister this afternoon, I will ask his advice. In any case, if the target of the plot is the JGB, this is more in the purview of the Budget Bureau which handles the government bonds.'

Trying hard to suppressing his disappointment and his exasperation, Ken responded with concern in his voice, 'Yes, I'm aware that the evidence is not conclusive. And I'm also aware that we must be prudent and that the JGB are the bailiwick of the Budget Bureau. But I'm convinced this is a credible international plot which, if carried out as I believe it will be, cannot but affect exchange rates. This means our bureau needs to stay on top of it too. I fully understand what you've said, sir, but I think it's time to alert the banking community. I know we don't have enough evidence to put out a general warning. But I think it would be both wise and politic to warn the largest banks and insurance companies that hold so much JGB.'

The director thought for a moment. 'I don't think we can go so far as to officially contact the biggest JGB holders yet. But, yes, I take your point.' Then, as if he'd made up his mind, he said more firmly, 'All right. Why don't you try to see Genya Ozawa. He's semi-retired but he's still president of the Bankers' Association. He's very level-headed and may have some suggestions. And he's been around long enough. If you tell him everything you've told me, I'm sure he'll understand why you wanted to talk to him. Be sure to tell him that you've talked to me but that you are talking to him in your personal capacity and not as the deputy director of our bureau. He might well have some advice.'

Ken agreed, thinking, *As expected, my boss is a cagey bureaucrat. But this will have to do for now.*

Four hours later Ken arrived at a large mansion in Setagaya, a well-to-do section of Tokyo. He was a little nervous. He knew Ozawa by reputation—'very intelligent and a true gentleman'—and was slightly intimidated at the thought of persuading the elderly banker that a credible international plot, very possibly an attack on the JGB, was no more than a week away. He pushed the bell at the gate, and a middle-aged woman wearing a maid's uniform let him in. She escorted him to a large reception room decorated in an opulent Western style. The two oil paintings on the wall were clearly genuine. *Wow, just like the rooms I've seen in the movies!*

A tall, silver-haired man wearing an ascot entered, asked the maid to bring coffee and walked over to Ken. Ozawa smiled, extended his hand and said, 'Deputy Director Murai, a pleasure to have you here. But if you had asked me to meet at the ministry, I'd have been pleased to spare you this visit.'

'I requested this meeting so it's only right for me to come to you. Thank you very much for giving me time today.'

Ozawa bade Murai to sit down, and almost immediately a young woman arrived with coffee and cookies. When she had served them and left the room, Ozawa took a sip of coffee and asked, 'You said you wanted to talk about the possibility of an international plot to attack government bonds—the JGB. Why isn't someone from the Budget Bureau here today instead of the deputy director of the International Bureau?'

Ken was prepared for this question and others that Ozawa asked. He explained that he had very reliable information that strongly indicated a major attack on Japanese stocks or the JGB was imminent. 'But the information seems to suggest the attack will be on the JGB.' As expected, Ozawa asked many questions about the sources of the information, who the plotters were and when the attack was expected. After Ken answered them, providing as much detail as he had given to his director, Ozawa chewed over what he had heard and then said softly, 'As you know, the banks in our association now have much more JGB than I think is prudent. If the price of the JGB declined by any appreciable amount, their balance sheets would take a very serious blow.'

The elderly banker looked straight at Ken, his eyes smiling. 'Deputy Director, if you tell the top officers of banks and insurance companies what you've just told me, I think almost all of them would say an attack on JGB won't get anywhere—it will fail. Well, I've lived a long life, and I can well remember Black Wednesday—16 September 1992. That day George Soros made a billion dollars by short selling the British pound, forcing the British government to pull the pound from the European Exchange Rate Mechanism. So I am well aware of what havoc one individual or a small group can do with sufficient resources.'

He paused, looked thoughtful and took another sip of his by-now-cold coffee. 'Is it possible that the Chinese man—Fan, I think you called him—and his cohorts in the plot have enough funds to mount a successful attack on the JGB? I am assuming they'd do their trades on the margin and they'd be very savvy, strategic traders—like Mr Soros.'

'Sir, I just don't know,' replied Ken ruefully. 'I've told you all I've been able to learn.'

'Well, we ought to be prepared. Your ministry and, of course, the Bank of Japan must do all they can to thwart the attack. Just think of the consequences—not only to our banks but also to our economy —should they be able to bring down the JGB! So, Deputy Director, if you are going to ask the banks in my association not to sell their JGB or even buy more JGB at the first sign of a credible attack, you know my answer has to be yes—for the sake of all the banks in my association and for our country.'

'Thank you, sir. I appreciate your cooperation. I will personally keep you posted on any further information we receive.'

'I will start communicating with some of our largest banks. I don't want to alarm them but I will talk about the necessity of backing the JGB should there be any signs of a large sale of the bonds. Some of the senior officers of the largest banks who opposed my becoming the president of our association may not listen to me. They may argue that we should sell some JGB instead of buying before the price goes down . . . to minimize their banks' potential loss. But I will do all I can to ensure that no one breaks rank.'

Ozawa stood up. The meeting was at an end.

Ken remained deep in thought on the subway as he travelled back to his ministry. He had done what the director of his bureau had permitted him to do based on the still insufficient and conjectural evidence he had come up with. *I'm almost certain 'the 10-year thing' Tanaka and the Osaka banker were talking about meant the 10-year bond. But the question is: How are they going to attack it? The attack has to be on a very large scale. Will they really have enough money to successfully attack the JGB even by doing margin trades? If the attack succeeds to any appreciable degree, it will mean a serious drop in the price of stocks and a big spike in interest rates . . . and yes, that will mean another real, long recession—or even worse.*

Before he knew it, the subway train was leaving his stop. *Well, I can get off at the next stop.* He was about to stand up but abruptly sat back down, to the disappointment of the man standing in front of him, hoping for his seat. He had some time to spare and so, on the spur of the moment, he decided to stay on the train and get off at Otemachi in the financial district. He would go to Sumida Bank and see what he could learn. He knew his director wouldn't approve, and that he had to be very careful. But he felt he simply had to try and see the president of Sumida Bank, which held a dangerous amount of government bonds. It was also a key member of the Mitsumoto consortium and where none other than Shigeo Tanaka was the vice president.

Although he had no appointment, he found that saying he was from the Ministry of Finance easily got him into the inner sanctum of the president's office. And here he was in luck. The president, Daisuke Honma, was in.

Honma, almost obese, stood and rather too effusively welcomed his unexpected visitor. 'Well, well, what brings a deputy director from the International Bureau to Sumida? I hope we haven't violated any regulations,' he said with a jocular laugh.

'No, no, I just happened to be in the area and thought I would bring you up to date on some information that has come to our attention. Your bank is important in helping our economy by holding so much JGB. So, I thought I should keep you posted on anything that might affect the price of our government bonds.'

'What could that be?' Honma said a little uneasily. But quickly managing a smile, he urged, 'Do sit down,' as he led Murai to the side of his large office where there was a suite of brown leather chairs. 'Can I get you something to drink?'

'No thank you, sir. I won't take up much of your valuable time.' *How much can I really say? Well, here goes.* He took a deep breath and began. 'President Honma, I'm here unofficially. The reason I wanted to see you is that there have been some rumours of a plot to bring down the price of the JGB. We don't know how credible they are. But I wanted to let you know so that you'd keep your eyes on any changes in price trends and sales volumes extra carefully.'

Honma sat up straight. Ken watched his flaccid face turn pale as he mumbled, 'A plot to attack the JGB?'

Ken said quietly, 'Yes, sir. But, as I've said, it's a rumour.'

Honma said nothing for a long moment. Then, 'Yes, you said that . . . just a rumour. You're from the International Bureau. Do you mean a big foreign bank or hedge fund is planning on dumping its holdings of the JGB?'

'No, sir, we have no specifics as yet, but we wanted to warn you. Your bank has a lot of our government bonds, and we appreciate your support of the Japanese economy. So we felt we should do everything we can to protect your interests.'

Honma asked a few questions, trying to find out more about the rumour. Ken hedged, saying that there was no credible evidence yet. To deflect more questions, Ken decided he would try a little flattery. So he said that the MOF had been pleased when Honma had been persuaded to stay on, though they had heard he wanted to retire. 'Everyone thinks you have done a superb job. The grapevine had it that your vice president, Mr Tanaka, wanted to drastically reduce the amount of JGB the bank holds. That would have been a bad day for Japan, I can assure you.'

Honma was duly flattered. 'I can assure you there is no danger of our reducing our government bond holdings. And you don't have to worry about Mr Tanaka. He's been sidelined. Just between us, I can tell you the board listens to me and not to Tanaka. And he's in rather dubious health.'

'Oh?'

'Yes. When his personal assistant arrived on Friday, she found a message from Tanaka on her answering machine. He said he had developed a serious health problem that needed immediate treatment. He expected to have to take leave for as much as two weeks.'

'That does sound serious,' said Ken, hoping for more information.

'I have no idea what the problem is or when he will return,' replied Honma, irritated. 'So far I haven't heard anything from him.'

'You don't know which hospital or clinic he's gone to?' asked Ken.

'No. All I know is what I've just told you. But then a senior executive doesn't have to ask permission for sick leave.'

Honma stood up and said, 'Deputy Director, thanks for taking the time to come and tell me about the rumour. Please tell the people in your ministry that they don't have to worry about Sumida's patriotism.'

Ken left the bank more worried than when he had arrived. He was sure that Honma didn't have a clue about his vice president being up to his ears in a major international plot. And he was very sure that Tanaka hadn't flown to the US for his health!

25

New York, 11 August

'You're certain that you were being spied on?' asked Peter Scheinbaum, frowning as he poured postprandial cognacs for Shig Tanaka, Josh Fried and himself.

Tanaka turned away from the window where he had been admiring the glittering nightscape of Manhattan from Scheinbaum's opulent Park Avenue penthouse. 'I'm certain—there were too many signs. Over the past few weeks—since I returned from a trip to Africa—people have been asking about me. A staff member at the bank and a neighbour both told me that a man had been making enquiries. So I kept my eye out for anyone tailing me. Almost every day I spotted the same car following me around during the day and a second car sitting outside my house until late in the evening. Rank amateurs—I don't know who they are.'

'So we have to assume that someone in Japan definitely suspects something. I hope it's not what we are planning. What do you think?' Scheinbaum was concerned.

Tanaka shook his head. 'I can't see how they could be on to our project. Since my smart phone is issued by the bank, I bought another under a different name to contact you and the others in the group. So if my phones were tapped or my house and office bugged, they wouldn't catch any of the calls or messages I've made to anyone in the group.'

'But you don't know for sure how long you've been under surveillance? What about calls or messages you sent before your trip? Whoever's spying on you must know you've come to New York,' Scheinbaum persisted.

Tanaka replied with some acerbity. 'No, I can't tell you for certain when the spying began, but I've followed all the rules set up by our group for communicating. And there's no way anyone can know where I am now except for you two. Officially I'm on sick leave. When I left Japan, I took a taxi to Narita hours before the first tail showed up. If it's the government checking on me, they can find that I flew from Narita to Washington, DC. But nothing after that.'

'So whoever "they" are probably know you're in the US,' noted Scheinbaum, disgruntled.

'Yes, but I don't see how anyone could find out where I went after I passed through immigration at Dulles International. I immediately took the train up to New York, and Josh has been kind enough to put me up. I made sure no one was tailing me. And I haven't used a credit card.'

Fried chuckled. 'I'm doing all I can to tuck Shig away so no one gets wise to our project.' He turned to Scheinbaum. 'If he keeps a low profile here in New York, you have nothing to worry about.'

Still looking dubious Scheinbaum said, 'But someone has suspicions, or otherwise why the surveillance?'

'Well, I can think of just one possibility. I did an errand for Fan in Benin about three weeks ago. I saw both the Japanese ambassador and the head of the Mitsumoto office there. So it's possible—actually probable—that one of them reported my visit to people in Japan.'

Both men, of course, wanted to know what the errand was. When Tanaka summarized Fan's proposal to MTC, Fried commented drily, 'Of course, he's not going to keep his word. I like his devious mind.'

Still unhappy, Scheinbaum added: 'OK, assuming your visit triggered the surveillance, who do you think is doing it? You said "if it's the government" earlier.'

'Well, since I talked to the ambassador there, he could've noted I came to see him in his routine report to the Foreign Ministry. And someone at the Foreign Ministry could have told someone at the

Ministry of Economy, Trade and Industry. Then this bureaucrat at METI, who knows about the Benin's oil reserves and the upcoming bid, might have wanted to find out what I'm really up to and asked the Metropolitan Police or a private detective agency to spy on me. Mind you, this is just a wild guess. But I'm 100 per cent certain that no one could know anything about the project from my visit to Benin and whatever else I've done.'

There was no way that Tanaka was going to admit that he never should have gone to Benin to meet the people he had met for 50,000 dollars. But before either Fried or Scheinbaum could question him further, the intercom buzzed and Scheinbaum went to let in a fit-looking middle-aged man with a full head of hair.

While Tanaka was wondering who this could be, the newcomer greeted the group and apologized to Scheinbaum for missing the dinner because he was on a diet. Hearing the voice and accent, Tanaka realized that the man was Markus Adler, even though he didn't have the slouch, the pouch or the combed-over thinning grey hair he had seen in Dresden.

The German held out his hand to Tanaka, saying, 'Mark Arnold. You met me in Dresden as Markus Adler.'

'Mark' declined cognac and sat down. Without waiting for Scheinbaum to start the discussion, Fried jumped in: 'Gentlemen, now that we're all here, let's go over our final plans. Shig, you start by telling us all about your friends who are joining our group. Peter has to know all the details so he can set up the margin trades and execute their trading contracts.'

Tanaka pulled a thick envelope from inside his jacket pocket and handed it to Scheinbaum. 'It's all here, but let me summarize for Josh and . . . Mark.'

'Two American friends are in. Tim Ogilvy, a billionaire international investor, is putting in 450 and Devra Berger, president and the majority shareholder of DevraStyles, an apparel company, came up with 50. And two Japanese, one the president of a bank and the other of an insurance company, are putting in 300 and 150 respectively. That's a total of 950 million dollars.'

Josh, smiling broadly, said, 'Shig, you've done well—that's almost 10 billion when used doing 10-to-1 margin trades. It's going to be a big help.'

Tanaka wondered if Fried or Scheinbaum was going to ask him how much of his own money he was putting into the project, but neither man did. Tanaka was confident that he could count on what Fried had told him soon after the project started: 'You bring in as much as you can from your friends in Japan and elsewhere who can be counted on to be discreet. I'll talk to Scheinbaum and make sure you'll get a fat "finders fee".' Tanaka was also relieved because this spared the need for him to give a lame excuse for not putting any of his own money in the project. He could have come up with at least 7 or 8 million dollars, putting together all his savings and what he could get by selling or mortgaging all the stocks and properties his rich, deceased wife had inherited and left him. Yet he had to admit that he preferred not to risk it, though he certainly didn't want to tell this to the others.

Scheinbaum said, 'Yes, we already have their contributions, which we'll use like all the others, to buy JGB and then dump the bonds strategically in Tokyo, New York and elsewhere starting on August 17 . . . all on 10-to-1 margin trades. Of course, as agreed, everyone can also short sell the Japanese stocks of their choice on a 10-to-1 margin trade using the money they sent for the project as their margin deposit. That is, there is no need for anyone in the group to make a separate margin deposit.'

Hearing Scheinbaum's magnanimous sounding words, Tanaka thought, *Yeah, but your brokerage will be charging a spiked-up interest rate and a fat commission and will be taking no risks. You aren't requiring a margin deposit because you consider our project foolproof.* Aloud he said, 'Peter, you wanted to know the exact terms of the trades my American and Japanese friends want to do when they short sell the Japanese stocks they choose. The details are in that envelope, but let me summarize them for you.'

Tanaka explained that Devra Berger wanted to short sell only KLOZ stock on a contract for just three days. Seeing Scheinbaum's quizzical expression, he added, 'KLOZ is the largest clothing-store chain in Japan and has many outlets abroad. She'd like to own stock in the same business she's in. She wants the short contract because she had a very hard time putting together 50 million and can't afford to take risks. Her thinking is that is that KLOZ stock will nosedive for three days after we dump the JGB, but by the fourth day bargain hunters will show up to buy the stock. So she wants to settle her contract on August 20 at the close of the market in Tokyo.'

Fried shook his head. 'I don't agree with her thinking. She'll be doing a 10-to-1 margin trade with her 50 million—that's short selling 500 million dollars' worth of KLOZ stock. I think the price of the stock will keep going down as the price of the JGB keeps tumbling. So she could make a hell of a lot more if her contract went for five days . . . or even seven. But, of course, the lady gets what she wants.'

Tanaka made no comment on Fried's interruption. When he could, he continued with his report. 'What the two Japanese investors and Ogilvy want to trade is more complex, which is why I've typed it out. They seem to be sure what kind of stocks will take a big hit when the price of the JGB plummets. Ogilvy wants the short selling contracts to go for seven working days, settling on August 26. The two Japanese . . . Mr Nakai and Mr Seki want their contracts to run for five days, settling on Friday, August 21, at the close of the Tokyo market.'

The new Mark Arnold had been quiet throughout the proceeding discussion. Now he suddenly spoke up: 'I think Mr Ogilvy became a billionaire because he knows what he's doing. A seven-day contract makes sense because if the government bonds take a dive, Japanese stocks are going to fall even more and won't come back up for some time.'

Fried said, 'I tend to agree with you on that, Mark. Peter and I already know what you plan to kick into the project and how you plan to use it, but Shig I don't think does.'

The German smiled at Tanaka and said proudly, 'I managed to come up with 250 million euros, just about 300 million dollars. The money is already with Peter. I picked seven Japanese stocks to short sell using my equations which tell me which stocks will get most pummelled when the government bond tanks. My equations worked well in the German market and should also work in the Japanese market. I want my short selling contract to go for seven days, though my equations say I can go for 10 days or longer. But the Japanese market may be a little different, so I've decided to be cautious.'

Tanaka nodded as Fried said, 'Now, while we are all here, let's review how much money we currently have for the project and make sure we're all on the same page. Peter, give us the picture, please.'

Peter seemed to take it in stride that Fried had taken over the meeting, though they were meeting in his apartment and he was handling all the trading. Scheinbaum cleared this throat and, looking down at his notes, said, 'Everything is looking good. Shig and Mark managed to come up with 950 and 300 million respectively, for a total of 1.25 billion. My hedge fund is putting in 4 billion, and Josh is kicking in 2 billion. That's 7.25 billion. Added to that is Fan's slightly more than 2 billion. The yuan appreciated as his money reached me via Singapore, so his total comes to 2.035 billion. So, we've got a kitty of over 9.285 billion dollars. Since we are using all the money to buy the JGB and then short sell them at 10-to-1 margin trades, we are talking about nearly 93 billion dollars of trades. It's a little shy of at the 100 billion that Josh and I wanted for the project. But it's close enough. We should be able to achieve our goal.'

He stopped, and the room went quiet. Josh broke the silence: 'Yeah, I wish I had more . . . but 93 billion dollars should be enough. We will buy the JGB very, very discreetly and then sell carefully and strategically. So we should be able to start a tsunami. Many big banks, insurance companies, pension funds in Japan and elsewhere, which hold a huge amount of these bonds are already very weary, worrying about the risk of the bond price collapsing suddenly. And we are going to let these big bondholders know they ought sell their JGB as soon as they can. I don't see how our attack can fail.'

Peter seconded Josh's view, choosing words carefully as if to convince everyone, including himself: 'The JGB market is huge—more than 10 trillion dollars—but I agree with Josh. As I've said already, I too wish we had more in our war chest. Still, I'm confident our attack will succeed. Japan has the highest ratio in the world of government debt to GDP, and more and more people are saying the JGB can crash without warning. Few economists and pundits are as concerned as they should be because their analyses are based on logic. They ignore the reality—that markets really work based on psychology, gut feeling and herd-like reactions. So 93 billion should blow up a small, critical section of a dyke to start a huge tsunami if we handle it right.'

Scheinbaum turned to Tanaka. 'You're Japanese. Doesn't it bother you that what we are about to do will almost certainly wreak havoc with your already long-suffering economy? I've long wondered why you were so eager to join us.'

Tanaka wasn't fazed by the question. His answer was almost vehement. 'No country should keep piling up such a huge amount of debt. And Japan could use a big shake up in the market to change our ossified laws and regulations relating to corporate governance, laws that over-protect entrenched management. My bank owns way too much JGB despite the fact that just a nudge could cause the collapse of the JGB price. I tried to get the board to listen to reason, but they decided to be "patriotic" instead. And I was ignored. Neither my bank's board nor Japanese politicians seem to realize what can't go on has to stop sooner or later.'

'Hmm,' sniffed Fried. 'It doesn't bother me if someone makes a killing on the JGB or even on our own treasuries. That's how capitalism works. If a government makes stupid financial decisions, it deserves to learn a lesson. It deserves to pay for making the same stupid decision year after year of selling more and more government bonds. Same goes for the people who keep buying them.'

As he listened on saying little, the German quant wondered, *Why are these people going on so about what's damn obvious?* But now he decided to ask Scheinbaum a question that had been puzzling him.

'Herr Scheinbaum, I'm wondering why your brokerage can't let the group do a 20-to-1 margin trade, which would double the amount of JGB we can dump on the market. You have our money . . . So even if, in the totally unlikely event, the price of the JGB goes up as much as 5 per cent, you wouldn't be taking any risk because 20 times 5 per cent is 100 per cent. You'd just keep our contribution, which in effect is collateral for nominally borrowing your money to do 20-to-1 trades. The chance of starting a tsunami increases if we had 186 billon dollars' worth of JGB to dump instead of 93 billion dollars worth.'

Trying to hide his annoyance, Scheinbaum responded slowly and deliberately: 'As you can surmise from what I said earlier, I am of course aware of what you've just said. But I own only 18 per cent of the brokerage. I'm the major shareholder but don't have enough shares to dictate what the brokerage does. In short, I can't do as I please at all times. Several members of the board are already pretty antsy about our group doing 10-to-1 trades. Given the nature of the project, no other major brokerage would let us do even a 10-to-1 trade, let alone 20 to 1. We just have to live with 10-to-1 trades.'

Arnold nodded, but his face said he wasn't happy. Looking at him, Fried said, 'Mark, don't worry. We can't miss. The price of the JGB is going to dive when we sell our bonds.'

Arnold put a good imitation of a smile on his homely face, 'Ja wohl, Herr Fried. Ich verstehe.'—'I understand.'—but his look said he was still less than satisfied.

Tanaka and Fried arranged to meet with Scheinbaum in the morning to organize the careful purchase of more JGB over the next week, making phone calls to the 'discreet brokerage firms' in New

York, Tokyo, London, Shanghai and Singapore that had agreed to do the trades for the group for a slightly higher than prevailing commission.

Shortly after 10.30, Fried adjourned the meeting. 'Well, gentlemen, long before the end of this month we will find how much richer we will be. Sweet dreams and good night.'

While seeing his guests to the elevator, Scheinbaum said, 'Now we've got to do everything very carefully so no one gets wind of what we're doing.'

As the elevator descended, Fried and Arnold jabbered in German while Tanaka thought, *In for a penny, in for a pound. I'll do everything I can to make the project succeed. I'll make a bundle and that fat Honma will get the sack.*

26

London, 14 August

Shortly after three on Friday afternoon, Sir Ian Smyth-Felton, president of the Royal Trust Bank, the fourth-largest bank in the UK, was interrupted during a meeting with the head of the loan department. His secretary, Siobhan Murphy, apologized as she handed him a white envelope. 'I'm sorry to disturb you, Sir Ian. The courier has just delivered this letter. It's from your daughter and marked "Personal and Urgent".'

Surprised, the banker said, 'Thank you, Siobhan,' glanced at the envelope and put it aside his desk. As soon as his meeting was over, he slit open the envelope, both worried and vexed about its likely contents. Just last week he had spoken to his only daughter, Stacey, now living in Santa Barbara, California, after a messy divorce only a year ago. She had told him she was 'beginning to enjoy the single life again' and that she was planning to travel to Honolulu with 'a friend'. *What now? Does she need money again? Or has something happened?*

As soon as he saw the first paragraph of the one-page letter, he sat up straight.

Dear Sir Ian,

We apologize for using your daughter's name to send this letter but we wanted to make sure you would read it as soon as you received it. The reason for this subterfuge is simple —the price of the Japanese government bonds, large quantities of which your bank owns, is going to plunge very soon, starting in all likelihood this coming Monday.

We regret that we cannot tell you who we are. The purpose of this letter is to suggest that your bond traders reduce your bank's exposure to the bond as soon and as much as possible. No reputable financial institution such as yours should suffer the consequences of the folly of the Japanese government selling so much of its sovereign bonds. As you must know, Japan's debt to GDP ratio is already very close to 300 per cent, by far the highest in the world.

Of course, you can ignore what we say. But since we are providing the same information to a score of the largest holders of Japanese government bonds, your failure to liquidate the 10.428 billion pounds' worth of these bonds your bank now holds could cost the bank dearly.

Sincerely,

Your friends in the financial community.

Sir Ian's immediate reaction was: *You scheming bastard! You're telling me to sell all the JGB my bank holds in order to help make the price go down! I should just ignore this damn letter—it's obviously from a hedge fund or a group of speculators planning to short sell the bond!*

But then he remembered reading in the *Financial Times* only a week ago that Japan's national debt was far greater than Greece's ever was, and its debt to GDP ratio was only exceeded by that of Zimbabwe before that country suffered hyperinflation and its economy crashed. Sir Ian knew the experts were split on whether or not they thought the price of the JGB would fall in the near future, but he recalled that the author thought it would be foolhardy to ignore the risk of their price plummeting.

Sir Ian was also taken aback by the accuracy of the letter in stating the exact amount of JGB his bank held—10.428 billion pounds' worth. It would be possible for someone to find out the general amount the bank held, but knowledge of the exact amount told him that whoever had sent him the letter had succeeded in hacking into his bank's highly protected computers. *Perhaps, after all, I should give some serious thought to the suggestion?* He decided he should at least talk to Naveen Kapur, the bank's chief bond trader.

Kapur was a burly and strikingly handsome Anglo-Indian in his 40s and a wizard at his job. As soon as he finished reading the letter Sir Ian handed him, he pursed his lips and said in his Oxbridge English, 'I've been meaning to talk to you about this. For the past few months, the guys in my unit have been telling me we ought to unload the JBG we hold. My traders have been hearing from those in other banks and brokerages that the JGB could crash. I've heard the same rumour myself. And this letter reminds me about what Alice Janowicz told me just yesterday—her job is to get any information that could affect the price of all the bonds we hold. She told me that a couple of her American friends have told her that a few big American hedge funds have very recently been accumulating a huge short position on the JGB. And what Alice hears is usually quite credible.'

'So you think the letter could be from one of these hedge funds?' asked the usually unflappable president, now a little unnerved.

'Could be. My guess is that a hedge fund guy wrote this letter. He wants our bank to sell the JGB we have, so that he can make a killing. It galls me to help him make money, but this letter persuades me to think seriously about unloading some . . . if not all . . . of the JGB we now hold as soon as possible.'

Looking at the undecided expression on Sir Ian's face, Kapur continued: 'The Bank of Japan bought about another 40 billion pounds' worth of JGB this past month. So its price notched up a bit . . . not by much, but enough to enable us to make good money if we now sell all our JGB. I need to see the price we paid for each lot since we began to accumulate the bonds. But my guess is we'd make about 170 million pounds. That's if we sell the JGB before it crashes. And, of course, we'd sell the JGB short at the same time to make some easy money.'

'So . . . if we do sell . . . do we sell as soon as possible?'

'Yes, Sir Ian. Immediately. The New York market is already open. So we should be able to unload some of the bonds without bringing down the price very much.'

'You're sure it's the right thing to do? I don't want to be second-guessed by some members of the board.'

'Yes, I'm very sure. The BOJ can't keep buying huge amounts of government bonds because their balance sheet is already bloated with them. Now is the time to sell the bond before its price tumbles. Because this letter says they are sending similar letters to a number of big financial institutions around the world, the sooner we unload the JGB the better.'

'All right, Naveen, let's go for it. Let me know what you plan to do.'

'I suggest selling the bond short . . . going for a week, doing a margin trade of 20 to 1. If we put up 50 million of our own money, we can short 1 billion pounds' worth of the bond to easily make 20 or even 30 million pounds.'

'OK, talk with Oliver Zilver right away. We need the CFO's approval for such a move. Tell him I approved selling the JGB we hold—at a pace both of you deem best. Also, take a short position on the JGB. The two of you can decide the specifics of the contracts.'

'Right. I just need to make one call before I talk to Oliver . . . to make doubly sure we're doing the right thing.'

As soon as Kapur left, Smyth-Felton picked up the letter again, sighing deeply. *Damn, the financial world had become so globalized and so bloody complicated. All this electronic trading and snooping lets crooks get hold of all kinds of information, including details about my private life and my bank's confidential data.*

Sir Ian had no way of knowing that he had just read one of 14 letters carefully crafted by Marilynn Tran, Josh Fried's Vietnamese-American personal assistant, a Cal-Tech grad and a whiz at mining the Internet for nuggets of information. Each letter had been written under the supervision of Fried and Tanaka.

On the same day that Sir Ian received his letter, others nearly identical in content reached the presidents of the eight largest banks in Japan, the two largest Japanese insurance companies, two banks in New York and the second-largest bank in Shanghai. They had been carefully chosen from among the world's largest holders of JGB. And Marilynn Tran had arranged for every letter to arrive at its destination by Friday mid-afternoon.

Only the presidents of two Japanese banks and the bank in Shanghai did nothing in response.

One Japanese bank president had already gone off to play golf when the letter arrived. No one in his secretariat dared read a letter marked 'Personal and Urgent', supposedly sent from the president's older brother in Kyoto. The letter sat on the president's desk until Monday afternoon when he decided to check his mail.

The president of the bank in Shanghai did nothing because his secretary was used to getting the letters to the president marked 'Personal and Urgent'. She disliked the Chinese practice of overusing the phrase to get special attention. Seeing that the letter was from the president's second son, now attending Tsinghua University in Beijing, made it easy for her to decide to show the letter to the president on Monday instead of breaking into the all-afternoon meeting he was in with the president and the CEO of China's largest steel maker. Her guess was that the son was again asking for money.

And the president of the second Japanese bank did nothing either, and for a very good reason—he could not tell the board that a huge amount of his bank's JGB should be sold immediately because he had been successful in keeping his position only by convincing the board that 'the price of the JGB will never collapse'.

So as soon as he finished reading the letter, he tore it up and threw the pieces into the wastebasket. *No one can short sell the JGB and make a killing. Its market is too big. This must be from a hedge fund trying to make a bit of money by scaring people to sell their JGB.* As he started towards the door, on his way out to lunch, the irritation on his face was replaced with a smirk. *Why don't I make a bit of money too? I can let Mayumi handle it for me.*

All the other recipients of the letter reacted immediately. Most believed it likely to have been sent by a hedge fund that was planning to short sell the JGB, though there was the possibility that it was bogus. Nevertheless they acted on it, smelling a chance to make easy money for their bank and for themselves. Some directed their key officers to 'look into what the letter says', while others told their chief bond trader 'to unload the JGB starting on Monday if the price isn't going down too fast. And be sure to make some contracts to short sell a reasonable amount of the JGB at the same time.' Six of the recipients asked the brokerage or hedge fund managing their personal wealth to 'immediately' short sell the JGB in amounts ranging from 8 million to as much as 50 million dollars.

In New York, on the afternoon of Friday, 14 August, the price of several exchange-traded funds, which specialized in bonds that included a substantial amount of the 10-year JGB—the most traded among all Japanese government bonds of differing lengths of maturity —lost almost 0.6 per cent. The unusually large fall could have been much greater had it not been for nearly 4.5 billion dollars' worth of buy orders that came from the sharp-eyed managers of several large pension funds. They did this to counteract the sudden sell orders of almost 6 billion dollars that had come during the final hour of trading. Most of the nearly 50 bond traders in the major financial institutions in New York, London, Tokyo and Singapore, who were not accustomed to seeing the price of the ETF for bonds suddenly falling as much as 0.6 per cent, spent a very busy weekend discussing with their colleagues and superiors if, come Monday, they should sell the JGB their institutions owned.

27

Around the World, 14 August

James Gao and his wife had just turned out their bedroom light when his phone rang. When he saw who was calling, he got up immediately and went to his study to take the call.

'Naveen, what's up?'

'Sorry to disturb you. I know it's very late for you, James, but it's rather urgent.'

'Don't worry, it's only 11 here in Singapore. Why did you call?'

Naveen told him of the letter his boss had received and of the decision to sell the bank's JGB in as prudent a manner as possible, but as fast as possible. 'But before we take this rather drastic step of selling a lot of the JGB we own, I wanted to know if you had heard anything, just a rumour even, that could affect the price of the JGB.'

'Interesting,' commented Gao. 'Several days ago, my immediate superior at Rubin-Hatch, Nick Koyama, asked me to keep my eyes open for any information or rumours relating to the JGB. He intimated he had some information that an attack was planned on the 10-year JGB. But in the past few days I haven't seen or heard anything unusual, though I've kept my ears and eyes open. Although based on what I know about the JGB, I must tell you that holding on to any substantial amount of the JGB wouldn't be wise.'

'So it does sound like there might be something to that letter. I don't know Mr Koyama, but I really respect your firm. I guess I'd better sell as planned. Thanks, James. I'm glad I talked to you.'

Gao asked if Kapur would fax him a copy of the letter. Naveen promised to do so immediately. Within five minutes a copy arrived and Gao phoned Nick. Since Singapore was exactly halfway around the world from New York, Gao knew it would be 11 in the morning there, also on Friday.

Nick was in a staff meeting when his personal assistant came quietly into the conference room and handed him a note. When he saw that James Gao wanted to talk to him 'urgently about the JGB', he slipped out of the room.

After listening to Gao about the letter sent to the president of The Royal Trust Bank in London, Nick said, 'So it's started! That can't be the only letter that was sent out. And if the Royal Trust is going to dump its JGB on the market, the others are more than likely to do the same. Even though we don't know how many have received the letter, this could start a tsunami that will tank the price of the JGB. And if the JGB goes down, so will Japanese stocks. I know you can't do much over the weekend, but do your best to figure out how to protect our customers who hold those bonds. Warn them, and if anyone wants to short sell JGB or some Japanese stocks, help them do it. I owe you a big one on this. By the way, can you send me a copy of that letter?'

Gao said, 'I'll fax it right away.'

'Thanks, James. I know it's near midnight in Singapore and that you won't get any rest tomorrow. Have a good night's sleep.'

'You think I'm going to get much sleep after this conversation? You know me, Nick, I'll do my best for our clients.'

Nick ended the call and looked at his watch. Noon. That meant the selling of JGB in the New York market must have already started; Gao said Kapur was going to start dumping the Royal Trust's holdings immediately. *Too bad, but I have to wake Ken.*

Emiko woke first when Ken's phone rang. 'Oh dear, who could be calling at this hour?' Ken quickly gathered his wits and answered his phone.

'It's Nick,' he said to his wife, and into the phone, 'Just a sec, Nick. Let me go downstairs.'

Even as Ken clambered down the steep wooden stairs and into the living room, he said into his phone, 'It's the JGB, right?'

'You got it!' said Nick. 'I just got a call from James Gao in Singapore, who had a call from a friend at the Royal Trust Bank in London. The plotters sent out an anonymous letter to the bank's president, warning him that the price of the JGB was going to fall and that he'd better sell as much as he could right away. Gao's friend wanted some confirmation . . . even a rumour . . . that an attack on the JGB was impending. When Gao told him that I'd heard a rumour about the JGB, the guy in London decided the bank had better get rid of its Japanese bonds.'

Nick went on almost breathlessly: 'So the date, August 17—the "Monday in the mid-August" we got from Mimi—is turning out to be right. And the date makes sense. Their attack will get the result they want . . . if they succeed . . . just before the bidding date for the Benin oil. As we all know, in summer when the trading volume is low, Monday is the day with the largest volume. So the plotters can more easily hide who is trading and how much. The Fan group must've sent the same letter to many financial institutions holding a lot of JGB. So we can now safely assume that a full-scale attack will start this coming Monday.'

Ken continued Nick's line of thinking. 'The price of the bonds could take a real hit. And if the JGB price tumbles . . . which is the same thing as the interest rate of the government bond shooting up. And everyone knows Japan can't afford to pay a higher rate of interest when we have to keep selling more bonds to refinance our maturing bonds and to make up the shortfall in tax revenues.'

Nick could hear the despondency in Ken's voice as he told Nick what Nick knew well already.

'Don't despair yet, Ken. We don't know how much damage the group can do. Let's not forget the JGB market is huge. And to do any serious damage, the Fan gang has to have hundreds of billions of dollars in their war chest. And they'll have to know how to use it very skilfully. To worry about their attack is to assume that they have enough money in their war chest *and* that they are very clever. We know a couple of American hedge funds are in the group, but they are known more for being shady than being the smartest players in the game.'

'I guess you're right. We shouldn't panic yet. They could start an avalanche of sell orders to make the JGB price tumble. But we've no evidence they have sufficient funds to do that. Besides, we shouldn't forget that the interest rate on the JGB is still lower than that for your Treasuries and Japan is still the biggest net creditor in the world. On the other hand . . . '

Ken paused mid-sentence, prompting Nick to ask, 'On the other hand what?' He heard Ken exhale.

'The market doesn't always behave rationally as we all know. History is full of panic situations caused by irrational market behaviour. And what worries me is that the new governor of the Bank of Japan isn't like the last one who kept buying the JGB in huge amounts. That's not all. Our prime minister and my own minister . . . '

Nick cut in. 'Ken, I read you. But we shouldn't be wasting time speculating about what could happen. I'll do what I promised I'd do if or when we became sure of an attack on the JGB is imminent. I'll call my friend Uberschall at the Fed.'

'Please do. As we discussed, it's better for you as an American business consultant to call him rather an MOF official, even though I know him.'

'I understand. I'll get in touch with him as soon as I can.'

Nick called Peter Uberschall at 1 p.m., hoping to reach him on his return from lunch. He had met the first vice president of the Federal Reserve Bank of New York four years ago at a conference on 'The Fed Policy and International Capital Flows'. Since then, they'd met several times as friends. Having both received PhDs in economics from Harvard just three years apart, they enjoyed exchanging views on many economic issues.

Uberschall, who was having a sandwich in his office, took Nick's call on the second ring. Cutting pleasantries short, Nick plunged into his 'urgent concerns about the Japanese government bonds'. He explained what he had just heard from James Gao and his discussion with Ken, and summarized as best he could everything he knew about the Fan group. It took some time because Ubershall was very surprised and, naturally, full of questions.

'Nick, that's quite a story,' he finally said. 'I'm really glad you called. Holy smoke! If the JGB takes a hit, so will our Treasuries. Japan has more than 2 trillion dollars' worth of US Treasuries. And if the JGB tanks, the Japanese economy will be in dire straits in no time at all. The BOJ and other financial institutions that own our Treasuries will be forced to dump a lot of them. And if both Japan's and our government bonds go down, almost anything can happen. Christ, we've got to talk about this with a few other people as soon as we can. I'm going to call Janet Krueger and try to have a conference call with you on a secure line. I'll call you back as soon as I can, OK?'

To Nick's surprise, Peter called back in less than 20 minutes. Janet Krueger, a board member of the Federal Reserve Bank in Washington, DC, whose work Nick knew well because she was a former professor at Stanford, was also on the line. 'You're right to have warned us, Nick. What many at the Fed think—that no group of speculators has enough money to attack the JGB successfully—is not important. We just can't take the chance. I saw our financial institutions freeze up and the euro totter only a decade ago. The JGB could go down. I still remember hearing years ago on TV the Irish finance minister stating that the price of Irish bonds would never tank. But it did only four days later, and that made the euro crisis worse. We . . . I mean the Fed . . . ought to do all it can to make sure any attack will fail. I'll talk to the chairman as soon as I can. That should give us time to get something in place by the time the market opens in Tokyo on Monday.'

Nick tried to get a word in to thank her, but Kruger didn't pause.

'There are several things we can do . . . including having the Fed accept the JGB as collateral for a loan at a favourable rate so American banks would buy the bonds. And we can issue some kind of a statement that even the group you're worried about would take notice.'

Peter cut in: 'In New York, we can "leak" something. Such as the Fed is thinking of buying a fairly large amount of the JGB . . . '

For the next few minutes, they speculated on various possible 'horrendous and immediate world-wide consequences' of the collapse of the JGB and 'some feasible effective countermeasures' besides the obvious ones they had already discussed. The three agreed to stay in touch.

'Oh, Lord,' Peter concluded just before hanging up, 'what a world we live in!'

28

Tokyo, 15 August

At the moment, Daisuke Honma wasn't looking anything like the president of one of Japan's largest banks. He lay between rumpled sheets, his bulging belly making a white mound on the bed. As the bathroom door opened and a figure entered the bedroom, Honma pushed himself up on the pillow and with a plump arm reached for the cigarettes and lighter on the bedside table. A gap in the curtains revealed an attractive naked woman with a figure as lovely as any 25-year-old, though Mayumi was almost a decade older. Honma ogled her as usual, although today his mind wasn't on her shapely naked body but on his finances.

A house in Azabu, a wife with expensive tastes and three nearly grown daughters who took after their mother meant that even a bank president's finances were stretched thin. Though he had found ways to augment his regular income by getting under-the-table 'appreciation money' for the loans his bank made to companies with dubious collateral and business prospects, inflating the expenses of his trips and entertaining clients and by other devious means, he found himself using much of these earnings to pay for this expensive apartment in Roppongi he rented for Mayumi. And he had already poured a small fortune into keeping her foundering bar afloat. But he simply had to have these afternoon trysts with her.

Ordinarily the pair would banter as Mayumi dressed, putting on each garment with the lascivious movements a stripper would use to undress. But this afternoon Honma stared at her without seeing her as he smoked a cigarette and mulled over the letter he had received on Friday afternoon, which had confirmed what a deputy director had warned him about during a surprise visit to his bank last Monday.

Worry over what the MOF official had told him and the anonymous letter had kept him awake much of the night. *If the price of the JGB drops badly, my bank could go bankrupt and I'll lose my job because I'm the one who always argued for buying more and more JGB.* But sometime in the wee hours he had come up with a plan to at least ameliorate his personal finances. *I can't defend the price of the JGB, but I can make some easy money using Mayumi to short sell the bonds*!

Mayumi noticed that Honma was unusually quiet. She pulled the curtain partially open and looked over at him.

'Why did you suddenly decide we would meet today instead of Tuesday? You usually see me on Tuesday, not Saturday.' There was a mix of curiosity and concern in Mayumi's voice.

'I had idea I thought you might like. But if you do, we need to act fast.'

'To do what?' Mayumi pulled on her sweater and sat down on the foot of the bed, her full attention on Honma.

'Do you know what short selling stocks or bonds is?'

Mayumi, although surprised by the question, answered almost proudly. 'I do. A few of our regular customers work at brokerage firms and they can't stop talking about selling short and buying long. On Monday I promise someone to sell him a stock on Friday at 100 yen. Then the price goes down to 80. So I buy the stock at 80 yen and sell it at 100 yen . . . and I make 20 yen. Correct?'

Honma smiled broadly. 'You got it. Well, this makes it easier to tell you what I've decided to do. I've heard from a very reliable source that the price of our government bonds is going to drop very soon. So I'm going to let you have some money to go to a broker on Monday morning, before the market opens at nine. You'll make a contract to short sell the 10-year government bonds. You'll do the trade on your own and we'll split the profit you make. Obviously I can't be openly involved in this trade because my bank owns a lot of the bonds.'

Mayumi adjusted her sweater and looked straight at Honma. 'How much money are you letting me have . . . to do this trade?'

Honma had already decided he would use the money in the shell company in Hong Kong he had set up two years ago in order to funnel money to Mayumi's bar and to deposit appreciation money he got for making dodgy loans. 'I'm thinking of 200 million yen.'

Mayumi looked a little bemused. 'That's a lot of money . . . almost 20 times what I can make from my bar in a year.' She paused and looked questioningly at Honma. 'You said I'd get half of what we make short selling those bonds. What is your guess on what my share will be?'

Honma explained that Mayumi could use the money to do a 10-to-1 margin trade. 'A brokerage will let you do the margin trade at a reasonable cost.' Mayumi caught on quickly when Honma said that if the JGB price fell by only 3 per cent, they could net as much as 60 million yen. Her share would be almost 30 million yen, a sum nearly three times what she was making a year.

Mayumi was all smiles. 'Wow! Thirty million without doing a lick of work! Could the JGB price go down by more than 3 per cent? By 6 per cent? So my share could be 60 million yen?'

Honma laughed. 'Don't be greedy. It's not likely the JGB price will drop by 6 per cent. Only if the holders of JGB panic and unload a lot of the bonds they hold.' Even as he answered Mayumi, Honma thought, *God forbid*! *If that happens my bank will go belly up.*

Mayumi saw the sudden change in Honma's expression.

'What's the matter? You look worried.'

'No, no, it's nothing.' Honma forced himself to smile. 'So, can you go see a broker first thing in the morning and set up a short selling contract? I'll give you the name of a reliable man. Drop my name carefully—he'll let you do a margin trade. But be sure my name isn't on the contract. Do a 10-to-1 margin trade with the contract going for five days, to be settled at the close of the market on Friday.'

'How will I get the money for the trade?' asked Mayumi, making sure she had all the details down pat.

Honma reached for his large leather briefcase next to the bed and from it took out a smaller leather case. He handed it to Mayumi, saying, 'With this, no one will know where the money came from.'

When she unzipped it and looked inside, her eyes widened. She had never seen so many 10,000-yen notes before. 'You said 200 million yen. That means there are 20,000 notes here! No wonder it's so heavy.'

Honma smiled. 'That's to make you rich and keep your bar going.'

But as she closed the leather case, she felt dirty rather than happy. *When Honma saved me from bankruptcy, I had to go to a hotel with him 'to celebrate' the survival of my bar, the beginning of the relationship that has always made me feel like a whore. What will he expect from me now?*

Honma took a business card out of his wallet and gave it to Mayumi. 'This is the broker to go see tomorrow. Be sure to see him as soon as you can in the morning.'

'I know how things work,' Mayumi assured him. 'You can count on me.'

Honma looked at his watch and sighed. 'Time to be going,' he said, tugging off the sheet and standing up. As he crossed the floor to the bathroom, his naked belly wobbling, he said, 'Call me sometime Monday afternoon . . . tell me how it went.'

Mayumi said, 'Fine,' and went into her small sitting room. As she quietly closed the door behind her, she thought, *I'm tired of feeling like a whore all the time.*

29

Tokyo, 15–17 August

Ken spent a nerve-wracking weekend. His first instinct after talking to Nick in the wee hours of Saturday morning was to call Baba and his immediate superior, the director of the International Bureau. But he quickly dismissed this urge. *Neither can do anything on Saturday. I'll see what's happening on the off-hour trading of the JGB and call them tomorrow.* To the annoyance of Emiko, he spent most of Saturday glued to the Nikkei, CNBC and Bloomberg, changing channels frequently to make sure he wouldn't miss any important developments regarding the Japanese government bonds. Since all markets were closed, news was scanty. When he checked the online trading, he found the price of the JGB was changing as usual within a very narrow range, and this held true for the futures of the 10-year JGB too. But after observing the very slight but worrisome volatility in the price of the JGB on Friday, he was convinced that this could very well be the calm before the storm.

Twice during Saturday Ken talked on the phone to Baba, first to tell him of Nick's call and later to confer about whether the PM should be alerted on the weekend. Baba was as worried as Ken, but said, 'I can't disturb the PM on the basis of one letter when the market isn't showing signs of anything drastic happening.'

By Sunday morning, Ken decided he simply had to talk to his boss. He called the director at 7.30, fully aware that he would more than likely wake him up, although he knew the director often left home very early on Sundays to go play golf. Ken did wake him, and the usually very civil man was distinctly annoyed. But as Ken explained why he had got in touch on a Sunday and at such an unusual hour, his boss became extremely disconcerted and said, 'Thank you for calling me. I'll get in touch with the minister of finance. He'll be dumfounded. My guess is he'll talk to the director of the Budget Bureau who's been telling him the JGB is immune from attacks. I'll call you if he tells me something you ought to know.'

Ken barely touched the delicious Japanese breakfast Emiko set before him, though he loved these weekend treats that included his favourite salted salmon. His mind was on his agenda for the day. After hurrying through his meal, he called Baba. Before Ken said anything, Baba spoke.

'Morning, Ken. You just caught me—I have to fly out to Okinawa with the PM this morning. He's trying to calm the crisis that's building up again. He says some of these lingering issues relating to the American military bases are international as well, so I've been ordered to accompany him.'

Ken expressed his sympathy for Baba's Okinawa visit on a Sunday and then reported his conversation with his boss. 'Bach, it's time to clue the PM in about the real possibility of an attack on the JGB tomorrow and what it means for our economy. I know he'd rather do backroom political deals than worry about government bonds. But if the attack is successful, it will trump politics and any issues relating to the military bases. Remind him that if the price of our bond goes up by just half a per cent, the interest rate we'll have to pay to sell it will go up by the same amount. Given the condition of our budget, we can't afford this. I don't even want to think about what will happen if the price goes up more than that!'

'Don't I know it.' Baba sighed and promised to talk to the PM.

At a little after 10, just when Emiko had convinced Ken to take a walk with her to work off some of his nervous energy, he had a call from his director. 'I just finished talking with the minister. He thinks we should alert the holders of the largest amounts of JGB that there might be a crisis in the making. As we speak, his secretary is calling all the senior officers of the ministry to come to an emergency meeting at the Budget Bureau at one today, even though it's Sunday. The meeting is to decide who is going to contact which of the largest holders of the bonds. The minister says these meetings with the top executives should be informal and face to face.'

Half an hour later, the minister's secretary called Ken to request him to come to the one o'clock meeting and 'explain the situation, starting from when he first learned about the Fan group, up to the letters the group had sent to the largest holders of JGB'.

Ken was pleased the minister was taking the situation seriously but he was taken aback at his instructions. *How on earth am I going to 'explain the situation' to senior officers of MOF who I know won't believe there could be an attack on the JGB? Anyway, at least the minister is doing something*!

Nick had a quick lunch and then took a cab to the ministry.

The meeting opened with the minister of finance saying, 'First, Deputy Director Murai is going to explain why he is convinced a serious attack on the our bond is impending and could start tomorrow.'

As Ken spoke, he noticed, as he had expected, that virtually all the senior members of the ministry in attendance looked glum and dubious. The deputy director of the Budget Bureau looked like he was going to have apoplexy. Ken wasn't surprised because this was a man who often appeared on television touting 'the unsinkable JGB'. When Ken had mentioned to him a few days before the possibility of an attack on the bonds, his response had been. 'No one, not even a group of big American hedge funds, would ever have enough money to attack our bonds because the outstanding amount of the JGB is over 11 trillion dollars.'

When Ken finished his 'explanation', the director of the Budget Bureau was the first to react.

'Heavens! This was the first I've heard of an international plot to attack the JGB. Deputy Director, despite your able presentation, I have to admit I'm not convinced. But this is not to say what you've told us isn't plausible. What's important is why weren't we told about this much sooner? Our bureau is responsible for the budget . . . so dealing with the JGB is in our bailiwick!! Yes, of course we must warn the biggest bondholders.'

Ken said nothing. *All he's worried about is his turf! But, thank God, he is agreeing to warn the major JGB holders.*

With the minister himself pushing the idea of warning the biggest holders of the bond and saying he would visit Genya Ozawa, the president of the bankers' association, no one objected to issuing warnings to the top executives of the financial institutions in question. They quickly worked out who would contact which executives and then the meeting was over.

Ken immediately went to his office and called Ozawa, asking him not to tell the minister when he came to see him that Ken had already 'informally' warned him about a possible attack. Ozawa chuckled and said, 'Deputy Director, you told me your visit was informal. Don't worry. I know how the bureaucracy works. I'll certainly contact the members of my association again . . . telling them I'm conveying "an informal request from the minister of finance".'

By late Sunday night, the group had managed to contact 21 of the 24 presidents of the largest banks, insurance companies and pension funds, requesting them not to sell their JGB 'even if the price declines, possibly starting tomorrow'. Just before 11 p.m., Ken returned home totally exhausted after his 'team'—Ken and a senior man from his bureau—had visited the presidents of two large pension funds and a large insurance company. As Ken headed to bed, he said to Emiko, 'I'm bushed. I just hope what we did today will help. But I've a foreboding that the JGB will have a bad day tomorrow. I hope I'm wrong.'

Monday, 17 August, was a beautiful summer morning in Tokyo, neither too hot nor too humid, and a nice breeze keeping any incipient smog at bay. The perfection of the day, though, was at odds with Ken Murai's intense trepidation that today the price of JGB would start to plunge, portending the beginning of a long recession in the Japanese economy, or worse.

Ken arrived at his office a few minutes past eight, almost an hour earlier than usual. He knew there had been little movement in the price of JGB overnight, but no markets had been open. *Anything can happen.* He checked his calendar. A Monday in the middle of August—usually he'd expect to find little on it but he did have three meetings he couldn't get out of. Baba hadn't contacted him yet, so Ken didn't know exactly what he'd told the prime minister and how the PM had reacted. This morning Ken was more than usually unhappy with both the PM and the minister of finance, 'politicians' in the worst sense of the term—shortsighted, reactive rather than insightfully proactive and economics ignoramuses.

Sighing, he reached for a folder whose contents he had to read before he met with a delegation from the Diet. At least he should be able to inform them of a possible imminent attack on the JGB. But he found it hard to concentrate and kept checking his computer. At nine, when the market opened, Ken gave up all pretence of working and sat there, staring at his monitor. Surely this was what the fishermen must feel when they see dark storm clouds rapidly approaching their boat.

Immediately after the market opened, the price of the 10-year bond started to drop and continued to do so. Ken stared with dread at the falling price. Within the first 10 minutes, the price had plummeted by almost half a per cent, the Nikkei index was down almost 1 per cent, led by bank stocks, and the yen had lost 1.8 yen against the dollar. Sumida and other large banks had lost about 2 per cent of their stock prices.

Oh, shit! *It's started with a vengeance*! Thinking of the international market, he quickly calculated how much more it would cost to sell about 11 billion dollars' worth of the 10-year JGB, which the government was planning to market next month. The additional cost of the interest rate rising by half a per cent came to 550 million dollars over 10 years. He shook his head. *This amount will play havoc with government finances as well as party politics.*

Ken checked the time on his computer: 9.26. Less than half an hour since the market opened. He was meeting with the Diet delegation at 10.30. *I have to have someone monitor the market and send me messages at regular intervals! Why didn't I think of this earlier? Who can I get?*

He thought of several candidates in his bureau and decided on a young woman who was a new hire. *She'll not only be dependable but is also working on a report without an imminent deadline.* He called her in.

Juri Hoshi, slim and attractive, arrived within seconds and looked at him expectantly. She had never been in Ken's office and her expression that was both curious and a bit apprehensive.

'Come in, Hoshi-san. And come and sit next to me so you can see my monitor.

Ms Hoshi timidly sat down but said nothing. Ken thought he'd better help her relax. He had temporarily forgotten how intimidating someone with his title was for a new hire. He asked her about her name. 'I know your first name is Juri. It doesn't sound like a Japanese name.'

The young woman smiled shyly. 'No, it doesn't. But it's my legal name and is written in two Chinese characters that mean pearl and reason. My parents wanted to give me a name that could be pronounced by people in most countries.'

'Foreigners are going to think your name is Julie.'

'You're right,' she said with a small laugh, 'That's exactly what my American friends call me!'

'Now, let me explain what I want you to do today. It looks like a foreign group has just launched an attack to bring down the price of our 10-year government bonds.' Ken pointed at the monitor. 'Look, the price of the 10-year JGB just dropped again. They most likely want to short sell them and make a mint. The price has already dropped enough to increase the interest rate by a little more than a half per cent.'

'Sir, we all know the price of bond going down means the interest rate on the bond will go up. So, even a half per cent rise is very bad for our government finances and for our economy.' Juri was clearly concerned.

'Yes, indeed. Look, I have a series of meetings today but need to be kept abreast of what is happening. I'd like you to monitor what is happening and report to me via text messages while I am at my meetings.'

Juri smiled. 'I gather you want to be updated *not* on the price but on the interest rate. If the interest rate goes up to, say, 2 per cent, the government will have great difficulty in paying it. And if it goes up to 3 or 4 per cent, there will be a national crisis. Japan could end up defaulting on its bonds.'

'Yes. You remember that several European countries defaulted some years back? But we now have much higher ratio of the JGB to our GDP than these countries ever did.'

'Sir, I did analogous calculations on interest rates and the prices of corporate bonds for a paper for one of my classes. There is a website that gives a conversion table between the price and the interest rate of corporate bonds. There ought to be a similar conversion table for the JGB on the Internet. If not, it shouldn't be difficult for me to make one.'

'Excellent,' Ken said with a smile. 'Please focus on the 10-year bond. It's the benchmark bond, the most traded and its price changes set the tone of the market. I'd like you to report to me by text message if the price changes, say, by more than 0.2 percent or even if it stays stable. Just keep me abreast of the market.'

Juri smiled. 'I understand, sir,' She left his office and Ken gathered his notes for the meeting, but before he could leave, his phone rang. It was Baba.

'Ken, sorry I couldn't call you until now. There was a problem with the plane and we didn't get back to Haneda until a couple of hours ago.'

'Were you able to talk to the PM about the JGB?'

'Yes, but his concern was with the politics of the American bases in Okinawa. So all I could do was to tell him about the letters the Fan group sent out. His response was to wait and see what happens. Very frustrating.'

'Well, he may pay more attention now. The price of the JGB has been falling steadily since the market opened.'

'How much?'

'A bit more than half a per cent as of now. It's a big drop. If it goes down even more, we'd be in a very big trouble.'

'Keep me informed.'

'I'm going to couple of meetings but I have someone monitoring the price changes. I'll have her text you as well. The minister and a number of us talked to bankers yesterday. If the JGB price keeps dropping, it may become necessary for the PM to act. Neither he nor the minister of finance can tell the Bank of Japan what to do. But knowing the PM, he'll know how to pressure the BOJ. We may need to have it buy a lot of JGB if the price continues to drop as it has immediately after the market opened. And we have to worry about stock prices and the yen as well.'

'If prices of stocks and JGB plummet, the PM is going to have a heart attack!'

Ken looked at his watch. 'I'll keep you posted. Gotta run.'

Ken grabbed the file containing his notes for the meeting and rushed out of his office. *How much further will the JGB price drop? How much JGB does the Fan group have to sell?*

Ken was able to check his phone once during the meeting. Juri's message said that the bond price had not dropped since around 9.40. And in the markets in Shanghai and Hong Kong the prices of the JGB and the yen were slowly matching those in Tokyo. Ken had a premonition that the stabilizing of the price was only temporary.

His meeting finally over, Ken dashed back to his office minutes after the market closed for the midday break and checked with Juri. She reported that not much had changed during the last hour of the morning session. 'The JGB rate is staying put . . . so is the yen. Several bank stocks are down by a bit more . . . because of it, the Nikkei lost 0.02 per cent. The Chinese markets are still tracking the Tokyo market.'

Ken thanked her and told her to go to lunch and come back at 12.30 when the market would open for the afternoon session. He asked his secretary to get him a sandwich from the ministry canteen. Worrying about what would happen in the afternoon session, he had little appetite and finally gave up and threw almost half his sandwich into his wastepaper basket. He had a meeting scheduled for 1.30, a weekly session of the four senior members of the General Affairs Secretariat section. Instead of reviewing a report on trends in the trade balance and capital inflows and outflows to be submitted to the minister, they discussed the probable impact of this sudden drop in the price of the JGB.

Ken arrived back at his office at three, just as the stock market closed. His secretary informed him that Counsellor Baba wanted him to call as soon as possible. Ken said he would but first he called Juri in. 'Sir, at the close of the market, the JGB rate was up another 0.15 per cent because the price of the JGB fell during the final 20 minutes. The story is very similar for stocks. The Nikkei also went down by another 0.07 per cent. But the yen is holding . . . no change all afternoon . . . in both the Tokyo and Chinese markets.'

Ken thanked her for her monitoring, then called Baba.

Baba said without preamble, 'I had a good 10 minutes with the PM. He had one of the guys in his office check the market. He is now very concerned and wants to talk to you, to hear what you have to say. I'm going to have his secretary get you on the line. Just wait for the call.'

Within minutes, Ken's office phone rang. The gravelly voice of the PM came on the line asking Ken for his assessment of the situation.

'Prime Minister, please allow me to come to the point. Today the price of our 10-year bond, and the most important bond traded among all JGBs, dropped enough to raise the interest rate on it by 0.65 per cent. As a consequence, the Nikkei index fell by about 2 per cent and the yen a bit less than 2 yen. The fall of the Nikkei led by the bank shares is bad news. But what's most important is the rise of the interest rate of the 10-year JGB's by as much as 0.65 per cent. And judging from how the price was still gyrating all afternoon, the interest rate on the JGB could go up more tomorrow.'

'Deputy Director, 0.65 per cent is bad enough. It's going to be a big mess, fiscally speaking, if we have to pay that much more when we have to sell more JGB again, and that's going to be very soon. I have to act.'

There was a brief pause, and then the PM said almost as if talking to himself, 'Hmm. I think I should get in touch with the governor of the Bank of Japan and ask him to buy JGBs if the situation warrants doing so. He must call an emergency meeting of his board. What do you think?'

Ken was not surprised to hear this, but running through his mind was the thought, *You can, sir, of course, even it means you'll be violating the independence of the bank from political interference. But it's going to be extremely difficult for the governor to get five members of his board of nine to go along with buying even more bonds. This governor isn't like the last one who was willing to do almost everything you wanted him to.*

Aloud he answered, 'Yes, sir. The governor knows full well the rate reached today is bad enough . . . we can't have it going up any more tomorrow.'

'I rather think the governor will go along . . . he has no choice. Well, thank you, Deputy Director.'

Within minutes after the call with the PM, Baba called Ken on his personal phone. 'He's really taken the situation seriously. He's already on the phone to the Bank of Japan. Thanks, Ken, for your help.'

'I only hope he can get the board to vote to support the JGB.'

'I don't know what the PM has up his sleeve,' replied Baba, 'but he was very determined and said he'd make sure he got the five votes. I don't think I want to know what he's going to do—just as I don't want to see how sausage is made!'

30

Tokyo, 18 August

Professor Susumu Toda strode down the street to the corner where he often caught a taxi. Today he was going to an emergency meeting of the policy board of the Bank of Japan scheduled to start at 9.30. It was now the height of the rush hour and he didn't have any time to spare. But Toda was lucky—he found a cab sitting at the corner where he usually took one. As he neared it, the door to the back seat opened automatically, beckoning him to get in. He gratefully climbed in. 'Please take me to the Bank of Japan in Nihonbashi. You know where it is?'

'Yes, sir,' the driver said. As the taxi started off, Toda pulled out of his briefcase the three-page note from the bank's governor, faxed late last night to all nine members of the policy board. As Toda reread the note, he grimaced and shook his head. The note was a summary of what the governor had said when he called to inform him of the meeting: the Bank must buy more JGB 'as necessary'. *I'll be damned if I'll vote to buy more government bonds when the bank's balance sheet is already overloaded with them! The politicians ought to learn that they can't keep balancing the budget by selling more and more bonds year after year.*

Suddenly Toda became aware that the taxi was travelling faster than he expected during rush hour. He looked around to see where he was—he certainly wasn't on the usual route to the Bank of Japan. The taxi was passing stores and houses that were unfamiliar to him. Perplexed, he asked, 'Where are we? Are you taking a short cut?'

'Yes, sir. The direct route is very congested this morning. This way we'll save some time.'

'OK, you're the expert,' said Toda. And then took a good look at the man, both at the back of his head and at what he could see of his face in the mirror. Unlike most taxi drivers who were middle-aged or older, this man was young with powerfully built shoulders. Oddly enough, he was wearing dark glasses, though the weather was cloudy. *Unusual, but why shouldn't there be young drivers?*

After a few more minutes, Toda grew concerned. 'Look, I have to be at the Bank by 9.30. Are you sure this route will save time?'

Instead of answering, the driver accelerated and almost immediately turned into a road next to a large park that Toda had never seen before. Now he knew something was wrong. Uneasy and not a little frightened, he loudly demanded, 'Stop the car!'

The driver said nothing. Toda yelled, 'Stop, let me out!' The driver turned into the park and suddenly stopped the car, saying, 'Sure.'

Toda madly pushed at the door handle but it was locked. He immediately moved over to the door on the other side, but that door was locked too. In the meantime, the driver got out of the car and, opening the door, said, 'Get out.'

Toda was in a panic. They were in the middle of what seemed to be a large park. There was not a soul in sight. *Why has he brought me here? What does he want? I've only got 60,000 yen on me. He can have it and my Rolex watch.* These thoughts flew through the mind of the recently retired economics professor as he sat there, staring at the driver and unable to move.

The driver grabbed Toda's arm. 'Get out.' Toda screamed for help at the top of his lungs. The driver yanked Toda out of the car and then, before Toda could find his feet, gave him a fierce rabbit punch at the base of his neck. Toda's legs buckled under him and he hit the ground with a thud. Barely conscious, he desperately tried to deal with the pain that seemed to fill his head. He felt the driver squat beside him and then a strange odour filled his nostrils. *What is he doing?* He opened his eyes for a few seconds, just as the driver held a cloth over his nose and mouth. Toda instinctively jerked his head away and yelled, 'No!' Pain seared through him as he breathed in the fumes. The driver pushed him back down. Toda felt nauseated and disoriented. And then everything went dark.

There were never many people in Soshigaya Park in the Setagaya Ward on a weekday morning. And this was fine by Makoto Suzuki, a web designer who worked from home and who ran in the park almost every morning to get himself going.

Suddenly, he heard a scream. A male voice yelling what sounded like, 'Help, help!' Without another thought, Suzuki took off in the direction of the scream.

He arrived at the road running through the park and saw a taxi make a screeching U-turn and speed down the road towards the main street. He was too far away to see the driver or the name of the cab company. But he knew something was wrong. He surveyed the roadside across from him, and his eyes lit upon a dark form lying on the ground.

Quickly Suzuki ran across the road and discovered a man in a dark suit. He knelt by the inert figure. The man was still breathing though his eyes were closed. Suzuki tapped his shoulder, but he couldn't rouse the man.

As Suzuki debated what to do, a tall man in his 30s jogged up, accompanied by a large white dog on a long leash. 'I heard someone scream,' he said to Suzuki as he looked at the man on the ground. 'Is he OK?' He asked Suzuki.

Suzuki looked up and said, 'I dunno. I heard a scream too, so I came to investigate. A taxi was making what looked like a hasty getaway and I found this man lying here. He's breathing but unconscious. We've got to do something. Do you have a phone on you?'

'Yeah. I'll dial 110 to get an ambulance.'

'You'd better dial 119 to get the police as well. I'm almost sure the taxi driver had something to do with this man lying here. You don't scream like that if you're collapsing for a medical reason.'

Both the police and an ambulance arrived within minutes. Suzuki answered the senior of the two policemen's questions and told him about the scream he heard and the taxi racing away. An ambulance attendant leaned over the man and examined him. 'His vitals are stable. I smell chloroform.' The policeman leaned over and sniffed. 'You're right.'

They searched the man's pockets for his ID but found no wallet. The younger of the two policemen said, 'From the look of the skin on his left wrist, I think his watch was stolen as well. Probably a carefully planned robbery.'

After the ambulance drove off, the officers quizzed Suzuki and the jogger again until the two wished they hadn't come across the scene. But they had nothing helpful to add.

'Just what we need,' groused the senior officer after they let Suzuki and the jogger with the dog depart. 'An unconscious man in his 60s, expensively dressed and no ID. Certainly a robbery. Guess we'd better get back to the station and write up a report. I hope the man regains consciousness soon. And I hope he isn't someone important. Because if he is, we'll have a helluva mess on our hands.'

31

Around the World, 19 August

After the close of the market at 3 p.m. in Tokyo on Wednesday, 19 August, nearly everyone having anything to do with Japan's government bonds was either extremely apprehensive or unhappy.

On Monday, the price of the 10-year JGB had fallen to the extent that it raised the interest rate on the bonds by 0.65 per cent. The price continued to decline in the morning session of the market on Tuesday, raising the interest rate by another 0.51 per cent, making the total increase since Monday morning 1.16 per cent. This meant that Japan would have to pay interest of at least 2.3 per cent—the rate last Friday plus the increases on Monday and Tuesday—on the JGB it was planning to sell during the coming few months. This rate was not high by international standards; it would make the Japanese rate almost comparable to that of the American 10-year Treasuries. But the new rate was more than double the one that had prevailed for so long and would seriously imperil the government's finances. This would further debilitate the economy and sharply decrease the stability of the government.

The decline in the bond price had suddenly halted in the afternoon session of the market on Tuesday. But relief was short-lived because this Wednesday morning the price of the JGB began to steadily fall soon after the market opened, only coming to a halt at 10.40 by which time the rate had risen by 0.63 per cent. The halt occurred because the Bank of Japan announced that it would buy the JGB, and the US Federal Reserve Bank said it would provide 'emergency' funds—under some vaguely specified conditions—to American banks that would consider buying Japanese government bonds. So at the close of the market, the interest rate on the 10-year bonds stood at 2.95 per cent. When the market closed, Ken Murai was much relieved that the rate had not exceeded 3 per cent, which he reckoned was the maximum Japan could pay without playing havoc with the government's finances.

Yesterday Ken had been informed by the director of his bureau that the Bank of Japan's policy board had voted four to four to purchase more government bonds 'should the need arise'. He wondered which of the members had been absent for the vote and why, but he knew that, with a tie vote, the governor's decision had prevailed, as stipulated in the bank's voting rules. He had no idea how much JGB the bank was going to buy in the coming days. Moreover, he knew that, if bondholders panicked, many of them would sell their JGB even when it was not rational to do so. In fact, Ken had said at a meeting of senior men in his ministry on Monday, 'It's not rational calculation but psychology . . . the gut feeling . . . that's going to decide what bondholders will do . . . and which way the JGB price will go. This means that anything can happen unless the Bank of Japan buys enough JGB to halt the run on the bonds.'

By 6.30 on Wednesday evening, Ken realized that he had just read through an entire document but couldn't remember a word. 'Time to go home,' he mumbled to himself, 'Worrying won't change anything.'

Most of the officers in Japan's financial institutions were as worried as Ken about the JGB. One bank president, Daisuke Honma, was more than worried. Alone in his study, clutching a glass of whisky, he was in a state of panic. If the JGB price continued to fall, his bank would become insolvent because its ratio of JGB holdings to its total assets was so high. But whether the bank failed or not, this was perhaps the end of his career because he had so vociferously argued that the bond was totally safe.

But as Honma sipped his whisky, he began to relax. *Even if the bank fails, I'll have a nice nest egg in the account of the sham company I've created in Hong Kong. Nearly 6 million dollars in kickbacks over the past few years from the loans my bank made. And my nest egg will become bigger once I get my share of the profit Mayumi makes by short selling the JGB. No need to worry, I'll be able to live comfortably even if Sumida fails.*

The paunchy president scratched his belly and grinned. *Hell, when I leave the bank, I'll leave my wife too and go live with Mayumi.*

Unlike Honma, Professor Toda had nothing to grin about, languishing in a hospital in Setagaya with a sore neck, a pounding headache and nausea. When he regained consciousness and saw his wife's worried face, the first thing he said was: 'What time is it?' When he was told 'almost noon', he said with regret, 'I missed the meeting at the bank this morning.' His wife said, 'You mean the meeting yesterday morning . . . today is Wednesday . . . you've been out cold for over 24 hours.'

When he hadn't come home for his four o'clock dental appointment the day before, his wife had called the bank and been told he had never arrived. She had waited another hour and then called the police. By 10 that evening the police told her they had located him in a hospital in Setagaya. 'He was robbed . . . all his money, his watch . . . and rendered unconscious by the chloroform and some long-lasting chemical the robber used.' He had suffered a concussion but the doctors expected him to make a full recovery.

Today, a day later and still groggy by evening, Toda glanced at the TV screen positioned above the foot of his bed—the news was on. But then he heard the words 'Bank of Japan'. He grabbed the remote and turned up the volume, just in time to catch the words ' . . . Voted to buy government bonds as much as it deems necessary.

But it seems what the bank bought today wasn't enough because the price of JGB fell again in today's market.'

Toda muttered, 'Damn! The vote must've been four to four. So the governor got what he wanted. I should have been there.' As he shook his head, wincing in pain, he thought, *What a stupid thing to do—when the bank already has so much JGB on its books!*

Was it really only a coincidence that he had been attacked yesterday and prevented from casting the deciding vote not to purchase more bonds? That afternoon two police officers had arrived to question Toda about what had happened. He was mortified that he could be of no help whatsoever. He couldn't identify the driver, except to say that he was youngish, with strong arms and fairly tall. He had no idea what company the cab belonged to. He had just jumped in when he spotted it at the street corner. The officers asked whether it had just pulled up or been waiting. But Toda couldn't remember. 'I think someone didn't want me to attend an important meeting at the bank, so I was attacked and drugged. Then the assailant took my money and watch to make you think it was a robbery. I don't think he meant to kill me.'

But when the senior policeman, dubious about Toda's speculation, asked who the 'someone' could be, Toda couldn't come up with a name. He couldn't imagine the governor of the bank or a member of the policy board, the only people who knew of the emergency meeting, having anything to do with something like this. 'Right,' the policeman nodded as he got up to leave, 'it was a carefully planned robbery of a man who looked as if he might be carrying a considerable amount of cash and other items worth stealing. These days Tokyo isn't as safe as used to be.'

As people in Tokyo settled down for the night on Wednesday, half way around the world in New York it was early Wednesday morning. The Tokyo stock market had closed at 2 a.m. EDT, so Peter

Scheinbaum had come in hours earlier than usual to check the markets. At just before eight, Josh Fried called. He was practically yelling and less than coherent, but the gist of his rant was why hadn't the JGB price dropped more in the Tokyo market.

When Fried finally ran out of steam, Scheinbaum said, 'Josh, calm down. We did exactly what we agreed to do. On Monday and Tuesday, we sold 40 billion of the JGB in Tokyo, 10 billion more here in New York, and the rest in other markets. We did it very, very carefully, using a few dozen brokers who promised to be "very discreet". I understand you're disappointed and upset because it seems our sales . . . and these letters we sent to the biggest JGB holders . . . didn't really start the tsunami of sales we'd expected.'

'It sure hasn't. All we've done so far is to drop the JGB price by a middling amount and the prices of the Japanese stocks I'm short selling have fallen by only about 3 to 4 per cent! What's wrong with the guys who got our letters? Why weren't they scared enough to dump a hell of a lot more of the JGB than they did?'

'First let me correct you on what you just said, and then I'll answer your questions. You said the price of JGB went down only a middling amount. Josh, you should know better than to say that! The price of JGB dropped big. I'm sure the Japanese government and banks are shitting in their pants. The government won't be able to sell as many billion dollars' worth of bonds as it has in the past because it can't afford to pay the new higher rate. And banks have taken a colossal hit on their balance sheets. With the Nikkei and the yen also taking a dive, anything can happen now to the Japanese economy.'

'I know that,' Fried said disparagingly. 'I was telling you what happened from my perspective. I was hoping for a much bigger drop in both the JGB and stock prices. Our short selling contracts of the JGB are up next Monday. Christ, I won't be making as much money as I thought I would unless the price of JGB drops more!'

'Just be patient, Josh. You still might. Some of the guys who got our letters are too scared to sell. Because if they do, the book value of the bonds they hold will go down even more. Besides, I seriously doubt the Bank of Japan will buy enough bonds to affect the market much. Hell, their balance sheet is already overloaded with the JGB. And the announcement by the Fed doesn't mean shit because no one going's to borrow from them to buy Japanese bonds.'

Scheinbaum hurried on before Fried could interrupt. 'Look Josh, as you well know, if the JGB tanks more, so will the price of the stocks you are shorting. So let's wait and see what happens over the next few days.'

After speaking to Josh, Scheinbaum sat back, frowning. *What a bloody pain in the ass Josh is turning out to be! He's such a greedy son of a bitch. I can guess why he's so insistent that I send him all of Fan's money when the project is over. I promised him I would but I'm not going to. I'll send it to Fan's account in Singapore. Trusting Josh to send Fan's money on to Singapore is like trusting a fox with a chicken!*

Then Scheinbaum's frown turned into a grin. *Josh, I have huge short-selling contracts on the JGB and side bets even you don't know about. If the price of the JGB and the stocks I'm short selling drop a little more, as I expect they will, I'll make at least 2.4 billion dollars!*

Luckily Scheinbaum managed to calm Fried so that Fried could, in turn, placate President Fan. Minutes after Fried's conversation with Scheinbaum, his personal phone rang. It was the president of SAEC, in an extremely foul mood. After carefully checking the news of the Tokyo and other Asian markets and learning the JGB price had fallen by much less than he had been anticipating, he was now violating his own strict rule of never talking directly on the phone with

Fried. When Fried answered, a voice with a strong foreign accent hesitantly said, 'This is a friend . . . in Shanghai.'

'In Shanghai? Sounds like . . . '

'Don't say my name. I called because I have to hear directly from you. After all the things we've done . . . why aren't the fish biting? Only a tiny nibble since Monday! We've rented the boat until Friday . . . so we've got only two more days to fish. From where you sit, do you see any chance of much bigger fish biting?'

'Anything can still happen. A few big fish may suddenly get hungry. You know we've agreed . . . '

Even before Fried finished his sentence, Fan cut in. 'I hope you're right, Josh. You may not realize this, but I've a couple of people who are going to be very unhappy if we don't make as much money as I thought we'd make.'

'Who?' asked Josh, surprised.

There was a long pause before Fan answered, 'Forget what I just said. I sure hope you're right . . . and a few big fish suddenly get hungry before Friday!'

As Fan ended the call, Fried rubbed his chin wondering why Fan had violated their understanding never to talk to each other on the phone except in a dire emergency. Fried was very disappointed with what had happened in the market since Monday but he didn't think it constituted a dire emergency. So wondered what was going on. *Is Fan not as tough as he makes himself out to be? Or does he have partners he's never mentioned before who can pressure him about the project? . . . No, he just brought up these people to justify breaking the rule about calling.* 'Damn these inscrutable Orientals!'

While Fried was on the phone with Fan, Nick Koyama's phone rang. *Who's calling me so early in the morning?*

As soon as he answered, he heard the agitated voice of James Gao, the head of the Shanghai branch of Rubin-Hatch Associates.

'Nick, my apologies. I know it's early but I urgently need your advice.'

'On what?'

Gao sighed. 'It's related to the JGB and the yen getting hammered. This has to do with one of my client here in Singapore . . . Mr Poh Zenming who came to see me just after the market here closed.'

'Who is he and how can I help?'

'Say, it sounds like you're in a cupboard!'

'If you must know, I'm in my bathroom, shaving. Keep talking. Who is Poh and what does he want?'

'He's a very wealthy man and a very shrewd international investor. He made money in real estate and then invested in foreign stocks and bonds. And for the past several years he's been doing more and more of private equity investment . . . you know . . . buying and selling companies.'

'So what does he want that's so urgent?'

Nick, out of the bathroom by now, sat down on a stool by the kitchen counter. He was determined not to lose his temper, even though trying to get Jim Gao to share information or come to the point was like pulling teeth. He reminded himself that Gao was one of the best analysts at Rubin-Hatch.

'Well, Poh thinks the Japanese stocks and yen will go down even more. He wants me to help him buy a dozen large and medium-sized Japanese companies. He came with a list. If I may say so, a damn good list . . . well selected. He wants us to do due diligence on these Japanese companies. Because we charge a lot for thoroughly checking out a firm, this will be very lucrative.'

'Why call me? Why not just do the due diligence and earn the fat fee we charge.'

'Because two big companies and one medium-sized one on his list are firms you've been advising.'

Surprised, Nick asked, 'Which ones?'

Gao named them and Nick said loudly, 'Damn! I've been aware that a few Chinese companies had their eye on these firms for some time but couldn't afford them. I'm sure Poh wants to get them for their technology. He can buy them now when they are cheap and sell them later to the highest bidders.'

'Precisely. If the Japanese stocks and yen go down even more, they'll be easy prey. So what do you want me to do?'

It was Nick's turn to be the slow responder. After a long pause, he said, 'Go ahead and make an honest and thorough report. When both stocks and the yen are down as they are now, it can't be helped.'

'Are you going to tell these companies about Mr Poh?'

'Leave it to me. But if this trend continues, more and more Japanese companies are going to be bought by foreigners . . . especially the Chinese. They'll be easy targets. Thanks, Jim, for your heads-up.'

After the call ended, Nick thought, *This is what happens when a country piles up a debt that's as huge as Japan's! President Fan and his friends . . . and now Mr Poh of Singapore and many more just like him are going to make their fortunes at the expense of the Japanese who worked so hard to build up their firms!*

Unlike others this Wednesday morning, there were two very happy investors, Tim Ogilvy and Devra Berger. Tim called Devra soon after nine.

'Good morning. Devra. And it's a really good one for you! Have you seen the closing data from the Tokyo stock market for Wednesday?'

'Yes, of course, Tim. I've been following it very closely. I think I've done rather nicely. I've made just a little shy of 30 million dollars by short selling the KLOZ stock, thanks to Mr Scheinbaum letting me do a 10-to-1 margin trade. And of course I'll get more . . . my share of profit our group makes by short selling the JGB. Thirty million plus my share are going to add up to a terrific return on my 50 million investment even after I pay interest and the commissions.'

'And I think the price of KLOZ shares will fall even more. This means you can buy a lot of cheap KLOZ shares to do what you said you want to do . . . buy as much KLOZ stock as possible.'

Devra wondered, *Why is Tim telling me this? Of course I'm going to buy more KLOZ shares so the company can't refuse to tell me, an important shareholder, all the tricks and strategies that had made KLOZ so big internationally . . . the things I've got to learn to make DevraStyles as big.*

But Devra only said, 'Exactly, Tim. I'm planning to buy as many shares as I can.'

'Good thinking. Devra, I'll call again soon with more news.' Ogilvy shut his phone smiling broadly. *She is going to be even happier when I call her next*!

32

Shanghai, 20 August

The former head accountant of SAEC's office in Nigeria had just made the biggest decision of his life. Ye Lixi was back in Shanghai on extended sick leave due to encephalopathy, an increasing brain dysfunction, resulting from malaria. His kidneys were also failing and, over the past week, he'd started having seizures. He hadn't forgotten what his doctor had told him only last week: 'Mr Ye, we are extremely sorry but we don't know how to cure your kind of malaria. Since you've asked, we can tell you that you'll be lucky to be lucid a month from now and still alive in three. We are truly sorry.'

What triggered his decision to act was the notification he received yesterday—that President Fan had formally replaced him as head accountant of the Abuja office, SAEC's biggest branch office abroad. This meant he would be forced to 'retire'. So he finally resolved to act on the plan that had been brewing in his mind since he had heard that Ma Jianrong's death was no suicide. *Before I join my wife in heaven, I've got to avenge the murder of Mr Ma, who got me my position in Abuja.*

While wracked by pain and intermittent fever, Ye had gone over and over what must have happened on the day he was to meet Ma and hand over to him the documentation he had obtained in Abuja—undeniable evidence that top executives of SAEC were systematically looting SAEC's funds in Nigeria. He also had collected evidence that Fan was getting huge bribes and kickbacks from the Nigerian authorities on the investments SAEC had been making in Nigeria as well as buying oil at above the market price. Despite Ma's earnest request to Ye to find out who was siphoning off money from SAEC's African accounts, Ma had failed to show up the evening they had planned to meet.

Even after more than 10 weeks, Ye remembered everything clearly. The day after Ma failed to show up for the meeting at his hotel, Ye was at the SAEC headquarters for a meeting with the CFO. He had asked an assistant about Ma where he was. She had said, 'Mr Ma took time off yesterday to attend a funeral, but no one in Accounting knows why he hasn't come to work today.' And while Ye was still in the accounting department, Mrs Ma had shown up, frantic because she hadn't seen him since he left the wake for her father after getting a text message on his phone. He hadn't returned home the night before, he wasn't answering his phone and she had no idea where he was.

Ye had returned to his post in Nigeria before Ma's body had been found. From a SAEC email bulletin sent to all branch offices, he learned that the police had decided Ma had committed suicide. *Why? Was he being blackmailed? Why hadn't he kept his appointment with me?*

And then a colleague had emailed him that the Ma's demise was being viewed as murder. Surprised, Ye had written to Ma's assistant, asking for details. She had sent a long message back with everything she'd gleaned from office gossip and the press reports.

Mrs Ma had been persistent in denying the possibility that her husband had taken his own life, and the police hadn't liked the odd circumstances—Ma killing himself with a pistol in his mouth in the warehouse of a bankrupt firm, located in an isolated, industrial area of Shanghai. One detective who had quizzed Mrs Ma at length had found out that her husband had been left-handed. 'He ate and wrote with his right hand like most left-handed Chinese, but for everything else he used his left.' The detective checked the photos taken by the Scene of Crime Team—the gun was by Ma's right hand. He checked and found that the fingerprints on the gun were only from Ma's right hand, which was odd because people handled a gun with both hands. The pistol was an old army issue, not readily available on the market.

But Ma had never served in the army. All this, taken with Mrs Ma's statement, made the police change the verdict from suicide to homicide. But no one had been caught and the assistant wrote that she hadn't heard of any suspects being questioned.

When Ye heard Ma had been murdered, he grew very concerned about his own safety. The documents that he was to hand over to Ma confirmed Ma's suspicions that large-scale embezzling was taking place, and all the evidence pointed to President Fan.

Ye had been able to acquire records of wire transfers of money. He had obtained them from a clerk in the Union Bank of Benin. Also, copies of emails Fan had exchanged with several high officials of the Nigerian government. Ye had worked for SAEC for over three decades and he was well aware of the sleazy side of SAEC's business. But all this had been done for the sake of SAEC, a key player in making China the greatest nation on earth. This he considered justifiable, but not what Fan had done.

Now back in Shanghai, Ye was gripped by constant fear. *Any day now Fan will be sending someone to kill me just as he had Mr Ma killed!* Fan must have had his suspicions that Ma as a competent accountant would find out that the accounts were off. And so he had had Ma's phone tapped, probably his computer hacked too. This was why Fan had known about Ma trying to meet Ye. To prevent Ma from obtaining the evidence against him, Fan had had Ma killed.

Today, Ye was lying on the bed in one of the two small rooms he had rented from an elderly couple. He was feeling even weaker than during the past few days, with disjointed thoughts running through his mind as if he was dreaming. *Mr Ma helped me get the job in Abuja. Fan didn't pull the trigger, but he hired the hit man! To kill Mr Ma! I don't want to live like this any more . . . I feel terrible . . . my seizures are increasing . . . good thing my days are numbered. I'd better do what I've got to do while I still can.*

With great effort, Ye sat up and reached for his phone on the bedside table. He thought for quite some time and then sent a message:

President Fan: I suggest you come to my apartment at nine tonight. If you do not come, documentary proof will be sent to the appropriate authorities detailing the embezzlement of a huge amount of the SAEC money. If you come, you will get the proof in exchange for a small request. Ye Lixi

Ye sat back exhausted. Ten minutes later he realized Fan didn't know where he lived. So he sent a second message. He knew he really couldn't hang on to this life much longer.

When Fan read the email, he was both angry and alarmed. The very idea of that lily-livered Ye 'suggesting' that Fan come see him was insulting. But Ye might have evidence against him, so he could not just ignore the email. However, Ye's request was most inopportune, especially now when Fan was preoccupied with monitoring the price of the JGB. As he reread the message, another thought crossed his mind: *I can't risk the sick fool sending anything to the authorities. He is going to shake me down for money. No matter what the sum is, I'm not going to pay him—blackmailers always ask for more. I've got to go see him and find a way to get the evidence . . . without killing him.*

Fan called home next and informed the maid that he would not be back for dinner. On the way to Ye's apartment, he stopped for a bowl of noodles, then got into his Mercedes and headed to the southwest of Shanghai where Ye's apartment was located.

Ye had been waiting for Fan and let him into the apartment as soon as he knocked on the door. He led him to his sitting room, saying, 'Thanks for coming, President Fan.'

Fan grunted a greeting. He was startled to see how old and sick Ye looked. The small sitting room reminded him a room in a hospital, reeking of illness and air freshener. He sat down on a shabby-looking chair and, without preamble, said, 'Let's get this over with quickly. What's this nonsense about the documentary proof of embezzlement and your small request?'

'I'll come to that. First, please indulge me and have a drink with me. Yes?'

'If you wish. A quick one and we'll get down to business.'

Ye walked haltingly over to a small cabinet and got out two small glasses. Into each he poured a finger of Chinese whisky from a green bottle. He handed one glass to Fan and said, 'Bamboo Leaf brand. Hope it's OK.'

Ye slowly sat down on a straight-backed chair and held up his glass. 'Here's to SAEC.'

Ye took a big gulp. Fan wordlessly sipped the cheap whisky. After Ye took another gulp, Fan said, 'OK, we've had our drink. Now let's discuss the documentary proof and your request.'

'President Fan, you know the evidence I have. Let's not play games. We'll talk about my request. I want 500,000 yuan to be deposited in my bank account. This is my only request because I'm dying. I want to send it to my dead wife's parents in Chongqing.'

'That's a lot of money . . . almost what you make in salary in several years. And don't forget, you are still getting paid even though you haven't been working for several weeks now.'

'I know it's a lot of money, but I also know you can easily come up with that amount.'

'I get the documents as soon as I pay you?'

'Yes, the documentary evidence of your looting SAEC . . . and my silence.'

Fan looked at Ye without saying a word. Ye could see from Fan's expression that he was very angry but thinking. Ye coughed a couple of times but said nothing. They could hear Ye's clock on the cabinet ticking.

Fan broke the silence. 'If you cross me . . . or get any funny idea about duping me . . . '

Fan didn't finish the sentence because Ye suddenly reached into his shirt pocket, took out a small vial of liquid and poured it into his nearly empty whisky glass.

Baffled, Fan asked, 'What are you doing? Are you OK?'

Ye didn't respond. He closed his eyes, gulped down the mixture and gasped. Ye's face began to contort immediately. He grabbed the front of his shirt with both hands and began to breathe rapidly, his face slowly turning red.

Fan couldn't believe what he was seeing. He stared at Ye, speechless. Then to Fan's astonishment, he saw a strange smile fleetingly cross Ye's face, even though he was gasping for breath in pain.

Fan cried out bewildered, 'What's the matter? What's funny?'

Ye, now gulping for air, said in a rasping voice, 'I'm dying. I've just taken poison.'

Before Fan could say another word, Ye keeled over with a thud. Fan stood up and gaped at him. Within seconds Ye stopped breathing.

Why did he do that? I didn't say no to the money!

The former colonel and current CEO of SAEC took hold of himself and slowly regained his composure. Instinctively he bent to check the pulse in Ye's neck. *He's dead. I've got to get out of here! I can't leave any trace of my having been here. I had nothing to do with his death—but I'll never be able to prove it.*

Fan took out a handkerchief and wiped his glass and put it down on the wooden table. With a final glance at Ye, he silently shut the door behind him. There was no one in the narrow and dingy hall as he let himself out and then hurried out of the building.

Why did Ye kill himself in front of me? He could've got money from me. He had no answer. But he knew he was missing something. Bewildered, he jumped into his Mercedes and drove off, tires screeching, into the quiet night. *At least now I don't have to think about sending any 500,000 yuan to Ye!*

33

Shanghai, 21 August

At eight on Friday morning, Ye Lixi's landlady knocked on his sitting-room door, wanting to give him his cup of morning tea. Hearing no response, she poked her head in, calling out his name. Then she entered and started for his bedroom but stopped short when she saw his feet sticking out from under the table. She put her hand on her month to stop from crying out and dropped to the floor beside him. As soon as the former nurse saw his face, she knew even without checking his pulse that he had been dead for hours. 'I knew he was going to die, but, oh, not this soon!' she moaned softly. Then she took another look at the dead man's face and decided to call the police.'

Two policemen arrived within 15 minutes, and, soon after, an ambulance. The senior of the two policemen noted the small vial and, given the landlady's description of the dead man's health, assumed the vial had contained medicine. But when he sniffed it and detected a faint odour of almonds, he shook his head and carefully sealed it in a plastic bag. Suspicious now, he looked around. Why were there two glasses for drinks? He lifted both in turn with his gloved hand and sniffed at each. Both smelt of whisky. He then looked at both glasses carefully and found one had fingerprints and the other none, seemingly wiped clean. He directed his colleague to help him search Ye's rooms for anything 'unusual'. Minutes later the colleague came out of the bedroom with a large buff-coloured envelope that he found stuffed under the mattress. The senior man pulled out a sheaf of papers and glanced through them. The first page read, 'This contains documentary evidence that proves Fan Zhipeng, the president of Sino-African Energy Corporation, is guilty of major financial malfeasance.' Intrigued, he quickly scanned the rest and then returned them to the envelope, folded it in half lengthwise and put it into his jacket pocket.

After the ambulance took away Ye's body, the policemen finished their search of the apartment, packed up the two glasses, the bottle of liquor, and the small vial. Leaving the younger policeman to guard the apartment, the senior man took the bag of evidence back to the Huangpu Municipal Police Station on Jingling East Road, a short distance away. There the contents of the envelope and the bag were examined and headquarters notified.

By two in the afternoon, the coroner who had made 'a preliminary examination' of Ye's emaciated body agreed with the detective that the cause of death was 'most likely due to poisoning'. Even though the poison involved was yet to be confirmed, the coroner said he would bet his pension that Ye had died by ingesting cyanide. And after the senior policeman and the station chief finished reading the contents of the envelope, the chief said, 'Fan has to be considered the prime suspect. It's very probable he had a drink with Ye and poisoned him.'

Shortly after three, on the sixth floor of headquarters on Foochou Road, the chief of police finished reading the documents in the thick envelope he had received half an hour earlier from Huangpo Police Station. The chief, who had dealt with numerous corruption cases since the anti-corruption campaign by the government in Beijing started almost a decade ago, had seen only a few cases as blatant as this one.

By four that same afternoon, two detectives brought President Fan in for questioning. Believing no one had seen him visit Ye's apartment late at night and knowing he had wiped his fingerprints off the glass, he vigorously protested his summons. 'I'm heartbroken to hear of the death of my valued employee. You've got the wrong man. You know who I am. As the president of a major state-owned corporation, I have a lot of good friends among the leaders of the Party here and in Beijing. They will testify that there is no way I am guilty of anything.'

Despite Fan's position and his connections, an arrest order was issued by the Chief of Police, not for the murder of Ye but for corruption. 'We have evidence that you've taken millions of dollars of kickbacks from officials of a foreign government.' Fan was momentarily taken aback. *Ma de!! They must have found the evidence Ye was talking about. I should have stayed and searched his rooms!*

Fan quickly regained his aplomb and demanded to make a phone call. He was allowed to make not one but two calls—to high-ranking members in the Party in Shanghai, the chairman of the party secretariat and the president of the Shanghai branch of the People's Bank. But he was curtly told neither was available. After the futile calls, Fan requested to go home and speak to his wife and get the things he would need. His intention was to get as much cash as possible to use to bribe the officers who could help him escape from the imminent detention. But this request was denied. 'You are a high flight risk,' he was told, 'and these days we make sure no one—however high in the party hierarchy—gets away with corruption.'

Fan was hauled off to the Tilanqiao Detention Centre in the Hongkou District at the northern edge of the city. He was booked and taken to a small, dank cell in the basement. Without even looking to see what it was, he refused to eat the food a prison employee brought to him.

Now at almost 11 at night, he was hungry and the smell and noises from the adjoining cells were almost driving him to distraction. *I've got get out of here before I go crazy like Ye. Why did he do it? Granted, he lost his position in Abuja and was very sick. But surely he could see that the important Nigerian office couldn't remain without its head accountant for months. He was on sick leave with full pay. Why did he commit suicide in front of me? And why won't my friends in the Party in Shanghai take my call? How can I get enough money to bribe anyone?*

His head whirling with thoughts, Fan lay back on his hard bunk and wrapped the thin blanket tightly around him. His stomach growled. He closed his eyes, though he was sure he wouldn't be able to sleep.

The next thing he knew, someone was gently shaking his shoulder. He opened his eyes to see Lei Tao standing over him. At first he thought he was dreaming. But when he realized he wasn't, the surprised Fan said, 'You?! What are you doing here? How did you know I'm here?'

Lei put his fingers to his lips and whispered, 'Keep your voice down. I came to get you out. Because of my uncle, I've excellent *guanxi* with the top people in the Party and the police here. When the police called SAEC to find you, I heard what had happened. It took a little time but it's all arranged . . . follow me . . . we will walk out of here and then you can fly to a place where the police will never find you.'

Before Fan could say anything, Lei whispered again, 'Hurry!'

Fan quickly put on his shoes and followed the CFO out of the cell. Lei locked the cell door and put the key in his pocket. The two hurried down the dimly lit corridor to the desk where the guard assigned to the corridor seemed to be dozing. Lei slipped the cell key into the sleeping guard's pocket and led Fan out. To Fan's surprise, he saw no guards until they reached the gate. And he was even more surprised when he saw one of the two guards at the heavy, metal gate open the gate for the pair. The guard said not a word but nodded at Lei.

Outside, a small, black car was parked with a middle-aged man in the driver's seat. Lei opened the back door and motioned Fan inside, and then got in next to the driver who quickly turned on the engine and drove off. Fan was too dumfounded to ask any questions.

After a few minutes, Lei turned to Fan, 'President, you are going to fly out of Shanghai to a place where the police will never find you.

The Party doesn't want to see another important man . . . a Party member and the president of one of our biggest stated-owned companies . . . getting caught with his hand in the cookie jar. And, in your case, a possible murder conviction, unlikely as I think the accusation to be.'

'Where are you taking me now?' asked Fan.

'Tonight you'll be staying at a safe house and then flown out tomorrow. The man you'll meet tonight will tell you where you'll be going.'

Exhausted and hungry as he was, and totally perplexed by everything that had happened to him in the last 24 hours, Fan was at last beginning to have a glimmer of hope. *This man I'm going to meet must be someone high up in the Party. If he can fly me out, I'll ask him to fly me to Hong Kong. From there I can contact Josh Fried, get a new passport, my share of the profits plus my own funds, and I'll be on my way to a new life.*

And with this thought, Fan leaned back in the seat with a long sigh of relief. Fan had no idea where he was going but the car kept on, speeding through the darkness.

34

Tokyo, 23 August

K en Murai couldn't sleep. The flashing blue numbers on his computer registering ever lower prices for the 10-year JGB flickered before his eyes, and in his ears rang the panicked voices of the minister of finance and his colleagues. What would happen to the government's finances and to the Japanese economy if the JGB price didn't go up in the coming weeks? He turned over yet again and knew he wouldn't be able to sleep. Emiko was breathing softly beside him. He guessed it must be past 1 a.m. He gave up. Careful not to wake her, he got up and, quietly closing the bedroom door, went downstairs to the living room.

Ken turned on the light next to the comfortable chair with the footstool, his favourite. Then he got himself a finger of Scotch from the drinks cabinet and sat down. *Music? No, not now . . . it's unlikely to help me stop thinking. Why not some mindless, late-night movie on TV?* He surfed through the channels until he found an old Hollywood movie with Japanese subtitles. He saw three unsavoury looking men digging a narrow tunnel with pickaxes. Listening to their conversation, he quickly caught on. This was a thriller and they were trying to get into a bank vault.

As he sipped his drink and watched the men argue as they dug, he finally started to relax. Just when the roof of the tunnel caved in exposing the floor of the bank vault to the delight of the three men, a message ran across the top of the screen: EARTHQUAKE OFF WAKAYAMA . . . MAGNITUDE OVER 8 . . . TSUNAMI LIKELY.

Ken was used to seeing these news flashes about Japan's frequent earthquakes, but this was a big one. His first reaction was: *Is this the huge earthquake everyone has been dreading? As big or even bigger even than the 9.1 Tohoku Earthquake in 2011?* Like nearly all Japanese, he knew that the Pacific side of Western Japan could expect a disastrous earthquake because of the continuing shift in tectonic plates along the deepest trough in the Pacific Ocean. 'Off Wakayama' could mean this was the dreaded earthquake along this Nankai Trough, one that could be worse than the Tohoku Earthquake that created the monstrous tsunami and killed nearly 20,000 people, destroyed or damaged over a million homes, and resulted in the Fukushima nuclear disaster.

He quickly switched to a news station. He caught a sombre, middle-aged man reporting on the quake: 'What we know is still very sketchy. But the initial estimate of this earthquake is a magnitude 8.1 and tsunami warnings have gone out for all coastal areas in western Japan.'

The announcer was handed a sheet of paper, glanced down at it, and continued: 'The epicentre was off Wakayama, and reports are coming in of very severe damage in the Kii Peninsula. We also have reports of severe damage on the southern coast of Shikoku and as far as Nagoya and Osaka. These are just initial reports and we have no figures yet on the number of people affected.'

Ken's immediate thoughts were of Emiko's sister Rika, her husband Kazuya and their two small children who lived in Kushimoto at the southernmost tip of the Kii Peninsula where Kazuya managed a hotel. Ken knew Kushimoto had been devastated by tsunamis in the past. *Should I wake Emiko or let her sleep? There's really nothing she can do tonight.*

But then he heard his wife call softly from the top of the stairs, 'Ken, Ken? What are you doing up?'

'I couldn't sleep. Emi, I've just heard there was big earthquake in Wakayama. Come downstairs, please.'

As Emiko hurried into the sitting room in her nightgown and robe, she heard the announcer say, 'More news is coming in. We can now confirm a big tsunami has struck the eastern coast of the Kii Peninsula. We have no video as yet.'

Emiko gasped. 'The Kii Peninsula . . . Is this the big one everyone has been talking about? Oh God, this means Kushimoto and my sister's family!!'

'I know. But remember, Emi, Rika and Kazuya found a house above the tsunami zone and had it fortified against earthquakes. It's the middle of the night so they must have been in bed. They should be safe,' Ken said reassuringly.

'But what if Kazuya was at the hotel? I've got to get in touch with Rika.'

She ran to the phone on the side table.

Meanwhile, the news on TV continued: We're informed a tsunami of possibly 2 metres struck the east coast of the Kii Peninsula just minutes ago. There are tsunami of varying heights all along western Japan, including Osaka and the coast south of Nagoya.'

'Two metres! That's the height of a very tall man!' Visibly shaken, Emiko punched in her sister's telephone number on their landline. No response. Then she got out her smart phone and tried to reach both Rika and Kazuya. Again no luck. Ken concluded, 'All lines of communication were severed after the 2011 quake in Tohoku, so presumably everything's down now on the Kii Peninsula.'

Emiko sent both a text message and an email to Rika. 'I hope she'll get my message and respond. She has to be awake and know we are worrying.'

'Emi, calm down. Rika must think we are in bed asleep, as usually we would be.' Emiko went over to the sofa and slumped down. On the TV, the announcer continued to report extensive damage, especially in low-lying areas of Nagoya and Osaka as well as the coastal areas along Honshu and the island of Shikoku.

'There's not much specific information we can give you now. The power is out in the stricken areas and it's too dark for helicopters to fly over and assess the damage. Please stay tuned for more.'

Ken wasn't surprised to hear that an earthquake of this magnitude was causing damage even as far as Nagoya. Looking at Emiko's distraught face, he didn't say what was on his mind: *This disaster is certainly going to affect the market . . . especially the price of JGB.* For the next 10 minutes, the couple fruitlessly watched TV for further information and Emiko kept checking her phone for any messages. Shortly after 3 a.m., they gave up and tried to catch a few hours of sleep.

The couple was awakened before seven by a call from Emiko's mother who lived not far from them in Tokyo. She was frantic. She had only heard about the earthquake when she turned on the TV while eating breakfast. Before calling Emiko, she had tried to contact Rika but couldn't reach her.

With daylight, the extent of the devastation and the number of deaths and people unaccounted for were gradually becoming clear. Though it seemed likely the death toll wouldn't be as high as in the 2011 quake, the number of people affected was many times larger because the quake and tsunami had struck major urban areas in the Kansai Region. Much of Osaka was without tap water and electricity and it was reported that liquefaction had disrupted the gas lines. Communications were still out for the Kii Peninsula. Both Ken and Emi were aghast when they saw a helicopter view of Kushimoto and the surrounding areas, which had sustained the most devastating tsunami damage. Emiko, very much shaken, said quietly, 'The Kushimoto Resort Hotel must have been badly damaged or even completely destroyed. I sure hope Kazuya wasn't there last night.'

Both Ken and Emiko found it frustrating that there was nothing they could do and that they had no way to contact Emiko's sister. Emiko went over to her mother's to try to calm her. Ken was left with his depressing thoughts. By mid-afternoon, Ken was sure the market would take a serious beating as it had after the Kobe Earthquake of 1995 and the Tohoku Earthquake of 2011. He hoped the fall of the JGB price would be minimal, thus enabling the government to elude a financial catastrophe.

The group that plotted to bring down the Japanese government bonds couldn't have picked a better time. If they've arranged for short selling contracts for a week, they will make a killing for themselves!

35

Tokyo, 24 August

Ken felt like he had just got to sleep when he heard the phone ring downstairs. He looked at the bedside clock. It was 6.15. As the phone stopped ringing, he noticed that Emiko's bed was empty.

Ken went down to the kitchen where Emiko was on the phone with her mother, mostly listening. After Emiko hung up, he asked, 'Any news of Rika?'

'Nothing yet, and Mother is beside herself with worry.'

'What are you going to do today?' asked Ken.

'I can't do anything helpful here, so I'm going to work. And you?'

Ken sighed. 'I don't suppose I'll end up doing anything useful. I'm sure the earthquake and tsunami are going to make the JGB tank even further. So I expect I'll be in meetings all day. The finance minister has been holding meeting after meeting this past week where he keeps saying the JGB price will bounce back because "*it has to*". He's like a sick man who thinks denying his symptoms will make the illness go away. I just can't believe the PM appointed a finance minister with so little understanding of how the economy works.'

'He was a crucial supporter of the PM and the leader of his faction in the party and he wanted to become the minister of finance. You know how our politics works.'

Ken smiled. 'You're becoming as cynical as I am. Any chance of getting some coffee?'

After a quick breakfast, Ken left for work. His parting words were: 'Don't expect me for dinner. I have no idea when I can get back.'

As he passed through the bureau's large office, Ken heard everyone excitedly relating stories about the earthquake and tsunami, though Tokyo itself hadn't been affected. Several minutes before the market opened at nine, he booted up his computer. Within five minutes after trading began, the price of the JGB started to drop very slowly but steadily. The Nikkei index too was falling just as steadily, and the yen too wobbled downward. As he watched the changing numbers on the screen, he felt almost dizzy. *The Fan group and panicking Japanese banks must be selling the JGB and the Bank of Japan isn't buying enough of them. And a lot of foreigners are dumping the JGB, Japanese stocks and the yen because of the earthquake!*

For the next 30 minutes or so, Ken watched half-dazed while the price of both the JGB and stocks continued to slide. At around 9.40, the JGB price had fallen enough to raise the interest rate to 5 per cent. 'Five per cent? Three per cent is the upper limit we can manage without defaulting on our bonds. What everyone in the ministry said would never happen *has* happened!'

Ken finally roused himself to check his schedule. Fortunately, he had only one meeting and he could cancel that. But he wanted to make sure he wouldn't be getting calls from panicked Diet members and journalists asking him to explain what was happening and what the Japanese government intended to do to. When his secretary brought him coffee, he asked her to take messages. 'Just tell them I'm unavailable at the moment. And cancel my meeting with the delegation from the currency traders' association.'

For the next two hours, until the morning session ended, the JGB price continued to fall, except for a lull between 10.15 and 10.30 because, Ken guessed, the Bank of Japan had bought just enough of the bonds to temporarily stabilize the price. However, by the end of the morning market at 11.30, the interest rate on the bonds had risen to 6.032 per cent.

Carnage! We now have to pay over 6 per cent to sell our bonds! We simply can't do it . . . no way. His mind went over the causes besides the Fan group: the earthquake and the limited amount of JBG the Bank of Japan must be buying; the American banks not buying the JGB even with the help of the Federal Reserve Bank; the US Senate voting down that big infrastructure bill; the IMF further downgrading the prospects of the EU economies; and the Chinese economy now growing much slower. *But the biggest reason for this, of course, is our having piled up all those JGB for years.*

Despite cancelling his meeting, Ken was too agitated to sit and mull over the impending financial catastrophe staring Japan in the face. During the morning he spoke to his director four or five times, fended off two members of the press who had somehow gotten his private number, and held a staff meeting at the behest of his boss who was even more besieged with demands from inside and outside the ministry. He ordered the staff to decline all requests for interviews or statements, or even advice, and to refer all callers to him or the bureau director, who he knew had also ordered his secretary to say he was 'unavailable but will get back to you when he can'.

Just as Ken was vaguely thinking that perhaps he should go to lunch even though he wasn't hungry, there was a knock on his door. His secretary said, 'Deputy Director, you are wanted in the minister's office as soon as you can get there.'

What now? He grimaced and raced up the stairs to the fifth floor. He found the minister with the director of the Budget Bureau, both grim-faced. But that was the only likeness. Ken always thought when he saw them together what an incongruous pair they were: a fat and bald politician and a gaunt and bushy-haired bureaucrat! A voluble and street-smart ignoramus and a taciturn and pedantic functionary!

The minister said, 'Sit down, Deputy Director. I'm sorry to call you so suddenly. We've been talking about what's happened in the market. The director here has a bailiwick that covers the JGB, but I thought we should also hear what our Harvard-trained economist thinks. How soon do you think the JGB price will bounce back?'

Seated next to the director of the Budget Bureau, Ken looked straight at the minister of finance, hesitated only for a moment, and replied, 'Sir, I hope I'm not overstating it, but we have to face up to the fact that the market is telling us that Japan can no longer make fiscal ends meet by selling government bonds. The price of the JGB has dropped enough to force us pay over 6 per cent, if not close to 7 per cent on any more JGB we sell.'

The minister was stunned. He said nothing for nearly a minute. Then he started to ramble: 'You don't expect the price to rise? Won't someone . . . foreigners, for example . . . decide to buy the JGB when its price had gone down by so much—6 or 7 per cent—that's what the Italians and Spaniards had to pay some time ago. We are already spending more than 20 per cent of our total annual budget to pay the interest costs, so even a 5 per cent interest rate is absolutely out of the question. If you don't think the JGB price will bounce back soon, then when do you expect it to bounce back . . . next week? Within a month? What should I tell the media?'

'Minister, I'd like to think that the JGB price has dropped as far as it will go and will rebound soon. But I'm not sure what the market will do. As for what to tell the media, I'm afraid you have to be prepared to answer some very hard and pointed questions.'

'Minister and I have been talking about this,' interjected the budget director. 'Tell us what *you* think journalists will ask the minister.'

Ken answered carefully. 'Well, for starters, they will ask what the government will do when it has to sell more bonds to pay for the bonds that are maturing soon. And how can we balance next year's budget without selling more JGB?'

The minister answered rather testily, 'Yes, of course I expect those questions. But I can't say to them, "We simply can't pay the interest rate we will have to pay—6 per cent is impossible." If I say that, the market will drop even more and we'll have a recession worse than the one after the bubble burst in 1991. I have to announce that the price of the JGB will bounce back. But journalists aren't going to believe me if I say that. So, what I need is your advice on how I answer such questions.'

Ken understood his predicament but didn't have any good answers.

'Sir, I realize that for now, you have no choice but to sound optimistic. But, sir, since you have asked my opinion, I think we had better get busy to find ways to cope with the horrendous consequences we should expect if the price of the JGB doesn't bounce back soon.'

The minister nodded. 'I agree. I've already called the governor of the Bank of Japan. But he wouldn't commit to anything. I suspect you have some ideas. Please speak freely.'

Ken could tell that the minister was close to desperate. Suddenly an idea came to him. *Not much. . . but it has to do for now.*

'Yes, Minister, I do have an idea. We could try to co-opt the critics for a start. May I suggest that you organize a task force within the ministry that will also include some top economists to serve as advisors. The charge of this task force will be to draft a comprehensive, realistic plan of action. This way the chief critics will be brought into the fold and there will be less criticism because we will be making use of the best talents and ideas. I'm sure the public will see you as a leader who is taking action. And we may well get a usable plan.'

The minister stared at Ken for a long moment and then said, 'Hmm. Your proposal makes sense.'

The budget director frowned. 'It's going to be difficult to find top economists who will be willing to serve on the committee. Could you suggest a few candidates?'

'Well, I would certainly include Professor Mikio Higuchi for several reasons. He used to be an officer in this ministry before he became a professor, first at Hitotsubashi and then at Tokyo University. He has a PhD from Yale and has written a lot of excellent books about how to put Japan's fiscal house in order. I know he has been very critical of the government policy. But he is a top economist who is in the public eye and constantly appears for interviews on TV. If we could persuade him to serve on this committee, I think he will give us some useful advice and he will then be a voice inside the government and less able to criticize our ministry in the media.'

'Hmm,' said the budget director again, looking like someone chewing a sour lemon. 'He certainly has been a harsh critic of our policy. He's been nettling a lot of people in the ministry on how we can't get away with balancing our budgets by selling bonds up to 30 and 40 per cent of our annual budgets. He said we had to worry about our bond collapsing because we no longer have a consistent trade surplus and our saving rate is down sharply. I have to admit his prediction is coming true. So . . . even though I don't think he can tell us anything we can agree with, having him in the committee should help to make people think we are doing something . . . something new.'

The minister looked at his watch and then at Ken.

'Well, Deputy Director, I think you have come up with a good idea. Email my secretary your suggestions of four or five more economists to put on the committee. I'll pick a few from your suggestions and add a few of my own choices. I'm going to tell the media that this committee is being organized. And, to discuss what we should do, I've called an emergency meeting of all the most senior people in the ministry for six this evening. To open the meeting, I'd like to present my ideas . . . so I want you to give me what I can say as soon as you can. And I'd like you to attend and note how people respond.'

'Yes, sir. I'll jot down some ideas and give them to your secretary within a few hours.' responded Ken, inwardly amused at how the minister had co-opted his proposal and was asking him to give the minister ideas that he could present as his own at the meeting.

Back in his office, Ken quickly checked the market and found to his great relief that the price of JGB hadn't fallen further. He immediately got to work on 'the minister's ideas'. He listed only the three top priorities he thought the committee should focus on: to give 'guidance' to all major financial institutions to hold on to their JGB; to consider an emergency 'national solidarity' tax on luxury items to be selected in order to help the quake-affected prefectures; and to draft a law to prevent capital outflow from Japan under strict conditions that would comply with all international treaties and the rules of the World Trade Organization.

There was a soft knock on his door. It was his secretary. 'Sir, it's almost two. I know you didn't have time for lunch, so I've brought you some sandwiches and coffee. Is there anything more I can get you? Anything I can do to help?'

'Many thanks. I'd forgotten all about food.'

Ken watched the market as he ate, and kept an eye on it as he worked. By the close of the market at three, the Nikkei index had lost only another 0.2 per cent in the afternoon session, but there was no change in the price of the JGB and the yen. Ken's guess was that financial institutions were holding onto their bonds and the BOJ was buying just enough JGB to keep the price from falling. The exchange traded funds that specialized in the JGB listed in the Shanghai and the Singapore markets moved virtually identically with the price movements in Tokyo.

Ken finished his six-page draft of 'the minister's ideas' at 4.40. His secretary immediately took it to the minister's office.

As the ministry officials invited to the meeting trailed into the conference room just before six, most expressed surprise at seeing Ken seated at the bottom end of the long table. When the group had assembled—the political vice minister who was a politician and a member of the Diet and the administrative vice minister who was the highest ranked bureaucrat, five directors of bureaus and 10 senior counsellors, it was clear to everyone that the only official present with a rank as low as deputy director was Ken. He knew they all wondered why he was at this meeting.

When everyone had assembled, the minister arrived and opened the session. He briefly said that everyone was aware of the crisis and they were there to discuss a plan of action to deal with it. He then said, 'I want to suggest a few of my own ideas of what the ministry ought to do. I discussed them earlier with Deputy Director Murai. As I am exhausted from talking with the prime minister and several others for the past hour, I am asking Murai to summarize my ideas. Go ahead, Deputy Director.'

Ken did as he was told. Everyone pretended that what Ken outlined were the minister's ideas while knowing full well they were Ken's but fully supported by the minister.

The political vice minister was the first to respond. Looking at the minister of finance, he began sycophantically: 'Minister, I agree with you that we should provide "guidance" to the big bondholders. We need to have them protect our government bonds. However, talking about any kind of an emergency tax hike seems a little premature. And we've got no need to worry about a capital flight out of Japan—people have been buying the JGB for years. They will buy more. And we Japanese are not like greedy foreigners who do not think about national interest. I really don't think we need to worry about capital flight, sir.'

The farce continued with everyone agreeing with the political vice minister. Ken wanted to speak up to reiterate the need for an emergency tax of some kind and a carefully crafted law to prevent capital flight. They needed to send a signal to the market and especially foreigners, who now held around 10 per cent of the JGB, that the Japanese government was very serious in preventing the further slide of the JGB's price. But he knew better than to do that. So he kept his mouth shut. After nearly half an hour of a fruitless talk, the minister said, 'Good, then we're agreed that we'll issue guidance to all financial institutions, but we'll hold off for now on an emergency tax and capital flight measures. Now, let's discuss a bit about what is going to happen in the market in the coming days.'

Except for the minister and the political vice minister, several members of the committee who spoke up had dire predictions. The consequences identified included bank failures, 'a total credit freeze', a sharp rise in the interest rates and all its consequences, the drop of the yen by as much as another 10 yen to the dollar and all its consequences, unemployment shooting up and demand dropping to sharply increase bankruptcies of companies and many more.

As Ken listened, watching the grim faces of the others, he wanted to say that because of all the dire consequences members were predicting, there was sure to be a capital flight. Companies earning money abroad would keep their money abroad and a lot of rich individuals would take their money out of Japan. But Ken didn't say a word, knowing he should not speak up unless was asked to. He was more saddened than frustrated.

True to form, the meeting lasted almost two hours, ending a little before eight after the minister announced that a committee of economists would be appointed within a few days. Then, as if on cue, there was a knock on the door and fancy, lacquered wooden boxes containing sushi were passed around along with tea. A few people made excuses and left. Ken too declined the sushi and left quietly.

Ken arrived home just before nine to find that his wife had arrived only a few minutes before. 'Have you eaten?' she asked.

He shook his head. 'Not since a sandwich at two o'clock. I just couldn't stomach eating with the ministry bigwigs, so I turned down some expensive sushi.'

'Never mind. I'll fix you some noodles. I brought back greens from my mother's garden and there's shrimp in the freezer. I'm late coming back because I've been at my mother's.'

'Thanks. Any news?'

'Yes. Rika and her family are safe. She contacted Mother this afternoon.'

'What a relief,' said Ken. 'How are they faring?'

'Not as well as we could wish. Their house sustained only slight damage, but the aftershocks have really scared the children. And though Rika had stocked up on food and water, some of her neighbours hadn't, and so she is running short after sharing what she had with them. Kazuya was asleep at home when the quake struck but rushed down to the hotel, arriving just after the tsunami so he's safe.'

'What about the hotel?'

'It's standing, but two members of the staff on duty were killed by the tsunami. They did manage to get the guests to the higher floors. Kazuya spent all day yesterday helping evacuate guests by helicopter. Then, after only a couple of hours of sleep, he went out to help search for survivors in the town. Mother said that Rika sounded exhausted and distraught. So far the only way in or out of Kushimoto is by helicopter, but a road should be cleared soon.'

Ken, sighing as he slumped down in a chair at the dinner table. 'You know, the reverberations of the quake and tsunami will be felt all over Japan. There are millions of people living in the affected area. And they have family and friends all over the country. There will be higher prices of fuel and many other necessities because the yen had fallen so much. And more importantly, I can't begin to imagine how many homeless there will be—far more than we had in Tohoku in 2011—and people will lose jobs, go bankrupt, even commit suicide. I can't think what I can do to help.'

'Wait until you get some food inside you and then some rest. Don't despair. I'm sure you'll think of something!'

'At the very least I want to do something so those rogues who began the disaster in the JGB market get retribution! How? I've no idea yet.'

Then savouring the aroma of the meal that was nearly ready for him, Ken finally began to relax.

36

Around the World, 25 August

While most people in Japan and many others around the world were surprised and even aghast at what Japan was going through, there were some who rejoiced at these circumstances, which were bringing about their own good fortune. For them, a natural disaster in Japan brought them profitable business and it couldn't have come at a better time.

After the earthquake, people in the construction industry got more business than they could handle. Bankers who had heeded the letters they received on Friday, 14 August, warning of the impending collapse of the JGB, and who had sold their holdings, profited, as did those who had short sold the JGB and Japanese stock. And then there were the plotters who had schemed to bring down the price of the JGB and who had sent these warning letters. A few of those in the 'project' thought they should have been able to make even more money, but by and large they were very happy.

In New York, Josh Fried was gloating. His excitement at the price of the JGB and various stocks at the close of the market yesterday hadn't been diminished this morning. His Irish wife, who had been at the theatre with friends last night, came into the kitchen to find her husband uncharacteristically grinning while grinding coffee beans.

Christa greeted him with a kiss and asked, 'Josh, you look like the proverbial Cheshire cat. Did you get another juicy insider-tip you can use to make a few million dollars?'

'Not a few million, Christa, 2.5 billion dollars! That's how much I've made in the past week.' Josh spooned ground coffee into a filter and inserted it into the coffee maker.

'What! Did you say billion or million?'

'I said *billion*. I made 2.5 billion dollars as of the closing of the market yesterday.' Coffee was forgotten for the moment.

'How?' Christa was stunned.

'I short sold Japanese government bonds and a score of Japanese stocks. A group of us knew we could bring down the price of the bond and stocks even without the earthquake and tsunami in Japan.'

Shaking her head, Christa said, 'How can anyone make so much money? And in just a week? When I was a waitress, I never made more than $25,000 in a year.' She thought a minute. 'So, in just one week you made 10,000 times . . . no! . . . 100,000 times what a hard-working waitress makes in a year!!'

'That's because I took risks. I'm just making capitalism work. Our system works because some of us take risks and get rewarded for doing so. Hey, I've got an idea. How about we buy that castle we saw at Easter? You can have your own Irish castle.'

Christa was dumfounded for several seconds. 'My own Irish castle? You're not joking?'

'No, I've never been more serious. You take risks and get rewarded. Let's just say this is your due reward for taking the big risk of marrying a man who was once just starting a hedge fund with an uncertain future.'

Christa broke out into a big smile and hugged her husband. 'How lucky I am,' she said. To herself she thought, *Marrying you wasn't really such a big risk. I had to get out of bankrupt Ireland, my poverty-stricken village, my dead-end job as a waitress. And I did it!*

Two hours later Mark Arnold walked into Josh Fried's office. The former Markus Adler had a contented smile on his face.

'Josh, I'm going to Paris. It's a city I've always wanted to see but never before had the chance to. I stayed one night at a crummy hotel near the Gare de l'Est in July on my way to New York, but I didn't see anything of the city. This time I'll stay at a luxury hotel for a week or 10 days, just long enough to see if I want to live there now I've become very rich. I know Interpol is probably looking for Markus Adler. But with my new name, my new appearance, and my new American passport thanks to you, I've nothing to worry about. While I am away, you can use my new equations . . . the "trend-following algorithm" . . . and make some money.'

While the jovial Arnold prattled on, Fried thought, *I hope you're right and you don't get caught.* Aloud he said, 'Thanks for the offer of your new algorithm. Your mathematical models have done wonders for me since you came to New York. I really don't understand how they work, but I like the results. I want to increase the money we made by short selling the JGB and stocks last week, so I'll try your new equations. One can never make too much money!'

Arnold smiled. He was glad these Americans appreciated him. Not like his former German bosses in Frankfurt who had exiled him to Dresden. Fried stood and shook hands with Arnold, 'Markus, I mean Mark, have a wonderful time. Be sure to come to see me as soon as you get back to New York. We'll settle up then . . . so you'll get your hands on all the money you made last week.'

While all the plotters were totalling their winnings, Shigeo Tanaka was drinking overpriced whisky alone at the lobby bar in the Palace Hotel near the Imperial Palace. This was the bar he came from time to time when he wanted to think through a knotty problem.

Too bad the Sumida Bank is certain to go bankrupt because the stupid board of directors didn't listen to my objections about buying so much JGB. What idiots to keep that fat Honma on instead of promoting me. Hell, I'll be out of a job at my age and with the reputation for working at a failed bank . . . .

On the other hand . . . I've made a bundle, more than enough to live very comfortably for the rest of my life. Josh and Peter are giving me a generous amount out of what they have made for my bringing into the project the two rich Japanese and a couple of Americans. Josh said on the phone the total could be as much as 20 million dollars!

Just suppose . . . if I kept the 450 million the two Japanese put up for the project plus the profit they've made after Josh sends it all to me . . . what can they do? They can't go to the authorities because their money was purloined.

He finished his whisky in a gulp. *However, they have yakuza connections,* he reminded himself. Only two seats away at the counter, a lone woman, 30-ish and very alluring, smiled at him invitingly. But, still preoccupied, Tanaka stood up and left without even realizing what an opportunity he was missing.

Daisuke Honma, president of Sumida Bank, had a quandary of his own. His bank had bought way too much JGB because of his misguided advice. Even if by some miracle the bank managed to survive, he knew he wouldn't be able to keep his job. He was just thankful that at the last minute he had followed his instincts and short sold the JGB using 200 million yen of his nest egg as a margin deposit and Mayumi as cover. If the trade had gone as he was sure it would, he would be able to make his nest egg bigger. *This, added to my savings, should be enough to live on if I stop the profligate spending of my family.*

Unfortunately, he couldn't keep his usual Tuesday meeting today with his mistress because the board had called an emergency meeting at 2 p.m. *Well, I'll find out tomorrow exactly how much I've made,* he thought with satisfaction. *Mayumi will go to the broker today before she goes to her bar.*

Though she usually didn't get up until 10, today Mayumi was up at 8.30 and at the broker's by 10. She signed several documents to get all the money—the margin deposit plus the profit minus the fees and the interest charges. Then she had an interesting conversation with the woman helping her. The employee informed her: 'The total profit you made comes to just a little over 120 million yen. So your profit plus your capital of 200 million yen, minus our commission and interest charge for the margin trade, comes very close to 318 million yen.'

'A profit of 120 million yen?' Mayumi said too loudly in the small office. Then she quietly calculated, *Honma said I'd get half . . . so half minus half the expenses comes to 59 million. I'd never have to ask Honma for money again! But I'll still be obligated to him . . .*

'That's right, 120 million yen,' the employee emphasized. 'The price of JGB you shorted tanked more than 6 per cent . . . I've never seen the JGB price drop this much. So your 10-to-1 margin trade came up a very big winner. You are either very smart or very lucky. Well, how do you want your money?'

'Please send it to my bank.'

'Of course. Please just write down the name of your bank, the location of the branch and your account number on this form. I can fill in the rest,' the woman said as she placed a form in front of Mayumi.

Mayumi hesitated, then after a moment wrote with a shaking hand, overwhelmed both by the amount of money involved and disconcerted by the scheme she had in mind.

When she finished, she asked, 'I know I can pay bills from my bank account, but can I send a large amount . . . like the huge sum I'm getting . . . to another bank account?'

The woman laughed. 'Of course. All you have to know is the account number, and the name of the bank and its location. You can even send money to a bank abroad.'

'One final question: If you send my money now, when will the money arrive in my bank account here in Tokyo?'

'Within a few hours, say early this afternoon at the latest.'

Mayumi, now giddy, took a cab back to her apartment, her mind in a whirl.

My goodness, my share is 59 million yen! But wait . . what if I don't hand over any money to Honma? Then I'll have his 200 million and his share of the profit too! A total of 318 million yen!! That means if I were to go abroad . . . Hawaii or New York or anywhere . . . I could live like a very rich lady . . . start a new life. No sucking up to customers. No need for whoring to keep my bar going! No worries about how to support myself when I can no longer work! And I might get lucky and meet someone who wants to marry me!

When she got home, she plopped down on the sofa in her small sitting room and kicked her shoes off.

I shouldn't make a hasty decision. Honma has been very generous. He gave me the money I needed to save my bar. And now this 59 million yen! But I have to spend every Tuesday with him . . . a man old enough to be my father . . . and so fat . . . every time he touches me he makes me feel like a tart. Ugh!

Why shouldn't I keep all the money? It isn't as if Honma earned it or even needs it. The capital for the trade came from his secret stash from the kickbacks and bribes he got making those questionable loans. Even if I keep all the money . . . he can't complain to the police.

But can I really get away with it?

Just then Mayumi's phone rang. *Honma!* She quickly answered it. He was eager for the details. And then he informed her that he had to cancel their appointment for that afternoon because of an emergency meeting at the bank. He would call her as soon as possible and arrange to meet her as soon as he could.

Is this a sign from heaven? Mayumi wondered. *If I can get out of the country, I'll be free and clear—of my grubby life of running a struggling bar and servicing men like Honma.*

But where can I go on no notice? I've got to leave today if I'm going. Why not Hawaii? I sure enjoyed my trip there with Mr Yoshida. It's a wonderful place . . . nice and hot and there are so many Japanese there that I won't stick out. I can go as a rich tourist and see what happens.

She grinned.

Honma doesn't know my real name because I've been using Mayumi Kondo since I first began to work at a bar. In my business, it doesn't do to let people know your real name. But my bank account, credit cards, and passport are in my real name. Honma writes cheques to my bar, not to me. This means he won't be able to find either the money or me in Hawaii!

And then she realized something very important that ruled out any last doubts she had: *I didn't use the brokerage firm Honma told me to, but another one where a good customer of the bar works. I wonder if I intended all along to keep all the money?*

She checked her passport. It was still valid. She began to quickly and methodically prepare to leave. She found a Hawaiian Airlines flight leaving from Haneda at just before midnight and booked a seat. She also made a reservation at the Hilton Hawaiian Village where she had stayed with Mr Yoshida. The hotel was so large she would just be an anonymous Japanese guest. She packed a large suitcase and a carry-on, thinking whatever else she needed she would buy in Honolulu.

She was suddenly very hungry. When she looked at her watch, it was almost three. She had quick lunch of bread, cheese and a banana and then took a cab to her bank. The money had arrived! She withdrew 1 million yen in cash. This would be around $10,000 and should be enough to live on in luxury until the rest of her money arrived from Japan to an account she would set up at a bank in Hawaii as soon as she got there. She knew she could exchange the yen into dollars in Honolulu. Then she returned home. She thought of calling the caretaker of the apartment and the bartender-cum-assistant-manager of the bar but did not. *What would I say? Who cares? If I don't come back, they can have all the stuff I've got here and the bar can close.* She cleared her desk of all her personal papers. She took a shower and dressed for the flight and made a swift check of her apartment. *Good, It's neat with nothing personal left in it. Just food in the fridge. I'll just disappear.*

Shortly after six, Mayumi went onto the street in front of her apartment and caught a cab to Haneda. At a Japanese restaurant at the airport she had a final dinner of broiled eel, her favourite dish. When her plane took off, she looked at the lights of Tokyo become fainter and said to herself, *Sayonara, Tokyo. Sayonara to my wretched life.* She closed her eyes, and by the time a flight attendant came by with drinks, the tired new millionairess was sound asleep.

37

Japan, 28–31 August

Ken Murai was hard at work on the memorandum for the special committee the finance minister was in the process of forming, when his personal phone rang. *Emiko?* She almost never called him at work, and she had seen him less than two hours ago when they left the house together.

With trepidation Ken put the phone to his ear.

'Ken?' Emi's voice sounded strained. 'I have terrible news. Rika's husband, Kazuya, is dead.'

'What?' Ken was shocked. 'How?'

'He was working with the teams trying to rescue people . . . to find people still alive and trapped in collapsed houses and buildings. They thought they had got all of the living out, but yesterday one of his team members thought he heard a whine, a dog perhaps, still alive after five days. The sound came from a partially collapsed two-storey house. When they went in to search, there was a strong aftershock and the second floor caved in on them. Kazuya and another man were inside when it happened. It took hours to get them out from under the wreckage. Kazuya was unconscious and badly injured, the other man dead. They got Kazuya to the local hospital. He died early this morning. Rika is in shock and my mother nearly hysterical.'

Emiko sounded so upset that he wondered if she was crying.

'Surely Rika and the children are not going to stay there now!'

'No. Mother told me that Rika had already decided that they had to leave as soon as feasible. Despite all the emergency aid they've got so far, living conditions are still horrible. The carport collapsed on

Rika's car, so she can't drive it. So Uncle is organizing a van to go get them on Sunday. The main reason I'm calling you at work is that Uncle wants you to go with him to take turns in driving. It's a long way and some parts of the road will certainly be hazardous.'

Ken was taken aback. He hadn't foreseen venturing into the heart of the disaster area. He swallowed hard and then replied, 'Of course I'll go. I'll call your uncle tonight about the arrangements.'

'Good! I knew you would come through. So I hope you can clear your calendar for this weekend so we can make preparations tomorrow. Uncle plans to make the round-trip on Sunday so you shouldn't miss any work.'

Good old Emi, Ken thought, *organized and always up to the challenge. But Sunday is going to be a hell of day*!

Ken set off with Emiko's uncle at three in the morning on Sunday. The first few hours went smoothly with little traffic on the road. Three hours into the journey, they had breakfast at a small coffee shop, and they stopped again for coffee and a snack before reaching Nagoya. Uncle had chosen the longer route through Nagano Prefecture so as to avoid the damaged Ise Bay Expressway, a series of bridges connecting various promontories of land to the south of Nagoya.

Under good conditions, the drive from Ken's house in Tokyo to Kushimoto via Nagano would have taken at most eight hours. But while the highway down the coast of Wakayama Prefecture to Kushimoto was passable, they had to take a number of detours because some roads were being repaired and they had wait several times because convoys of trucks carrying in supplies and relief workers were given priority.

Ken was appalled by what he could see from the van. There seemed to be debris everywhere. Despite the shelters that had been provided, many people were camping out. *I knew from TV that*

*conditions were terrible, but what I'm seeing is much worse . . . it's
lucky that it's the height of summer, though lucky isn't the right word
for these poor people who have lost their homes.*

With all the delays, Ken and Uncle didn't arrive at Rika's until
two in the afternoon. Rika, looking exhausted, was ready. Neighbours had gathered to help unload the supplies the two men had
brought in the van, which was loaded to the roof with essentials such
as diapers, antibacterial hand wipes, foodstuffs and so on. One neighbour wanted to give the men some refreshments, but both refused,
knowing she had little to spare. Three quarters of an hour after the
van arrived in Kushimoto, the two men, Rika and her two children
were on the road headed for Tokyo.

Rika, subdued, said little and fed her daughters the rice balls and
fruit Emi had had Ken take with him. The two little girls were excited
and chatted to the men about what life was like after the earthquake
and tsunami.

'We couldn't use the toilet. There was no water. So we had to use
a bucket and Mama had to pour it down the street drain.'

'Honey, that's enough about that,' admonished Rika.

The older girl was most impressed by the use of disposable plastic
wrap to line bowls because there was no way to do dishes. When Ken
asked her what she wanted to do first when she arrived in Tokyo,
she immediately said, 'Take a bath!'

Rika commented that the few old people living in outlying dis-
tricts were actually better off than those in town. 'They have out-
houses, they rely on wood not gas, and they have wells. They also
have kitchen gardens and so they have enough food. I never thought
I would envy people who lived such an old-fashioned way of life.'

Ken's heart ached when he had to drive on without stopping to
help the people begging for food or water on the roadside. But at one
point when they were waiting to take a detour, an old woman came
up to the van, pleading for water for her grandchildren. Though Ken

had only four bottles intended to last them for the trip, he gave her all four bottles, thinking, *I can buy more once we're were in Nagano.*

When at last they had driven out of the area affected by the disaster, they stopped at a family restaurant on the outskirts of Nagano. Here the children happily gobbled down hamburgers, which they relished after their recent diet of instant noodles.

It had now grown dark, and Uncle was visibly tired. When Ken said he would drive the rest of the way to Tokyo, Uncle nodded and Ken took the wheel. It was just after one in the morning when the exhausted group arrived at the home of Rika and Emiko's mother. Emi was there with her mother waiting for their arrival.

Emiko pulled Ken aside and said, 'I know you are exhausted, but I have to tell you that Bach urgently wanted to talk to you. He couldn't get you on your phone so he called me about 11. He wants talk to you as soon as possible.'

'I can't call him at this hour—surely he won't still be up.' Ken sent a text message asking his friend to call as soon as he wanted to.

The Murais didn't get home and to bed until well after two. Ken felt as if he had just got to sleep when his phone rang. It was Baba calling and it was already seven.

'Sorry to call so early when you got home so late. Did everything go OK? Your message said you didn't get home until two this morning.'

'Yes, we brought my sister-in-law and her children safely back to Tokyo, but we had to go via Nagano and the road conditions held us up. It was a very depressing trip. But why did you want to talk to me so urgently?'

'Well, I was in the same area myself yesterday, but I saw the devastation mostly from a helicopter. Why I called was to tell you that the PM's had a heart attack.'

'Oh, no,' groaned Ken. 'That's what you were afraid might happen, isn't it? Tell me the situation—I haven't heard any news since Saturday.'

'I called you last night before the media got the information, but this morning it's breaking news. The PM finally flew to view the disaster area yesterday with a full entourage, Chief Secretary Fukunaga, the minister of internal affairs and communications, and yes, me included. The PM waited so long to go that he made a big deal of it and the trip proved to be too much for him. He collapsed on the plane on the way back. He was taken to Tokyo University Hospital and I was there until nearly midnight. The PM was in the intensive care unit but when I called this morning, I was told he is considered stable and has been moved to a private VIP suite. We tried to keep his heart attack secret, but unfortunately reporters were at the airfield when his plane touched down and they saw him loaded into a medical helicopter on a stretcher. '

Ken groaned. 'Just what we need on top of everything else! So who's in charge at the moment? Is it the PM or is it the finance minister who also serves as deputy prime minister?'

'It's not entirely clear.'

'Why not?'

'Last night everything was chaos and the concern was on the PM. Once in the ambulance, the PM was hooked up onto machines and at the hospital I was told he was out on medications. I talked to Fukunaga this morning before I called you and asked who was in charge. He reported that the PM refuses to see your minister of finance who should be taking over the PM's job. And from all what I saw, and from what Fukunaga said this morning, the PM is in no mental condition to make the decision he has to in order to govern.'

'Knowing how much the PM dislikes my minister and his faction, I'd put money on his not wanting to relinquish any power to him. It's well known that the PM had to appoint him minister of finance and name him as second in command should the need arise, in order to keep my minister and his faction happy. So what you're telling me is that no one is running the country?'

'Well, certainly not officially, but if you want to know anything or get anything done, you have to contact Chief Secretary Fukunaga.'

'What a mess,' bemoaned Ken. 'The economy is in terrible shape, the nation has just suffered a major natural disaster and our country is being run by the sly and street-smart Fukunaga!'

38

Hawaii, Tokyo and Paris, Week of 31 August

Mayumi was in desperate straits. She couldn't get at her money, still in her account in Japan. The account contained almost 320 million yen, close to 3 million dollars. This was more than sufficient to give her a new life in Honolulu, even if the yen dropped a little more. Last Wednesday, she had opened an account at the Bank of Hawaii and filled out the paperwork for the transfer of her money. But when she checked on Thursday, no money had been put into it, nor on Friday either. When she asked why, she was told there seemed to be some kind of hold-up—money usually came through within 48 hours. 'Please come back on Monday. I'm sure it will be there by then,' said the very solicitous teller.

So Mayumi, now using her real name, Kanako Matsuya, had enjoyed her weekend. She had exchanged the yen she brought with her for roughly 9,000 dollars, enough to make her feel comfortable about enjoying an ocean-view room at the Hilton Hawaiian Village and dinners at the posh tourist restaurants in Waikiki. She browsed the luxury boutiques on Kalakaua Avenue. But she refrained from buying anything, preferring to wait until her money was here and in dollars.

As soon as the bank opened on Monday, Mayumi was back again, inquiring about the transfer of funds. *Still nothing*! Now alarmed, she went back to her hotel and made a call to her bank in Tokyo. She was passed from the operator to a teller and then to a manager. Finally she was informed that because of the size of the sum she had requested be sent to a foreign country, it was being investigated by the section of the Financial Service Agency that monitored the international flow of money in order to prevent money transfers by terrorists or others for such purposes as tax evasion and money laundering.

Of course, the manager kept mum about the fact that he had tipped off the FSA when he saw a very unusual request by the holder of a small account who suddenly had a large sum she wanted sent abroad. He had been loath to see the money sent out of the bank because this would threaten his goal of having an increased amount of total deposits and cash in his branch at the end of the month, but there was no way he wanted to get caught by the FSA. He responded to Mayumi smoothly, 'I could put you in touch with the agent who is looking into your account, but he suggested that you return to Japan so you can provide evidence of how you had obtained this money and why you want to have it sent to Honolulu.'

Mayumi was staggered. She barely managed to thank the manager for this information and say she would be in touch. She had no idea what she could do, but for now she had to conserve her funds. *No more gourmet dinners—it will be cheap noodle shops from now.* She told her hotel that tomorrow she would check out of her corner room in the Rainbow Tower. She went online and found a satisfactory hotel two blocks back from the beach and less than a third of the price she was paying now. She booked a room for a week and then began to pack. And while she packed, she deliberated.

If I go back to Japan, how can I possibly satisfy the officer at the FSA? Could I tell him I made the money short selling government bonds? But they'll ask how I got the money to short sell in the first place. I can't tell them anything about Honma . . . If I do, they'll get in touch with him and he'll accuse me of theft. That would land me in jail. But . . . how can he accuse me? The money he gave me to short sell surely came from an illegal stash. But he could make up some story, and the FSA agent would be much more likely to believe a bank president than a bar owner who has barely managed to keep her bar afloat over the years. Why not brazen it out by telling the

FSA that I'm some important man's mistress and he had given me the money, but I can't tell the FSA the man's name because he is a married politician . . .

Mayumi, now back to being Kanako, felt wretched. There was just nothing she could think of that would get her the money. And she was losing money every day because the value of the yen was going down with Japan's economic woes. Dispirited, she lay on the king-sized bed and sobbed, oblivious of the paradise that lay just beyond her windows.

If his mistress was having a bad week, so was Daisuke Honma. Even as he calculated what he had made when his short-selling contract was up, he was aware that Sumida Bank couldn't sustain the losses they were facing since the price of the JGB tanked. The chairman of the board members had called an emergency meeting for Tuesday, when he usually met Mayumi.

The board meeting had gone even more badly than he had anticipated. The members grilled him on the bank's current balance sheet and questioned whether it would improve or further deteriorate in the very near future. Although Honma tried to prevaricate, saying that he would yet have to thoroughly investigate the bank's position, most of the members were not having his transparent equivocation. One member was furious, saying that Honma had promised that nothing of this sort could ever happen. He threatened to fire Honma on the spot. Finally the chairman calmed the man down and adjourned the meeting. He scheduled another for Thursday, informing Honma that he would be expected to present up-to-the-minute data on the bank's position.

Honma had gone home and cancelled his family's holiday to Hong Kong. His daughters were furious, saying this had been planned for months. All he said was: 'We have a perfectly good villa up in Karuizawa. Go up there for the week.' Then he went to take a bath.

He was sure his wife suspected that something had adversely affected their finances, but he had never let her know the family's financial position. He gave her a generous allowance for household and personal expenses, and she had never asked about the family's financial position. He certainly wasn't going to tell her now what he was worried about.

And the bank wasn't Honma's only worry. The meeting had lasted longer than he expected. When it was over, he tried to call Mayumi but she didn't answer her phone. He called the bar but was told she hadn't come in yet. He couldn't contact her either Tuesday evening or Wednesday.

Honma was so stressed by Wednesday evening that he developed a feeling of pressure just left of centre in his chest. No matter what he did, it wouldn't go away. *Am I suffering heart trouble on top of everything else?* He knew he was overweight, 'nearly obese' his doctor had said, and he was on medication for his high cholesterol.

The rest of the week was a nightmare. The chairman of the board hadn't liked the report Honma had managed to cobble together for the Thursday meeting. He was furious at Honma's numbers, which included the assumption that the JGB price would quickly bounce back. The chairman had called in an auditor from outside. His daughters were no longer speaking to him. And he simply couldn't get in touch with Mayumi.

Where is Mayumi? Where is my money? It was crucial that he get in touch with her—his nest egg would become critical should the bank fail and he lose his job—but Mayumi wasn't answering her phone. Finally, on Thursday, Honma had taken a taxi over to the bar and found a notice on the door that the bar was closed for 'personal reasons'. No one was there; it was dark.

Desperate, Honma hired a detective to try to trace Mayumi. No one in her apartment building could remember seeing her that week. The manager was annoyed because her mail was piling up and Mayumi hadn't left word about what to do with it, nor had she told him she would be away. The landlord of the bar let the detective into it and they discovered that there was no liquor and no money in the cash register. There was no trace of a Mayumi Kondo in any official record that the detective was able to check.

The detective told Honma, 'Women like her have a *genjina*, a professional name used in the demimonde. I'll keep trying to find her real name. But Mr Honma, hasn't she ever told you her real name, given your relationship with her?' Honma had only a vague recollection that Mayumi had once told him her real name but he couldn't remember what it was. The money he had given her to save her bar had always been paid into the account of the bar, which was incorporated, and the money he gave her to short sell the JGB was in cash.

Even while wondering whether the detective was incompetent or just prolonging his investigation to get paid more, Honma gave in and paid out more money to have the detective try to trace her. Two days later the man reported that he was sorry but he hadn't yet been able to find Mayumi's real name or where she was. As far as he could tell, 'She had simply disappeared into thin air. In Japan, about 80,000 people every year simply "evaporate" and she seems to be one of them.' Honma dumbly nodded, thinking that's why we have a word for it . . . *johatsu* . . . people disappearing like vapour.

So his ploy to increase his nest egg hadn't worked. The pressure in his chest worsened. *No time to see a doctor now.* He was about to be late for the board meeting at which he had been warned he would be asked to resign. *Maybe it would have been better if I had lost the battle with Tanaka over the bank's policy on JGB holdings. At least then I couldn't have been blamed for causing the bank to go under.* He sighed and heaved himself out of the chair that within a few hours would no longer be his.

In the meantime, Mark Arnold was exulting in his fortune. He had booked himself into a suite in George V, one of Paris' top hotels. He planned to live it up for two weeks in Paris, the city of his dreams. Luxuriating in a hot bath to recover from his travels, he did his best to forget the stress of his arrival at Charles de Gaulle.

Mark had thought that with his American passport he would sweep through airport immigration without a question. But the immigration officer had looked at his passport and asked him why he was in Paris, surely a routine question. He had replied that he was on holiday in what he thought was his best American English. But she had gone on to ask where he was staying, what he planned to do, a whole series of questions. By the end he had become rather flustered. He had thought she would let him go, but no, she had some kind of problem with her computer and asked him to be patient for a moment. Finally, with a smile she let him go, wishing him a good time in Paris.

Arnold had breathed a sigh of relief and gone to collect his suitcase from the carousel, now nearly empty. He had started to go through the Nothing to Declare exit when an agent had stopped him for 'a routine check'. But this check had seemed far from routine, and when it was discovered that he was carrying 50,000 dollars in cash, he was admonished, 'Monsieur, you can bring into France in cash only 10,000 euros or an equivalent amount in other currencies.' He was then made to fill out numerous forms. It had taken an enormous amount of time because the first agent had tried to communicate with him in French but had had to give up and go find someone who spoke English. But at long last he was let go and was in a taxi on his way to the George V.

Refreshed by his bath and a long nap, Arnold made his way to the hotel bar. He sat down on a stool, hoping to 'get lucky.' What he wanted was to meet a lovely lady here in Paris, someone he could have a relationship with, certainly not a whore. He knew it would be a long shot but he would do his best. He nursed a drink and watched the other patrons. He hadn't been there long when a stunning young Asian woman came in with a rather grizzled-looking middle-aged man with bushy eyebrows. They sat at a table just behind Arnold. The man got up to talk to the bartender and greeted Arnold. When he went back to his table, he and the Asian woman conversed in French. Just listening to her lilting voice, Arnold thought, *Wouldn't I love to meet that woman*!

The following day, Arnold wandered around Paris. He wanted to soak up the atmosphere, as he thought of it. He walked down through the Jardin des Tuileries to the Louvre, but when he saw the long queues outside, he crossed the river intending to go to the Musée d'Orsay. Again the queues were at least a block long. He gave up and wandered around the Left Bank, then had lunch at a small bistro just across the Seine from where he could see the Notre Dame. After a good lunch he made his way back to the George V. He went back to the bar with high hopes, but the woman didn't show up again, nor did anyone else he could talk to. Lonely and exhausted from so much walking, he went to bed early.

Arnold was enjoying a croissant slathered with strawberry jam when there was a knock on his bedroom door. *Has to be the housekeeper*, he grumbled to himself as he got up, brushed crumbs from the hotel robe, pulled the sash tighter and went to answer the door. He had opened it only a crack when it was pushed open and a middle-aged man and a young Asian woman burst into the room.

Startled, Arnold retreated a few steps and stared at the pair. *Yes, this was the couple in the bar two nights ago.* He recognized the bushy eyebrows on the man and it was certainly the same stunning woman.

The man held up his ID and said, 'Capitaine Jacques Roland.' The woman did the same, saying 'Lieutenant Simone Lam.'

'Marcus Adler,' said Roland in English, 'you're under arrest for stealing over 250 million euros from the Dresden branch of the Deutsche Wiederaufbaubank.'

Adler, utterly shocked, managed to protest in a squeaky voice, 'I'm Mark Arnold from New Jersey, in the US.'

Capt. Roland hid a smile. In his fright, Adler had spoken in a very strong German accent.

'Whatever you choose to call yourself, your fingerprints are those of Markus Adler of Dresden, wanted by Interpol for grand theft.'

Adler hollered, 'Was zum Teufel! Ich habe kein Verbrechen begangen. Sie haben den falschen Man!' And then, realizing he had just shouted in German, he turned pale.

'Herr Adler,' Roland said quietly, 'we'll clear this up at the police station. Please get dressed. Lt Lam will wait in the hall for us.' Turning to her, Roland said, 'Lieutenant, please ask Lt Girard to come in and take your place.'

The fight went out of Adler. He slumped down on the sofa. 'Why do you think I'm Adler? I came through Immigration yesterday with my American passport. How did you find out who I am and where I'm staying?'

'Monsieur, you came into France with an American passport. But our passport-control officer wondered why you had such a strong German accent when your passport says you were born in New Jersey. So she checked your passport with the American authorities and found it isn't valid, though it is a very good forgery. She alerted Customs who discovered that you were carrying a large amount of cash without declaring it. And then we were called in. We checked your fingerprints, which we got from a glass you drank from at the bar last night, and it matched with your fingerprints that Interpol has for Markus Adler. We knew where to find you because we had you followed when you left the airport.'

'So that's why it took me so long to get through all the immigration procedures,' he mumbled in German to himself.

Roland didn't understand German but could tell how utterly dejected Arnold was. Feeling a little sorry for the German whom the Interpol has categorized as a 'Category 1 Thief,' he said, 'If you hadn't tried to come back to Europe, you might have got away with it. Now with any luck, you'll be let out of prison in Germany in maybe 10 years.'

39

A Southwestern Province in China, 1 September

One of the original plotters wasn't making plans for spending his pelf—he didn't even know how much money he had made on his seven-day contract to short sell the JGB. In fact, he didn't even know where he was, other than somewhere in one of China's southwestern provinces.

This of course was Fan Zhipeng, who at the time of his arrest was the president and CEO of SAEC. That was on 21 August, 10 days ago, or at least he was pretty certain 10 days had gone by. It had all been a terrible shock, and he still didn't know exactly what had happened or why.

Lei Tao, SAEC's CFO, had come to help him escape and then taken him to a 'safe house' for the night, promising him that he would be flown out to a safe place the next morning. The manager of the safe house had treated Fan respectfully and kindly. He had been offered a drink and food and a soft bed. By the time he lay down, it was the wee hours of the morning. Exhausted, he had immediately fallen into a sound sleep.

When Fan finally awoke, he was bewildered to find himself on a narrow hard bunk. Someone in the bunk above his was snoring. Through the moonlight coming in through two small windows high in one wall, he could make out other bunks. He had no idea where he was or how he got there. He hoped this was some kind of nightmare from which he would soon awaken. He felt drugged. He dozed fitfully, but every time he woke he still found himself on the same hard bed.

In the morning he was told by the man in the bunk across from his that he was in a 'Re-education Centre.' His informant was a defeated-looking man in his late fifties who said, 'Whatever they call this place, it's a "black prison". It's where the Party . . . especially the Party leaders in the provinces . . . lock up people they call dissidents. I thought they'd done away with all these black prisons until I landed here, but they haven't . . . obviously.'

Fan had been about to tell the man that he was no dissident, but he was stopped when a guard unlocked the door of the room and ordered everyone up. He discovered the guards were Miao, one of the largest ethnic minorities in this part of China. However, the men who ran the centre were two Han Chinese. They called themselves 're-education officers' but looked like clever thugs. He was sure they belonged to one of China's 'triads' or 'black societies.'

Fan soon found out what 're-education' meant: long hours working in the vegetable gardens, doing laundry by hand and cleaning the entire camp, including the kitchen and latrines. The first few days were the hardest. Fan wasn't used to any kind of physical labour, particularly not long hours of back-breaking fieldwork, and he was always exhausted. His back ached and his hands had blisters. The Miao guards, all of them young and well built, who spoke only limited Mandarin, gave him orders never to ask questions, hurried the men over their meagre meals and kept the prisoners under constant watch except when they were locked up at night.

He gradually got to know the eight other 'candidates for re-education' in his room. Everyone had two things in common. First, they all knew or had some link to Lei Shuo, minister of ethnic affairs. Though Fan had never met him, Lei Shuo was the uncle of Lei Tao, and one of the most powerful men in China—a member of the Politburo, the principal policy-making body of the Party, as well as a member of the cabinet in the central government.

Second, they had all held important positions in local government or in state-owned enterprises in which Lei Shuo was involved directly or indirectly. Four of the prisoners had been a CEO or CFO in large enterprises located in provinces with a large number of minorities. They had tried to stop Lei's continuing expropriation of various ministry subsidies to assist minorities. Two had tried to prevent the misuse of funds by a CFO or chief accountant who got his position on the recommendation of Lei Shuo. All had either been forced to or had willingly cooperated in Lei Shuo's extraordinarily complex and avaricious schemes.

Fan had a lot of time to think. He berated himself for thinking that Lei Tao had been acting on his own in conniving with him to misuse more than 2 billion dollars of SAEC's money. Because Lei Tao had come to help him escape from the detention centre in Shanghai but then he'd ended up in this black prison, he now had no doubt that Lei Tao had been doing his uncle's bidding all along.

Even though Lei Shuo was a powerful figure in the Chinese government, Fan was surprised that he could operate his own black prison. This was completely outside the law in China. Gradually he pieced together how this was possible.

One of Fan's bunkmates told him, 'Because of Lei Shuo, I had to hire a man as the de facto vice CEO who was a leader in the triad in Guangzhou . . . one of the most notorious black societies in China.' Another man who had known Lei Shuo said, 'When he had a little too much to drink, Lei Shuo once boasted that he could get all the information and muscle he needed "from my friends in Shanghai, Tianjin, Shenyang and even Hong Kong". As you know these are cities where the triads are strong and entrenched.'

Fan of course knew of the triads in China—the organized and local crime gangs that were involved in armed robbery, racketeering, smuggling, narcotic trafficking, hacking into websites for gain, even contract murder—but he had never thought that the triad had anything to do with SAEC even indirectly. Now he knew better.

Although he now knew he was in Lei Shuo's black prison, he had no idea where it was located. He questioned the other men after they were locked in at night but didn't learn much. They had all been brought here in a plane or by a car 'from a safe house' and after being drugged. A man with a badly disfigured face said that there was a dense forest to the north and a mountain range to the south. 'My guess is that we are either in Yunnan or Guangxi Province.'

Another man, almost 70 and the oldest in the room, agreed. 'It has to be a place with a lot of Miao people and this ethnic minority is found primarily in the southwestern provinces.'

Fan's roommates had all been in the black prison longer than he had and were all dejected and demoralized, seemingly inured to their fate.

'Haven't any of you tried to escape?' he asked the man with the disfigured face on another night.

The man, the former president of a large state-owned steel company in Baotou, an industrial city in Inner Mongolia, whispered back in a tired voice, 'It's impossible. We're totally isolated. I wouldn't know even in which direction to go since I don't know where we are. We're under constant guard and locked in at night. We've checked the door and windows. To open them we'd need tools that we don't have access to.'

Fan didn't respond but thought to himself, *I'll do my best, however difficult it is, to escape from this black prison.*

Fan had been in the prison for more than a week before he was interrogated. Then one afternoon he was called out of the laundry and ordered to go to the office of the RO, the re-education officer. Fan was escorted there by a tall Miao, the guard who gave most of the orders to Fan's group.

The RO looked more like a thug than an officer. He sat behind a table and told Fan to take a seat opposite him. The tall Miao stood guarding the door.

'President Fan. We've decided it's time to ask you a few questions. You can make this easy on yourself or you can make this hard. It's up to you. If you answer my questions honestly, you can go to your evening meal. If not, Zha, my Miao friend here, will teach you manners. Believe me, he can quickly make you regret not answering my questions honestly.'

The RO glanced at a sheet of paper on the desk just in front of him.

'The numbers I see on this paper tells me that SAEC sent a huge amount of money—a little over 2 billion dollars—to a bank in Benin, Africa. I have been reliably informed that all the money was then sent to New York to be used for a financial project that a Joshua Fried handled for you. The project was successful, so all the SAEC money and the profit from the project have been sent to an account you have in a bank in Singapore. Is this correct?'

Fan was startled by all the details the RO knew. He replied, 'Yes, that's correct.'

'Now, tell me the name of the bank, the branch where the account is located, the account number and the PIN needed to have the money wired elsewhere.'

Fan thought, *If I don't give the special-code phrase Fried and his banker friend in Singapore devised in order to access the account, no one can get at the SAEC money.*

'Give me a piece of paper and I'll write it all down.'

The RO motioned Fan to come to the table and handed him a pen and paper. Fan carefully wrote down all the details to access the money, except for the special-code phrase.

'We'll soon find out if this is correct. You may go now.'

Fan tried not to show his relief as the Miao guard escorted him to the mess hall to join his roommates for the muck they called 'dinner'.

Once locked into the bunkroom for the night, Fan lay back on his bed and closed his eyes. He didn't want to talk to the others who were likely to ask about the interrogation. He needed to think.

The RO only quizzed me about the money related to the plot. But not about the money I got from the Nigerians. That should have been in the report that Ye was using to blackmail me with. If the police have Ye's report, why doesn't Lei Shuo know about this money? Or is Lei Shuo's chain of communications, which must include the thugs in the black societies, not as good as he thinks? This means I've succeeded in preventing even Lei Shuo from finding out about the kickbacks I got from the Nigerians and now waiting for me in Singapore.

By now Fan was having trouble concentrating because he was so exhausted. But one thing was sure—he had to keep Lei Shuo from getting the special-code phrase needed to get SAEC's money from Ing's bank in Singapore.

I am the only person who can get SAEC's money released from the Singapore bank. So Lei Shuo has to keep me alive. I had long thought that Lei Tao and I were just going to 'borrow' the funds for the short duration of the project and then return them. The huge profits were to be divided between Lei Tao and me, with a generous fee to Professor Du. But Du is dead, and I am here in this black prison. Now Lei Shuo is trying to get all the SAEC money we 'borrowed' plus all of the profits from the project! No, I'm going to do all I can to make sure he doesn't get any of that money!

I've got to think more about this tangled mess tomorrow. They're not going to leave me alone when they discover it won't be so easy . . . more likely impossible . . . to get the SAEC money and the profit from Singapore. But whatever happens, I'll still have the Nigerian payoffs.

And with that last thought, Fan fell asleep.

40

Shanghai and Singapore, 2–3 September

If President Fan thought being in a black prison was a harrowing fate, what happened to two men in Shanghai was far worse.

One was a giant, ne'er-do-well young man who on this Wednesday was sitting at a back table in a small noodle shop. He was built like a tank, and people who knew him were amused at the aptness of his name which meant 'small ox'. Ding Niu was more brawn than brains and so had never been regularly employed. Now he was desperate. The coming meeting with the small thug he had done so many 'jobs' with was his last chance to get hold of some money that he now desperately needed just to live on. And the man he called 'the lieutenant' was very late. Ding Niu glowered as he checked the clock again. It was already 12.20 and they had agreed to meet at noon.

He had nearly given up when the 'lieutenant' arrived, casually slumped into a chair opposite Ding and curtly apologized for being late without explaining why. The new arrival was clearly the dominant man of the pair, though he was short, squat and couldn't have weighed much more than half of what Ding Niu did. He was called 'the lieutenant' by his acquaintances because of his army tales, but in fact he had never been an officer. He was a very clever thug no one wanted a tangle with. What none of his acquaintances knew, however, was that he was a hit man for a highly placed person who had close ties with a black society and that he was a member of one as well. This was the only job he could get after he had been dishonourably discharged from the army.

Ding Niu grunted a greeting. He had never served in the army, but he rather liked the nickname 'Corporal' which the lieutenant had given him. Though he often resented the patronizing way he was treated, he had always done whatever was asked of him because he was paid enough for him to scrape by on. He had also been taught many interesting things about explosives and various electronic gadgets, such as detonators and timers when they did 'jobs' together.

As Ding Niu watched the lieutenant try to chat up a pretty waitress, he became even more certain that he had made the right decision. Not only was he in desperate need of funds, he was also fed up with the way the lieutenant treated him. So he had finally decided to kill two birds with one stone. Yesterday he had asked to meet the lieutenant 'just to have a chat'. The lieutenant had surprisingly agreed, suggesting lunch at this small restaurant near Century Park, the biggest park in Shanghai. Ding thought the place was an odd choice. . . very out-of-the-way . . . but he had agreed.

The lieutenant finally turned to him and said, 'Let's eat.' They both ordered the noodle dish of the day, and when the waitress had served them and left, the lieutenant said, 'Hey, Corporal, we can talk about anything except money.'

Ding Niu tried to chat. However, he couldn't keep the conversation going because he was distracted. The lieutenant noticed, and midway through the meal asked, 'What's the matter? You've always been a bit doltish but today I feel like I'm talking with a slow-witted 10-year-old. What's with you?' Ding replied, 'Oh . . . nothing. Excuse me . . . I've got to go to the john.' His companion, looking disgusted, nodded but said nothing.

Ding Niu stood up and went down the narrow hall that led to the toilet but passed it and continued on and out the back door. In seven or eight minutes he returned to the table. 'You OK?' asked the lieutenant. 'Yeah,' muttered Ding and sat down again. The lieutenant saw that Ding's face was flushed but he didn't comment.

They finished the meal without talking about money. Ding had repeatedly asked the lieutenant for loans in the past. But not today. This puzzled the lieutenant who asked why Ding had wanted to meet him.

'It's been a while, and I wondered if you had anything for me to do,' was Ding's answer.

'Not now, but I'll call you if something comes up.' The lieutenant pulled his wallet out. 'I'll treat you to lunch,' he said as he got up and went over to the waitress who flirted with him as he paid. Ding Niu thought he seemed in a hurry to leave, cutting the waitress short and walking out the door without glancing back.

Ding would have understood the reason for the lieutenant's actions had he known what the lieutenant's 'boss' had said to him very recently.

'Things have changed. I don't have any more jobs for you in the near future. And you need to lie low for a bit. I appreciate all you've done for me. Here's something to tide you over until I contact you again.' He had handed the lieutenant a thick envelope containing a lot of notes. 'Just one thing,' the boss added. 'Make very sure that the big half-witted guy who's helped you in doing jobs for me never says anything to anyone.'

After his companion in crime departed, Ding Niu stayed on, drinking a fresh cup of tea. He nervously kept checking the time, and five minutes later he left the restaurant and walked over to his six-year-old Geely. He stood outside the car and once again checked his watch. Then, in the distance, came the sound of a huge explosion. He muttered to himself, 'Vroom! The Nissan blows up!'

The Small Ox grinned. *The timer worked. The red Nissan must have exploded just when the lieutenant reached the tunnel below the Huangpu River. Five kilos of explosives would have made a fireball as big as the one that blew up Professor Du's car. The bastard deserved it! He can't just leave me to starve. But now I'll get all the fancy equipment he has in his apartment. I should get a lot of money for it. OK, time to go. I've gotta get to the lieutenant's apartment before anyone else does.*

He opened the door to the Geely, climbed in, and turned on the ignition.

The car exploded, sending a ball of flame skyward with a thunderous noise.

The waitress and several customers ran outside when they heard the earsplitting sound of the explosion. The cook and the dishwasher quickly joined them. The small group gawked speechless at the black smoke emanating from the burning Geely. Finally, the waitress said, 'That must be that big young man's car. The poor man must be totally charred. Horrible! I'd better call the police.' She hurried back into the restaurant. The cook and the dishwasher, shaking their heads, followed her.

'What's going on anyway,' nervously asked one of the customers. 'I heard the muffled sound of another explosion not five minutes ago.'

The customers continued to peer at the car, wondering if the big young man was really in it when it exploded. Then neighbours came to gawk, but when police sirens were heard, the crowd quickly dissipated, leaving only three men who kept staring at the smouldering car still sending black smoke skyward.

At about the same time the two hitmen blew each other up in Shanghai, the CFO of SAEC was 10,000 metres in the air on his way from Shanghai to Hong Kong. In Hong Kong he changed both planes and identities. He had a Hong Kong passport issued in the name of Lu Sanfu which he used to make sure no one would know he had gone to Singapore. No one at SAEC even knew he had left Shanghai.

Today, Thursday, he had an appointment to see Fan's banker. He planned to request that all the SAEC money, including the hefty profit, be sent to a bank in Liechtenstein as he had been ordered to do by his uncle. He smiled as he got out of his taxi at the bank, even as the midday heat seared his skin. He had no idea Singapore would be so hot, but then this was his first trip outside China other than a short holiday in Japan four years ago.

As he entered the impressive door of the bank, he smiled, pleased with himself. So far, everything had gone as planned. He told the guard that he had an appointment with Nelson Ing, and within minutes a young woman arrived to escort him up to the banker's private office. A short man with a pockmarked face had greeted him in very good English and cordially asked what he could do for Lei. He bade Lei to sit down.

Lei Tao explained in barely intelligible English that he had come for the money in the SAEC account. Ing's attitude changed subtly. He said in flawless Mandarin, 'Why hasn't President Fan come himself? I don't normally deal with agents for our clients.'

Lei Tao, too nervous even to realize Ing had switched to speaking Chinese, explained in Mandarin that the president couldn't get away from Shanghai and so had asked him to go see Ing. 'I'm the chief financial officer of SAEC. I have all the bank account information for you. I am not asking for the money for myself, but merely that the funds be transferred to another bank.' Lei took a piece of paper out of his pocket and handed it across the desk to Ing.

Ing scanned the sheet of paper, looked up at Lei, and said, 'I find it really odd that the president didn't call me to ask that the money be sent to another bank. I'll need to see your passport or a credible ID . . . and you also have to give me a code sentence. All the accounts like the president's need a pass phrase in order to access the money in them,' said Ing, smiling. But the look in his eyes was far from friendly.

'A code phrase?' blurted out Lei. 'The information I just gave you even includes the PIN . . . '

'This account was set up with an extra security precaution. In addition to all the information on this sheet, you have to give the code sentence attached to the account.'

Lei Tao was totally flustered and unable to reply. He'd never heard of a code sentence for accessing an account. Despite the air conditioning in the office, he began to sweat.

Lei stammered, 'I guess, well . . . President Fan must have forgotten to give me the code phrase.'

The banker rose and said in an officious tone, 'I find this most irregular. I won't waste any more of your time. Please tell the president to call me if he wants the funds sent to another bank. Please do remember, we are talking about a very large amount of money here.'

Lei stood up slowly and the banker started move towards the door and suddenly stopped and said in a mocking tone, 'We should have thought of this sooner. If he can't come himself, I could call him now. What about it?'

As flustered as he was, Lei managed to mumble, 'As I've said, he is busy. He is away . . . in Beijing . . . for meetings. So he sent me.'

Ing said with a disparaging smile, 'I have his personal phone number . . . '

Lei stood mute, and Ing ushered him out.

Seething, Lei caught a passing taxi a few minutes later and returned to his hotel. His return flight wasn't until the next morning but there was no point in staying in Singapore any longer. He checked for earlier flights and found one that would get him to Hong Kong just after midnight. *That bastard Fan! How did he think he was going to get away with not telling us the code sentence! We'll have it beaten out of him!*

Lei Tao packed his small carry-on and slumped down on the bed. There were hours before he had to leave for the airport, so he picked up the remote from the bedside table and turned the TV on to a news channel in Chinese.

More nonsense about that earthquake and tsunami in Japan. Why were they making such a big fuss over it? Tens of thousands of people died in earthquakes in China and they made the news only for a few days.

But wait? What's this news item from Shanghai?

Lei Tao was astounded at learning that car bombs had blown up two vehicles and their drivers yesterday at midday. There was no mention of the identity of the victims or who was behind the crimes. Lei Tao was momentarily distracted from his huge problem. *What's going on in Shanghai? More car bombings? Another one since Professor Du?*

41

Dublin, 3–4 September

While some of the original team that plotted to take down the Japanese government bonds had got their comeuppance, the Americans had more than fulfilled their hopes—or, rather, their unabashed greed. Shrewd but cautious Peter Scheinbaum had made nearly 4.2 billion dollars. He had short sold the JGB and a dozen Japanese stocks as a member of the Fan group, and got his share of what his brokerage had made from commissions and interest, both charged at considerably higher than the going rates from each member of the group. Then, without telling Josh Fried, he had short sold the JGB and various Japanese stock on his own.

Josh Fried hadn't made quite as much money, but he became so fantastically rich that he decided he deserved a real holiday. After a stopover in London, he would take his Irish wife back to Dublin to enjoy the luxury she had never had while she lived there. He booked them into a suite at the Four Seasons for a week and arranged for the hotel's car to pick them up at the airport. Christa would arrive in style.

Fried knew why his wife was unusually restive as they arrived in Dublin. At 18, she had escaped from the drab little town of Wexford on the southeast coast and made her way to Dublin where she had worked as a waitress and a sometime model. But by the time she was 25, her modelling career was virtually at an end, so she had moved to London and another restaurant job. Seven years ago she had met Josh, who was in London on business.

Divorced from his second wife the year before, Josh was 'entranced' by Christa. He gave her lavish gifts, took her to Paris a few times and finally proposed. Though he was old enough to be her father, and overweight, with a large bulbous nose, she had accepted his proposal. He was not certain that she loved him, but he hoped she might in time. He was always considerate, often amusing and he made her feel like a queen—at least at first. For the past several years he had been working almost all of the time, and often cancelled dinner engagements, forgot to show up at the theatre and was out of town on business far too often. She hadn't complained, but he was aware that despite their opulent apartment in Manhattan and all the luxuries he showered upon her, she was bored, lonely and unhappy.

But now Josh could reward her patience. When they were alone at last in their suite, Josh revealed more about his business than he ever had before.

'Sweetheart, since I've made a fortune, I can now pay back the 600 million I owe to banks and almost 150 million dollars in bonuses to my senior guys and the best quants in the firm. They've learned to use an algorithm a German guy cooked up. I didn't want to worry you by telling you that over the past few years my hedge fund had been doing rather poorly and I had to max out the credit lines my banks gave me. But now, even after paying everything I owe, I'm richer by almost one and a half billion dollars!'

'One and a half billion dollars! I can't even imagine that much money, Josh.'

'You better—because it'll be all yours when I'm gone. I'm 62 . . . so maybe you don't have long to wait. You know I'm leaving everything to you.'

'Don't talk nonsense, Josh. You've got at least 20 or 30 more years to go.'

Her husband of seven years smiled at her as he took her hand. 'Tomorrow we'll go to a realtor and find out if the castle you have your eyes on is available. Price is no object!'

Fried kept his promise. The following morning they visited an estate agency. A very deferential realtor had been waiting with a list of Irish castles for sale. Christa was disappointed that the one she had seen at Easter was no longer on the market, but there were quite a few others that looked promising. They promised to return the following day for more details on the two properties they decided to view.

The couple spent the rest of the day going their separate ways. Josh, who was exhausted with jet lag and his last few hectic days in New York, hung around the hotel's pool. Christa went shopping, and returned with so many packages that a porter had to help carry them up to their suite. For dinner they took a short cab ride to Dunne and Crescenzi, an award-winning Italian restaurant that the concierge recommended.

Josh was in a cheerful mood. He ordered 'the best Chianti you have' and an antipasto to start. They had just begun to eat when Fried's phone chirped. He apologized to Christa, looked at the caller ID and said, 'Damn, I've got to take this.' He listened for a minute and Christa saw the colour slowly drain from his face. 'I'll be back,' he said, and walked out of the restaurant, his ear still glued to his phone.

When he returned to the table after several minutes, he said abruptly, 'We're leaving . . . we have to go. I have to make some calls and I need to make them from our suite.'

Christa could tell that something serious had happened. 'What about dinner?'

'The hell with dinner! The roof's caved in. That kraut Adler and his damn algorithm! Come on!! We can get back to the hotel quicker if we walk instead of waiting for a cab.'

By the time he said, 'Come on!' Josh was practically yelling at Christa. A middle-aged woman at the next table stared at him. He pulled out a wad of notes and thrust some at the waiter, then strode out of the restaurant without waiting for Christa.

As they had hurried down Sandymount Avenue, it began to drizzle. 'What happened Josh?' Christa asked, by the time she had caught up with him.

'My hedge fund just lost 2.45 billion dollars! I'm out of the office for less than a week and this happens! Jim Kirkpatrick called to tell me he and Glen Evers . . . our quant . . . used Adler's algorithm to make more money—just as we've been doing recently. Well, they bet big last Friday on the derivatives involving the oil futures and they got wiped out. To cover the loss, they bet even more and that lost even more. Jim did everything he could, but nothing doing. Snake eyes are snake eyes. In the financial community, news travels fast. Come next Monday, most of our clients will be pulling their money out of my hedge fund. We are going to be bankrupt . . . penniless, Christa.'

She was aghast. 'Did they have your permission to use . . . what you called algo . . . ? How could anyone lose so much money?'

'Algorithm . . . a bunch of complex equations we use to help us trade. Yeah, they did because it had been working like a charm. Easy. The financial market is nothing but a big casino. If you make a good bet, you can make billions. But make the wrong bet and you can lose billions. They bet on the derivatives they were very sure of . . . but they bet wrong. Morgan Stanley, Société Général, Sumitomo and UBS lost from 2 billion to 9 billion some years back and Greenfield and Stern lost 4.2 billion last year.'

By now he was almost running. Christa was having a hard time keeping up.

Josh muttered to himself, 'Damn! Why did I listen to Adler? Why did I let my people use something that I don't think even my best quant fully understood?'

As they crossed the rail line at Sandymount station, a dozen people who had just got out of a train crowded onto the pavement. Josh elbowed his way through them quickly but Christa could not.

Josh kept going without looking back. Christa followed him as best she could, getting wetter by the minute, her thoughts muddled. *Oh damn! I'm getting wet. Why can't Josh wait for me? Are we really penniless?*

Christa finally caught up with her husband at the traffic lights. By the time they reached the gate of the hotel, it was raining in earnest and they nearly sprinted into the building. As soon as they were in their suite, Christa hurriedly took off her wet coat and shoes and turned to her husband.

'You said we're penniless. Do you mean we now have to worry about how we live? Day to day?'

Fried, heedless of the water dripping water off his clothes, answered in a much quieter voice: 'Yes. My hedge fund will be finished when my clients pull their money out. That's why I'm going to call some people to see if someone can lend me a couple of billion dollars. Although I know my chance of getting a loan big enough to help me is zilch, I'm going to try to get as big a loan as I can. I should've done what an old president of a big Spanish bank did to sail through the 2008 financial crisis without a government bailout—he didn't allow his bank to use any algorithm in trading derivatives because he didn't understand how algorithms worked. So his bank traded in only very simple derivatives. But I had to deal in lots of derivatives using the best algorithms I could get because I'm running a hedge fund, and until now we made a lot of money.'

'You've no personal savings? Some money no one can get at?'

'I've only about a hundred thousand left in several accounts. But when we pay our outstanding bills, that'll be gone.'

'What about our apartment? Surely you can sell that and get enough money to tide us over for a while.'

'I'm sorry, Christa. The bank will take the apartment because I included it as a part of the collateral for a loan I took out some years ago. We've got to look for a cheap apartment somewhere. At my age and because of what's happened, I doubt I can get a high-paying job to let you live anywhere near the way you've been living since we got married. But at least we have each other,' her husband said, looking at Christa pleadingly.

Christa looked away and grabbed an apple from a dish of fruit on the coffee table without saying a word. She went into the bedroom and closed the door behind her.

Josh decided to let her be for a while to absorb what was going to happen to their life. *I know she won't like it, but it'll still be better than the life I rescued her from. She's now in her 30s—she surely doesn't want to return to the hard life of a waitress, on her feet for eight hours at a time. And I know she won't—and can't—go back to Wexford where her father ekes out a living as a fisherman. There's nothing for her there. But I won't give up yet! I don't think anyone can help me save my hedge fund, but I have to try.*

For over an hour he made calls, pleaded and begged, but the answers were what he had expected, 'Sorry, Josh, but given the size of a hole your hedge fund dug, I can't help you.' After making the last call, he cautiously opened the bedroom door to Christa fast asleep with the lights out. He crept into the bathroom and took a sleeping pill, and then a second. He knew he wasn't going to get any sleep without help. He crawled into his side of the huge king-sized bed. He felt like screaming out of despair and frustration as he listened to Christa's rhythmic breathing next to him, but within minutes he fell into a deep, drug-induced sleep.

Josh awoke with a foggy brain, a hangover from too much medication. *It has to be morning because I can see daylight through a crack in the drapes.* He looked over to Christa's side of the bed. She wasn't there. *What time is it anyway?* He looked at the bedside clock. *Past nine.*

Still groggy, he got out of bed and pattered to the door to the sitting room. Opening it, he found an empty room. *Where's Christa?*

Did she go down to the dining room for breakfast? He went back to the bedroom to the closet to get some fresh clothes. It was half empty—only his clothes were hanging in it.

Startled, Josh rushed to the bathroom. All Christa's toiletries were gone. He went back to the bedroom and opened the drapes. His wife's suitcase was gone, as was her handbag. He searched the entire suite but couldn't find a trace of his wife except for two large empty paper bags and a cardboard box in which Christa had brought back the things she had bought yesterday. And then his eyes lit on an envelope on the desk marked 'Josh'.

Josh knew without even opening the envelope that his wife had left him. *Christa is gone! Should I ask the people at Reception if they know where she's gone? No . . . that would just be too humiliating.*

Crushed, Josh slumped into a chair and put his head in his hands. He had lost everything—his business, his money and his beloved young wife. Finally he summoned the courage to open the envelope.

Dear Josh,

Forgive me for taking off, but I can't bear the thought of living hand to mouth again, always wondering if we can pay the bills. You have been very good to me, and I am ashamed that I am abandoning you when your fortunes are down. And I am too ashamed to tell you to your face that I cannot face poverty again. Please forget me. Do what you have to, but without worrying about me. I am not worth it.

May you find happiness in the future with someone who can support you through thick and thin.

Your very grateful Christa.

While Josh was reading the letter, Christa was settling into her seat on a plane bound for London's Heathrow Airport. As she fastened her seatbelt, once more she went over her decision to leave her husband.

Josh might be penniless, but I'm not. I have the 120,000 dollars in two savings accounts in New York that I've saved away from my housekeeping money, almost by instinct. I hated relying on the money that Josh handed me, generous though he always was. I also have all the jewellery he's given me, most of it in the safe in our New York apartment. I don't know how much I can sell it for, but certainly tens of thousands of dollars. As she thought about her future, a tear slowly rolled down her cheek. *From Heathrow, I'll fly to New York and get to the apartment before Josh can. I'll take my jewellery and my clothes, but that's all. I don't want anything else. Then what? I'm not going back to Ireland! And I can't stay in New York because that's where Josh will be. Maybe California? I can try my luck there. I just have to! I'm not going back to Josh. He's an old man already and I remember my mother change the diapers of her demented grandfather. I'd rather go back to waitressing than get stuck doing that!*

Christa's plane took off with a roar. She looked out her window at Ireland's emerald-green landscape. *Goodbye Ireland . . . Goodbye Josh . . . Hello San Francisco?*

42

Around the World, 5 September

On Saturday, 5 September, three potentially life-changing phone calls were made. One was from the vice mayor of Shanghai to his daughter on a remote farm on New Zealand's South Island, an hour's drive from Christchurch. At four in the afternoon in Shanghai, Mimi's father, Xia Xinbi had returned to his office after a meeting with the mayor. Smiling, he looked at the time, picked up the phone he was using to contact his daughter and called her in New Zealand. After seven rings, Geoff answered, rather to Xia's surprise.

'Mimi's out in the barn. I'll just take the phone out to her.'

Several minutes later Mimi came on the line, terribly excited. 'Father, I've just helped with the birth of twin lambs!' Then her voice changed. 'Why are you calling? Is everything OK?'

'We're OK, but I have news for you. Lei Tao has been arrested.'

'What? The CFO of SAEC? What for? Last week when we talked you told me Fan escaped from the Shanghai prison and the authorities didn't know where he was . . . Why Lei Tao?'

'From what I've heard, there seems to be enough evidence to show Fan is corrupt. And it appears that so is Lei Tao.'

Mimi was astonished. 'He's such a nice man! It's hard to believe he's a criminal.'

'The authorities have evidence of his involvement in embezzling large sums of money from SAEC. They were looking into SAEC's financial records after Fan's arrest. They also found evidence in the apartment of a SAEC employee, the man who committed suicide or was killed by Fan—the police aren't sure which. Then this week, Lei Tao didn't come to work and no one knew where he was. The investigating team took the opportunity to search for more records at SAEC. And it was your friend Bingbing who found a second set of books well hidden in a supply cupboard. It seems she's been suspicious for some time about how Fan, the CEO, could be embezzling funds without the CFO's knowledge.'

Mimi was stunned and needed a moment to absorb all this alarming information. Finally, she said, 'So Fan and Lei were in it together? You said President Fan could've killed the man from whom the authorities got more evidence. Could they . . . I mean Fan and Lei . . . also been in cahoots and responsible for the disappearance and deaths of at least three men working for SAEC?'

'We don't know. Obviously that will be looked into. We don't know yet if other employees were involved. But Lei Tao is safely in jail. He was arrested yesterday when he returned home from a secret trip to Singapore.'

'Singapore!' Mimi almost shouted. 'What was he doing there?'

'I don't know. My friend in the police told me that Lei Tao travelled under an assumed name and using a forged Hong Kong passport and that he was arrested when he came back to Shanghai. The police are questioning him about what he was doing in Singapore. I'm telling you all this to let you know that I think it's safe now for you to come home.'

'But Father, you told me earlier that President Fan escaped from prison and that no one knows where he is. I think I'd better stay here until you know everything that's going on. If someone like Lei Tao is involved, we can't be sure about mostly anyone else at SAEC. And if Fan is still at large, he still could have someone . . . '

Mimi didn't finish saying what was one her mind because she still hadn't told her parents about her terrifying trip to Tokyo. She was still very afraid that Fan would send someone after her.

'I know you're worried. But I doubt that Fan will be sending anyone to harm you. I'm sure he's preoccupied in trying to find a way out of his plight. Your mother and I miss you! And aren't you lonely in such an isolated place? So different from Shanghai with all cultural amenities!'

'I miss you too, but I feel safer here for the time being.'

Because her father didn't push her to come back to Shanghai 'for now', Mimi didn't go on to explain that she did feel much safer out in the foothills of the mountains on a remote station accessible only across a riverbed. And when that had water in it, only by helicopter. And that the attraction of the station was the lambs, one or more born daily now, and even more her New Zealand companion who had brought her here.

In Tokyo, on the same Saturday, Shig Tanaka saw his future brighten. Yesterday he had submitted his letter of resignation to the woman who served as the secretary to the chairman of the board. Honma was sure to be fired and the bank was almost certain to go bankrupt. He thought it prudent to gracefully leave now. At least he had more than enough money to live on very comfortably.

This morning Tanaka sat at home having a leisurely second cup of espresso. It was really quite a relief to be free of the bank. He hadn't realized how stressful the summer months had been. But he no longer had to worry about the bank's impending insolvency or his relationship with Honma and the board members. With what Scheinbaum had sent him, his deceased wife's legacy and his small savings and investments, his total wealth was almost 20 million dollars.

As he contemplated how he was going to live as a very wealthy man and if he would miss working, his thoughts were interrupted by his phone. To his surprise, the call was from the board chairman of Sumida Bank.

'Vice President Tanaka, I'm at the bank. I know it's Saturday, but can you come meet me in the boardroom as soon as possible? I'll send a car.'

Tanaka was surprised. *What does he want? He knows I've sent in my letter of resignation. The fact that he's offered to send a car means he knows I no longer have the use of one. Why does he still refer to me as vice president?'*

'I'll be waiting for the car, sir.'

As soon as Tanaka entered the boardroom, Chairman Kawata stood up to greet him, all smiles. 'Thank you for seeing me on a Saturday.'

What's going on? Why is he being so gracious to an employee who's just resigned? Tanaka was thoroughly puzzled. Kawata waved him to a seat and as the two sat down, he began to explain why he had called Tanaka in.

'Vice President, I'm so glad I caught you. The board was so sorry to receive your letter of resignation yesterday . . . after all these years you've given us. So very sorry.' Kawata said, still smiling, 'We've decided we don't want to accept your resignation.'

Kawata went on as if he couldn't see the look of astonishment on Tanaka's face.

'The board has requested that I ask you to reconsider your decision.'

'You mean, you want me to stay on as vice president?' Tanaka was incredulous.

'No, no, that's not what the board wants at all. We would like to you take the leadership of the bank, to become president.'

Tanaka was dumfounded. Then his face clouded over as he realized what this meant. *Wily Kawata is offering me to become president of a bank that's going bankrupt! He wants me to deal with the mess . . . the creditors, the courts, the unions! How stupid!*

Kawata continued to smile. 'I understand your reaction. We are offering you a promotion you didn't expect. But if you would be so kind, would you come to a special meeting of the board tomorrow morning at 10 and hear us out? I have called an emergency meeting with the approval of a majority of the board members because we need to move fast. I've called you in today so that you'll have time to think over the bank's plans and our offer.'

'Sir, I appreciate the offer . . . but the days of our bank are numbered . . . '

Kawata held up his hand. 'Yes, against your repeated warnings, we hold an unusually large amount of JGB. As a result, Sumida can't survive as it is now. So for the last several days some of the board members and I have been in talks with the Manhattan Trust Bank, which we know has been looking for a bank to buy in Japan. I talked with Tom Kendall, the president, whom I have known for the past 20 years, and Manhattan Trust has agreed in principle . . . that is, subject to due diligence . . . to buy 51 per cent of our shares but keep the name Sumida. Tom says he wants a Japanese president "for the foreseeable future" . . . so I recommended you and he accepted my proposal. He says he knows you already from your years in New York. Of course, Honma will be formally dismissed at tomorrow's meeting. We obviously can't make you an offer while he is still nominally president.'

Tanaka was silent, taking in what he had just heard. *I've met Kendall a few times . . . an able . . . and shrewd banker. For the foreseeable future? It could be long enough till I'm ready to retire.*

At last he said, 'I know Tom . . . he was the chief loan officer at Manhattan Trust when I was in New York and I've done some business with him. I am honoured by the board's decision to offer me the job, but I need to think. Of course, I'll come to the meeting tomorrow. By then I'll have made up my mind.'

As Tanaka took his leave, he smiled. *I already know I'm going to accept the offer. To finally become president of Sumida Bank! Now I know what makes me really happy isn't a fortune but getting the job I've coveted for so long!*

'Now make a giraffe,' demanded Mikey of his father who was cooking animal pancakes for his little son.

'How about an elephant instead,' suggested Nick as he turned a hippopotamus over with a spatula just as his phone rang.

'Hey, Bess, can you come tend to the animals?' Nick called out to his wife. 'I've got to take a call from Ken.'

His wife hurried into the kitchen and grabbed the spatula while Nick took his phone into the living room.

'Nick,' said a familiar and excited voice. 'I hope I didn't wake you up. I had the most amazing conversation this morning. I don't want to talk about this with anyone in Japan. So I could scarcely wait to call you.'

'Hey, Ken, you sound more cheerful than I've heard you in weeks. Who were you talking to? It's Saturday evening for you, right?'

Without answering the question, Ken said, 'I still can't believe it, but I got a phone call from the leader of the opposition party.'

'You mean Torao Nishi? A very smart guy . . . I've heard him speak a few times on American TV. He sounded more like a thoughtful European social democrat than the leader of a centre-left Japanese party.'

'Right. He wants me at a meeting tomorrow. He hinted that he wants me to do something very important even though he wouldn't say what it was.'

'Don't be too self-deprecating, Ken. In my book, you are as good as the best economist in Japan. That's great news. Do you think Nishi is planning a move to try to oust the PM?'

'I'm certain he is. The prime minister focused on dealing with the effects of the earthquake and tsunami and did nothing about the effects of the JGB's collapse on our economy. Now he's in the hospital, and no one else is doing anything either. The finance minister's just as useless. In the meantime, our economy continues to go to hell.

I hope Nishi succeeds in getting enough support to become prime minister.'

'You have to do your best to help Nishi come up with the policies Japan needs to adopt immediately.'

Ken stopped for a moment and then, surprising Nick, said in an anguished voice, 'We're only just beginning to find out the real impact of the tanking of the government bonds. Everything I expected is happening with a vengeance. Long-term interest rates have gone up, which means people aren't buying houses or cars and people who need to repair their property damaged by earthquake and tsunami are struggling. A lot of businesses, including some big firms and banks, have gone under or are about to go under . . . more people are losing their jobs . . . money is leaving Japan. And you know how most Japanese think and behave—if other people are having a hard time, you shouldn't be having a good one. So even people who can afford to take a holiday or buy a new appliance aren't doing so . . . '

Nick interrupted, 'Ken, stop! I know all that. But it sounds like you'll have a chance to really affect what happens to Japan and its economy by advising Nishi at the meeting tomorrow!'

'I sure hope so. I'm not sure if Nishi can get together a coalition to obtain a majority in the Diet, but he seems to have got a promise from a number of members in the PM's party that they'll help him head a new government. If that happens, I think a few dozen more members from the PM's party will abandon the sick, old PM and vote for Nishi.'

'This is an extraordinary time for Japan . . . and extraordinary things can happen . . . they've happened before . . . ' Nick did his best to sound upbeat.

'Yes, we made almost revolutionary changes after the Meiji Restoration of 1868 and again after the Second World War. Now we need to do it again. For starters, I know Nishi is in favour of changing the electoral system so the farmers' votes for the PM's party don't count three times as much as urban votes for the opposition parties.

But that's the easy part. We have to create demand by investing in the future and paying for it, not by selling more and more JGB but by raising taxes on the rich, on big corporations and on financial institutions. We can't continue to raise the regressive sales tax, which gives the people less money to spend. That's going to take some doing. But we have to make a start!'

'Good luck! We've talked about capitalism needing a serious overhaul—to make it less plutocratic, more equal in distributions of income and wealth and a lot of other deep systemic changes like the US had made during the 1930s.' Before Ken could end the call, Nick asked, 'How is your family faring?'

'Coping, but barely. My sister-in-law's moved in with her mother for the time being and the kids have been enrolled in school here. They'll survive, but it's been tough.'

Before Nick could respond, he heard a shout from the kitchen.

'Daddy, Daddy! Mommy's made a giraffe with a long neck and she didn't break it. Come see and have breakfast!'

Nick grinned and said, 'Ken, did you hear Mikey?'

'Yup. Loud and clear. Now go have breakfast. Thanks for talking to me. Give my best to Bess and Mikey.'

Ken hung up, thinking, *If Nishi succeeds in creating a governing coalition and can be persuaded to adopt the policies Nick and I just talked about, the Japanese economy might be able to get out of the disastrous mess in maybe five or six years.*

43

Tokyo, 6–7 September

'I'm hoping to be discharged by the middle of the week. Can't govern a country from a hospital bed!' The prime minister started out in a firm voice, which dissolved into a quiver and then a coughing fit.

His senior counsellor, Saburo Baba, moved to his bedside and propped him up, then handed him a glass of water. The PM didn't look or sound fit enough to govern Japan, and Baba doubted whether the doctors would let him return to the official residence so soon. He looked as if he had aged almost a decade since he'd had the heart attack.

While the PM tried to stop coughing and compose himself enough to explain why he had called Baba in on a Sunday, Baba went over to the window and looked down at the street below. It was a lazy Sunday, a few people were strolling down the street and there was only the occasional, muted sound of traffic. But Baba noticed a shabbily dressed man standing across the street and staring up at the hospital. Baba could swear that the man was looking at him. *It has to be the same man I saw when I visited the PM two days ago.* He remembered the dirty white bucket hat that hid the top part of the man's face and large black-rimmed glasses. The same black shirt, black pants and dirty white trainers. Suddenly the man turned away and hurried off down the street. *Who could that be? Should I tell someone that I've seen a suspicious character looking up at the PM's room?*

The PM suddenly began to give Baba a laundry list of requests— personal errands and phone calls, including one to the American ambassador, requesting he postpone their scheduled meeting by a week. Baba knew he was not the right person for any of these tasks but he dutifully took notes on his iPad. He would figure out later how to get most of them done by the PM's chief secretary. *I appreciate his trust in me, but I'm not his errand boy—I'm his senior advisor on international issues.*

The PM, tiring quickly, fell silent and Baba, promising to get everything done, prepared to leave. As he went over to draw down the Venetian blinds, he glanced out of the window and saw the same man back at the same place, looking up at the window again. *Yes, I should tell someone about this guy.*

Baba quietly left the room, and on his way out told the officer on the PM's security detail, sitting in the suite's outer room, that the PM was resting. He went down to the lobby and at Reception asked for the PM's chief security officer. The woman on duty directed him to the hospital's cafeteria.

Capt. Oka greeted Baba warmly and suggested he get some coffee and join him.

'What's up?' asked Oka when Baba came back with his drink.

'There's a guy out on the street staring up at the PM's room. He was there two days ago and he's there again this afternoon.'

'Yeah, we're aware of him. He concerns us too.'

'Do you know who he is?' asked Baba.

'Not yet. We can only tell you what he isn't,' said Oka. Baba looked puzzled. Oka smiled. 'He comes into the hospital daily and asks at Reception about the PM. He's been doing this for most of the past week. The same woman was on duty on three of the days and was puzzled by this scruffy-looking man hanging around and asking about the prime minister. Fortunately, she told one of our guys about him. So yesterday I put one of our female officers on Reception duty.' Oka paused for a few sips of his coffee.

Baba said, 'And . . . ?'

'Well, when he came in yesterday to inquire after the PM again, our officer chatted him up. She said that, as far as she knew, the PM is out of the woods and would be discharged soon. She fibbed and said she had the date and time of his discharge on a form and pretended to look for it in a drawer. As she'd hoped he would, the man leaned over the counter to try and look what she was doing. So, we managed to get his fingerprints off the edge of the counter.' Oka laughed. 'Of course, she had to tell him she couldn't find the information because someone must have taken it away.'

'And . . . ?' inquired Baba, now very intrigued.

'Our comprehensive database says he has no criminal record, so we don't know who he is. He could just be some kind of a nut. But we're keeping an eye on him.'

'You can't question him?'

The security officer gave Baba a condescending look. 'Senior Counsellor, of course we can, but only informally, since he hasn't done anything. Inquiring about the prime minister's health isn't a crime. Trust me. I know what I'm doing to guard the PM. I told my men about this guy and I'm keeping my officer at the Reception desk. So, are you satisfied?'

'I'm just glad you're aware of this guy. His staring up at the window of the PM's room rather unnerved me.'

A day later, Baba was back at the hospital to report to the PM. As he neared the entrance, he was relieved to see that the scruffy man was gone. *Well, that's one thing less to worry about.*

Baba had turned over to the PM's housekeeper the few personal requests he had made, then given Chief Secretary Fukunaga the other messages and finally called the American Embassy himself.

As he reflected on how the PM, once a wily politician, was now looking and behaving, he was convinced that the country's leader was, as his American friends would say, 'losing it'. *If he weren't, he wouldn't mix up his private and public life and ignore our economic crisis. And why does he refuse to let the deputy prime minister act in his stead? So what if he's the leader of another faction, he's in the same political party.*

Baba walked past the nurses' station, greeting them with a nod. And then he saw a doctor walking towards him from the other end of the corridor, heading for the PM's suite. The doctor reached the door, pushed it open, and walked in.

Baba didn't want to disturb the PM while a doctor was examining him so he slowed his pace. *Wait a minute! Something isn't right! What is it? Damn! The shoes . . . the dirty white trainers!* Instantly Baba was on the run. He shoved open the door to the suite with such a bang that the security officer in the outer room looked up, startled.

'Check the man who went into the PM's room. I don't think he's a doctor. Hurry!'

The security officer moved before Baba finished speaking. He threw open the door to the bedroom, Baba just behind him. The man with a crazed expression on his face was holding a four-inch knife over the sleeping PM. *It's him, the nut who's been staring at the PM's window!*

The officer yelled at the man, 'Drop the knife!'

The man whirled around, then slashed at the air with the knife. Baba froze, and saw, out of the corner of his eyes, the officer hesitate, then touch his gun. *Don't, it's too dangerous . . . in this small room.*

The man suddenly raised the knife as if to charge. The policeman lunged to one side, grabbed the man's left leg and pulled it towards himself. The man yelled and fell to the floor on his back, still holding the knife. The officer kicked the man's hand and the knife clattered to the floor. Then he grabbed the man's right arm, twisted it and shoved the man over onto his stomach. Within seconds he had handcuffed the man. That done, he pulled out his phone and called his superior.

Baba looked at the man who stared back at him, his flushed face contorted with pain.

And through all of the commotion, the PM slept on.

The man started gabbling. 'He ruined my life! He ruined our country! He doesn't deserve to live! My company went bankrupt and my employees have no jobs! It's all because of him!

As the man ranted on, Capt. Oka and a uniformed officer rushed into the room, two nurses on their heels. The noise woke up the PM who groggily asked, 'What is this? What are all of you doing here?'

Hearing no answer, the prime minister seemed to have gone back to sleep. Baba followed Oka, leaving the two nurses with the PM.

Baba was more concerned than ever. He believed the man had really meant to kill the PM. But what he found even more worrisome was the PM's condition. He was obviously on medication so strong that it made him sleep through the ruckus. Even when he woke up, he seemed totally disoriented. Baba hoped this incident could be kept from the media—it would make a field day out of knife-wielding assailant and the PM's befuddled reaction.

Hours later Baba called Ken Murai. He simply had to talk to someone who would be discreet. Ken answered on the fifth ring.

'Did I catch you at a bad time?' asked Baba.

'No, it's fine. We've just finished a late dinner. I had to fish my phone out of my briefcase in another room. What's up?'

'Are you alone? This has to remain just between you and me.'

'Just a sec. I'm going to my study. What's happened?' Baba could hear the sound of a door closing and Ken said, 'OK, what's up?'

'A crazy man tried to kill the PM.'

'What? How? Is he OK?' Even the usually calm Ken was shaken.

'He's OK, a security guy got him before he could get at the PM. But, as you'd expect the chief of the PM's security team is mortified.'

'What happened?'

Baba told him, and then said, 'I had a long talk with the chief of the PM's security detail a couple of hours ago. The man was the owner of a small factory in Osaka that subcontracts odd metal bits for cars. He went bankrupt and had to let his 12 employees go. Then he lost his house in the recent earthquake. His family is currently living in a school gymnasium and subsisting on what little savings he had. The guy couldn't take it any longer. He blames the PM for everything. So he came up to Tokyo several days ago determined to get revenge.'

Ken responded, sighing audibly. 'I feel for him. Because the Bank of Japan has been printing money to buy government bonds and making the yen cheap in order to increase our exports, car manufacturers have been selling more cars cheaply overseas. But the subcontractors have to buy the raw materials they need at higher prices and the companies they were supplying haven't been paying enough to keep them in business.'

'Yes, Ken, even I know taxes for ordinary people have gone up but wages haven't. Then came the earthquake and tsunami. The PM didn't cause that. But the government hasn't done anything to help the victims. The guy couldn't stand seeing his family and his long-time employees suffer. He felt had to do something to stop the PM from continuing to harm everyone. He said he had nothing to live for so decided to act.'

'Bach, you said the chief of security is mortified. How did the guy manage to get into the PM's room?'

'I think the security was a bit sloppy. The man figured out that the easiest way to breach security was to pose as a doctor. Anyone can buy a white coat and stethoscope. Maybe he even stole them from somewhere in the hospital. The hospital is easy to get into. The security chief had been prepared for this guy trying something, but no one thought to look for him disguised as a doctor. It's just lucky a very good security officer was in the outer room of the suite.'

'So he is the hero of the day. I take it this isn't going to make the news?'

Baba didn't mention that it was he who recognized the assailant and alerted security. He merely answered Ken's question.

'The security chief doesn't want the news to come out for obvious reasons. And I agree with him. We don't need such news when our country is already in a big mess. But if one of the hospital staff relates the attack to someone, even in confidence, it's going to spread like wildfire and the mass media will be on it in no time. You know how these things go.'

'Don't I know it! But, Bach, the PM is safe and the guy will go to jail. So all's well that ends well'.

'Not quite, and that's what worries me! I'm no longer certain our PM is mentally competent, at least not at present. I know he's on strong medication, but even after he woke up he didn't seem to comprehend what was going on. I mean, he didn't react like a normal person would in the same circumstances. And he's been making such strange requests of me lately that I'm beginning to worry whether he's competent to do anything . . . let alone govern the country . . . especially given the crisis we're in.'

This time Ken had no words to allay his friend's anxiety.

44

Kunming and Haikou, China, 8–10 September

Three weeks after the earthquake and tsunami, the situation in Japan was still grim. The search for bodies had ended, but there were still over 1,000 people unaccounted for. While the death toll would likely be less than a quarter of that of the 2011 disaster, the number of people affected was far larger. Millions of people lived in the Nagoya and Osaka areas and all along the coast of the islands facing the Pacific. Surprising many, the biggest problem turned out to be Osaka. Built on soft ground, many parts of Osaka had suffered far more liquefaction that anyone had anticipated, and houses that looked sound from a distance were no longer habitable. More than a million people were still without electricity and running water.

The economy, too, was worsening by the day. The rates of bankruptcy and unemployment were continuing to rise steadily and, because of the much-depreciated yen, the prices of petrol, electricity and food were skyrocketing. Rumours that Japan could default in paying the interest on its government bonds had started to be bandied about, even in the responsible media. Crimes were increasing in a country long vaunted for its low crime rate. And the number of suicides was rising at an alarming rate.

What was compounding the nightmare was the veritable political paralysis. The ailing prime minister was hanging on to power despite a brewing rebellion by almost one-third of the Dietmen of his own party. Neither he nor his cabinet, especially the finance minister, seemed to comprehend the gravity of the crisis. Not only were the politicians allied to the PM squabbling, so also were the various opposition parties. Voices in various foreign countries were sounding the alarm about the crisis confronting the third-largest economy in the world.

TV news, newspapers, online articles and especially CNN kept Japan's troubles at the forefront of the news. But deep in the mountains of southwest China there was a group of well-educated Chinese men who had not heard of the Japanese disaster. They not only didn't know what was going on in the world, they didn't even know where they were. All they knew was that they had been transported, unconscious, to this black prison which they were sure was run by members of a local triad, the black society of criminals. They had simply disappeared from their former lives and had no hope of release.

Until this morning.

This morning was different. Fan opened his eyes to find light streaming in through the small windows. They had never been allowed to sleep past dawn. He saw two men sitting on the edge of their bunks, looking around with puzzled eyes.

Fan got up and went to the door. When he turned the knob, the door swung open. Astonished, Fan announced, 'We're not locked in!' Another man shouted, 'Hey, the door's unlocked!' Others, awakened by the shout, began to talk and soon the room was abuzz with speculation. Fan pulled on his jacket and shoes and went out, followed slowly by the others.

The small group made its way to the shack where they cooked and ate. No guards appeared. Fan heard a clamor of voices from within and opened the door to find several Miao excitedly jabbering in their own language. 'What's happened?' Fan asked in Chinese. 'The door of our room was unlocked.'

The young guard named Zha responded. 'The centre has been closed,' he said in much better Chinese than Fan had heard him use before.

'Closed?'

'It's no longer in operation. The Han Chinese criminals in charge left in the middle of the night. We don't know why. We're on our own. We've all lost our jobs,' Zha said, looking glum. 'You are luckier . . . now all of you can leave.'

Fan's first thought was: *Now I can leave this godforsaken place and get at my money.* 'Why did the Chinese leave so suddenly?' he asked.

'We don't know,' said Zha, 'They told us nothing. In the middle of the night we heard two vehicles start up. By the time I came out I saw the second pick-up truck pull out. Loaded with boxes and other stuff.'

This is my chance . . . I've got to get the hell out of here as soon as possible. 'Where are we?' he asked Zha. 'I mean . . . exactly where is this centre?'

'In the Miao Autonomous Region, deep in the mountains of Yunnan Province.'

'What's the nearest city or town?'

'Kunming, about 60 kilometres north.'

'Almost 5,000 kilometres from home,' sighed someone behind him. 'We don't have any money, so we'll just have to wait until someone comes and rescues us. Someone must have found out about this illegal prison.'

Another voice said, 'Well, we might as well have breakfast.' The small group trooped over to the kitchen.

I've got to get out of here before any police arrive and realize I'm supposed to be in jail in Shanghai. Let's see if my treating the Miao guards as human beings has worked.

Fan tapped Zha on the arm, 'Can I talk to you a minute? Outside?'

Zha looked at him quizzically but followed Fan out of the shack.

'I have a proposition for you.'

'A proposition?'

'I'm going to make you a very rich young man.'

'I know you don't have any money,' Zha jeered at Fan.

'I can get it . . . so listen to me.'

'Talk, I'm listening.'

'I didn't give out the critical code words needed to access my bank account in Singapore. I also have another account at the same bank that the Chinese . . . the RO . . . didn't know about. So my money is still there.'

Zha's brows knotted as tried to decide whether Fan was making up a story to dupe him.

In fact, even as he spoke, Fan was worried about the SAEC money and the profit he had made from the project. He had expected that within a few days of giving out the account information, he would be called back into the office again and beaten for not giving what was needed to access the account. But a week had passed and he hadn't been called back again.

Had Ing ignored the need for the added code and handed over all of SAEC's money? Well, if that's happened, there's nothing I can do about it. But I still have 8 million dollars in my 'private account'. I really have to convince Zha that I'm not bullshitting him.

Fan hurriedly said, 'I swear I can get money from either one of these accounts. Just trust me. I'm willing to pay you handsomely if you'll help me get to Kunming. I know there's no public transportation and I can't walk 60 kilometres. Can you get me there?'

Zha was still unconvinced so Fan plowed on: 'Kunming is a big-enough city . . . it must have a few big banks that do a lot of wire-transferring of money. If I can open an account, my bank in Singapore can wire me money.'

'Not so fast. Before we talk about how I'll get you to Kunming, I want you to know that if you are making up stories about having money in Singapore just to get you to Kunming, I can make you regret it *very*, very painfully. Got it?'

Fan nodded. 'Got it. I have money in Singapore. I swear. You heard the RO ask for details.'

'How long will it take to wire-transfer money from Singapore to Kunming?'

'Today is Thursday. We should have the money by tomorrow.'

'How much?'

'These days I can get the wire-transferred dollars in yuan. I'm going to ask for 200,000 dollars to be wired . . . and I'll give you half. Close to 600,000 yuan.'

Zha's jaw dropped. Fan smiled. He guessed it was easily more than 10 times Zha's annual income. Finally, smiling for the first time since Fan had met him, Zha said, 'You've been decent to me. Treated me like a human being, not like these crooked Han Chinese treat us Miao.'

Fan mentally breathed a sigh of relief.

'So, it's a deal? You give me 100,000 US dollars' worth of yuan and I'll take you to Kunming.'

Fan nodded. 'Yes, it's a deal. But how are we going to get there?'

Zha smiled again. 'The minivan's still here. But we need to get going before everyone wants to use it to leave. Come on. Let's go while they're at breakfast. Let me grab my bag.'

Fan had nothing worth going back to the barracks for. He had arrived at the prison with nothing but his clothes, and the only clothes he had now were his prison garb. He ambled off to the lot where the old TJ110 minivan was parked. Zha jogged up minutes later and they drove off, through a dense forest and on an unpaved track until at last they arrived at a paved road that led into Kunming.

Since Zha no longer needed to concentrate on his driving, Fan asked, 'Do you have any cash? We'll need some place to stay.'

Zha laughed. 'You Han Chinese! You think all minorities are uncivilized and have never heard of credit cards. Even though my credit limit is only 10,000 yuan, that's enough to stay at a decent hotel for several nights in Kunming.'

They arrived in Kunming in the late morning. Zha knew the city well and wove his way through the city to an unprepossessing hotel in a working-class district. 'This is owned by a Miao. Cheap and clean.'

A woman in colourful traditional clothing checked them in. She was a little surprised to see Fan, but she gave him a clean, small room on the second floor, next to Zha's. Zha went to buy toiletries and clothes for Fan and came back half an hour later with a small bag containing a toothbrush, toothpaste, soap and a razor, plus a set of inconspicuous clothing. Since neither man had eaten breakfast, they were very hungry. As soon as Fan changed clothes, Zha took him to a small restaurant and introduced him to the famous Yunnan Cross Bridge Rice Noodles.

Once his stomach was full, Fan went back to planning. He knew he wasn't safe yet. He broached the subject of documents to Zha. Did he know anyone who could get some ID for him?

Zha nodded, 'Yeah. I'll take you to my friend. He's a town clerk. What name do you want to use?' he asked with a sly smile, making Fan aware that Zha was more worldly wise and astute than he had assumed. *I picked the right man.* Relieved, Fan thanked Zha and asked if the friend could make two IDs for him. Fan had been worried about using his real name because the authorities could trace him, but he needed ID in his own name to open a bank account and get money from Singapore. However, he also needed a false ID to get safely out of Kunming. Zha thought it wouldn't be a problem.

From then on everything went smoothly, though it all took longer than Fan would have liked. The town clerk was more than happy to issue two IDs for a friend of his old friend Zha, who advanced Fan 5,000 yuan to pay for them. Fan tentatively broached the possibility of obtaining a false passport, but the clerk shook his head, saying that would take some time. So Fan settled for the two IDs, thinking he could easily have Fried send him a passport.

Once Fan had ID in his real name, he was able to open an account with the local branch of HSBC and make arrangements for a bank transfer from his private account in Singapore.

Fan ended up having to spend two nights in Kunming because the funds from Singapore wouldn't arrive until Thursday. He spent an anxious 48 hours worrying that a local policeman or two might suddenly show up to arrest him.

When the money arrived, Fan transferred half of it plus what he owed Zha to an account Zha had set up in a different bank. Then Fan withdrew the rest in cash except for the 2,000 yuan the bank insisted remain in the account. Fan borrowed Zha's phone and found there was a China Southern flight to Haikou at 6.35 p.m. He got one of the last seats on it. Fan was pleased because he knew there were many flights daily between Haikou on China's resort island, Hainan, and Hong Kong.

Zha drove Fan to the airport with little time to spare. As Fan got out of the minivan, Zha said, 'I really am grateful to you. I never thought a Han Chinese incarcerated in the black prison would give me the funds to start a new life. Who knows . . . with the kind of money I got, I might start some business, find a nice Miao girl and get married. Good luck to you!'

Fan reached over and shook hands with Zha and watched him drive away. At last he was free from that nightmarish prison and had become Li Huanwen. *Now to get to Haikou, check into a decent hotel and call Fried for a Hong Kong passport. Then to Singapore where I can get my hands on my funds . . . and SAEC's as well! More than 2 billion dollars just waiting for me!*

When the plane made a stop in Guangzhou, the thought occurred to Fan that he could probably have got away with offering half the amount to Zha. *Oh, well, too late now. He did get me out of a jam.*

Fan, rather Li Huanwen, arrived in Haikou on the northern end of Hainan Island just after 11.30 that night. He felt wonderful breathing in the cool ocean breeze. As the passengers deplaned, he followed a stolidly built woman with a fancy hairdo who, from the rear, reminded him of his wife. Only then did he think of her. *Was she already asleep or still frantically searching for him?* He really didn't care. By the time his cab was heading to a hotel the cab driver suggested, the new Mr Li was feeling like a billionaire.

46

Haikou and Tokyo, 11–12 September

Fan gazed out of the window of his room in the luxurious Haikou Ocean-View Towers Hotel located on the coast of Hainan. The hotel was no match for a five-star hotel in any major international city, but it was a far cry from the black prison he had endured for nearly three weeks. When the doorbell rang, Fan, wrapped in a toweling robe, went to let in room service with his lunch.

Half an hour later, ensconced in a comfortable chair and sated with the first really good meal he'd had since he was arrested, Fan was congratulating himself on how well things were going. He had checked into a cheap airport hotel after his arrival in Hainan late last night. After sleeping until nine this morning, he had booked a room in what was reputed to be the best hotel on the island and moved to this opulent ocean-view room. Now he had to make plans to collect his private stash and SAEC's money as well and then get out of China.

The first thing to do was to open a bank account in Haikou so he could have more funds transferred here. The funds he had received in Kunming were rapidly dwindling after paying for his expenses there, his plane ticket to Hainan and the very expensive but very necessary pieces of ID he had purchased through Zha. Reluctantly, Fan abandoned his comfortable chair and got dressed to pay a visit to the city centre.

The first purchase Fan made was a phone on which he could make international calls and use the web. He found a quiet cafe where he could check the Internet and put in a call to Nelson Ing in Singapore. He was a bit taken aback to hear that Mr Ing was out of the office and wasn't expected back for some time. *Well, at least I should be able to obtain funds from my private account as I did when I was in Kunming. I'll get money from the SAEC account when he returns.*

Next Fan went to a bank to set up an account using his real name so he could obtain money from Singapore. He requested a transfer of 50,000 dollars and told the manager he would return on Monday to get his money. In the meantime, he had enough cash to tide himself over for more than a few days even at an expensive hotel. Then he went shopping for clothes befitting his status as a guest in a luxury establishment. He returned to the hotel, took a swim in the hotel's large pool and then enjoyed the sauna. Feeling on top of the world, he put on his new clothes and gorged on a multi-course dinner. Smiling broadly he kept thinking, *This is the life!*

He was back in his room well before 10. Since New York was exactly 12 hours behind China, this was a good time to contact Josh Fried, who was to have sent all his money from the project on to Singapore. Fan thought Fried would certainly know what the situation was in Singapore and how Fan could retrieve the SAEC money even if Ing wasn't there. He called Fried's office but no one answered the phone, even after 10 rings. He checked the number and tried again. No one picked up, this time even after 20 rings. *This is odd.* On his phone Fan checked the holidays in New York, but this Friday wasn't one. And there wasn't even a message to the caller about when the firm could be contacted.

Since he couldn't contact Ing or Fried, there was nothing to do at this hour but go to bed.

Fan had an uneasy night. Finally he got up at six. He had to decide what to do, but first he would order coffee from room service. While waiting for it to arrive, he decided to check the website for Fried's firm to find out what its hours were. When he typed in 'Joshua

Fried Hedge Fund' on his browser, the first item to come up was not the firm's website but an article with the headline: JOSHUA FRIED'S HEDGE FUND FILES FOR BANKRUPTCY

Bankrupt? Fried must've made a few billion. Fan couldn't believe it. He reread the article. Shaking his head, he read another entitled 'Fried's Hedge Fund in Sudden Insolvency'. The content was the same—Fried had been forced to file for bankruptcy. He felt sick. *Where is the SAEC money and all the profit from the project? If Scheinbaum sent SAEC's money to Fried's hedge fund while I was in the black prison, then it could be lost in the bankruptcy. Could it have been sent to my account in Singapore before Fried went bankrupt? Ing is away from the bank, so I can't contact him. And why is he away and for how long?*

Now his only hope was the 7.8 million dollars in his private Singapore account. He was sure of it, because $200,000 out of that total of 8 million had been sent to Kunming. So he would have enough to go on for a time, though not the vast fortune he had imagined possessing. He would have to wait until Monday to collect the transfer and then try to contact Ing again. In the meantime he had better decide what he wanted to do, where he wanted to go in the long run.

Fan sighed and thought about getting dressed. But then his eyes lit on the local paper, the *Hainan Ribaou*, delivered with his coffee. He picked it up and began to thumb through it. It was full of local news and held no interest for him until he got to page five. Stunned, he saw his photo, and a headline that read: FAN ZHIPENG OF SAEC SOUGHT IN NATIONWIDE DRAGNET. The article went on to describe Fan as 'the embezzler of over 10 billion yuan from the Sino-African Energy Company and suspected of receiving a huge amount of kickbacks from an African government'. He was also considered 'a person of interest' in the death of a SAEC employee and thought to be at large anywhere in China and possibly even abroad.

The photo was a good one. Anyone who saw it could identify Fan. He slumped back in his chair. *This is disaster.* His world had collapsed. It was worse than being in the black prison where he could dream of what he would do with his riches once he got out. But now most of his money was probably gone and there was a nationwide manhunt on for him. That he was considered a person of interest in the death of a SAEC employee meant he was still considered a suspect in Ye's death. And murder was a capital crime in China.

He had to think, but his brain seemed enveloped in a fog. There was no one he trusted to turn to in China. No longer anyone at SAEC. He couldn't go home. Certainly the police would be monitoring his wife, and his house would be under surveillance. Fried would be of no use, and he had never met Scheinbaum. Who could he go to for help?

There was only one person he might contact: Shig Tanaka in Japan. Tanaka had gone to Benin for him and was a fellow Asian. But how could he get in touch with him? It was Saturday and unlikely the bank would be open. How about a coded email? No, that wouldn't work because he hadn't memorized the code. He would have to try to call him, hoping Tanaka might be working on a Saturday.

Fan picked up his phone and entered the words 'Shigeo Tanaka' and 'Sumida Bank'. And up popped an article about Tanaka being the new president of Sumida Bank. *Finally a piece of luck! Now to figure out how to contact him. But will he help me? He's now the president of one of Japan's largest banks and I'm on the run from the law.*

And then a thought occurred to him: a bank president won't want to have his role in a plot to bring down his own country's government bonds exposed! Nor will he want Japan's tax authority to learn about the millions he garnered from the plot and on which he most certainly paid no taxes. No, *I won't even have to threaten him, or even suggest that I might. Tanaka is a bright man and knows he has to help me! He should be able to give me a 'loan' of a few million! And get me a fake passport too.*

He found the number of the bank and called. He would have to disguise his call but in such a way that Tanaka would know who was calling. When the call went through, he said to the young woman who answered that he wanted to speak to the president. In his accented English, he said, 'Tell him it's a good friend from Shanghai and I'd like to see him for dinner this weekend.'

It worked! Tanaka was at the bank. He greeted Fan without using a name, said he was in the middle of something and that he would call Fan back. Fan spent an anxious 20 minutes until Tanaka called and said that the line would not be monitored. Nevertheless, Fan was cautious. He briefly said that he would like to visit Japan because he needed to take 'a long, quiet holiday'.

There was a long pause, and then Tanaka said, 'I think I get the picture. Where are you now?'

Fan hesitated and then said, 'Haikou, on Hainan Island.'

There was another pause. Then Tanaka asked, 'Would it work to call you back at this same number in 24 hours?'

Fan agreed and Tanaka hung up.

Now Fan had to think about how to stay out of sight until he left Haikou. He briefly thought of moving to a cheap place down in the heart of the city. But the more he thought about it, the fewer people who had an opportunity to see him, the better. He was already ensconced here under an assumed name. The police would scarcely think he would be living openly in an expensive resort hotel on Hainan. More likely they would be looking for him near Kunming, or Shanghai, or even Hong Kong. And they would be searching the plane manifests for flights to Taiwan, the US, Africa or Europe. Who would ever think he would go to Japan?

No, he would stay quietly in this hotel until Monday and then collect his money from the bank. He could make arrangements to fly to Tokyo right after Tanaka called back. In the meantime, he'd get dressed, go down to the hotel shop and buy some dark glasses and a sun hat appropriate for this resort.

Tanaka put his phone down and groaned. *Everything was going so well. Too well, I guess. Now what do I do? Fan must be in deep trouble or he wouldn't have contacted me, and that too at the bank. There must be no one in China who can help him. But why me?*

The new president of Sumida Bank sighed again as he pondered his dilemma. He barely knew Fan, had met him with Fried back in Shanghai at the economic forum, once more when he'd gone to Shanghai on business and then in Cotonou. But Fan hadn't even been at the meeting in New York when the group had discussed the plans at Scheinbaum's penthouse. The logical person would have been Fried, but that wasn't on with his recent bankruptcy. *Why did he call me? Because I'm in Tokyo and closer to Hainan? Or because I've done something shady, like going to Benin and making a bid-fixing proposal to Mitsumoto for him . . . so he thinks I'll do something shady for him again? Will he blackmail me for attacking the JGB, now that I've become the president of Sumida? Well, I've got just 24 hours to decide what to do. I thought once I collected my profits from the project, I wouldn't have to see any of the others again. And if he's on the run, does that mean he needs a fake passport? The authorities will catch him if he tries to fly out of China using his real name. He didn't say he couldn't travel, just that he needs a place to go. I sure don't want to go looking for false travel documents for him. Where would I put him if I said he could come? Does he have any money? I wonder if he lost it all when Fried went bankrupt? And what has he been doing for the past several weeks? I haven't seen anything in the Japanese papers.*

Tanaka decided to search the Internet. He put in Fan's name in a search in English. *Nothing.* He looked into the web site for SAEC and discovered that Fan was no longer listed as president. He couldn't read Chinese and he didn't know the Chinese characters for Fan Zhipeng, so he gave up.

Tanaka continued to sit and stare at nothing, his mind going round in circles. What if he didn't call Fan back? How much trouble could Fan make for Tanaka if he did nothing?

Suddenly there was a tap on the door. His secretary poked her head in and asked, 'Sir, can I get you some coffee or perhaps a sandwich if you are going to be working here this afternoon?'

Tanaka looked at his watch. It was way past the quitting time for the staff who came in on rotation on Saturdays. This was kind of his secretary, but more likely a hint that she would like to leave. Tanaka apologized and thanked her. 'I won't be much longer. Please go home now—I'm sorry to have kept you.' She nodded and excused herself.

There was no point in his staying any longer either, so he shut down his computer and prepared to leave. Nothing awaited him at home, but he didn't want to keep his chauffeur on duty any longer than he had to, so home he went. He cobbled together a lunch from leftovers in the fridge, but later couldn't remember what he had eaten. All he could think of was what to do about Fan.

47

Tokyo, 12–13 September

Even as Ken Murai was ushered into a private room in a French restaurant not far from the Imperial Palace, he was still uncertain about why he was there. Torao Nishi, the leader of the largest opposition party, had asked to meet him, but his reason had been vague. All he had said was: 'I want to get your views on various important economic issues.' Ken had agreed to serve on an advisory committee of economists but thought it unusual for a committee to meet in a restaurant on a Saturday evening.

Ken had met Nishi only once, at a meeting with some Diet members about a year ago. He had answered a few questions Nishi had asked him but he no longer remembered what about. Although he did remember that the questions had been pointed and informed and that answering them had taken time and special care.

Unusual for a Japanese politician, Nishi had earned his MA at the London School of Economics after graduating from the University of Tokyo where he studied law. Ken often read or heard Nishi's views in the newspapers and on TV and was sure that Nishi was a European-style social democrat like himself. But Nishi, he thought, carefully pulled his punches because Japan's politics was dominated by conservatives, just as the Ministry of Finance was. The number of politicians who openly espoused a European-type social democracy was limited. Virtually all the small parties were more conservative than the PM's, and the Socialist Party had only three members in the Diet. Whenever Ken heard or read about Nishi's unusually articulate and frequent criticism of the policies of the current government, he wished that Nishi would become prime minister some day, although it seemed unlikely this would happen.

When he entered the room he found four men and one woman already seated around a table. He knew who they were, though he hadn't met three of them. *This isn't a meeting of Nishi's economic advisors. It's a meeting of his inner circle of Dietmen.*

With Nishi was another member of his party, Kenta Fujino. Then, somewhat to his surprise, he found two members of the PM's party— Eiji Hirose and a woman, Chieko Motoi. But both were leaders of 'the anti-PM faction' of the ruling party. And of course he knew Ken-suke Den because he had been the finance minister when Nishi's party held power for just three years a decade ago. Den had been the minister of finance the year Ken had joined it. So here were members of two parties, but all they had in common was a reputation for being extremely well informed about and vocal in their criticism about recent economic policies.

Nishi and the former finance minister greeted Ken, and then Ken and the three members of the Diet he had never met exchanged Japanese-style brief introductions of name and title. Just as Nishi was about to speak, a waiter came to take orders for the main course. This took several minutes, affording time for Ken to muse. *Aha, now I know why Nishi asked me to come! He is organizing a coalition to form a new government. But what do they want to ask me or talk about tonight? It's extraordinary for me to be invited to a gathering of this very select group which is hoping to topple the government.*

The orders taken, the waiter left, and Nishi began. 'Thank you for coming tonight, Deputy Director. But I'd like to start out with all of us as friends and on equal terms for our discussion, so let's dispense with titles and use names. Is that OK with all of you?'

Everyone smiled and nodded assent. Nishi continued: 'As you have probably guessed, Murai-san, we are here because we know we must do something, and as soon as possible, to deal with the current economic crisis. Mr Den, your former boss at the Ministry of Finance, recently gave us copies of two articles that you wrote after receiving a doctorate in economics from Harvard University. I found them extremely valuable in thinking about our current crisis, so I wanted to have you give us your thoughts on what we should be doing to work our way out of the horrendous situation we find ourselves in.'

Before Nishi could continue, there was a soft knock on the door and two waiters brought in plates of mixed hors d'oeuvres, which they served along with a French Chardonnay. When they left, Nishi proposed a toast 'to the future of our country' and the group began to eat.

Neglecting his appetizer, Nishi said to Ken, 'Correct me if I'm wrong, but you argued in these articles that the most critical reason for the slower economic growth since 1980 of the major economies, including the US, Japan and Europe, was a slowdown in the growth of consumer demand. By the early 1980s, most people in these economies already possessed everything they needed. So most of the increase in demand had to come from people buying luxuries and things they really didn't need.'

'Yes, like more clothes than we can wear, knick-knacks and electronic gear,' commented Fujino.

'Right,' Nishi went on, 'And another reason demand didn't increase much is that, on the other hand, poor people, whose numbers have been steadily increasing, couldn't buy even the necessities of life. And we all know income distribution has been becoming more unequal every year in Japan as well as in other rich countries. Yes, you also wrote consumer demand in Japan is especially slow to increase because we have the most quickly ageing society with a very low birth rate.'

Ken was both amazed and amused to hear Nishi summarizing the academic articles he had published in English some years back. Nishi went on to give the statistical evidence from one of the articles while the others quietly ate. At one point Nishi asked Ken if the trends of his statistical evidence still supported Ken's analyses and Ken answered, 'Definitely, Mr Nishi. I keep abreast of these data and they continue to show that what I argued in my articles is even better supported today than when I wrote them.'

Ken had to answer several more questions about the most recent trends of the still-increasing disparities in both income and wealth distributions, persistent excess-productive capacities in many industries across the rich economies, the continuing trend of the declining birth rates in Japan and Europe and several other issues. Ken was surprised to see everyone raptly listening to him rattle off statistics most people would find mind numbing.

The talk was interrupted by another soft knock on the door. Two male waiters removed the appetizer plates—Nishi's and Ken's nearly untouched because they had been talking so much—and brought in the main course. Conversation was general as the group tucked into the traditional French cuisine this restaurant was known for. When most had finished eating, Nishi began again. 'So Murai-san here argued that cutting taxes in order to make the economy grow won't work.' He nodded at Ken. 'Do you still believe this?'

'Absolutely,' Ken said earnestly. 'There's no shortage of capital. In fact, interest rates have continued to fall steadily in all the rich economies since the 1980s. If we reduce corporate taxes and the Bank of Japan cuts interest rates further, investments won't increase, because demand isn't increasing. And our growing inequality in incomes means that there is a growing segment of the population who can't afford to buy the goods produced. Increasing their taxes with regressive taxes on consumption simply means they have even less money to spend on even the necessities. But Japan also has a special problem—its population is shrinking year after year and, unlike all the other rich economies, it has virtually no immigrants coming in.'

Motoi, the only woman in the group, spoke up in a low voice. 'That's why I voted against a cut in the corporate tax last year, especially after we raised the consumption tax again. Our party has things backwards. We don't need more capital. We need more money in the pockets of consumers, especially those in the lower-income brackets.'

Ken remembered that Motoi, along with about 20 members of the PM's party, had voted against the cut in the corporate tax rate and lost. The law had been passed because the very conservative opposition parties had supported the tax cut. Ken had a faint recollection that, because of her vote, Motoi had been relieved of the chairmanship of some committee in the Diet.

Hirose from the PM's party asked, 'OK, we seem to have a number of problems here. A large segment of the population has most of their needs sated, while a growing proportion can't afford to satisfy their basic needs. Plus we have a shrinking population and one that's ageing as well. What's your solution?'

The man sounded a bit belligerent, but this was an easy question for Ken. 'We should increase expenditures for infrastructure, education, research, environmental protection and a whole range of similar concerns we have so far neglected. We need to stop thinking about growing the economy by increasing the production of things, stuff. So much of it is goods that by any rational standard we don't need ... things we buy on a whim or to satisfy our vanity, electronic toys for adults and many other kinds of junk.'

Before anyone could object, Ken hurriedly continued. 'And we should pay for what we do need, not by raising taxes on the poor but by increasing taxes on the rich, on companies and financial institutions, and on luxury goods and services. The rich are now paying far lower taxes than they did until the 1970s—that's half a century ago. And companies don't need more tax breaks—they are now sitting on huge amounts of cash, what they call "internal reserves". I checked last week. As of the end of June, Japanese companies had internal reserves totalling 2.5 trillion dollars, just about the same amount as American companies, though the US economy is more than twice as big.'

'But won't increasing taxes hurt the economy?' asked Hirose. 'I'm with you so far, but I'd like to hear how changing our tax structure will get us out of the crisis we are in now.'

Ken nodded. 'To answer this question, I have to restate some of the things I've already said. Please bear with me. We can change the tax structure in such a way that will put more money in the hands of poor and middle-class consumers, so they will buy more of the goods and services they really need. And if we decide to invest more to meet our societal needs, we will create more demand. I mean demand that really improves the quality of our lives—not demand for more frivolous services for the rich. Making the tax structure more progressive is a win-win strategy. Incomes will rise, the disparity in wealth will decrease, there will be more demand for the goods and services we really need and our economy will grow instead of being stuck in a very low growth rate and chronic deflation.'

'You make a very sound argument,' declared Nishi's colleague, Fujino. 'But it's going to be a hard sell. We all know most people in the rich countries scream against any kind of tax increase.'

Ken agreed, saying that there needed to be a lot of public education. 'It's ridiculous how the public has bought into the idea of a "small government" with low taxes and almost no government regulations of any kind, despite the fact that it's been clear for years that a small government doesn't solve our economic problems. The rich will benefit most from the increased taxes they have to pay, because the value of everything they own will decline over time if the economy continues to grow slowly and the government has no money to invest to prevent the further degradation of the environment. We have to forge ahead with a fundamental systemic change in capitalism if we are going to save our capitalist democracy, especially with our country in such a mess.'

Ken looked around the table. He had everyone's attention but he knew he had to be succinct and not patronize or bore the people sitting around him.

'Let me give you two examples from history how my solution works.'

Aware that a lecture on economic history would be out of place, Ken quickly summarized how, in the UK, during the nineteenth century, Gladstone abolished more than 1,000 tariffs designed to protect the income of the aristocrats and industrialists. He singled out the case of the notorious Corn Laws, tariffs that raised the price of foodstuff for the poor in order to enrich landowners. These laws, along with the effects of industrialization and urbanization, created an unprecedented inequality in the distribution of income. By abolishing tariffs, adopting the first income tax and factory laws and strengthening Poor Laws and so on, British capitalism managed to survive without the revolution that Marx predicted would take place.

All this was clearly news to the listeners who hadn't read Ken's articles. Everyone was even more interested when he described how, during the period, from the progressive 1890s through the New Deal in the 1930s, the US system had been drastically changed by introducing an income tax, adding three amendments to its Constitution, enacting anti-trust and social-security laws and making other significant changes. 'In both the English and the US cases, capitalism survived because the systemic changes made both societies substantively better. There was less political corruption, much less inequality in income distribution and more investments for the future. The only problem was that, in both cases, it took nearly half a century to change the system. Learning from these examples, what we should do is to change our economy systemically without taking so long. But this is a tall order.'

As Ken finished, Nishi spoke up in agreement. 'A tall order indeed. England in the nineteenth century was able to fundamentally change its system because they were facing a real possibility of a revolution. And the US changed its system because it had to. From the late nineteenth century, America had become dominated by big companies and corrupt politicians. And then came the Great Depression. But, Murai-san, the Japanese situation is different. We've had a very stagnant economy for several decades but there's no imminent danger of a revolution or another great depression. So we face the difficulty of having to convince both the politicians and the voters that we need to overhaul our system but without taking decades to do so.'

Former finance minister Den spoke up, picking his words carefully. 'The key is whether we . . . politicians . . . and the voters too of course . . . are smart enough to realize that we need to change our rotten system before it caves in from a revolution or a great depression. I hope Nishi-san and everyone here will do their utmost to get rid of the incompetent government we now have and start making the systemic change we've been talking about.'

While Den spoke, the waiters returned, removed the dishes from the main course and then served a small green salad. *This really is an authentic French restaurant, from the professional waiters to the food and the order of service*, thought Ken as he started in on his salad.

The waiters hadn't been gone for more than a couple of minutes when the door of the room burst open and a tall young man dressed in a waiter's uniform and carrying a large paper bag rushed in and asked in a loud voice, 'Mr Nishi?'

Startled, Nishi said, 'Yes, that's me.'

As soon as Nishi responded, the man whipped out a large bottle from the bag and a lighter from his pocket and tried to light the cloth sticking out from the neck of the bottle. Someone yelled, 'Duck!' As Ken started to dive under the table, he thought, *Oh my God, it's a Molotov cocktail!* But before the cloth caught fire, a well-built middle-aged man who'd followed the 'waiter' into the room lunged at him and batted the lighter from the young man's hand. The man winced but managed to throw the bottle with his left hand where it shattered against the wall beside Motoi's chair.

The room quickly filled with the familiar nauseating fumes of gasoline. Two men were gagging. 'My hand is bleeding,' wailed Motoi, 'The glass . . . ' She couldn't finish as she began to retch. Ken, holding a napkin to his nose like others, watched as the middle-aged man handcuffed and frog-marched the assailant out of the room. 'Thanks. Well done,' Nishi said to the departing middle-aged man. Ken stood aside to let Fujino help Motoi out of the room. She was holding a napkin to her arm in an effort to staunch the blood dripping onto her pale pink suit.

Once out in the corridor, which was crowded with waiters, guests and security people, Ken spotted an ashen-faced Den. 'Are you OK, sir?'

'Thanks. I'm fine. Never thought this could happen to me. The sign of times, I guess. Good thing Nishi had a guard watching over him.'

Early Sunday morning Ken Murai phoned his friend, Saburo Baba.

'Are you OK, Ken?' Baba's was very concerned.

'I'm a bit shaken and my good suit is a mess, but yes, I'm OK. I called because I thought you'd like to know what happened.'

'It would be helpful. I'm not sure what to believe from the media reports. They didn't mention you, but I knew you were supposed to be at that dinner. How bad was it?'

'It could have been worse . . . someone could have been killed if the attacker managed to ignite the Molotov cocktail and if Nishi hadn't had a security guard with him. The fumes were terrible. But he missed his target, which was Nishi. The only person injured was Chieko Motoi who cut her hand on some glass.'

'I didn't know Nishi had a security guard,' commented Baba. 'That's not usual for a Dietman.'

'Mr Den, the former finance minister, told me that Nishi's father-in-law is a retired official from the Tokyo Metropolitan Police Department. He was concerned about the hate mail that Nishi's been receiving recently. So he hired a private security guard. Luckily for

Nishi and for all of us, the father-in-law hired a guard who's very good.'

'Do you know who the assailant was?'

'No. Just some tall guy . . . I didn't even get a good look at him. It was a good salad—too bad I didn't have a chance to eat it,' remarked Ken in an attempt to lighten the conversation. It didn't work.

'Things seem to be going from bad to worse,' sighed Baba. 'This shows that the kind of policies Dietman Nishi and his group are proposing could be very divisive in Japanese politics.'

'True, but we simply have to do something to turn Japan's economy . . . our country . . . around! Bach, we just can't go on as it is!'

Baba was surprised by Ken's vehement tone, but Ken immediately calmed down. 'Sorry about getting worked up. We couldn't finish the meeting last night, but Nishi phoned me this morning and almost implored me to meet with the group again.'

'Be very careful,' cautioned Baba.

From the tone in his old friend's voice, Ken knew he was now very genuinely afraid for him.

48

Haikou and Tokyo, 13–14 September

Fan spent an unsettled weekend, unable to concentrate on anything or make any plans. All the pots of room-service coffee combined with his worries and ended up giving him a headache. So he stayed in his room all Sunday waiting for Tanaka's call, but it never came. *Well, everything's closed on Sunday, including Sumida Bank. He's probably having difficulties contacting people to make arrangements for me. I'm sure he'll call tomorrow.* Fan tried to comfort himself with this thought, though it did little to ease his tension. Finally in the late afternoon, when his headache eased off a little, he went down to the pool for a swim, making sure he took his phone with him.

As he towelled himself off, Fan wondered what had happened to him. Gone was the leader of men he had been as a colonel in the army. Gone was the self-confident CEO who had so efficiently commanded one of the largest state enterprises in China. And gone also was the man who all his life had so competently made decisions affecting not only himself but also hundreds, even thousands, of people. Now he was cowering in fear, hiding from the world, nervously awaiting a phone call from a man he barely knew.

On Monday morning, Fan ordered in a room-service breakfast again and desultorily watched TV while waiting for Tanaka's call. But it didn't come. He skipped lunch because he was not hungry. At two he decided to call Tanaka. But when he called Sumida Bank and asked for the president, he was told he was busy with meetings for the rest of the day. 'Can I take a message?' he was asked. 'No, I'll call back,' he answered.

By mid-afternoon Fan decided he had to take control of his life once again. And he needed money if he was to do anything. He decided to risk a visit to the bank. He donned his hat and dark glasses, and took a taxi.

Soon Fan was walking into the bank's lobby. *So far so good.* He saw the teller he had dealt with on Friday and walked over towards him. But before he reached the window, he saw the teller nod at someone at the side of the lobby.

It was all over for Fan in seconds. Unlike his arrest in Shanghai the month before, there was no bluster left in him. *Can't make a break for it . . . this is the end!* A dejected man, he slumped as one of the officers handcuffed him. He was so dispirited he didn't even feel angry at the teller who was being congratulated by one of the policemen for recognizing Fan and alerting the authorities.

Just before five, Tanaka returned to his office. His secretary handed him his messages, saying, 'There was also a call from a man who spoke in English. But he didn't leave a name, said he would call back.'

Tanaka thanked her and went into his private office. *That had to have been Fan. Damn! I can't postpone calling him any longer. I can't have him keep calling the bank. But what am I to say? He'll get caught sooner or later. I guess I'll just call and tell him I need more time.*

Tanaka picked up his private phone, checked the number Fan had called from on Saturday and put through the call. He could hear the phone ring, and then keep ringing. He was just about to give up when the phone was answered.

'Wei,' said a strange voice.

Not Fan! He said he got the phone to talk to me. Fan is awaiting my call . . . no one else should be answering this phone!

Confused, Tanaka blurted, 'President Fan?'

'Zhe shi shui?' Then there was a pause. 'Who is this?' asked the same voice. This time Tanaka couldn't miss the gruff, almost authoritative tone.

Definitely not Fan! Someone got his phone. Police? Yes, must be!

Tanaka hung up instantly and slumped back in his desk chair. He began to grin. *He's been caught! I'm off the hook.*

49

Tokyo, 15 September

Saburo Baba surfed through the news channels while he ate a quick breakfast. There was nothing of interest. The police had identified the man who tried to kill Nishi and his colleagues at a meeting on Saturday evening. He was an unemployed young man who admitted he had been hired by 'someone who paid me 500,000 yen'. Although the man refused to say who the 'someone' was, after intensive questioning he admitted he had met the man in a bar near the headquarters of the smallest right-wing party. The police were now trying to identify the man who'd hired the ineffectual assailant from the description he had given them. However, the public-relations officer briefing the media admitted that 'it may be extremely difficult to tie anyone connected to the right-wing party to the crime.' Baba muttered, 'It figures. Anyone, let alone a Dietman, who wanted to harm Nishi and his group would be smart enough to use a middleman.'

It was a depressing start of the day for Baba. He was already so disheartened by his job that he had put in a carefully worded request to the foreign minister asking for a transfer back to the Foreign Ministry. It wasn't usual to ask to be relieved from serving the PM but he had argued that, given Japan's current economic crisis, the PM would be better served by having someone with an economics background advising him on international economic issues. His hope was that his own minister, a leader of an important faction in the PM's party and close to the PM, would be able to persuade the PM to approve his request. But he was not especially sanguine about the prospect of it being granted any time soon. The PM was still in hospital and still unwilling to give up the reins of government. Thus almost everything either remained undone or was being done at a snail's pace.

Baba arrived at his office to find a message that the PM's chief secretary, Fukunaga, wanted to see him as soon as possible.

Now what does he want? Baba straightened his tie and went to see Fukunaga.

The chief secretary, who looked like an owl, seemed oddly ingratiating, unlike his usual officious self.

'Have you a lot on your plate today, Counsellor? I wonder if you could do an errand for the PM, if you have time. Normally I'd undertake the task myself, but I can't leave my office today.'

'I expect I could. What is it?' asked Baba now very curious about Fukunaga's unusually solicitous manner.

'We need to have some very sensitive documents picked up from the CFO of Mitsumoto Trading, from their head office in Otemachi. Could you go by taxi?'

Baba usually used an official car and driver to go to meetings. *This is very curious*, he thought, but all he said was: 'OK. When do you want me to go?'

Fukunaga suggested early afternoon, and they agreed that Baba would go after lunch. Though he thought it an odd request, Baba asked no questions. Due to all the business between Mitsumoto and Benin, he couldn't but wonder, *What kind of sensitive documents am I being sent to collect, and why me?*

Just before 1.30 Baba went out to the street and hailed a cab. 'The Mitsumoto Building in Otemachi.' The taxi sped along for 10 minutes and then came to a sudden halt near the Imperial Palace. Baba could hear voices amplified through megaphones, but he couldn't make out what the shouting was about.

'Looks like we'll be here for a while,' groused the unhappy driver. 'Same thing happened yesterday. Protest after protest. About rising unemployment, lack of disaster relief, anything you can think of. I don't blame them for being mad at the government but they should be in front of the Diet or the PM's office. I reckon they are here because there's more space for a larger crowds.'

'Looks and sounds like at least a couple thousand people, if not more!'

'More than yesterday, that's for sure. I'd join them, but I've got to make a living, such as it is. Can't make any money when I can't move. Didn't you see the demonstrations on TV last night?'

When Baba said he hadn't because he'd been busy, the cab driver described in detail the protests in Tokyo and other cities by thousands of people. 'Most were young but some were middle-aged men and women, and at times they were very rowdy.' The driver sighed. 'This economy is the pits. Either you work 35 hours a week as a part-timer on peanuts, or you have a full-time job working 10, 12 hours a day without overtime. Japan is finished. Me, I'd like to live in Italy. *La dolce vita.*'

Baba laughed and said he would too, without mentioning that the Italian economy had been 'in the pits' too for the last few years. Finally the taxi was able to move again. When Baba arrived at the CFO's office nearly 20 minutes late, the executive waved away his apologies saying, 'I'm not surprised. More demonstrations? We had them here yesterday and no one could leave the building until after seven. The grave crisis facing our economy now is, I fear, going to continue even longer than the one after the bubble burst in 1991.'

Without offering Baba tea or coffee or even suggesting he sit down, CFO Akita handed him a thin, black plastic attaché case, 'This is for Mr Fukunaga. Thank you for coming to get it on his behalf.'

The CFO escorted Baba to the elevator. As they waited for it to arrive, they could hear someone on the loudspeaker haranguing Mitsumoto.

The CFO said, 'They're back again. I'd better let you out the back way.'

As he was led to the back stairway, Baba asked, 'Who are they? Any idea what the man is saying?'

'My assistant told me they're a mob of young and middle-aged men, making all kinds of accusations against banks and big business.'

'Like what?'

'They accuse the biggest banks in Japan . . . the Sumiyoshi Bank in the next building and the Mitsuda-Kanto just across the street . . . they say these banks have been buying billions of dollars since the yen started to drop. They say the banks make a lot of money by buying the dollar, and this causes the yen to drop even more, making the lives of people even more difficult. The demonstrators don't understand that banks have to buy dollars so they won't lose even more money than they have already. A few big banks and a dozen smaller ones have already gone bankrupt. Our economic system wouldn't function without banks.'

At the door to the stairwell, the CFO said, 'When you get down to street level, please go out the door to the alley and turn left. If you walk a block or two, you should be able to avoid the mob and catch a taxi.' But when Baba reached the end of the alley, he found there was no way he could cross the street or even walk along it—the crowds were so thick. He clutched the attaché case tightly under his arm and wondered what to do.

'Hey, Buddy, you OK? What are you doing here? You don't look like one of the mob,' shouted a voice over the din of voices. Baba turned around and saw a stout man in a dirty chef's uniform.

'I'm trying to figure out how to get out onto a main street and get a cab,' Baba said.

The man motioned Baba. 'Getting to the main street isn't going to be easy and you'll have trouble finding a cab because they avoid the mob. Here, come in until they go by.'

Baba thanked him and entered the kitchen of a restaurant. He apologized for the intrusion.

'No problem. No customers at midday for a couple of days now. No one's going to try to break through that crowd. They got it tough, but they sure make it tough on the rest of us who are just trying to make a living.'

The chef led Baba into a corner of the closed restaurant. Baba sat down and ordered an espresso and some spumoni. *It's the least I can do*, he thought.

As he waited alone in the restaurant, he looked at the attaché case lying on the table in front of him. The black case was totally ordinary and nondescript. It was zipped shut but not taped or locked. Baba hesitated, but the phrase 'very sensitive documents' made him curious. Feeling a bit guilty, he carefully pulled open the zipper and put his hand in. Expecting to find sheets of paper, he was surprised to find a dozen or more cheques.

Just as he began to examine the cheques, he heard the kitchen door open and hurriedly stuffed the cheques back into the case. The chef put the coffee and ice cream down in front of him. Baba thanked the chef who hurried back to the kitchen where the phone was ringing.

Ignoring his food, Baba took the cheques out again. They were all bankers' drafts. The check on top was for 1.2 million dollars, drawn on a bank in Sydney, Australia, in favour of Takako Fukunaga. The only person he knew by that name was the wife of the chief secretary. As far as he recalled, she worked for a large real-estate company somewhere in Tokyo. Intrigued, he examined the others. There were 13 more and were all drawn on banks outside Japan, mostly in the US, China and Europe. All were issued in favour of Takako Fukunaga. His quick calculation told him that all the cheques added up to just under 17 million dollars.

It did not take long for Baba to deduce what these cheques were.

Each was drawn on a bank in a city where Mitsumoto Trading had a branch office. Cheques were issued in favour of the wife of the chief secretary, so it would be difficult to connect them to the PM. There was absolutely no doubt that the money was a totally illegal 17-million-dollar war chest for the PM. If the PM lost a confidence vote in the Diet and called a snap election, he would need these funds and more to try to help his supporters in his party win a general election. And, given the current political and economic situation, it was very likely the PM could lose a confidence vote.

Now I know why Fukunaga didn't come to pick up this money. He knew about the demonstrations and the media coverage, and he didn't want to been seen anywhere near the Mitsumoto office. It also explains why he told me to take a taxi and not an official car. Since he couldn't go himself, it had to be someone CFO Akita would recognize, and I met him at the meeting at the Forest Inn.

Baba now very much regretted seeing the cheques. He knew he couldn't live with himself if he kept this secret.

Wondering what to do next, he put sugar and cream into his now-cold coffee and ate the melting spumoni. He could no longer hear the roar of the mob, so it must have passed by. Still alone in the restaurant, he pulled out his phone and called his Tokyo University classmate, Koji Osada, now head of the administration section of the Metropolitan Police Department. He must have sounded worried because his friend agreed to see him at a coffee shop near Metropolitan Police headquarters in an hour, even though Baba said he couldn't tell him what it was about over the phone. Baba knew that Osada would be the best man for advice in this situation.

Baba paid for his snack, thanking the chef for saving him from the crowd and went out to catch a cab back to his office in Nagatacho. In the cab, he put the attaché case on his lap. It felt like a live grenade.

As soon as he was back in his office, Baba locked the door and quickly made copies of all the cheques to take to Osada. Then he went to see Fukunaga with the attaché case.

Fukunaga was waiting for him.

'Counsellor Baba, you are a bit later than I expected. I called CFO Akita and he told me you arrived late because the demonstrations and the traffic.'

Baba nodded. 'And the crowd delayed me from leaving as well.' He handed over the attaché case, 'Here is what the CFO gave me.'

Fukunaga gave Baba a long, searching look, like an owl regarding a prey. Then he took the case. 'Thank you, Counsellor Baba, for giving your time.'

50

Tokyo, 18 September

The raid by the authorities was so sudden and so totally unexpected that Fukunaga had no time to remove from his desk drawer several documents he didn't want anyone to see. But when he heard the team of officers walk through the door to his outer office, he did manage to grab and shove into his jacket pocket the small black notebook in which he jotted down details about confidential meetings and other extremely sensitive subjects. He stood rigidly next to his desk as the men from the Public Prosecutor's Office marched into his office with their cardboard boxes. His owlish face turned red and his clenched fists shook as they seized everything they could from his office, including those documents in his desk drawer.

The lead investigator approached Fukunaga and ordered him in an officious tone 'to accompany us when we take these documents to the headquarters of the Public Prosecutor's Office. We want to ask you to answer some questions . . . voluntarily, of course.' Infuriated, Fukunaga sputtered, 'Do you know who I am?' The investigator quietly replied, 'Yes, that's why we're here.'

'The PM will call the minister of justice!' Fukunaga had yelled, but it had no effect on any of the men.

The search of the spacious office and the small adjoining room where Fukunaga's two assistants worked began a few minutes before nine and ended within an hour. The team of eight officers carried away seven boxes full of files, Fukunaga's laptop, the large computer on his desk, his assistants' computers and the contents of his desk drawers. Finally, the lead investigator said, 'Shall we go now?' and Fukunaga numbly nodded and followed the officers out. The two assistants were standing in the hall. One, a young woman, was sobbing while the other, a middle-aged man, glowered at the officers.

As Fukunaga emerged from the building, nearly a dozen journalists and cameramen crowded around him. He shook his head as they shouted questions at him until he was almost shoved into a car.

Halfway down the hall, Baba had heard Fukunaga's voice and immediately realized what was happening. From his window he watched the PM's chief secretary being driven away.

The scheduled staff meeting was cancelled. Baba's phones were ringing, both his office landline and his personal phone. He decided not to answer either until he could decide what to say. Since he wasn't sure how to handle any inquiries, he booted up his computer and finished organizing all the reports he'd written for the PM and saved them on the Cloud. It seemed futile to finish any current assignments at this point.

At one, Baba decided it was time he had something to eat and went to the canteen to buy a sandwich. He was very relieved to see that no journalists were around. The last thing he wanted was questions about why Fukunaga was being investigated.

But Baba couldn't get away from the gossip. Four young women in the canteen were talking about what had happened that morning. 'What do you think he's done?' 'I didn't think they could do such a thing!' and 'He looks like an owl. I never liked him.'

Baba took the sandwich back to his office, and continued organizing his files. At about four, he got an email from Osada at the Metropolitan Police: 'Call me.' He left his private phone number for Baba to use.

Baba called Osada immediately. Osada was amused.

'That was fast! I tried to call you a couple of times and then I realized you weren't answering either of your phones. Wise man! I thought you might like to know what's happened so far. I just got a call from my friend—you know who I'm talking about. As expected, the Public Prosecutor's Office found Fukunaga to be a pretty tough and shrewd man. At first he refused to answer any questions. But the prosecutors are used to his type. When they showed him copies of the cheques, he tried to say they were for his wife. He said she acted as an intermediary for Mitsumoto when it bought properties abroad. But after one of the team came in with emails he'd exchanged with Mitsumoto, it didn't take long before he gave up spouting that nonsense.'

Baba sighed. 'I suppose he knows who ratted on him.'

'I rather think so. We've kept your name out of the interrogation so far, but since the primary evidence was the photocopied cheques, who else could have made the copies and turned them over to the police? Certainly not the Mitsumoto people, though it's possible some secretary who handled the cheques could have done so. There's no proof it was you—just circumstantial evidence. But it's very strong, I should add.'

'What have you gleaned so far from all those boxes of material and the computer files?'

Osada answered at length and almost gleefully: 'Well, they haven't had time to go through it all, but the team has reported that there are a lot of incriminating files showing a long and sordid relationship between the PM and several big companies and banks, in addition to Mitsumoto. And scores of emails and files revealing a dozen things the PM has done that are going to crucify him in the Diet. Two emails Fukunaga sent to a guy called Gomajiri and one he got from Gomajiri show that Fukunaga hired Gomajiri to recruit someone to "deal with" a "Professor T".' Osada paused. 'Gomajiri is a very unusual name.'

Baba cut in, 'Even I've heard of Eiji Gomajiri! He's the leader of a yakuza group.'

'Right. We are quite sure that's the Gomajiri to whom Fukunaga sent the emails. And we've established from the police files that Professor T could be Professor Toda who was kidnapped, assaulted and drugged on his way to an emergency meeting at the Bank of Japan. The dates of these emails fit because they were only a day before the meeting. So we can use these emails to try to get both Fukunaga and Gomajiri for instigating and being an accessory to kidnapping and assault, both very serious crimes. And you can guess who "suggested" the whole thing to Fukunaga.'

Baba was horrified. 'Fukunaga had Professor Toda kidnapped and drugged? How much of this is going to come out? I mean get into the media?'

'The Public Prosecutor's Office will sanitize everything a bit "in the national interest", so as to protect the dignity of the PM's office. But the main facts will come out. The opposition parties are going to make the most of this in order to topple the government. It's a godsend for Nishi, if I'm reading the media rumours correctly.'

'And it's going to hit the market. With the price of stocks and bonds where they are now already . . . this is going to be very bad,' Baba said sighing. 'What happens next?'

'After discussions between the higher-ups in the Ministry of Justice, the Interior Ministry and those in the Public Prosecutor's Office, we've agreed about what to do with the banker's drafts Mitsumoto Trading gave to Fukunaga. The election commission, a part of the Interior Ministry, will start a formal investigation of Fukunaga. He'll be charged with gross criminal violation of the election laws. There's no doubt he'll be found guilty in the end, but it could take at least three years, if similar cases are any guide. It's going to be very difficult to connect the PM because he'll say he had no knowledge of what Fukunaga was doing even when we all know that's a crock of shit.'

Baba could hear Osada draw on the pipe he usually had in his mouth.

'But you will do something?' asked Baba rather anxiously.

'Yes, of course. To start with, Fukunaga will be indicted for masterminding the violation of the election laws. And I'm going to talk to some people to see if we can find a few shareholders of Mitsumoto stock willing to sue the company for illegally using corporate money.'

'I'm very glad to hear all this. If Fukunaga is indicted, politically it's as good as indicting the PM.'

'Yes, certainly. But I have a question for you. First, a lawsuit against Mitsumoto will require your sworn statement that you got those banker's draft from Mitsumoto, gave them to Fukunaga and got in touch with the authorities with copies of the drafts. Some people are going to accuse you of being disloyal to the PM and doing things a true Japanese should never do. Are you willing to do that?'

Baba sighed deeply and thought for a moment. Then he replied, 'I suspect my name will come out in the end. If I'm considered disloyal by some—so be it. But others will applaud me for helping turn the wheels of justice. I'm ready to face the consequences of my actions. I did what I felt I had to do. I couldn't let myself be a part of the corruption of our government.'

'Hmm. I realized that when you first called me,' remarked Osada approvingly.

Baba was thoughtful. 'Osada-kun, with the PM in the hospital and heavily medicated, and unwilling to let anyone in his cabinet to do his work, it's not too far-fetched to say that Fukunaga has been usurping the PM's power in various unsavoury or even criminal ways. Chief secretaries always try to cover for their boss, to keep their boss squeaky clean. But in this case, given the evidence and since everyone knows the PM's reputation, going after Fukunaga will implicate the PM. I've no doubt at all about this. The government will go down. Well, *c'est la vie*. Whatever the new government, it couldn't be worse . . . less effective than this one.'

After the talk with Osada, Baba thought for a moment and then called Ken Murai but his secretary said he was in a meeting, most likely until six. While he waited, Baba methodically cleaned out his office, packing up personal belongings. He knew his time in the PM's office was at an end.

At 6.15, he called Ken again. This time, Ken took the call.

'I know you called earlier, and from the office gossip here, I can guess what's up.'

'I really would like to talk to you. And I think you should hear about what's happening from me and not TV news. Would it be possible to meet this evening?'

Ken could detect what he thought was quiet desperation in his friend's voice. 'Sure. Come to my house at 7.30. I may be late. I can't ask Emiko to cook because she has been putting in long hours in her office, but we'll order in some sushi or Chinese.'

By 8.30, dinner was over. Baba had related the events of the day to the couple, and Emiko had listened wide-eyed. Now she asked, 'Will this bring the government down?'

'If the PM had resigned because of illness, it might have been possible for the party to put someone else in as PM, but there's no way the government can stay in power with all these revelations. So Nishi and his group now have a real chance of putting together a coalition government from the dissidents in the PM's party plus members of opposition parties.'

Ken nodded as he listened to Baba's astute reading of the situation. It was Emiko who voiced concern for Baba. 'But what about you, Bach? Fukunaga . . . and the PM . . . are going to find out you're the person who gave those cheques to the police. And even though the PM's still in the hospital, how can you go to work tomorrow and face Fukunaga. I mean, Fukunaga will be back tomorrow, won't he?'

Baba gave a short laugh. 'Yes, I'm sure he will be. But I won't. I cleared out my office and dropped the stuff off at home before I had the cab bring me here.'

'*Cleared out?*' asked Emiko.

'I've known for some time now that I had to get out of the PM's service. What happened during the last couple of days hastened my departure.'

'Knowing how these things work,' Ken began, 'I can pretty much guess what's happened. You talked to the foreign minister, who is a leader of a big faction in the PM's party . . . and a good friend of yours. He told you he understands your situation well . . . so he'll have the PM release you from your secondment as a senior counsellor. He will give you a temporary non-demanding job in the Foreign Ministry until he finds you a new assignment.'

Baba laughed and said, 'It was a bit more complicated than that, but you're right.'

Still concerned, Ken said, 'I'm glad you are getting out of the PM's service and away from Fukunaga, but aren't you going to be in the media spotlight?'

'Not if we can help it, though I suspect my name will come out at some point. Neither the Public Prosecutor's Office nor the Foreign Ministry wants my role to be made public. The only danger would be if Fukunaga decided to avenge my turning copies of those cheques over to the authorities. But why would he want to make things worse for himself? I doubt he'd be stupid enough to hire someone to teach me a lesson or worse. So my future is safe, unlike Fukunaga's and the PM's.'

'Our country is like a ship in a huge storm with no captain at the helm,' said Ken sadly, 'Here we have a sick PM . . . and a political situation that is already weak. It could well implode when the news of this scandal breaks. If that happens, the stock and bond markets and the yen are all going to take another hit . . . the last thing our reeling economy needs.'

'If the economy gets worse . . . ' Emiko began to speak but stopped when she saw Baba's worried face. She did not finish. There was no need to do so.

51

Tokyo, Cambridge and Beijing, 21 September

Ken Murai spent an anxious weekend. Fearful of how the Fukunaga affair was going to affect the market, he had kept his eye on it on his laptop in his study. To his relief, the prices of the Japanese stocks and bonds or the yen didn't seem to be moving any more than they usually did over a weekend. Today, Monday, he booted up his computer as soon as he arrived at work and when the market opened, he immediately checked the Bloomberg and the Nikkei-CNBC.

His fears were justified. By 10.30, the Nikkei 225 Index was down a little over 2 per cent and bank stocks were falling by close to 3 per cent. The yen dropped 2.16 yen against the dollar. Worse, the Japanese government bonds had become very volatile. And by 11, it was clear that the bond price was trending downwards, raising the interest rate by between 0.3 and 0.5 per cent. Ken thought, *I've become inured to terrible market news during the last month, but we can't take any more of this*!

Shortly before the market closed for lunch at 11.30, the Nikkei-CNBC's crawler read: DIETMAN TORAO NISHI SAYS A FURTHER DROP IN THE NIKKEI INDEX IS A NAIL IN THE COFFIN OF THE CURRENT GOVERNMENT.

Ken's secretary frowned when he asked her to get him a sandwich so he could spend the lunch hour watching the news on several stations. Afraid that he had offended her, he apologized for asking her to do a personal errand, but she replied, 'No, that's no problem. I'm just concerned because recently you never seem to take a lunch break.' He smiled and thanked her for her concern.

Munching on his lunch, Ken watched NHK's special coverage of 'Mitsumoto-gate' and 'another major debacle in the market'. The opinions expressed by pundits were predictably harsh against the PM. On one station, a well-known financial maven intoned, 'The already grave situation in the economy has been made worse by the news of this major corruption scandal. I am reliably informed that a large bank in Tokyo, four large regional banks and two insurance companies will be declaring insolvency today or tomorrow, and these will most likely lead to more bankruptcies. And . . . '

The expert was suddenly interrupted. A grim-faced female news-caster announced that 'Mr Fukunaga, the chief secretary of the prime minister, has been formally indicted for various serious violations of the campaign-finance laws and complicity in the abduction and assault on a member of the board of the Bank of Japan. There is no word yet from the prime minister's office.'

Ken shook his head in despair. *That group of miscreants who triggered the drop in the price of government bonds must be laughing all the way to the bank.*

One of these miscreants was a banker in Singapore. Almost a month ago, when Nelson Ing read the news in *Lianhe Zaobao*, Singapore's largest Chinese newspaper, that the SAEC president had been arrested in Shanghai, he had begun to formulate an audacious scheme to make himself truly wealthy. He had been slowly and care-fully carrying it out—with Fan in prison, there was no hurry. How-ever, when he suddenly had the request from Fan to transfer money to a bank in Kunming, Ing knew that somehow Fan was free and that he had to act immediately.

Ing had efficiently transferred all the remaining money in both of Fan's accounts to some 14 different accounts belonging to six dummy corporations he had created in Hong Kong, England, Germany and the US. These accounts were in six banks in the Channel Islands, where the banking laws were still lax despite recent pressure from the G20 to tighten them. When Ing had everything in place, he had taken leave from the bank, shut up his apartment in Singapore and flown to Zurich using a false passport. He had no intention of returning to Singapore, but he didn't want to close the door if for any reason he changed his mind. *This way it will be at least a month before anyone realizes I've gone for good.*

From Zurich, Ing had made his way to London via Paris on the Eurostar, and then taken the short train ride to Cambridge. He had long believed that becoming a billionaire would make him truly happy. But today, sitting in his penthouse suite in a hotel on the bank of the River Cam, just 10 days after leaving Singapore, he felt desolate. When he had felt despondent in Zurich, he'd thought it a momentary pang because he was travelling alone. But the feeling had persisted and grown.

He had a new name, Neal Tan, and a British passport, albeit forged. He kept telling himself, *Don't be stupid, Nelson! You're a billionaire. How could you not be happy? Is it because you don't know what to do with so much money?*

He sighed as he gazed out the window, idly watching a punt go down the river, a young man trying to impress his girl friend but clearly in danger of losing his balance and falling in. But it wasn't the couple that made him sigh. It was the utterly unexpected conundrum that he should have considered before fleeing from Singapore: *Yes, I've more money than I could ever spend, but I'm now spending every minute of the day worrying about getting arrested.* He tried to think of something positive. But nothing seemed to be working.

All of SAEC's money plus that in Fans' personal account have been wired from one bank to the next within the network I so carefully created . . . and all of it in amounts never exceeding 50 million dollars. So far no one knows where the money from Singapore has ended up. I can send the money anywhere. But where? Where do I want to live? And with whom? With all the money I have now, will I be able to trust anyone enough to get close to them?

He had belatedly realized that he could not invest his money in large chunks in hedge funds or investment banks in any rich country as he had planned to do. After arriving in England, he discovered that because of the recently strengthened regulations in the OECD countries, he was going to be asked too many questions that he could not answer. Many institutions had recently paid so much in fines for accepting shady money, mostly for tax evasion, that they had become downright legalistic. A few banks in Europe had indicated interest in accepting his money, but these banks, he quickly found, were run by bankers like himself, the last people to whom he would entrust his money. Several American hedge funds had said they would take his money, but they had been quick to smell its likely origin and had asked for not the usual 2-to-20 rule but a 4-to-30 rule—charging 4 per cent to manage his money and taking 30 per cent of all returns earned on investment. And Ing was aware that they were hedge funds, like Fried's, that could go bust without warning. Desperate, he had even contacted several investment banks in Africa and Latin America, but after hearing what he had to say they had either hung up on him or offered deals worse than 4-to-30 rule.

So Nelson Ing, or Neal Tan as he had to remember to call himself, had had 150,000 dollars wired from one of his banks in the Channel Islands to a bank in Cambridge. Years before he had studied economics at the university and he thought Cambridge was a good place to think things through and decide what to do next.

His watch told him it was a little after three. Watching punts on the Cam wasn't helping him ease his feelings of desperation enough to make any decisions. *Maybe a little exercise will help.* He decided to try out the hotel's swimming pool. Unfortunately, it turned out to be much smaller than the photo he'd seen on the web. Four boys were noisily playing in the water and the smell of chlorine made him cough. He saw a door to a sauna and escaped to a very small, double-decked sauna.

Ing went to the upper deck, leaned against the wall and closed his eyes. Within minutes, sweat began to run down his face and chest. *Too hot for my liking.* He realized he was feeling even more miserable.

Some Chinese sage once said there are two kinds of misery: too little money and too much of it. I now know why I'm miserable. What good does it do to have so much money but on the lam with no friends, no wife? Why didn't I know too much money, especially purloined money, is like having fetters of anxiety and misery?

His head swimming from the heat, he was about to leave but a man entered, blocking his way. The man looked like any Englishman but spoke with a slight accent.

'Stay a bit longer, Mr Ing, We need to talk.'

Startled, Ing said, 'Sorry, you have the wrong person. My name is Neal Tan.'

'By now I ought to know you, Mr Nelson Ing. My colleague has been following you since he got a tip from a man in the ethics compliance department of a bank in Guernsey that you use.' He shook his head in reproof. 'You gave us such trouble. Following the money you wired crisscrossing banks in Europe and Asia was difficult and time-consuming. Especially since you chose your banks well . . . they were very difficult to get straight answers from . . . quickly. We might not have cottoned on to you were it not for the tip.'

Ing felt dizzy. 'Who are you?' he sputtered.

'I'm Maurice Fremont of the Financial Fraud Division of Interpol. My colleague and I were assigned to your case when your bank in Singapore found you'd taken leave after wiring so much money. The bank reported this to the authorities and the government of Singapore asked for our help. You are an able man, Mr Ing. The network of shady banks you created and all the details you took care of . . . all this took much more time for our team than we first anticipated.'

'Mr Fremont, I'm a little dizzy from the heat. Can we please talk outside?' pleaded Ing, overwhelmed both by the sauna and the imminent arrest.

'Oh, sorry. *Certainment.*'

They went down to the pool and sat on the plastic chairs. The boys had left and the two men were alone. Oddly, it did not occur to Ing to run away. It wasn't because he knew it was futile. It was because . . . he didn't know exactly what . . . but suddenly he was no longer desperate. He suddenly felt . . . lighter . . . calmer. Smiling weakly, he asked, 'So . . . are you going to arrest me now?'

'Not yet. No handcuffs, if you cooperate. I want to talk to you, and if I get the information we need and you agree to accompany me back to Singapore, there will be no handcuffs. We can behave like two gentlemen.'

Ing stared at the officer in disbelief.

Maurice Fremont changed his tone. 'It wouldn't do at all for you to clam up or give us the runaround because then you will be arrested like a common criminal. My superior thought my idea was fine. The Interpol is, I think, more civilized than most police organizations.'

What Ing said next surprised himself. 'Having so much money is like a shackle around my neck. Two billion dollars, I believed, would make me very, very happy. But it hasn't. Living on the lam from one hotel to another, always worrying about getting caught, became very old very quickly.'

'Became very old?'

'Tedious . . . wearisome. I guess I could have gotten about 10 million dollars in several banker's drafts and forgotten about the rest of the money. Ten million would have been enough to live on nicely . . . somewhere nice . . . '

Fremont nodded. 'But you'd be still on the lam. It's better to pay the debt to society and live in peace . . . the life of an ordinary person. I know the prisons in Singapore are better than in most other countries and you'll get, my guess is, about five years at most. You'll be only 47 when you are released.'

Ing sighed deeply. 'OK, I'll tell you everything Interpol wants to know. What will happen to all the money? Will it go back to China?'

'That's my understanding. To the Chinese government. *Bon*, we'll have dinner here and leave tomorrow morning early for Heathrow. I have a tentative booking for us on the midday nonstop Singapore Airlines flight.'

'And you trust me to go with you quietly?' asked Ing with amazement.

Fremont smiled. 'Within limits. While we are at dinner, my colleague will go through your belongings—with your permission, of course. Please leave your safe open. We will control your documents. We know you aren't a violent man, Mr Ing.'

Ing had the strangest dinner he ever had in his life. He sat with the handsome man from Lyon in the hotel restaurant at a window table with a view of the Backs. The Frenchman treated him like 'a gentleman' and, while dining on good English steak, told Ing about how he joined Interpol nine years ago after serving as a detective in Paris. In turn, Ing told him about his poverty-stricken childhood and how he had won a scholarship to Cambridge after doing exceptionally well in high school. After the unlikely pair shared cognac, Ing went to bed undisturbed, but with the knowledge that Fremont's colleague was spending the night in the living room of his suite. He had no idea where Fremont was staying.

It was the best night's sleep that Ing had in a long time. He had fulfilled his lifelong ambition to become one of the wealthiest people in the world, but it hadn't made him happy. All those billions of dollars had done was to give him unimaginable stress and constant worries. Now he was free from all that. *Thank God. No more misery. No more living as a fugitive.*

In Beijing, on the same day, Lei Shuo, minister of ethnic affairs, found himself running for his life. Bent over, he scampered through a narrow tunnel that ran from his house to the edge of a wooded area in a western suburb of Beijing. When he neared the exit and stopped to catch his breath, he looked up and was horrified to see light seeping through the camouflaged exit hole to his emergency tunnel. *Why is there a light so late at night? It's totally dark out tonight. No one but my nephew and the workers sent by the black society to dig the tunnel know it even exists.* His old heart pounding, he tried to think but his brain wouldn't work. *I know I can't think as well as I used to, but this is totally confounding!*

As he stopped to catch his breath, he heard the voice of the man who had come to his house so late at night with a team of six officers, the captain of the People's Prosecutor's Office.

'Minister Lei, you can't run way. We have the tunnel covered at both ends. My men are waiting for you here and back in your house by the toilet. It would be best for you to come out quietly. If you wait until daylight, the media will be here with cameras while you're being led away in handcuffs.'

Lei Shuo squatted down to think. Had he come to the end of his attempt to avoid arrest and prosecution? There was no escape from this tunnel. He had tried to cover his tracks by closing down the black prison. There was no way his role in the embezzlement of more than 2 billion dollars of SAEC money could be detected. Fan would take the fall for that. *Nor can they connect me with any of the murders committed by the men the black society sent me. What happened? I totally covered my tracks, erasing everyone who might foil my plans. OK, I couldn't get at that young Chinese woman . . . she disappeared. But she couldn't have set the authorities on me. And I know my nephew would never rat on me. He owes me everything! His educa-tion, his position in SAEC—I've even hidden his sexual misadven-tures. So, I'll be OK in the end.*

Lei yelled, 'I'm coming, I'm coming,' even as he thought, *Damn the idiotic anti-corruption campaign of the Beijing government!*

Lei crawled to the exit where two officers gripped him under his arms and hauled him to his feet. The captain looked at him coldly. 'Let's go! It's after midnight.'

Lei stumbled along the dark path to his residence and the official vehicles. His mind worked slowly and disjointedly. Images of the things he had done over the years to accumulate his enormous wealth went through his mind. And he mistakenly believed he was the only one who knew where most of it was stashed away. *I'll have the last laugh. As soon as I get rid of these cops, I'll find a way to disentangle myself from these devils of the black society. They've got their claws a little too deeply into my business. I'll be back to the good life.*

The small group arrived at the gate. One of the men went into Lei's house to get the men guarding the toilet where a hole in the floor led to the tunnel. Lei exhaled deeply. *Why not try? No one is immune to a bribe if the amount is big enough.*

'Captain, I'm wondering if you'd consider letting me get away . . . say, for 30 million yuan for each of you. Everyone will get his money within a couple of days . . . all tax free . . . how about it?'

One of the officers looked at Lei open-mouthed. The captain laughed. 'You senile old man. That's about 5 million dollars! Don't add another crime to your murders, extortion, and embezzlements . . . and, let's not forget your black prison. And your cosy arrange-ment with a few big black societies. We've known for weeks what you've been up to but only tonight we got the go-ahead from the Party to take you in. It's way too late for your bribes. No more busi-ness as usual.'

As the group stood waiting for the three officers to return, the captain looked at Lei and asked, 'What were you going to do anyway when you came out of the tunnel into the woods? There was no one waiting for you—we checked.'

Lei didn't answer. He hadn't known what he was going to do. A short man known as the 'Lieutenant'—belonging to a black society—had suddenly stopped answering his calls. Had Lei been able to contact him, the Lieutenant would have been at the exit of the tunnel, with a car.

'How did you know about the secret tunnel? Even my servants don't.'

'Your nephew.'

'Lei Tao?' The old man gasped.

'He kept silent until he was told he was to be tried for multiple murders. Then, to save his neck, he told us everything. He'll still get a life sentence, but I expect his full confession will save him from the death penalty.'

That stupid nephew . . . I should've thought of leaving China as soon as I got the first whiff of this lot starting to stick their noses into my business . . . .

The three officers arrived from the house. Lei was led to the police van. He felt on his cheeks the cold midnight air. The leafy neighbourhood was as quiet as a tomb. Lei felt dejected. *I've got to think. I'm in a bad spot, but I've been in several before. I'll get out of this one too. Just wait, I'm going to . . .* '

But his thought was abruptly cut short as an officer unceremoniously shoved him into the police van.

52

Tokyo, 24–25 September

Saburo Baba looked at his watch again. He was waiting for Ken Murai at a sushi restaurant where the two sometimes had lunch. But Ken wasn't late—Baba was early.

Ken arrived on time, greeted his friend and sat down beside him. 'You look great, Bach! Being back at the Foreign Ministry seems to agree with you.'

'Working from nine to five is almost like being on holiday.'

'So what have you been doing with all your free time?'

'Trying to get my life in order. Going to the dentist,' Baba replied with a laugh. 'And although I'm not supposed to know what post I'll have next, I've been told on the QT that I'm most likely to be sent abroad because of the brouhaha over Fukunaga and the PM.'

The sushi chef had served both men large cups of green tea and was hovering for their orders.

'Let's start with tuna,' suggested Baba. 'This lunch is my treat. I'm celebrating getting out of the clutches of the sick old man.'

Ken thanked his friend, and the chef placed plates in front of them with wasabi and pickled ginger at the edge. So far the two men were the only customers in the small shop. As the chef began to slice the lean, red tuna for the sushi, he conversationally asked Ken, 'Deputy Director, how much worse is our economy going to get? I mean, when will we see bankruptcy and unemployment rates stop rising? Since mid-August, my business has dropped so badly, it's hardly worth opening the shop for lunch any more.'

'No time soon, I'm afraid,' responded Ken. 'Be prepared for the long haul. Things will be far worse than in the 1990s or the big recession that started in 2008. Our economy could shrink by as much as 5 to 7 per cent if not more during the next 12 months and won't grow again for some years.'

He decided not to cast more gloom on the lunch by saying what he was really thinking: *Our government is facing the distinct possibility of defaulting on its bonds, because now we'll have to pay 7 per cent or more in November when we have to sell new bonds to refinance the ones maturing. We're already spending 20 per cent of our budget to pay the interest on our current outstanding bonds that are now paying far less in interest. Unless we get a new government and adopt some drastic policies, we are headed for a default on the JGB and economic chaos.*

As the chef placed sushi on the plates before his two customers, he turned to Baba. 'Counsellor, pardon me for asking, but why does the prime minister want to hang on to power? He's been in the hospital for some time now. Can he really be running our country from a hospital bed? But the newspapers say he is doing all he can to remain in office.'

Baba smiled. Given his position, he didn't think it politic to respond. He just said, 'Beats me. I sure wouldn't want to be in his shoes.'

The chef took the hint and asked the pair what they would like next.

Murai wasn't happy by the way the conversation was going, but he knew that the chef and just about everybody else in Japan was concerned with both what was happening in the economy and the state of the country's political leadership. He decided to change the subject.

'Say, how's your son Genya doing? Does he like working at that famous sushi shop near Shimbashi?'

The sushi chef suddenly became long-faced.

'Two weeks ago he was let go. Their business dropped badly and they couldn't keep on an apprentice. He's now looking for a job. And he's boning up on English. Sushi remains popular everywhere and shops in other countries aren't particular about how much training their chefs have. My wife and I hate the thought of him emigrating.'

All Ken could think to say was: 'Very sorry to hear that.'

Before the chef could respond, the sliding door to the shop opened and three boisterous young office workers burst in. They seated themselves at the opposite end of the counter from Ken and Baba and immediately ordered beer.

'We're celebrating!' one declared.

'Congratulations,' returned the sushi chef. 'What are you celebrating?' he asked as he got their beer from a refrigerator.

'Our good-for-nothing government is collapsing,' replied one of the young men.

The sushi chef stared at them, puzzled. It was clear that he thought the collapse of the government to be a disaster.

'Did you hear something on the news?' asked Ken. 'You said the government is collapsing.'

'Some of the Dietmen in the prime minister's party have had enough. And Horie, the Dietman who heads the biggest faction, has called a meeting of all members in his faction for this evening. A major defection is in the works!'

One of the other men poked the speaker in the arm and said something to him in a low voice. The man bragging about the possible downfall of the government turned to Ken and, in a worried tone, asked, 'Say, you two aren't reporters are you? We're really not supposed to know about this meeting. I heard about it only a little while ago from my girlfriend who works at the Diet. She said the defection of at least 30 Dietmen in the prime minister's party is definite and will become public by this evening.'

'No, we're just bureaucrats having lunch,' replied Ken. 'But that's interesting news and I can understand the celebrations. Don't worry, though, we won't broadcast it.'

The young man's girlfriend was right about the news, but not the timing. By the time Ken got back to his office, the media had reported that the PM's party had splintered, even though no one could yet be certain how many Dietmen in the PM's party were deserting him.

As Ken had dreaded, the news was dismal on the following day. By the time the market closed, it was reported that, 'So much stock was sold that the Nikkei dropped by 3.4 percent. But the price of the JGB has remained unchanged because many investors who sold stock bought government bonds to park their money.'

The TV news programmes and Internet reports were wild with speculation. A majority of the pundits Ken heard sounded as if they welcomed the splintering of the PM's party 'even if it meant the fall of the government and weeks under a caretaker government that can do little to help the economy'. That the current PM had just been released from hospital was barely mentioned.

Ken was of two minds about the news. He was glad to be rid of the old PM, but he knew the task of forming a new government would be formidable. Even if most of the Dietmen who deserted the PM's party decided to support Nishi, whether Nishi could get a majority in the Lower House was still uncertain. Should the PM call for a snap election, it would mean at least three or more weeks of nothing being done to alleviate Japan's economic crisis. And the cries of the millions affected by the August earthquake and tsunami were growing louder by the day.

When Ken talked to his friend Nick in New York late that night about the political situation, they chatted at length about the Japanese and American economic news. When Ken mentioned Nishi, Nick commented, 'Aah, Torao Nishi. I know his politics well enough to like him, as I told you when we first discussed him. If he were an American politician, his nickname would be the "Tiger of the West".'

It took Ken a few seconds to realize that Nishi meant 'west' and the 'tora' of Torao meant 'tiger'. He laughed. 'I've no doubt he'd be a tough and able PM. I hope he'll get enough support in the Diet to be so. His policies just might pull our country out of our crisis.'

Nick laughed in turn and the call ended on a cheerful note. Ken couldn't remember the last time he had laughed at anything.

53

Tokyo, 3–4 October

K en had just turned out his bedside light when his phone rang. 'Who's calling you after 11 on a Saturday evening?' mumbled Emiko, half-asleep.

'Don't know. No caller ID,' her husband replied, even as he answered.

'Murai-san?' a voice asked.

Ken instantly knew who it was from the distinctive voice.

Nishi Torao said, 'I'm very sorry to bother you so late at night, but could I come over to see you? It's very important that I talk to you tonight. I can be at your house in 10 or 15 minutes.'

Ken was so taken aback that all he could say was: 'Of course. I'll be waiting. I take it you know where I live?'

'Yes, my secretary told me. Thanks. See you soon.'

As Ken closed his phone, Emiko asked, 'Who was it?'

'It's Dietman Nishi and he'll be here in about 10 minutes. I don't know why—he just said it was something very important.'

'He's coming to talk to you at this hour? Whatever could be so urgent?'

'Maybe he's much closer to forming a government than we know. He may want to take some decision on economic policy to secure the support of the last few undecided Dietmen.'

'Where are you going to talk to him? In the living room?'

'Yes, it's more comfortable than my study.'

'Fine, I'll stay here and read. But I'll get dressed. If he wants something to drink, just call, and I'll get it.'

As the couple talked, Ken was throwing on some clothes. He had barely time to comb his hair and then check that the sitting room was in order before the bell rang.

Nishi, a handsome and robust man, looked exhausted. He was in his late 50s, but tonight he looked at least a decade older. He turned down Ken's offer of tea or a drink, asking only for a glass of water. Ken quickly got him a glass of water from the kitchen. The house was so quiet that Ken could hear Nishi gulping it down. Putting the glass down on the coffee table in front of him, Nishi breathed in deeply.

'I've just come from my last meeting . . . one of more than I can count over the past couple of weeks. To make a long story short, the five of us . . . those you met the other day . . . have succeeded in getting at least nine more than a majority of Dietmen to vote for a new coalition government. We'll have everyone from my party, at least a third of the PM's party, all three Socialists and six from other small parties. By abandoning their parties and joining us, at least 40 or 50 current Diet members could lose their seats in the next election. But they all know we have to do something to turn our country around.'

'Wonderful! Congratulations! Great!' Ken was so overjoyed he couldn't compose a sentence. Although he knew that 'at least nine more than a majority' constituted a very slim margin in the Diet, he was truly surprised to learn that Nishi and his closest allies were about to achieve a veritable political coup.

Nishi managed a tired smile. 'No less important, when the most senior of the defectors from the PM's party reported how many in his party are now supporting me, the PM promised to step down instead of calling a snap election. It means the new coalition can govern the country for two years at least before the next general election has to be held.'

'No snap election? Two years will be time enough to make some real changes!'

Nishi smiled again. 'We spent most of this afternoon discussing cabinet members. Deciding which party gets how many cabinet positions . . . and who gets which portfolio. As you can guess, it was extremely difficult. We had to twist some arms . . . rather brutally. But we've agreed on the line-up of the core members of the new cabinet. We are keeping a couple of the cabinet positions of less important ministries and eight positions of political vice ministers in reserve, to use them to entice still wavering Diet members to vote for the coalition at the Diet vote next week.'

'I'm sure it's a tough call for some Diet members. But the most important thing is that you'll have a majority and you'll be the PM.'

'For now, that's the plan. I wouldn't mind taking the Foreign Ministry and making Motoi the first female PM in Japan. But she strenuously objected and said I ought be the prime minister.'

'Very glad to hear it, sir.' Ken was genuinely pleased.

'If you are beginning to wonder why I came to tell you all this . . . things you'll be reading in the paper and hearing on TV tomorrow . . . The core members of the new coalition have succeeded in persuading a large majority of the Dietmen who agreed to join the coalition to ask you to become minister of finance. I know this is a totally unexpected request . . . and the job will be extremely demanding. But if we are going to deal with all the grave problems our economy is now facing and will face in the foreseeable future, we need you. We need your help in making the systemic changes you've written about in your articles.'

Ken was so overwhelmed he was speechless. Nishi mistook his prolonged silence for hesitation. 'In the postwar period, we've had three finance ministers and a score of other cabinet members who were not members of the Diet. The law requires only that a majority of cabinet members be Diet members. So your becoming a minister wouldn't be unprecedented. I'm keenly aware that we will have to have a general election in two years and we could lose the control of the Diet then, and you'd be jobless. Whereas you can stay on in the

Ministry of Finance until you retire. So accepting the position certainly poses some risk for you.'

Ken, still silent, nodded. Nishi went on, his expression earnest. 'However, I had my assistants do some research. They told me that you are from Kobe. It so happens that the Dietman in my party from the Kobe area is 72 and barely won the last election. He could be persuaded to retire in two years' time so you could run for his seat.'

Ken felt he had to say something. 'Sir, I'm very honoured by your request . . . and, I admit, very surprised. It certainly is very tempting. But as you will easily understand, I have to think about your offer and discuss it with my wife. I'll admit that I've never once thought of becoming a politician. But the idea of being able to do something to put our country back on track, to pull it out of the dire straits it's currently in, is very, very enticing.' Ken hesitated. 'Have you thought of giving the position to a Diet member and keeping me on as an advisor.'

'Certainly, I've thought of that,' Nishi said. 'That would be the normal procedure.' Then he added, with a smile, 'Wouldn't I be correct in thinking that you imagine you could do a better job than the current finance minister?'

'I can't deny that, sir. But . . . '

'I already have your advice. And I hope you will continue to advise me no matter what your decision is.' Nishi leaned forward, 'Murai-san, I will need all the help I can get as prime minister. I'm hoping I can do the job, but if I said I'm 100 per cent confident that I can do the job as it must be done, I'd be less than totally honest.'

Touched by Nishi's candor, Ken said, 'I understand, sir. As I've said already, I am very honoured by your offer. But it's come out of the blue and it's late at night, and I don't think I'm thinking very straight at the moment. How much time can you give me before I have to answer you . . . ?'

'Seventy-two hours. I hope that's enough time. Sooner would be better if you find you are absolutely certain of your decision. I should add that if you end up running for the Diet seat, my party will do all it can . . . including getting the necessary campaign funds.'

Nishi stood up slowly like an old man. Ken walked beside him as the pair slowly made for the front entrance.

Nishi said solemnly. 'That's it—72 hours. I'm hoping we can keep this meeting tonight from the media. But my discussion with the Dietmen is getting out. I suspect the media is going to hound you in a few days if not sooner . . . whatever you decide. Thanks for seeing me at this ungodly hour. My secretary is waiting outside in a car.'

Even though exhausted, Nishi shook Ken's hand vigorously and then plunked heavily down on the bench by the door to put his shoes on. Ken was very glad that Emiko had thought of setting the bench by the door so people didn't have to balance on one foot while putting on their shoes.

No sooner had Nishi gone than Emiko came down to the sitting room.

'I heard him leaving. What did he say to you? You look shell-shocked.'

'Emiko, sit down. I'll tell you everything he told me.'

And Ken proceeded to do so. Neither he nor Emi got much sleep that night.

Sunday morning Ken decided he had to consult other people before he made his decision. After tossing and turning much of the night, he and Emiko had gone over and over the pros and cons of Ken's accepting Nishi's offer. They had got nowhere. If Ken could have taken leave of his job to become the minister of finance, as can many senior European bureaucrats, there would have been no question that he would accept. The problem was that, in Japan, it was not possible for anyone to become a minister for a time and then return to the same ministry as a bureaucrat. Japan's centuries-long culture of observing a rigid hierarchic system made it impossible for a former minister to serve under a current minister regardless of age. This meant Ken had the problem of what he would do in the future. He had always thought he would serve in the Ministry of Finance until he retired.

'I have a secure position in the Ministry of Health, Labour and Welfare. So you could always become a house husband,' Emi joked.

Ken laughed. 'You know, if it were you being asked to do something risky while I had the secure position, we probably wouldn't even be having this discussion. I guess we haven't progressed very far on gender equality.'

By mid-morning he knew he should talk to Baba, whose judgement he always respected. He asked Baba to lunch, saying he had something important to discuss with him. Intrigued, Baba accepted the last-minute invitation.

Emi made *chirashi-zushi*—bowls of rice topped with a variety of vegetables and egg—which she knew Baba liked. Baba was both surprised and delighted with the idea of Ken becoming the finance minister. But as a bureaucrat himself, he quickly saw Ken's dilemma.

'That's quite a decision you have to make. Having been minister of finance, you can't go back and work in the ministry as a regular officer. That's not possible.'

Ken sucked in his breath. 'Yes, I'm aware of that. Nishi suggested I run for a Lower House seat in Kobe area, but I'm not sure I'm cut out to be a politician. Or even if I can win an election. Possibly I could get a teaching job at some university.'

Baba strongly encouraged Ken to take Nishi's offer because 'things have the way of working out . . . especially with your credentials and experience.' But Emiko sounded less than eager to see Ken taking on 'an impossible job' and then being forced to look for a position afterwards. Ken mostly listened.

After Baba left, Ken called Professor Sada, his mentor at the University of Tokyo and from whom he had sought advice from time to time over the past two decades. Apologizing profusely, he asked if he might call on the professor that afternoon. Sada seemed pleased to hear from Ken and immediately suggested he drop by for tea. He arrived at the professor's home just before four, where Mrs Sada graciously served tea and cake, then left the two men alone.

Professor Sada was delighted with Ken's news. 'Murai-kun, that's wonderful! Japan really needs you. I do hope you'll accept. But obviously you have some reservations or you wouldn't have come all the way to talk to me. Tell me what's on your mind.'

'Sir, do you think I can make a real difference, to bring our economy around? There are so many people out there still stuck with the totally misguided idea that we need lower taxes on the rich and on corporations so that they invest and create more jobs. It's been clear for years that this hasn't worked. But because of our national debt and low taxes, we don't spend enough on important things such as education, the environment and infrastructure. Things were getting worse even before the recent increase in the regressive consumption tax. The real-wage level has been stagnant for years for most workers and more people are having difficulty buying even the necessities. We are in a real mess because of the collapse of the government bond price and the earthquake. Sir, I could go on and on,' Ken ended, almost bitterly.

'I understand and I agree with you. Our capitalism needs a serious overhaul. As you argued so well in your articles, we have to realize that most of us in rich economies are sated with consumption goods and demand is not increasing fast enough to need more investment to create jobs. This means the "small government" mantra of low taxes is ideological dross that has got us into the mess of perpetual slow economic growth and all its consequences. I too could go on and on. So . . . Murai-kun, go for it . . . and become the minister of finance. If Nishi has managed to form a new government, it means you truly may be able to accomplish something.'

'Sir, that's why from the start I wanted to accept Nishi-san's offer. But there is something else, something personal I wanted to talk to you about,' said Ken. 'This may be selfish but I have to consider my options when my term as finance minister has ended. Nishi-san has assured me that he'll help me become the Diet member from my home district in Kobe, but I'm not at all certain I want to become a professional politician.'

'Hmm. You are still young, so you are entitled to think about your future. And I'll admit I can't see you as a politician,' said Sada thoughtfully. 'But I don't think you need to worry. Remember that you not only have a degree from the University of Tokyo but also a doctorate in economics from Harvard. You've published a couple of excellent academic articles that continue to be cited by many economists. I am sure that many a university in Japan would happily hire you as a professor. With your English, you would be an attractive prospect for a foreign university too. As I've told you more than once over the years, you'd be a very good professor. I truly think you will have a number of great opportunities ahead of you. And a more interesting future than just going up the ladder in the Ministry of Finance, eventually becoming an administrative vice minister but still under the whims of the minister whoever happens to be the current political appointee.'

Professor Sada was so upbeat and reassuring that Ken returned home rather light-hearted. When he told Emiko about his talk with Professor Sada, Emiko said thoughtfully, 'I've been thinking, and I think what Professor Sada told you is right. Go for it and take the job Nishi-san is offering. It's a rare opportunity—to do something important.'

Ken and Emiko sat down to watch the news on TV. All the stations were broadcasting details relating to Nishi's coalition, including speculation on 'the expected line-up' of the new cabinet. Apparently a paparazzi reporter had been tailing Nishi and been so adept that neither he nor his secretary-driver had realized they were being followed when Nishi came to see Ken in the middle of the night. Now a pundit was speculating on what the purpose of the secret meeting could be. Was Ken to be an advisor or did Nishi have other plans for him? He switched channels to find the head of a tiny reactionary party excoriating 'the socialist revolution' that would be carried out by the new coalition government. He accused Ken of being 'the mastermind behind making Japan into a socialist country that will doom the economy'.

Ken was surprised to hear himself branded as someone opposed to capitalism.

'How can they get it so wrong?' he complained to Emiko. 'I clearly believe that capitalism is the most efficient economic system. I want to preserve it, but it needs to be overhauled in order to thrive. I've said this since my Harvard days!'

With all the gossip bandied about in the media, he realized that the sooner he made up his mind, the better it would be for both him and Nishi. But there was one more person he wanted to call before he called Nishi, just to make sure there was no substantive counter-argument for accepting Nishi's offer. *Nick. He is outside Japanese culture and politics but he knows it almost as well as I do. He'll give me his usual candid and constructive advice!*

He looked at his watch. Too early—Nick would still be asleep. He'd wait until eight. In the meantime, he and Emiko had a snack as he answered her questions. She seemed to have decided that Ken was taking Nishi's offer and was already wondering what his policies would be.

Finally, at just a few minutes past eight, Ken called Nick. The phone kept ringing, and just before Ken nearly hung up Nick answered in a very sleepy voice.

'Hey, Ken. Why are you calling me at seven on Sunday morning?'

'Sorry, but I really need to talk to you.

'It's OK. What's up?' Nick sounded wide awake very quickly.

Ken told him of Nishi's offer, and briefly summarized the advice of Baba, Professor Sada and Emiko. 'They all think I should accept. What do you think?'

As usual, Nick got to what was on the top of Ken's mind instantly. 'What you really want to know is how much you think you can accomplish during the term in office, which could be as short as two years. Right? Whether you can start Japan on the way to the "systemic change of capitalism" you've been arguing the country needs.'

'Right.'

'You really believe that our current system of capitalism needs to be substantially modified to make it more fair and more efficient. But the kind of deep systemic change of capitalism you have in mind will take decades. But the current system here in the US and in Japan is so entrenched that what you can accomplish to change it in two years will be very limited.'

'That's precisely my concern,' conceded Ken.

'You know damn well you'll have trouble getting your Diet to vote for increasing taxes on the rich, the middle classes and large corporations. But this will be necessary to create the tax-financed demand that can make the economy grow again. Not to mention investing in the future in education and the environment. Your opponents will argue that your idea of systemic change is an argument for bigger government, which will stifle private initiative and entrepreneurship and put the economy on the slippery slope towards a wasteful and inefficient socialism. I can guarantee you when your tax and other ideas are made clear, the small majority Nishi now has could quickly dwindle.'

Ken was silent. *Nick is right*. But it was depressing to hear it.

But Nick wasn't finished. 'I've been playing devil's advocate, Ken. Or the devil may call it the voice of reason. But if we are always reasonable by the standard of what we usually think, we wouldn't have had many path-breaking scientific discoveries, no French Revolution, no American Independence . . . you know what I mean. If you accept Nishi's offer, you could end up failing and jobless—though I know it won't be for long. You'd be taking a risk, but Ken, you have to start somewhere. Japan has to change its system because the current system has gotten it into a mess. And from what I see in the news, things are only getting worse.'

Nick paused and then said, 'I strongly encourage you to take the first step. Go for it, Ken.'

'Thanks, Nick. That's really what I wanted to hear. If we don't start now to change the system and revive our economy, when will we?'

'Ken, you have an incredible opportunity! Nishi has given you the possibility of trying to carry out in real life the ideas you have written about and you still believe in very strongly. My congratulations!'

'Thanks, Nick, I knew you'd help me decide. Sorry for waking you up . . . and on Sunday.'

After Ken hung up, he took a few deep breaths. Then he went to tell Emiko that he was going to phone Nishi and accept his offer. Emiko hugged him. 'I knew you'd take up the challenge.'

54

Honolulu, Tokyo and Beijing, 1 January

Ken Murai gazed out at the scene from his eighth-floor lanai at the Kahala Hotel. He was entranced by the azure ocean, the water glittering in the sun, and the children playing on the beach and in the gentle waves. *I can see why they say that Hawaii is a paradise in the Pacific. I should enjoy it before I get back to Tokyo and worry about the new bill raising the tax on the profits from trading stocks. And I've got to deal with . . .*

Emiko, a large straw hat in her hand, walked into the sitting room of their suite. 'Ken, are you ready? I'm sure Nick and Bess will already be waiting for us at the restaurant.'

His ruminations interrupted, Ken came back inside. 'Be right with you.' He walked over to a closed door on the side of the living room and knocked on it three times. When he heard two knocks back, he and Emiko left the suite, carefully checking to see that the door was locked as they went out.

Out in the hall, they met two Japanese men, one young, the other middle-aged. Ken nodded a greeting and the four set off for the elevators, the two men a short distance behind the couple.

Emiko said sotto voce, 'Don't you think all this security is a bit ridiculous in Honolulu? I understand why in Tokyo, but do we need it here too?'

Ken nodded. 'Nishi insisted a special police unit team protect all cabinet members, and I can't go against the PM's orders. After what happened to Motoi, I admit I feel better when these guys are nearby, even here in Hawaii.'

Emiko decided to drop the subject because she knew that when Foreign Minister Motoi visited Okinawa last month, someone had taken a pot shot at her with a long-range rifle while she was standing at the window of her hotel room. The bullet shattered the large window but luckily didn't harm Motoi. The police had not yet been able to apprehend the shooter who the media was speculating was 'hired by some right-wing group.'

When the Murais entered the Plumeria, the hotel's open-air restaurant, they found Nick and Bess Koyama seated at an outside table near the shore. After the four had ordered and been served with iced tea, Emiko said, 'I am really looking forward to this lunch, Nick. It was lovely of your parents to host us for a New Year's Eve buffet last night and we loved seeing how Mikey has grown. But I'm dying to catch up on all the news we couldn't talk about last night.

'Me too,' said Bess. 'We hear about the trials and the work of rebuilding the earthquake damage on a daily basis, but how is your family faring, Emiko? You wrote that your sister and her children have moved to Tokyo to live with your mother. How are they doing?'

'I guess OK, though they are still grieving. But the older girl has stopped having nightmares and my sister is going to enroll in April in a special programme to train as a counsellor to children who have experienced grief or trauma. And they are luckier than all the people still stuck without adequate housing especially now that it's winter.'

'I guess, Ken, that you really have a double problem to deal with, rebuilding so much of Japan from all the earthquake damage as well as handling all the aftermath of the crash of the government bonds,' Nick commented. 'I sure know that since you became finance minister, you haven't had time for the long chats we used to enjoy. I manage to get most of the financial and economic news, but I'm eager to find out if you know what's happened to some of the miscreants involved in the various plots. I keep my eye on the news in Japan, but there are still loose ends I can't account for. I read that the chief secretary of the former prime minister was being indicted for violations of the campaign fund law. What do you know about Fukunaga?'

Ken grinned and explained what he knew about what Fukunaga and his wife had done, as well as the CFO of Mitsumoto Trading. He added, 'People who know these things tell me they'll be sent to prison for at least a couple of years.'

Nick said, 'But I'll bet the former PM won't be indicted.'

Ken laughed. 'No, there's no evidence to connect him to the cheques from Mitsumoto. We all know the money was intended for the PM's political war chest, but both the former PM and Fukunaga were too devious to leave any kind of evidence tying the PM to the money. And you can bet that none of the others involved are going to rat on a former PM, old and sick as he is.'

Nick asked, 'If no one ratted as you say, how did police or the election commission . . . and you . . . find out about the illegal contribution by Mitsumoto?'

Ken summarized what Baba had done to expose the illegal contribution to the police. Very surprised, Nick said, 'It must've been a very difficult thing to do. I applaud his moral courage. I hope Bach didn't get into any trouble over it. What's he doing now?'

'So far no trouble for him. Not only that, he's going to become Japan's ambassador to Canada come April. It will be formally announced soon.'

'That's terrific!' said Nick. 'They must think really highly of him to get such a posting in his 40s.'

'Yes, they do. He certainly deserves to be ambassador. Speaking of miscreants, do you know anything more about the gang who attacked the JGB in August? I know only that Fried went bankrupt and Fan was arrested. Do you know anything I don't know?'

'Yes, we do,' Bess spoke up excitedly. 'My friend Belinda, who put us on the trail when she decoded their messages, was in Hawaii a few days ago on her way to Boston to spend the New Year with her family. She had a lot of astonishing news. It turns out that it wasn't just President Fan of SAEC who was corrupt. The CFO of SAEC . . . someone called Lei Tao, was working with him, and behind the scenes was the CFO's uncle, Lei Shuo, minister of ethnic affairs and a member of the Politburo. Belinda read about their arrests in the news in China and then did a lot of checking on the Internet.'

Ken, who was listening open-mouthed, asked as soon as Bess stopped to take a breath: 'So this wasn't just Fan's plot? We assumed he was the kingpin behind the "Shanghai Intrigue". So who was responsible for the murders Mimi told us about? And for what happened to Mimi when she went to Tokyo?'

'The man behind both the murders and Mimi's kidnapping was almost certainly Lei Shuo. Belinda thinks Fan was behaving like he was the key person, and he may have thought he was, but in fact the Leis were using him as a front man. He had the best command of English and the ability to organize the group that triggered the fall of the JGB. Belinda is convinced the Leis planned to have him become the fall guy.'

'Why does she think that?' asked Ken.

'She said Lei Shuo had been investigated for financial shenanigans more than once in the past, but each time the investigation was dropped mysteriously. I guess he went too far this time. And his nephew, Lei Tao, was caught as well and is being tried for embezzlement. The old uncle has now been tried for multiple crimes including multiple murders. It came out that he was not only very corrupt but for years had ties with what the Chinese call "black societies". These are the counterpart of the criminal groups you call yakuza in Japan.'

Emiko looked shocked and baffled, and Ken was astonished. 'So the man behind the murders wasn't President Fan after all, but a member of the Politburo?'

Bess responded, 'Yes. He's the only one of the trio charged with murder. Belinda is convinced that everything was very carefully planned, starting with Lei Shuo "inserting" his nephew into SAEC as the CFO.'

'Mimi was so sure that the villain was President Fan,' commented Ken.

'What I couldn't figure out,' said Bess, 'is why Mimi was targeted even after her trip to Tokyo. But after talking to Belinda, I think there was no rational reason. I think that Lei Shuo was paranoid about anyone who could possibly jeopardize his corrupt schemes. And he could dispatch black-society thugs to "silence" anyone he ordered. Belinda suspects from all she's read that Lei Shuo could now be senile or demented.'

After taking a moment to digest all of this, Ken asked, 'Does Belinda know what happened to Lei Shuo?'

Bess responded, 'I asked her the same question, but all she could find was that he was arrested. Nothing about if he was convicted . . . '

Ken nodded and said, 'I wonder what happened to Mimi?'

'Mimi came out of all of this with a fiancé,' said Bess with a big smile. 'Geoff Mitchell, her instructor at the University of Minnesota.'

Emiko, who had been listening quietly to the conversation between Bess and her husband, spoke up, 'How nice. When will they get married?'

'In a Christmas card, she said this coming spring. Now that the villains at SAEC have finally been caught, Geoff has gone back to Minnesota to finish up his PhD and Mimi has rejoined her family in Shanghai to plan the wedding. She said his family is giving them a honeymoon in Paris.'

Hearing Bess mention Paris, Nick laughed.

'What's so funny?' asked Ken.

'Well, when Bess said Paris, I couldn't help thinking about the German in the plot. From the start we knew a German was involved in the plot and I know who it was because he was arrested in Paris,' replied Nick, grinning.

At the same time Ken asked, 'Who was it?' Emiko said, 'Paris! What was a German doing in Paris?'

Nick grinned. 'Just living it up. It was the man from Dresden, a banker named Marcus Adler. He'd stolen millions of euros from the bank he managed in order to join the plot. He'd gone to New York on a forged passport in the name of Mark Arnold and disguised his identity. I guess he figured that it was safe for him to squander some of his ill-gotten gains on a posh trip to France. The Interpol was looking for a Marcus Adler who robbed a bank of millions, who looked very little like Mark Arnold. But some pretty savvy officers checking arriving passengers at Charles de Gaulle thought there was something fishy about Mr Arnold, supposedly born in the US but with a strong German accent . . . so, they contacted Interpol.'

'How do you know all this?' Ken was stumped.

'Quite by accident,' admitted Nick. 'Wolfgang Reichmann, who heads the Zurich office of Rubin-Hatch, was in New York for meetings at the head office. A bunch of us went out for dinner and starting telling stories. Wolfgang was in Frankfurt when the story about Adler broke. He got interested in the story and followed it for a few days.'

'I'm glad that at least some of the perpetrators of that plot got their just deserts.' Said Ken with irony. 'I was disgusted when it was announced that Shigeo Tanaka was made president of Sumida Bank. The American bank that bought up Sumida must've thought highly of him for having told the bank it was dangerous to hold so much JGB. Tanaka sure came out smelling like roses!'

Contrary to the speculations of the foursome having lunch at the Plumeria, Shigeo Tanaka, at home in Tokyo, was far from enjoying life. He had just woken up and was downing black coffee in an attempt to clear his fuzzy head. He had drunk far too much whisky the day before, and he groaned when he remembered why he had done so.

He had worked long hours this past week, plus attended an end-of-the-year party every night, even he thought these parties were a silly Japanese custom that just gave many people an excuse to get drunk. He'd gone to work on New Year's Eve to make sure that he had done everything he should to end the year cleanly, as was the Japanese custom. To his surprise, just before 10 he'd received a phone call from Tom Kendall who was not only in Tokyo but calling from the office of the chairman of the board. Tanaka had assumed that Kendall, president of the Manhattan Trust Bank, the American owner of Sumida, was in New York.

Why is Tom in Tokyo just before the New Year holidays? And why didn't he let me know he was coming? Something's odd.

But he didn't have time to speculate because Kendall asked him to come to the boardroom immediately.

As soon as Tanaka entered the room, Kendall said, 'Sit down. I have to tell you something you don't want to hear.'

Surprised at the lack of the usual preliminary chat, or even New Year's wishes, Tanaka asked, 'You don't like these two banks I've recommended that Manhattan Trust buy?'

'No. They're fine. We'll buy them. I like the locations of their branch offices and their books are just as your guys who did due diligence said.'

The cold look in the American's grey eyes made Tanaka uneasy.

'I've known you for nearly 20 years, Shig, since you were first posted in New York. So this is difficult. But I've no choice. The board is unanimous and I concur with their decision.'

'What decision, Tom?'

'Shig, we have to let you go. You are being dismissed for cause . . . so there'll be no golden parachute. Sorry.'

Tanaka was totally taken aback. 'You're firing me? For cause? What cause?'

'We discovered you were a key member of a group that attacked the JGB in August. You must've made a pile, though by doing so you made Sumida insolvent. All the board members think what you did was unconscionable . . . an act of betrayal.'

What he heard hit him like a thunderbolt. Tanaka blustered. 'What were you told? Why do you think I went against the bank's interests?'

Kendall raised his hand to stop Tanaka from saying any more. 'Don't try to deny it. There were rumours in New York about what seemed to be a clever attack on the JGB. So one of our board members, an old Japan hand, asked around. No one in the banking world thought there was any truth to the rumour, but then he happened to meet an acquaintance, a high government official who used to advise your prime minister. Off-the-record he confirmed you had taken part in a plot to make money by short selling the JGB. And we've had this information confirmed by our sources in the Fed in the US.'

Tanaka could hardly believe what Kendall was telling him, although he had known he had been under surveillance. He slumped as he recalled this.

Kendall continued. 'The Japanese authorities did nothing because what you did was unethical but not criminal. And even though all of us do a lot of short selling, none of us would short sell the stock of our own bank. Nor would we short sell the government bonds we own. In your case, you were fully aware what attacking the JGB would do to Sumida and to Japan. For years now, we bankers have been criticized for being unethical and many of us deserved the criticism. But we don't need a blatantly unethical president for our bank here, especially one we can't trust to work in favour of the bank. Our contract with you states that we can dismiss you for cause if we find you've done anything unethical. You can keep your ill-gotten gains— whatever you've made should be sufficient for you live on.'

Tanaka stared at Kendall. He had nothing to say.

'I'll give you 24 hours to clear out of your office,' Kendall said, his voice now very cold. 'But I'm sure you don't want to suffer the ignominy of staying for the rest of the day and walking out in front of everyone who'll know you've been fired. Given the Japanese custom of having everything in order by the end of the year, I'm sure there's nothing left for you to do here. So I'll walk with you to the front door and see you into a taxi. Then I'll have one of the assistants pack up the personal things in your office and send them to your home.'

Assailed by a mix of conflicting emotions, Tanaka could only nod assent.

The last thing Kendall said to him as the taxi door closed was: 'Shig, I'm sorry it had to end this way. You were a very good banker.'

As the leisurely lunch at Plumeria came to an end, the four friends discussed how they would spend the afternoon. The two men didn't want to waste a minute of what they considered a perfect day for swimming, while the two women decided to go get Mikey and bring him over to the beach so he could play in the sand.

After a brisk swim in rather chilly water, Ken and Nick lounged on beach chairs to warm up in the sun. Without their wives to stop them from talking shop, they went back to their favourite subject—the economy.

'Nick, besides the couple of bills pending now in the Diet, our government now has to really worry about the trade balance. Even though the yen tanked, our exports aren't increasing but the price of imports has gone up. And since we import so much oil, our not getting the Benin oil has been adding a few billion dollars to our trade deficit. It's ironic that because of all the machinations by the Leis and Fan at SAEC and because of what had happened to our economy, neither SAEC nor Mitsumoto got the right to exploit the oil.'

'Yeah, but neither did anyone else.' Nick reminded him. 'Even though Benin postponed the bidding date to October, only one French company made a bid, and it was so low that the Benin government decided not to accept it. So, Ken, cheer up. When Benin solicits new bids sometime in the near future, the Japanese might still have a chance. With the US producing so much shale oil and the Chinese economy growing more slowly, I suspect Benin will have to accept bids lower than they would like if they want to make anything from those four tracts.'

Ken said, 'I hope you're right. I have to talk to Nishi about what our government can or should do when Benin calls for new bids. I'm sure China will also bid but I'm also sure it'll take time for the Chinese to reorganize SAEC.'

As three young women in bikinis passed by, Nick and Ken grinned at each other and then watched them prance down the beach. When they were gone, Ken resumed the conversation on a new topic.

'I'm still amazed that behind the plot to bring down the JGB was that old man so high up in the Party. And with ties to the Chinese yakuza.'

'As Bess' friend in Beijing said, Lei Shuo is a real greedy bastard, most likely not in his right mind. He didn't care what he did to make money.' Nick said stretching his arms. 'But enough of this Shanghai Intrigue stuff, let's go for another swim.' Nick stood up laughing, and the two men headed for the water, under the watchful eyes of a nearby bodyguard assigned to the minister of finance.

A s Nick and Ken jumped into the ocean and raced to the small island, a black sedan was heading out of the centre of Beijing to the southwest. Two men, a police captain in his 50s and a young police driver, were in the front seat, and a middle-aged man in a civilian suit was in the back, next to an old man huddled in a corner. No one said a word, and with the windows closed, all that could be heard was the noise of the engine.

An occasional streetlight lit up the old man's tired and wrinkled face. He let out a dry cough. The man next to him looked over at him but said nothing. Then suddenly the old man burst out with a series of garbled words that sounded like he was having a nightmare. 'My disloyal nephew . . . where did the lieutenant go? . . . Why couldn't they get that stupid girl . . . bastards all of them!'

The car stopped at the gate of a large, grey four-storey building. The three younger men got out, and the officers helped the old man out of the car. The captain led the way to the entrance, while the other officer escorted the old man, catching him when he stumbled. Once in the building, the four walked through it and out into a large ground surrounded by a high wall. At almost 10 p.m. and on a holiday, the place was eerily quiet. Several lights on the second floor of the building and the three-quarter moon dimly lit the yard. When the four arrived, a floodlight suddenly turned the ground into daylight.

The old man looked up and saw to one side six men, dressed in olive outfits and olive caps, each holding a rifle. He watched as the police captain handed a piece of paper to the man in the civilian suit, whom he now recognized from the People's Court a week before. The man in the civilian suit took a pen out of his pocket and signed it. The police captain then walked over to the six men with rifles and issued instructions he couldn't hear.

The man in the civilian suit took the old man by the arm and led him to the wall opposite the men with rifles. He said, 'Here's a blindfold. It's customary.' He tried to hand it to the old man but the old man said, 'No. I don't need it. I'm going to the next world with my eyes open.'

As the man in the suit walked to the side of the yard, the old man suddenly started to walk unsteadily towards the men with rifles.

After he had walked several steps, someone yelled, 'Stop right there.' The old man stopped, smiled benignly at the civilian, and then turned towards the men with rifles, still smiling. Someone shouted,

'Ready, aim . . . fire!' The sound of rifle fire shattered the silence of the night.

An hour later, the man in the civilian suit arrived home and told his wife what he had been doing for the past few hours. He was so distraught he seemed not to care that the execution was strictly under wraps.

'The old man smiled at me just before he got shot. He seemed to be smiling at all of us, like he was demented. The police told me he was more than a little odd when they arrested him. In the car, he went from what seemed dejected silence to loud outbursts, much of which I couldn't make out. It beats me how he stayed a minister and a member of the Politburo. The police captain told me he'd done the kind of personal favours to some members of the Politburo that only a man with ties to the black societies can do. And because of those ties, people were scared to challenge him even when they knew he was utterly corrupt. But tonight it was hard to see how such a shell of a man could have been so powerful and responsible for so many deaths.'

His wife said, 'I think there are other reasons why he was able to keep his powerful positions, besides those that you've just mentioned.'

Her husband was surprised. 'What do you mean?'

'Our culture is *guanxi*-ridden and we revere older people. That's why our government's campaign to rout out corruption never really succeeds. Even men who become senile or unhinged, as you say, can often hang on to their high positions in the government. In China, personal connections can even trump laws and we always hesitate to act against our elders.'

Her husband thought for a moment and said, 'I think you're right. And that could explain why the government had Lei Shuo executed in secret, late at night. They couldn't take the chance of keeping him alive, what with his powerful connections. I sure hope I don't have to witness again what I saw tonight!'

In Honolulu, some five hours later, the Murais and Koyamas entered Hoku's, the Kahala Hotel's gourmet restaurant. They were warmly greeted by an attractive server. 'Mr Koyama's father . . . Professor Koyama . . . asked me to take good care of you tonight.' At her suggestion, they decided to order the restaurant's signature dish, a huge opakapaka fish cooked Chinese style.

Bess looked around and asked the Murais, 'Where are your minders tonight?'

Ken laughed, 'I convinced them they could sit at the Veranda bar next to the restaurant and enjoy a casual meal while keeping watch on the door to the restaurant. I think they are as tired of us as we are of them.'

'I never thought I'd have a friend who was so *erai* that he'd have government security,' commented Nick.

'*Erai*? What's that?' asked Bess.

'It means important in standard Japanese,' replied Emiko. 'But in western Japan, it means something is trying or tiring. And at the pace Ken has been working, I think the second meaning really suits him. We are both grateful to you for arranging this week in Honolulu for us!'

'I don't think I'd ever have gotten any time with you since you became the minister of finance if we hadn't gotten you outside Japan,' commented Nick.

'You're right, Nick. This would have been impossible in Japan where I seem to deal with crisis after crisis. But I'm not going to talk about our problems tonight because if I do it'll spoil our dinner.'

'Ken, I know what you mean. But please indulge me and answer just one question,' asked Nick apologetically. 'I know a few tax laws were passed and the next budget was finally approved about a month ago, each time with a thinnest majority. When do you think you'll see some results . . . and the Japanese economy begin to come out of the mess it's in now?'

The new minister of finance sighed and said, 'We're hoping to see some tangible results by summer. Surprising many right-wing pundits and politicians, the stock market is notching up very slowly and the JGB price has already stabilized. These are leading indicators and the unemployment and bankruptcy rates will go down at an appreciable rate much later. And the low yen will increase our exports. It's like turning a huge oil tanker around—it's a very slow process.'

Nick nodded. 'Right. Many of us are watching how Japan's economy will perform because you're trying an experiment, as it were, of how we can revitalize capitalism if we dump the stupid supply-side economics and invest in the future with increased tax revenues.'

'I am very aware of that,' Ken said smiling. 'In the budget committee meetings, I always remind the Diet members that we are trying to do the things all the other rich capitalist economies should be doing but can't because of strong opposition from short-sighted right-wing politicians. I think . . . I hope . . . we are doing the right things. But I think we should be coming out of the current mess by the time we have our next election in two years.'

Emiko added, 'Most major newspapers now seem to agree with Ken. They often quote what Ken says about how creating demand using tax revenues can reinvigorate our economy and help sustain the environment. I sure hope the new policies will work because my bureau, which helps the unemployed and the poor, can't cope with the current double-digit unemployment rate much longer.'

Conversation had turned serious despite themselves. But it was cut short by the arrival of a huge fish deep-fried whole, dishes of rice and vegetables, and three kinds of sauce. Emiko said she'd never eaten anything like this before. Talk turned to a comparison of food between Hawaii and Japan.

When slices of coconut cake had been set in front of them, their server brought them a bottle of champagne. 'A gift from Professor

Koyama who comes here very often,' she informed them. Nick suggested they raise a toast.

'To what?' asked Bess.

'To all our friends—may they be safe and happy,' suggested Emiko.

'To the future of Japan, which will lead the way to a new kind of capitalist economy for the benefit of everyone,' proposed Ken.

'To all of the above, and may the greedy reprobates have learned their lesson and *never* try it again,' Nick added, and the four raised their glasses.

Epilogue

New York, 4 January

'Let's start the new year right!' Peter Scheinbaum declared.

'*D'accord*,' replied his friend Etienne Mulsant with a smile. 'We're on the same page,' the French banker said, proud of his English prowess. The two were in Scheinbaum's New York office, the door tightly closed. Scheinbaum had requested that all calls be held while in conference with the vice president in charge of investments abroad for his French bank. The two had become friends a decade ago when Scheinbaum helped the Frenchman invest his bank's money in the US, resulting in far more profit than Mulsant had ever expected.

The Frenchman turned serious.

'Peter, we'd like to invest as much as 500 million euros if you can help me to make a good return. Of course, if we can make . . . *comment dit-on en anglais* . . . a bundle? a killing? . . . in the shortest possible time. Any ideas?'

It was Scheinbaum's turn to smile. 'Etienne, a bundle will do. More than *beaucoup*. And in the shortest possible time!' He was ready with an answer because he had been looking for a deep-pocketed investor for a new project he had been planning for the past month.

'Etienne, it's an omen your being a Frenchman. I've been doing a lot of research on a new project that involves the French government bonds.'

'Our government bonds? They're paying so little. And the rate has been notching up lately. Our bank has some of them. Their rates go up, the value of these bonds on our book goes down.'

Scheinbaum laughed. 'I'm not suggesting you buy the bonds. I'm thinking of *attacking* the damn bonds . . . short selling them. Your new government in the hands of that populist and xenophobic party has been spending a lot of money on vote-getting things . . . like increasing pensions and the salaries of government employees . . . while cutting taxes on small businesses. To get the money to pay for these schemes, it's been selling more and more bonds. That's why the interest rate has been going up slowly but steadily.'

'You can't short sell enough of the bonds to bring down the price. The outstanding amount is almost 4 trillion euros . . . more than our GDP.'

'It's 3.8 trillion and 112 per cent of GDP, Etienne. What's important is that all the bondholders are now very nervous. When I was in Paris two weeks ago, I talked to several CEOs of big banks and insurance companies. They're afraid your crazy government will sell even more bonds in the coming year and the price could suddenly tank.'

'Peter, if you put it that way, yes, the bond price could drop sometime in the near future. But that's entirely different from being able to make it drop and make money by short selling it. It would take billions . . . more likely tens of billions . . . to buy and short sell the bond at the time of our choosing.'

'You are wrong there. Look what happened to the Japanese government bond in August. All we needed was a little more than 9 billion dollars to do 10-to-1 margin trades.'

Etienne looked thoughtful but said nothing for a long minute. 'I thought the Japanese bond price dropped in August because Japan's government bonds totalled nearly 300 per cent of GDP and that combined with a shaky and imprudent government caused people to sell. I had no idea you had anything to do with the price dropping so much, so suddenly.' Mulsant looked straight at Scheinbaum. 'Tell me more exactly how you did it.'

When Scheinbaum finished describing the details of the attack by his group, the Frenchman said, '*Très bon*, I'll discuss this at my bank immediately and see if we can put in more than 500 million euros. I assume I can make a side bet for myself using whatever money I can get my hands on . . . '

'By all means, Etienne. If you hadn't brought up making a side bet, I've have been disappointed.'

'Well, as we say, *Aide-toi et le ciel t'aidera.*'

Josh looked puzzled, so Malsant translated: 'In English you say, "God helps those who help themselves." Surely God must be a capitalist.'

The two men guffawed, and then began to discuss others who could be invited to join the project. To attract deep pockets in France, they would call their project 'Le Complot Parisien'. Scheinbaum assured his French colleague that just as George Soros had triumphed over the British pound and he and his colleagues had started the crash of the Japanese government bonds, their project would be just as successful.

The Frenchman beamed and said, 'Bien sûr. Le capitalisme est merveilleux.' And this Scheinbaum knew meant 'capitalism is marvellous'.

Acknowledgements

The authors acknowledge with gratitude the following people.

Lin Xinru provided us with information and guidance relating to all things Chinese that we needed to write this book, and which only the gifted and generous 'Belinda' living in China could provide. Linda Glenn advised us on how to reorganize the sequence of the development of the story, which we hope made this a better book. And Sunandini Banerjee, the editor, and others at Seagull Books made myriad suggestions that substantively improved the quality of our writing and helped us reduce the number of errors. The remaining errors are the responsibility of the authors.

Despite the single pen name, this book has two authors—Kozo Yamamura and his wife, Susan Hanley. Like their previous novels, the core plot is the creation of Kozo, who is an economist, which readers can easily surmise. But providing the basic plot is no more than an architect coming up with a blueprint for a house because the construction requires the work of many skilled workers. Thus the pen name is made up from the Ko in Kozo and the Yama in Yamamura, while the S represents the contributions by Susan, a historian who loves the complex webs humans are capable of weaving. She is very happy with this recognition, because she finds fleshing out an intricate novel much more fun than writing history, which proscribes her from tampering with historical facts and forces her to add mind-numbing footnotes.